# *Praise for Iain M. Banks*

"Banks is a phenomenon... writing pure science fiction of a peculiarly gnarly energy and elegance." —William Gibson

"There is now no British SF writer to whose work I look forward with greater keenness." —*The Times*

"Poetic, humorous, baffling, terrifying, sexy—the books of Iain M. Banks are all these things and more." —*NME*

"Staggering imaginative energy." —*Independent*

"Banks writes with a sophistication that will surprise anyone unfamiliar with modern science fiction." —*New York Times*

"The Culture Books are not technological just-so stories. They're about faith in the future, about the belief that societies can make sense of themselves, can have fun doing so, can live by Good Works, and can do so in circumstances far removed from our own little circle of western civilization." —*Wired*

"An exquisitely riotous tour de force of the imagination which writes its own rules simply for the pleasure of breaking them." —*Time Out*

"Pyrotechnic, action-filled, satiric, outlandish, deep and frivolous all at once, these bravura space operas... juggle galactic scale... with a revelatory energy rarely matched in speculative fiction." —*Science Fiction Weekly*

"Few of us have been exposed to a talent so manifest and of such extraordinary breadth." —*New York Review of Science Fiction*

**By Iain M. Banks**

*Consider Phlebas*
*The Player of Games*
*Use of Weapons*
*The State of the Art*
*Against a Dark Background*
*Feersum Endjinn*
*Excession*
*Inversions*
*Look to Windward*
*The Algebraist*
*Matter*

**By Iain Banks**

*The Wasp Factory*
*Walking on Glass*
*The Bridge*
*Espedair Street*
*Canal Dreams*
*The Crow Road*
*Complicity*
*Whit*
*A Song of Stone*
*The Business*
*Dead Air*
*The Steep Approach to Garbadale*

# The Player of Games

Iain M. Banks

**www.orbitbooks.net**

*New York London*

Orbit
Hachette Book Group
1290 Avenue of the Americas, New York, NY 10104
www.HachetteBookGroup.com

This edition published in the U.S. by Orbit, March 2008
Originally published in Great Britain by Macmillan (London) Limited, 1988, and in the U.S. by St. Martin's Press, 1989

Orbit is an imprint of Hachette Book Group. The Orbit name and logo are trademarks of Little, Brown Book Group Ltd.



ISBN 0-316-00540-1 / 978-0-316-00540-1
LCCN 2007930990

15

LSC-C

Printed in the United States of America

# *Contents*

# The Player of Games

# 1

## *Culture Plate*

This is the story of a man who went far away for a long time, just to play a game. The man is a game-player called "Gurgeh." The story starts with a battle that is not a battle, and ends with a game that is not a game.

Me? I'll tell you about me later.

This is how the story begins.

Dust drifted with each footstep. He limped across the desert, following the suited figure in front. The gun was quiet in his hands. They must be nearly there; the noise of distant surf boomed through the helmet soundfield. They were approaching a tall dune, from which they ought to be able to see the coast. Somehow he had survived; he had not expected to.

It was bright and hot and dry outside, but inside the suit he was shielded from the sun and the baking air; cosseted and cool. One edge of the helmet visor was dark, where it had taken a hit, and the right leg flexed awkwardly, also damaged, making him limp, but otherwise he'd been lucky. The last time they'd been attacked had been a kilometer back, and now they were nearly out of range.

The flight of missiles cleared the nearest ridge in a glittering arc. He saw them late because of the damaged visor. He thought the missiles had already started firing, but it was only the sunlight reflecting on their sleek bodies. The flight dipped and swung together, like a flock of birds.

When they did start firing it was signaled by strobing red pulses of light. He raised his gun to fire back; the other suited figures in the group had already started firing. Some dived to the dusty desert floor, others dropped to one knee. He was the only one standing.

The missiles swerved again, turning all at once and then splitting up to take different directions. Dust puffed around his feet as shots fell close. He tried to aim at one of the small machines, but they moved startlingly quickly, and the gun felt large and awkward in his hands. His suit chimed over the distant noise of firing and the shouts of the other people; lights winked inside the helmet, detailing the damage. The suit shook and his right leg went suddenly numb.

"Wake up, Gurgeh!" Yay laughed, alongside him. She swiveled on one knee as two of the small missiles swung suddenly at their section of the group, sensing that was where it was weakest. Gurgeh saw the machines coming, but the gun sang wildly in his hands, and seemed always to be aiming at where the missiles had just been. The two machines darted for the space between him and Yay. One of the missiles flashed once and disintegrated; Yay shouted, exulting. The other missile swung between them; she lashed out with her foot, trying to kick it. Gurgeh turned awkwardly to fire at it, accidentally scattering fire over Yay's suit as he did so. He heard her cry out and then curse. She staggered, but brought the gun round; fountains of dust burst around the second missile as it turned to face them again, its red pulses lighting up his suit and filling his visor with darkness. He felt numb from the neck down and crumpled to the ground. It went black and very quiet.

"You are dead," a crisp little voice told him.

He lay on the unseen desert floor. He could hear distant, muffled noises, sense vibrations from the ground. He heard his own heart beat, and the ebb and flow of his breath. He tried to hold his breathing and slow his heart, but he was paralyzed, imprisoned, without control.

His nose itched. It was impossible to scratch it. *What am I doing here?* he asked himself.

Sensation returned. People were talking, and he was staring through the visor at the flattened desert dust a centimeter in front of his nose. Before he could move, somebody pulled him up by one arm.

He unlatched his helmet. Yay Meristinoux, also bare-headed, stood looking at him and shaking her head. Her hands were on her hips, her gun swung from one wrist. "You were terrible," she said, though not unkindly. She had the face of a beautiful child, but the slow, deep voice was knowing and roguish; a low-slung voice.

The others sat around on the rocks and dust, talking. A few were heading back to the club house. Yay picked up Gurgeh's gun and presented it to him. He scratched his nose, then shook his head, refusing to take the weapon.

"Yay," he told her, "this is for children."

She paused, slung her gun over one shoulder, and shrugged (and the muzzles of both guns swung in the sunlight, glinting momentarily, and he saw the speeding line of missiles again, and was dizzy for a second).

"So?" she said. "It isn't boring. You said you were bored; I thought you might enjoy a shoot."

He dusted himself down and turned back toward the club house. Yay walked alongside. Recovery drones drifted past them, collecting the components of the destructed machines.

"It's infantile, Yay. Why fritter your time away with this nonsense?"

They stopped at the top of the dune. The low club house lay a hundred meters away, between them and the golden sand and snow-white surf. The sea was bright under the high sun.

"Don't be so pompous," she told him. Her short brown hair moved in the same wind which blew the tops from the falling waves and sent the resulting spray curling back out to sea. She stooped to where some pieces of a shattered missile lay half buried in the dune, picked them up, blew sand grains off the shining surfaces, and turned the components over in her hands. "I enjoy it," she said. "I enjoy the sort of games you like, but . . . I enjoy this too." She looked puzzled. "*This* is a game. Don't you get *any* pleasure from this sort of thing?"

"No. And neither will you, after a while."

She shrugged easily. "Till then, then." She handed him the parts of the disintegrated machine. He inspected them while a group of young men passed, heading for the firing ranges.

"Mr. Gurgeh?" One of the young males stopped, looking at Gurgeh quizzically. A fleeting expression of annoyance passed across the older man's face, to be replaced by the amused tolerance Yay had seen before in such situations. "Jernau *Morat* Gurgeh?" the young man said, still not quite sure.

"Guilty." Gurgeh smiled gracefully and—Yay saw—straightened his back fractionally, drawing himself up a little. The younger man's face lit up. He executed a quick, formal bow. Gurgeh and Yay exchanged glances.

"An *honor* to meet you, Mr. Gurgeh," the young man said, smiling widely. "My name's Shuro . . . I'm . . ." He laughed. "I follow all your games; I have a complete set of your theoretical works on file . . ."

Gurgeh nodded. "How comprehensive of you."

"Really. I'd be honored if, any time you're here, you'd play me at . . . well, anything. Deploy is probably my best game; I play off three points, but—"

"Whereas my handicap, regrettably, is lack of time," Gurgeh said. "But, certainly, if the chance ever arises, I shall be happy to play you." He gave a hint of a nod to the younger man. "A pleasure to have met you."

The young man flushed and backed off, smiling. "The pleasure's all mine, Mr. Gurgeh. . . . Goodbye . . . goodbye." He smiled awkwardly, then turned and walked off to join his companions.

Yay watched him go. "You enjoy all that stuff, don't you, Gurgeh?" she grinned.

"Not at all," he said briskly. "It's annoying."

Yay continued to watch the young man walking away, looking him up and down as he tramped off through the sand. She sighed.

"But what about you?" Gurgeh looked with distaste at the pieces of missile in his hands. "Do you enjoy all this . . . destruction?"

"It's hardly destruction," Yay drawled. "The missiles are explosively dismantled, not destroyed. I can put one of those things back together in half an hour."

"So it's false."

"What isn't?"

"Intellectual achievement. The exercise of skill. Human feeling."

Yay just grinned. She said, "I can see we have a long way to go before we understand each other, Gurgeh."

"Then let me help you."

"Be your protégée?"

"Yes."

Yay looked away, to where the rollers fell against the golden beach, and then back again. As the wind blew and the surf pounded, she reached slowly behind her head and brought the suit's helmet over, clicking it into place. He was left staring at the reflection of his own face in her visor. He ran one hand through the black locks of his hair.

Yay flicked her visor up. "I'll see you, Gurgeh. Chamlis and I are coming round to your place the day after tomorrow, aren't we?"

"If you want."

"I want." She winked at him and walked back down the slope of sand. He watched her go. She handed his gun to a recovery drone as it passed her, loaded with glittering metallic debris.

Gurgeh stood for a moment, holding the bits of wrecked machine. Then he let the fragments drop back to the barren sand.

He could smell the earth and the trees around the shallow lake beneath the balcony. It was a cloudy night and very dark, just a hint of glow directly above, where the clouds were lit by the shining Plates of the Orbital's distant daylight side. Waves lapped in the darkness, loud slappings against the hulls of unseen boats. Lights twinkled round the edges of the lake, where low college buildings were set among the trees. The party was a presence at his back, something unseen, surging like the sound and smell of thunder from the faculty building; music and laughter and the scents of perfumes and food and exotic, unidentifiable fumes.

The rush of *Sharp Blue* surrounded him, invaded him. The fragrances on the warm night air, spilling from the line of opened doors behind, carried on the tide of noise the people made, became like separate strands of air, fibers unraveling from a rope, each with its own distinct color and presence. The fibers became like packets of soil, something to be rubbed between his fingers; absorbed, identified.

There: that red-black scent of roasted meat; blood-quickening, salivatory; tempting and vaguely disagreeable at the same time as separate parts of his brain assessed the odor. The animal root smelled fuel; protein-rich food; the mid-brain trunk registered dead, incinerated cells . . . while the canopy of forebrain ignored both signals, because it knew his belly was full, and the roast meat cultivated.

He could detect the sea, too; a brine smell from ten or more kilometers away over the plain and the shallow downs, another threaded connection, like the net and web of rivers and canals that linked the dark lake to the restless, flowing ocean beyond the fragrant grasslands and the scented forests.

*Sharp Blue* was a game-player's secretion, a product of standard genofixed Culture glands sitting in Gurgeh's lower skull, beneath the ancient, animal-evolved lower reaches of his brain. The panoply of internally manufactured drugs the vast majority of Culture individuals were capable of choosing from comprised up to three hundred different compounds of varying degrees of popularity and sophistication; *Sharp Blue* was one of the least used because it brought no direct pleasure and required considerable concentration to produce. But it was good for games. What seemed complicated became simple; what appeared insoluble became soluble; what had been unknowable became obvious. A utility drug; an abstraction-modifier; not a sensory enhancer or a sexual stimulant or a physiological booster.

And he didn't need it.

That was what was revealed, as soon as the first rush died away and the plateau phase took over. The lad he was about to play, whose previous match of Four-Colors he had just watched, had a deceptive style, but an easily mastered one. It looked impressive, but it was mostly show; fashionable, intricate, but hollow and delicate too; finally vulnerable. Gurgeh listened to the sounds of the party and the sounds of the lake waters and the sounds coming from the other university buildings on the far side of the lake. The memory of the young man's playing style remained clear.

Dispense with it, he decided there and then. Let the spell collapse.

Something inside him relaxed, like a ghost limb untensed; a mind-trick. The spell, the brain's equivalent of some tiny, crude, looping sub-program, collapsed, simply ceased to be said.

He stood on the terrace by the lake for a while, then turned and went back into the party.

"Jernau Gurgeh. I thought you'd run off."

He turned to face the small drone which had floated up to him as he re-entered the richly furnished hall. People stood talking, or clustered around game-boards and tables beneath the great banners of ancient tapestries. There were dozens of drones in the room too, some playing, some watching, some talking to humans, a few in the formal, lattice-like arrangements which meant they were communicating by transceiver. Mawhrin-Skel, the drone which had addressed him, was by far the smallest of the machines present; it could have sat comfortably on a pair of hands. Its aura field held shifting hints of gray and brown within the band of formal blue. It looked like a model of an intricate and old-fashioned spacecraft.

Gurgeh scowled at the machine as it followed him through the crowds of people to the Four-Colors table.

"I thought perhaps this toddler had scared you," the drone said, as Gurgeh arrived at the young man's game-table and sat down in a tall, heavily ornamented wooden chair hurriedly vacated by his just-beaten predecessor. The drone had spoken loudly enough for the "toddler" concerned—a tousle-haired man of about thirty or so—to hear. The young man's face looked hurt.

Gurgeh sensed the people around him grow a little quieter. Mawhrin-Skel's aura fields switched to a mixture of red and brown; humorous pleasure, and displeasure, together; a contrary signal close to a direct insult.

"Ignore this machine," Gurgeh told the young man, acknowledging his nod. "It likes to annoy people." He pulled his chair in, adjusted his old, unfashionably loose and wide-sleeved jacket. "I'm Jernau Gurgeh. And you?"

"Stemli Fors," the young man said, gulping a little.

"Pleased to meet you. Now; what color are you taking?"

"Aah . . . green."

"Fine." Gurgeh sat back. He paused, then waved at the board. "Well, after you."

The young man called Stemli Fors made his first move. Gurgeh sat forward to make his, and the drone Mawhrin-Skel settled on his shoulder, humming to itself. Gurgeh tapped the machine's casing with one finger, and it floated off a little way. For the rest of the match it mimicked the snicking sound the point-hinged pyramids made as they were clicked over.

Gurgeh beat the young man easily. He even finessed the finish a little, taking advantage of Fors's confusion to produce a pretty pattern at the end, sweeping one piece round four diagonals in a machine-gun clatter of rotating pyramids, drawing the outline of a square across the board, in red, like a wound. Several people clapped; others muttered appreciatively. Gurgeh thanked the young man and stood up.

"Cheap trick," Mawhrin-Skel said, for all to hear. "The kid was easy meat. You're losing your touch." Its field flashed bright red, and it bounced through the air, over people's heads and away.

Gurgeh shook his head, then strode off.

The little drone annoyed and amused him in almost equal parts. It was rude, insulting and frequently infuriating, but it made such a refreshing change from the awful politeness of most people. No doubt it had swept off to annoy somebody else now. Gurgeh nodded to a few people as he moved through the crowd. He saw the drone Chamlis Amalk-ney by a long, low table, talking to one of the less insufferable professors. Gurgeh went over to them, taking a drink from a waiting-tray as it floated past.

"Ah, my friend . . ." Chamlis Amalk-ney said. The elderly drone was a meter and a half tall and over half a meter wide and deep, its plain casing matte with the accumulated wear of millennia. It turned its sensing band toward him. "The professor and I were just talking about you."

Professor Boruelal's severe expression translated into an ironic smile. "Fresh from another victory, Jernau Gurgeh?"

"Does it show?" he said, raising the glass to his lips.

"I have learned to recognize the signs," the professor said. She was twice Gurgeh's age, well into her second century, but still tall and handsome and striking. Her skin was pale and her hair was white, as it always had been, and cropped. "Another of my students humiliated?"

Gurgeh shrugged. He drained the glass, looked round for a tray to put it on.

"Allow me," Chamlis Amalk-ney murmured, gently taking the glass from his hand and placing it on a passing tray a good three meters away. Its yellow-tinged field brought back a full glass of the same rich wine. Gurgeh accepted it.

Boruelal wore a dark suit of soft fabric, lightened at throat and knees by delicate silver chains. Her feet were bare, which Gurgeh thought did not set off the outfit as—say—a pair of heeled boots might have done. But it was the most minor of eccentricities compared to those of some of the university staff. Gurgeh smiled, looking down at the woman's toes, tan upon the blond wooden flooring.

"You're so destructive, Gurgeh," Boruelal told him. "Why not help us instead? Become part of the faculty instead of an itinerant guest lecturer?"

"I've told you, Professor; I'm too busy. I have more than enough games to play, papers to write, letters to answer, guest trips to make . . . and besides . . . I'd get bored. I bore easily, you know," Gurgeh said, and looked away.

"Jernau Gurgeh would make a very bad teacher," Chamlis Amalk-ney agreed. "If a student failed to understand something immediately, no matter how complicated and involved, Gurgeh would immediately lose all patience and quite probably pour their drink over them . . . if nothing worse."

"So I've heard." The professor nodded gravely.

"That was a year ago," Gurgeh said, frowning. "And Yay deserved it." He scowled at the old drone.

"Well," the professor said, looking momentarily at Chamlis, "perhaps we have found a match for you, Jernau Gurgeh. There's a young—" Then there was a crash in the distance, and the background noise in the hall increased. They each turned at the sound of people shouting.

"Oh, not another commotion," the professor said tiredly.

Already that evening, one of the younger lecturers had lost control of a pet bird, which had gone screeching and swooping through the hall, tangling in the hair of several people before the drone Mawhrin-Skel intercepted the animal in midair and knocked it unconscious, much to the chagrin of most of the people at the party.

"What now?" Boruelal sighed. "Excuse me." She absently left glass and savory on Chamlis Amalk-ney's broad, flat top and moved off, excusing her way through the crowd toward the source of the upheaval.

Chamlis's aura flickered a displeased gray-white. It set the glass down noisily on the table and threw the savory into a distant bin. "It's that dreadful machine Mawhrin-Skel," Chamlis said testily.

Gurgeh looked over the crowd to where all the noise was coming from. "Really?" he said. "What, causing all the rumpus?"

"I really don't know why you find it so appealing," the old drone said. It picked up Boruelal's glass again and poured the pale gold wine out into an outstretched field, so that the liquid lay cupped in midair, as though in an invisible glass.

"It amuses me," Gurgeh replied. He looked at Chamlis. "Boruelal said something about finding a match for me. Was that what you were talking about earlier?"

"Yes it was. Some new student they've found; a GSV cabin-brat with a gift for Stricken."

Gurgeh raised one eyebrow. Stricken was one of the more complex games in his repertoire. It was also one of his best. There were other human players in the Culture who could beat him—though they were all specialists at the game, not general game-players as he was—but not one of them could guarantee a win, and they were few and far between, probably only ten in the whole population.

"So, who is this talented infant?" The noise on the far side of the room had lessened.

"It's a young woman," Chamlis said, slopping the field-held

liquid about and letting it dribble through thin strands of hollow, invisible force. "Just arrived here; came off the *Cargo Cult;* still settling in."

The General Systems Vehicle *Cargo Cult* had stopped off at Chiark Orbital ten days earlier, and left only two days ago. Gurgeh had played a few multiple exhibition matches on the craft (and been secretly delighted that they had been clean sweeps; he hadn't been beaten in any of the various games), but he hadn't played Stricken at all. A few of his opponents had mentioned something about a supposedly brilliant (though shy) young game-player on the Vehicle, but he or she hadn't turned up as far as Gurgeh knew, and he'd assumed the reports of this prodigy's powers were much exaggerated. Ship people tended to have a quaint pride in their craft; they liked to feel that even though they had been beaten by the great game-player, their vessel still had the measure of him, somewhere (of course, the *ship* itself did, but that didn't count; they meant people; humans, or 1.0 value drones).

"You are a mischievous and contrary device," Boruelal said to the drone Mawhrin-Skel, floating at her shoulder, its aura field orange with well-being, but circled with little purple motes of unconvincing contrition.

"Oh," Mawhrin-Skel said brightly, "do you really think so?"

"Talk to this appalling machine, Jernau Gurgeh," the professor said, frowning momentarily at the top of Chamlis Amalkney's casing, then picking up a fresh glass. (Chamlis poured the liquid it had been playing with into Boruelal's original glass and replaced it on the table.)

"What have you been doing now?" Gurgeh asked Mawhrin-Skel as it floated near his face.

"Anatomy lesson," it said, its fields collapsing to a mixture of formal blue and brown ill-humor.

"A chirlip was found on the terrace," Boruelal explained, looking accusingly at the little drone. "It was wounded. Somebody brought it in, and Mawhrin-Skel offered to treat it."

"I wasn't busy," Mawhrin-Skel interjected, reasonably.

"It killed and dissected it in front of all the people," the professor sighed. "They were most upset."

"It would have died from shock anyway," Mawhrin-Skel said. "They're fascinating creatures, chirlips. Those cute little fur-folds conceal partially cantilevered bones, and the looped digestive system is quite fascinating."

"But not when people are eating," Boruelal said, selecting another savory from the tray. "It was still moving," she added glumly. She ate the savory.

"Residual synaptic capacitance," explained Mawhrin-Skel.

"Or 'Bad Taste' as we machines call it," Chamlis Amalk-ney said.

"An expert in that, are you, Amalk-ney?" Mawhrin-Skel inquired.

"I bow to your superior talents in that field," Chamlis snapped back.

Gurgeh smiled. Chamlis Amalk-ney was an old—and ancient—friend; the drone had been constructed over four thousand years ago (it claimed it had forgotten the exact date, and nobody had ever been impolite enough to search out the truth). Gurgeh had known the drone all his life; it had been a friend of the family for centuries.

Mawhrin-Skel was a more recent acquaintance. The irascible, ill-mannered little machine had arrived on Chiark Orbital only a couple of hundred days earlier; another untypical character attracted there by the world's exaggerated reputation for eccentricity.

Mawhrin-Skel had been designed as a Special Circumstances

drone for the Culture's Contact section; effectively a military machine with a variety of sophisticated, hardened sensory and weapons systems which would have been quite unnecessary and useless on the majority of drones. As with all sentient Culture constructs, its precise character had not been fully mapped out before its construction, but allowed to develop as the drone's mind was put together. The Culture regarded this unpredictable factor in its production of conscious machines as the price to be paid for individuality, but the result was that not every drone so brought into being was entirely suitable for the tasks it had initially been designed for.

Mawhrin-Skel was one such rogue drone. Its personality—it had been decided—wasn't right for Contact, not even for Special Circumstances. It was unstable, belligerent and insensitive. (And those were only the grounds it had chosen to tell people it had failed on.) It had been given the choice of radical personality alteration, in which it would have had little or no say in its own eventual character, or a life outside Contact, with its personality intact but its weapons and its more complex communications and sensory systems removed to bring it down to something nearer the level of a standard drone.

It had, bitterly, chosen the latter. And it had made its way to Chiark Orbital, where it hoped it might fit in.

"Meatbrain," Mawhrin-Skel told Chamlis Amalk-ney, and zoomed off toward the line of open windows. The older drone's aura field flashed white with anger and a bright, rippling spot of rainbow light revealed that it was using its tight-beam transceiver to communicate with the departing machine. Mawhrin-Skel stopped in midair; turned. Gurgeh held his breath, wondering what Chamlis could have said, and what the smaller drone might say in reply, knowing that it wouldn't bother to keep its remarks secret, as Chamlis had.

"What I resent," it said slowly, from a couple of meters away, "is not what I have lost, but what I have gained, in coming—even remotely—to resemble fatigued, path-polished geriatrics like you, who haven't even got the human decency to die when they're obsolete. You're a waste of matter, Amalk-ney."

Mawhrin-Skel became a mirrored sphere, and in that ostentatiously uncommunicable mode swept out of the hall into the darkness.

"Cretinous whelp," Chamlis said, fields frosty blue.

Boruelal shrugged. "I feel sorry for it."

"I don't," Gurgeh said. "I think it has a wonderful time." He turned to the professor. "When do I get to meet your young Stricken genius? Not hiding her away to train her, are you?"

"No, we're just giving her time to adjust." Boruelal picked at her teeth with the pointed end of the savory stick. "From what I can gather the girl had rather a sheltered upbringing. Sounds like she hardly left the GSV; she must feel odd being here. Also, she isn't here to do game-theory, Jernau Gurgeh, I'd better point that out. She's going to study philosophy."

Gurgeh looked suitably surprised.

"A sheltered upbringing?" Chamlis Amalk-ney said. "On a GSV?" Its gunmetal aura indicated puzzlement.

"She's shy."

"She'd have to be."

"I must meet her," said Gurgeh.

"You will," Boruelal said. "Soon, maybe; she said she might come with me to Tronze for the next concert. Hafflis runs a game there, doesn't he?"

"Usually," Gurgeh agreed.

"Maybe she'll play you there. But don't be surprised if you just intimidate her."

"I shall be the epitome of gentle good grace," Gurgeh assured her.

Boruelal nodded thoughtfully. She gazed out over the party and looked distracted for a second as a large cheer sounded from the center of the hall.

"Excuse me," she said. "I think I detect a nascent commotion." She moved away. Chamlis Amalk-ney shifted aside, to avoid being used as a table again; the professor took her glass with her.

"Did you meet Yay this morning?" Chamlis asked Gurgeh.

He nodded. "She had me dressed up in a suit, toting a gun and shooting at toy missiles which 'explosively dismantled' themselves."

"You didn't enjoy it."

"Not at all. I had high hopes for that girl, but too much of that sort of nonsense and I think her intelligence will explosively dismantle."

"Well, such diversions aren't for everybody. She was just trying to be helpful. You'd said you were feeling restless, looking for something new."

"Well, that wasn't it," Gurgeh said, and felt suddenly, inexplicably, saddened.

He and Chamlis watched as people began to move past them, heading toward the long line of windows which opened onto the terrace. There was a dull, buzzing sensation inside the man's head; he had entirely forgotten that coming down from *Sharp Blue* required a degree of internal monitoring if you were to avoid an uncomfortable hangover. He watched the people pass with a slight feeling of nausea.

"Must be time for the fireworks," Chamlis said.

"Yes . . . let's get some fresh air, shall we?"

"Just what I need," Chamlis said, aura dully red.

Gurgeh put his glass down, and together he and the old drone joined the flow of people spilling from the bright, tapestry-hung hall onto the floodlit terrace facing the dark lake.

Rain hit the windows with a noise like the crackling of the logs on the fire. The view from the house at Ikroh, down the steep wooded slope to the fjord and across it to the mountains on the other side, was warped and distorted by the water running down the glass, and sometimes low clouds flowed round the turrets and cupolas of Gurgeh's home, like wet smoke.

Yay Meristinoux took a large wrought-iron poker from the hearth and, putting one booted foot up on the elaborately carved stone of the fire surround and one pale brown hand on the rope-like edge of the massive mantelpiece, stabbed at one of the spitting logs lying burning in the grate. Sparks flew up the tall chimney to meet the falling rain.

Chamlis Amalk-ney was floating near the window, watching the dull gray clouds.

The wooden door set into one corner of the room swung open and Gurgeh appeared, bearing a tray with hot drinks. He wore a loose, light robe over dark, baggy trous; slippers made small slapping noises on his feet as he crossed the room. He put the tray down, looked at Yay. "Thought of a move yet?"

Yay crossed over to look morosely at the game-board, shaking her head. "No," she said. "I think you've won."

"Look," Gurgeh said, adjusting a few of the pieces. His hands moved quickly, like a magician's, over the board, though Yay followed every move. She nodded.

"Yes, I see. But"—she tapped a hex Gurgeh had repositioned one of her pieces on, so giving her a potentially winning formation—"only if I'd double-secured that blocking piece two moves earlier." She sat down on the couch, taking her drink with her. Raising her glass to the quietly smiling man on the opposite couch, she said, "Cheers. To the victor."

"You almost won," Gurgeh told her. "Forty-four moves; you're getting very good."

"Relatively," Yay said, drinking. "Only relatively." She lay back on the deep couch while Gurgeh put the pieces back to their starting positions and Chamlis Amalk-ney drifted over to float not-quite-between them. "You know," Yay said, looking at the ornate ceiling, "I always like the way this house *smells,* Gurgeh." She turned to look at the drone. "Don't you, Chamlis?"

The machine's aura field dipped briefly to one side; a drone shrug. "Yes. Probably because the wood our host is burning is *bonise;* it was developed millennia ago by the old Waverian civilization specifically for its fragrance when ignited."

"Yes, well, it's a nice smell," Yay said, getting up and going back to the windows. She shook her head. "Sure as shit rains a lot here though, Gurgeh."

"It's the mountains," the man explained.

Yay glanced round, one eyebrow arched. "You don't say?"

Gurgeh smiled and smoothed one hand over his neatly trimmed beard. "How *is* the landscaping going, Yay?"

"I don't want to talk about it." She shook her head at the continuing downpour. "What weather." She tossed her drink back. "No wonder you live by yourself, Gurgeh."

"Oh, that isn't the rain, Yay," Gurgeh said. "That's me. Nobody can stand to live with me for long."

"He means," Chamlis said, "that he couldn't stand to live for long with anybody."

"I'd believe either," Yay said, coming back to the couch again.

She sat cross-legged on it and played with one of the pieces on the game-board. "What did you think of the match, Chamlis?"

"You have reached the likely limits of your technical ability, but your flair continues to develop. I doubt you'll ever beat Gurgeh, though."

"Hey," Yay said, pretending injured pride. "I'm just a junior; I'll improve." She tapped one set of fingernails against the other, and made a tutting noise with her mouth. "Like I'm told I will at landscaping."

"You having problems?" Chamlis said.

Yay looked as though she hadn't heard for a moment, then sighed, lay back on the couch. "Yeah . . . that asshole Elrstrid and that prissy fucking Preashipleyl machine. They're so . . . unadventurous. They just won't listen."

"What won't they listen to?"

"Ideas!" Yay shouted at the ceiling. "Something different, something not so goddamn conservative for a change. Just because I'm young they won't pay attention."

"I thought they were pleased with your work," Chamlis said. Gurgeh was sitting back in his couch, swirling the drink in his glass round and just watching Yay.

"Oh, they like me to do all the easy stuff," Yay said, sounding suddenly tired. "Stick up a range or two, carve out a couple of lakes . . . but I'm talking about the overall plan; real radical stuff. All we're doing is building just another next-door Plate. Could be one of a million anywhere in the galaxy. What's the point of that?"

"So people can live on it?" Chamlis suggested, fields rosy.

"People can live anywhere!" Yay said, levering herself up from the couch to look at the drone with her bright green eyes. "There's no shortage of Plates; I'm talking about art!"

"What did you have in mind?" Gurgeh asked.

"How about," Yay said, "magnetic fields under the base material and magnetized islands floating over oceans? No *ordinary* land at all; just great floating lumps of rock with streams and lakes and vegetation and a few intrepid people; doesn't that sound more exciting?"

"More exciting than what?" Gurgeh asked.

"More exciting than this!" Meristinoux leapt up and went over to the window. She tapped the ancient pane. "Look at that; you might as well be on a planet. Seas and hills and rain. Wouldn't you rather live on a floating island, sailing through the air *over* the water?"

"What if the islands collide?" Chamlis asked.

"What if they do?" Yay turned to look at the man and the machine. It was getting still darker outside, and the room lights were slowly brightening. She shrugged. "Anyway; you could make it so they didn't . . . but don't you think it's a wonderful idea? Why should one old woman and a machine be able to stop me?"

"Well," Chamlis said, "I know the Preashipleyl machine, and if it thought your idea was good it wouldn't just ignore it; it's had a lot of experience, and—"

"Yeah," Yay said, "too much experience."

"*That* isn't possible, young lady," the drone said.

Yay Meristinoux took a deep breath, and seemed about to argue, but just spread her arms wide and rolled her eyes and turned back to the window. "We'll see," she said.

The afternoon, which had been steadily darkening until then, was suddenly lit up on the far side of the fjord by a bright splash of sunlight filtering through the clouds and the easing rain. The room slowly filled with a watery glow, and the house lights dimmed again. Wind moved the tops of the dripping trees. "Ah," Yay said, stretching her back and flexing her arms.

"Not to worry." She inspected the landscape outside critically. "Hell; I'm going for a run," she announced. She headed for the door in the corner of the room, pulling off first one boot, then the other, throwing the waistcoat over a chair, and unbuttoning her blouse. "You'll see." She wagged a finger at Gurgeh and Chamlis. "Floating islands; their time has come."

Chamlis said nothing. Gurgeh looked skeptical. Yay left.

Chamlis went to the window. It watched the girl—down to a pair of shorts now—run out along the path leading down from the house, between the lawns and the forest. She waved once, without looking back, and disappeared into the woods. Chamlis flickered its fields in response, even though Yay couldn't see.

"She's handsome," it said.

Gurgeh sat back in the couch. "She makes me feel old."

"Oh, don't *you* start feeling sorry for yourself," Chamlis said, floating back from the window.

Gurgeh looked at the hearth stones. "Everything seems . . . gray at the moment, Chamlis. Sometimes I start to think I'm repeating myself, that even new games are just old ones in disguise, and that nothing's worth playing for anyway."

"Gurgeh," Chamlis said matter-of-factly, and did something it rarely did, actually settling physically into the couch, letting it take its weight. "Settle up; are we talking about games, or life?"

Gurgeh put his dark-curled head back and laughed.

"Games," Chamlis went on, "have been your life. If they're starting to pall, I'd understand you might not be so happy with anything else."

"Maybe I'm just disillusioned with games," Gurgeh said, turning a carved game-piece over in his hands. "I used to think that context didn't matter; a good game was a good game and there was a purity about manipulating rules that translated perfectly from society to society . . . but now I wonder. Take this; Deploy." He nodded at the board in front of him. "This is foreign. Some backwater planet discovered just a few decades ago. They play this there and they bet on it; they make it important. But what do we have to bet with? What would be the point of my wagering Ikroh, say?"

"Yay wouldn't take the bet, certainly," Chamlis said, amused. "She thinks it rains too much."

"But you see? If somebody wanted a house like this they'd already have had one built; if they wanted anything in the house"—Gurgeh gestured round the room—"they'd have ordered it; they'd have it. With no money, no possessions, a large part of the enjoyment the people who invented this game experienced when they played it just . . . disappears."

"You call it enjoyment to lose your house, your titles, your estates; your children maybe; to be expected to walk out onto the balcony with a gun and blow your brains out? That's enjoyment? We're well free of that. You want something you can't have, Gurgeh. You enjoy your life in the Culture, but it can't provide you with sufficient threats; the true gambler needs the excitement of potential loss, even ruin, to feel wholly alive." Gurgeh remained silent, lit by the fire and the soft glow from the room's concealed lighting. "You called yourself 'Morat' when you completed your name, but perhaps you aren't the perfect game-player after all; perhaps you should have called yourself 'Shequi'; gambler."

"You know," Gurgeh said slowly, his voice hardly louder than the crackling logs in the fire, "I'm actually slightly afraid of playing this young kid." He glanced at the drone. "Really. Because I do enjoy winning, because I do have something nobody can copy, something nobody else can have; I'm me; I'm one of the best." He looked quickly, briefly up at the machine again, as though ashamed. "But every now and again, I *do* worry about losing; I think, what if there's some kid—especially some kid, somebody younger and just naturally more talented—out there, able to take that away from me. That worries me. The better I do the worse things get because the more I have to lose."

"You are a throwback," Chamlis told him. "The game's the thing. That's the conventional wisdom, isn't it? The fun is what matters, not the victory. To glory in the defeat of another, to need that purchased pride, is to show you are incomplete and inadequate to start with."

Gurgeh nodded slowly. "So they say. So everybody else believes."

"But not you?"

"I . . ." The man seemed to have difficulty finding the right word. "I . . . *exult* when I win. It's better than love, it's better than sex or any glanding; it's the only instant when I feel . . ."—he shook his head, his mouth tightened— ". . . real," he said. "Me. The rest of the time . . . I feel a bit like that little ex–Special Circumstances drone, Mawhrin-Skel; as though I've had some sort of . . . birthright taken away from me."

"Ah, is that the affinity you feel?" Chamlis said coldly, aura to match. "I wondered what you saw in that appalling machine."

"Bitterness," Gurgeh said, sitting back again. "That's what I see in it. It has novelty value, at least." He got up and went to the fire, prodding at the logs with the wrought-iron poker and placing another piece of wood on, handling the log awkwardly with heavy tongs.

"This is not a heroic age," he told the drone, staring at the fire. "The individual is obsolete. That's why life is so comfortable for us all. We don't matter, so we're safe. No one person can have any real effect anymore."

"Contact uses individuals," Chamlis pointed out. "It puts

people into younger societies who have a dramatic and decisive effect on the fates of entire meta-civilizations. They're usually 'mercenaries,' not Culture, but they're human, they're people."

"They're selected and used. Like game-pieces. They don't count." Gurgeh sounded impatient. He left the tall fireplace, returned to the couch. "Besides, I'm not one of them."

"So have yourself stored until a more heroic age does arrive."

"Huh," Gurgeh said, sitting again. "If it ever does. It would seem too much like cheating, anyway."

The drone Chamlis Amalk-ney listened to the rain and the fire. "Well," it said slowly, "if it's novelty value you want, Contact—never mind SC—are the people to go to."

"I have no intention of applying to join Contact," Gurgeh said. "Being cooped up in a GCU with a bunch of gung-ho do-gooders searching for barbarians to teach is not my idea of either enjoyment or fulfillment."

"I didn't mean that. I meant that Contact had the best Minds, the most information. They might be able to come up with some ideas. Any time I've ever been involved with them they've got things done. It's a last resort, mind you."

"Why?"

"Because they're tricky. Devious. They're gamblers, too; and used to winning."

"Hmm," Gurgeh said, and stroked his dark beard. "I wouldn't know how to go about it," he said.

"Nonsense," Chamlis said. "Anyway; I have my own connections there; I'd—"

A door slammed. "Holy *shit* it's cold out there!" Yay burst into the room, shaking herself. Her arms were clenched across her chest and her thin shorts were stuck to her thighs; her whole body was quivering. Gurgeh got up from the couch.

"Come here to the fire," Chamlis told the girl. Yay stood shivering in front of the window, dripping water. "Don't just stand there," Chamlis told Gurgeh. "Fetch a towel."

Gurgeh looked critically at the machine, then left the room.

By the time he came back, Chamlis had persuaded Yay to kneel in front of the fire; a bowed field over the nape of her neck held her head down to the heat, while another field brushed her hair. Little drops of water fell from her drenched curls to the hearth, hissing on the hot flagstones.

Chamlis took the towel from Gurgeh's hands, and the man watched as the machine moved the towel over the young woman's body. He looked away at one point, shaking his head, and sat down on the couch again, sighing.

"Your feet are filthy," he told the girl.

"Ah, it was a good run though," Yay laughed from beneath the towel.

With much blowing and whistling and "brr-brrs," Yay was dried. She kept the towel wrapped round her and sat, legs drawn up, on the couch. "I'm famished," she announced suddenly. "Mind if I make myself something to—?"

"Let me," Gurgeh said. He went through the corner door, reappearing briefly to drape Yay's hide trous over the same chair she'd left the waistcoat on.

"What were you talking about?" Yay asked Chamlis.

"Gurgeh's disaffection."

"Do any good?"

"I don't know," the drone admitted.

Yay retrieved her clothes and dressed quickly. She sat in front of the fire for a while, watching it as the day's light faded and the room lights came up.

Gurgeh brought a tray in loaded with sweetmeats and drinks.

* * *

Once Yay and Gurgeh had eaten, the three of them played a complicated card-game of the type Gurgeh liked best; one that involved bluff and just a little luck. They were in the middle of the game when friends of Yay's and Gurgeh's arrived, their aircraft touching down on a house lawn Gurgeh would rather they hadn't used. They came in bright and noisy and laughing; Chamlis retreated to a corner by the window.

Gurgeh played the good host, keeping his guests supplied with refreshments. He brought a fresh glass to Yay where she stood, listening with a group of others, to a couple of people arguing about education.

"Are you leaving with this lot, Yay?" Gurgeh leaned back against the tapestried wall behind, dropping his voice a little so that Yay had to turn away from the discussion, to face him.

"Maybe," she said slowly. Her face glowed in the light of the fire. "You're going to ask me to stay again, aren't you?" She swirled her drink around in her glass, watching it.

"Oh," Gurgeh said, shaking his head and looking up at the ceiling, "I doubt it. I get bored going through the same old moves and responses."

Yay smiled. "You never know," she said. "One day I might change my mind. You shouldn't let it bother you, Gurgeh. It's almost an honor."

"You mean to be such an exception?"

"Mmm." She drank.

"I don't understand you," he told her.

"Because I turn you down?"

"Because you don't turn anybody else down."

"Not so consistently." Yay nodded, frowning at her drink.

"So; why not?" There. He'd finally said it.

Yay pursed her lips. "Because," she said, looking up at him, "it matters to you."

"Ah," he nodded, looking down, rubbing his beard. "I should have feigned indifference." He looked straight at her. "Really, Yay."

"I feel you want to . . . take me," Yay said, "like a piece, like an area. To be had; to be . . . possessed." Suddenly she looked very puzzled. "There's something very . . . I don't know; primitive, perhaps, about you, Gurgeh. You've never changed sex, have you?" He shook his head. "Or slept with a man?" Another shake. "I thought so," Yay said. "You're strange, Gurgeh." She drained her glass.

"Because I don't find men attractive?"

"Yes; *you're* a man!" She laughed.

"Should I be attracted to myself, then?"

Yay studied him for a while, a small smile flickering on her face. Then she laughed and looked down. "Well, not physically, anyway." She grinned at him and handed him her empty glass. Gurgeh refilled it; she returned back to the others.

Gurgeh left Yay arguing about the place of geology in Culture education policy, and went to talk to Ren Myglan, a young woman he'd been hoping would call in that evening.

One of the people had brought a pet; a proto-sentient Stygian enumerator which padded round the room, counting under its slightly fishy breath. The slim, three-limbed animal, blond-haired and waist-high, with no discernible head but lots of meaningful bulges, started counting people; there were twenty-three in the room. Then it began counting articles of furniture, after which it concentrated on legs. It wandered up to Gurgeh and Ren Myglan. Gurgeh looked down at the animal peering at his feet and making vague, swaying, pawing motions at his slippers. He tapped it with his toe. "Say six," the enumerator muttered, wandering off. Gurgeh went on talking to the woman.

After a few minutes, standing near her, talking, occasionally moving a little closer, he was whispering into her ear, and once or twice he reached round behind her, to run his fingers down her spine through the silky dress she wore.

"I said I'd go on with the others," she told him quietly, looking down, biting her lip, and putting her hand behind her, holding his where it rubbed at the small of her back.

"Some boring band, some singer, performing for everybody?" he chided gently, taking his hand away, smiling. "You deserve more individual attention, Ren."

She laughed quietly, nudging him.

Eventually she left the room, and didn't return. Gurgeh strolled over to where Yay was gesticulating wildly and extolling the virtues of life on floating magnetic islands, then saw Chamlis in the corner, studiously ignoring the three-legged pet, which was staring up at the machine and trying to scratch one of its bulges without falling over. He shooed the beast away and talked to Chamlis for a while.

Finally the crowd of people left, clutching bottles and a few raided trays of sweetmeats. The aircraft hissed into the night.

Gurgeh, Yay and Chamlis finished their card-game; Gurgeh won.

"Well, I have to go," Yay said, standing and stretching. "Chamlis?"

"Also. I'll come with you; we can share a car."

Gurgeh saw them to the house elevator. Yay buttoned her cloak. Chamlis turned to Gurgeh. "Want me to say anything to Contact?"

Gurgeh, who'd been absently looking up the stairs leading to the main house, looked puzzledly at Chamlis. So did Yay. "Oh, yes," Gurgeh said, smiling. He shrugged. "Why not? See what our betters can come up with. What have I got to lose?" He laughed.

"I love to see you happy," Yay said, kissing him lightly. She stepped into the elevator; Chamlis followed her. Yay winked at Gurgeh as the door closed. "My regards to Ren," she grinned.

Gurgeh stared at the closed door for a moment, then shook his head, smiling to himself. He went back to the lounge, where a couple of the house remote-drones were tidying up; everything seemed back in place, as it should be. He went over to the game-board set between the dark couches, and adjusted one of the Deploy pieces so that it sat in the center of its starting hexagon, then looked at the couch where Yay had sat after she'd come back from her run. There was a fading patch of dampness there, dark on dark. He put his hand out hesitantly, touched it, sniffed his fingers, then laughed at himself. He took an umbrella and went out to inspect the damage done to the lawn by the aircraft, before returning to the house, where a light in the squat main tower told that Ren was waiting for him.

The elevator dropped two hundred meters through the mountain, then through the bedrock underneath; it slowed to cycle through a rotate-lock and gently lowered itself through the meter of ultradense base material to stop underneath the Orbital Plate in a transit gallery, where a couple of underground cars waited and the outside screens showed sunlight blazing up onto the Plate base. Yay and Chamlis got into a car, told it where they wanted to go, and sat down as it unlocked itself, turned and accelerated away.

"Contact?" Yay said to Chamlis. The floor of the small car hid the sun, and beyond the sidescreens stars shone sharply. The car whizzed by some of the arrays of the vital but generally indecipherably obscure equipment that hung beneath every Plate. "Did I hear the name of the great benign bogy being mentioned?"

"I suggested Gurgeh might contact Contact," Chamlis said. It floated to a screen. The screen detached itself, still showing the view outside, and floated up the car wall until the decimeter of space its thickness had occupied in the skin of the vehicle was revealed. Where the screen had pretended to be a window was now a real window; a slab of transparent crystal with hard vacuum and the rest of the universe on the other side. Chamlis looked out at the stars. "It occurred to me they might have some ideas; something to occupy him."

"I thought you were wary of Contact?"

"I am, generally, but I know a few of the Minds; I still have some connections . . . I'd trust them to help, I think."

"I don't know," Yay said. "We're all taking this awful seriously; he'll come out of it. He's got friends. Nothing too terrible's going to happen to him as long as his pals are around."

"Hmm," the drone said. The car stopped at one of the elevator tubes serving the village where Chamlis Amalk-ney lived. "Will we see you in Tronze?" the drone asked.

"No, I've a site conference that evening," Yay said. "And then there's a young fellow I saw at the shoot the other day . . . I've arranged to bump into him that night." She grinned.

"I see," Chamlis said. "Lapsing into predatory mode, eh? Well, enjoy your bumping."

"I'll try," Yay laughed. She and the drone bade each other good night, then Chamlis went through the car's lock—its ancient, minutely battered casing suddenly bright in the blast of sunlight from underneath—and went straight up the elevator tube, without waiting for a lift. Yay smiled and shook her head at such geriatric precocity, as the car pulled away again.

Ren slept on, half covered by a sheet. Her black hair spilled across the top of the bed. Gurgeh sat at his occasional desk near the balcony windows, looking out at the night. The rain had passed, the clouds thinned and separated, and now the light of the stars and the four Plates on the far, balancing side of the Chiark Orbital—three million kilometers away and with their inner faces in daylight—cast a silvery sheen on the passing clouds and made the dark fjord waters glitter.

He turned on the deskpad, pressed its calibrated margin a few times until he found the relevant publications, then read for a while; papers on game-theory by other respected players, reviews of some of their games, analyses of new games and promising players.

He opened the windows later and stepped out onto the circular balcony, shivering a little as the cool night air touched his nakedness. He'd taken his pocket terminal with him, and braved the cold for a while, talking to the dark trees and the silent fiord, dictating a new paper on old games.

When he went back in, Ren Myglan was still asleep, but breathing quickly and erratically. Intrigued, he went over to her and crouched down by the side of the bed, looking intently at her face as it twitched and contorted in her sleep. Her breath labored in her throat and down her delicate nose, and her nostrils flared.

Gurgeh squatted like that for some minutes, with an odd expression on his face, somewhere between a sneer and a sad smile, wondering—with a sense of vague frustration, even regret—what sort of nightmares the young woman must be having, to make her quiver and pant and whimper so.

The next two days passed relatively uneventfully. He spent most of the time reading papers by other players and theorists, and finished a paper of his own which he'd started the night Ren Myglan stayed. Ren had left during breakfast the next morning, after an argument; he liked to work during breakfast, she'd wanted to talk. He'd suspected she was just tetchy after not sleeping well.

He caught up on some correspondence. Mostly it was in the form of requests; to visit other worlds, take part in great tournaments, write papers, comment on new games, become a teacher/lecturer/professor in various educational establishments, be a guest on any one of several GSVs, take on such-and-such a child prodigy . . . it was a long list.

He turned them all down. It gave him a rather pleasant feeling.

There was a communication from a GCU which claimed to have discovered a world on which there was a game based on the precise topography of individual snowflakes; a game which, for that reason, was never played on the same board twice. Gurgeh had never heard of such a game, and could find no mention of it in the usually up-to-date files Contact collated for people like him. He suspected the game was a fake—GCUs were notoriously mischievous—but sent a considered and germane (if also rather ironic) reply, because the joke, if it was a joke, appealed to him.

He watched a gliding competition over the mountains and cliffs on the far side of the fjord.

He turned on the house holoscreen and watched a recently made entertainment he'd heard people talking about. It concerned a planet whose intelligent inhabitants were sentient glaciers and their iceberg children. He had expected to despise its preposterousness, but found it quite amusing. He sketched out a glacier game, based on what sort of minerals could be gouged from rocks, what mountains destroyed, rivers dammed, landscapes created and bays blocked if—as in the entertainment—glaciers could liquefy and re-freeze parts of themselves at will. The game was diverting enough, but contained nothing original; he abandoned it after an hour or so.

He spent much of the next day swimming in Ikroh's basement pool; when doing the backstroke, he dictated as well, his pocket terminal tracking up and down the pool with him, just overhead.

In the late afternoon a woman and her young daughter came riding through the forest and stopped off at Ikroh. Neither of them showed any sign of having heard of him; they just happened to be passing. He invited them to stay for a drink, and made them a late lunch; they tethered their tall, panting mounts in the shade at the side of the house, where the drones gave them water. He advised the woman on the most scenic route to take when she and her daughter resumed their journey, and gave the child a piece from a highly ornamented Bataos set she'd admired.

He took dinner on the terrace, the terminal screen open and showing the pages of an ancient barbarian treatise on games. The book—a millennium old when the civilization had been Contacted, two thousand years earlier—was limited in its appreciation, of course, but Gurgeh never ceased to be fascinated by the way a society's games revealed so much about its ethos, its philosophy, its very soul. Besides, barbarian societies had always intrigued him, even before their games had.

The book was interesting. He rested his eyes watching the sun going down, then went back to it as the darkness deepened. The house drones brought him drinks, a heavier jacket, a light snack, as he requested them. He told the house to refuse all incoming calls.

The terrace lights gradually brightened. Chiark's farside shone whitely overhead, coating everything in silver; stars twinkled in a cloudless sky. Gurgeh read on.

The terminal beeped. He looked severely at the camera eye set in one corner of the screen. "House," he said, "are you going deaf?"

"Please forgive the override," a rather officious and unapologetic voice Gurgeh did not recognize said from the screen. "Am I talking to Chiark-Gevantsa Jernau Morat Gurgeh dam Hassease?"

Gurgeh stared dubiously at the screen eye. He hadn't heard his full name pronounced for years. "Yes."

"My name is Loash Armasco-Iap Wu-Handrahen Xato Koum."

Gurgeh raised one eyebrow. "Well, that should be easy enough to remember."

"Might I interrupt you, sir?"

"You already have. What do you want?"

"To talk with you. Despite my override, this does not constitute an emergency, but I can only talk to you directly this evening. I am here representing the Contact Section, at the request of Dastaveb Chamlis Amalk-ney Ep-Handra Thedreiskre Ostlehoorp. May I approach you?"

"Providing you can stay off the full names, yes," Gurgeh said.

"I shall be there directly."

Gurgeh snapped the screen shut. He tapped the pen-like terminal on the edge of the wooden table and looked out over the dark fjord, watching the dim lights of the few houses on the far shore.

He heard a roaring noise in the sky, and looked up to see a farside-lit vapor-trail overhead, steeply angled and pointing to the slope uphill from Ikroh. There was a muffled bang over the forest above the house, and a noise like a sudden gust of wind, then, zooming round the side of the house, came a small drone, its fields bright blue and striped yellow.

It drifted over toward Gurgeh. The machine was about the same size as Mawhrin-Skel; it could, Gurgeh thought, have sat comfortably in the rectangular sandwich plate on the table. Its gunmetal casing looked a little more complicated and knobbly than Mawhrin-Skel's.

"Good evening," Gurgeh said as the small machine cleared the terrace wall.

It settled down on the table, by the sandwich plate. "Good evening, Morat Gurgeh."

"Contact, eh?" Gurgeh said, putting his terminal into a pocket in his robe. "That was quick. I was only talking to Chamlis the night before last."

"I happened to be in the volume," the machine explained in its clipped voice, "in transit—between the GCU *Flexible Demeanor* and the GSV *Unfortunate Conflict of Evidence,* aboard the (D)ROU *Zealot.* As the nearest Contact operative, I was the obvious choice to visit you. However, as I say, I can only stay for a short time."

"Oh, what a pity," Gurgeh said.

"Yes; you have such a charming Orbital here. Perhaps some other time."

"Well, I hope it hasn't been a wasted journey for you, Loash. . . . I wasn't really expecting an audience with a Contact operative. My friend Chamlis just thought Contact might . . . I don't know; have something interesting which wasn't in general circulation. I expected nothing at all, or just information. Might I ask just what you're doing here?" He leaned forward, putting both elbows on the table, leaning over the small machine. There was one sandwich left on the plate just in front of the drone. Gurgeh took it and ate, munching and looking at the machine.

"Certainly. I am here to ascertain just how open to suggestions you are. Contact might be able to find you something which would interest you."

"A game?"

"I have been given to understand it is connected with a game."

"That does not mean you have to play one with me," Gurgeh said, brushing his hands free of crumbs over the plate. A few crumbs flew toward the drone, as he'd hoped they might, but it fielded each one, flicking them neatly to the center of the plate in front of it.

"All I know, sir, is that Contact *might* have found something to interest you. I believe it to be connected with a game. I am instructed to discover how willing you might be to travel. I therefore assume the game—if such it is—is to be played in a location besides Chiark."

"Travel?" Gurgeh said. He sat back. "Where? How far? How long?"

"I don't know, exactly."

"Well, try approximately."

"I would not like to guess. How long would you be prepared to spend away from home?"

Gurgeh's eyes narrowed. The longest he'd spent away from Chiark had been when he'd gone on a cruise once, thirty years earlier. He hadn't enjoyed it especially. He'd gone more because it was the done thing to travel at that age than because he'd wanted to. The different stellar systems had been spectacular, but you could see just as good a view on a holoscreen, and he still didn't really understand what people saw in actually having been in any particular system. He'd planned to spend a few years on that cruise, but gave up after one.

Gurgeh rubbed his beard. "Perhaps half a year or so; it's hard to say without knowing the details. Say that, though; say half a year . . . not that I can see it's necessary. Local color rarely adds that much to a game."

"Normally, true." The machine paused. "I understand this might be rather a complicated game; it might take a while to learn. It is likely you would have to devote yourself to it for some time."

"I'm sure I'll manage," Gurgeh said. The longest it had taken him to learn any game had been three days; he hadn't forgotten any rule of any game in all his life, nor ever had to learn one twice.

"Very well," the small drone said suddenly, "on that basis, I shall report back. Farewell, Morat Gurgeh." It started to accelerate into the sky.

Gurgeh looked up at it, mouth open. He resisted the urge to jump up. "Is that it?" he said.

The small machine stopped a couple of meters up. "That's all I'm allowed to talk about. I've asked you what I was supposed to ask you. Now I report back. Why, is there anything else you would like to know I might be able to help you with?"

"Yes," Gurgeh said, annoyed now. "Do I get to hear anything else about whatever and wherever it is you're talking about?"

The machine seemed to waver in the air. Its fields hadn't changed since its arrival. Eventually, it said, "Jernau Gurgeh?"

There was a long moment when they were both silent. Gurgeh stared at the machine, then stood up, put both hands on his hips and his head to one side and shouted, "Yes?"

". . . Probably not," the drone snapped, and instantly rose straight up, fields flicking off. He heard the roaring noise and saw the vapor-trail form; it was a single tiny cloud at first because he was right underneath it, then it lengthened slowly for a few seconds, before suddenly ceasing to grow. He shook his head.

He took out the pocket terminal. "House," he said. "Raise that drone." He continued to stare into the sky.

"Which drone, Jernau?" the house said. "Chamlis?"

He stared at the terminal. "No! That little scumbag from Contact; Loash Armasco-Iap Wu-Handrahen Xato Koum, that's who! The one that was just here!"

"Just here?" the house said, in its Puzzled voice.

Gurgeh sagged. He sat down. "You didn't see or hear anything just now?"

"Nothing but silence for the last eleven minutes, Gurgeh, since you told me to hold all calls. There have been two of those since, but—"

"Never mind," Gurgeh sighed. "Get me Hub."

"Hub here; Makil Stra-bey Mind subsection. Jernau Gurgeh; what can we do for you?"

Gurgeh was still looking at the sky overhead, partly because that was where the Contact drone had gone (the thin vapor-trail was starting to expand and drift), and partly because people tended to look in the direction of the Hub when they were talking to it.

He noticed the extra star just before it started to move. The light-point was near the trailing end of the little drone's farside-lit contrail. He frowned. Almost immediately, it moved; only moderately fast at first, then too quickly for the eye to anticipate.

It disappeared. He was silent for a moment, then said, "Hub, has a Contact ship just left here?"

"Doing so even as we speak, Gurgeh. The (Demilitarized) Rapid Offensive Unit—"

"—*Zealot,*" Gurgeh said.

"Ho-ho! It was *you,* was it? We thought it was going to take *months* to work that one out. You've just seen a Private visit, game-player Gurgeh; Contact business; not for us to know. *Wow,* were we inquisitive though. *Very* glamorous, Jernau, if we may say so. That ship crash-stopped from at least forty kilolights and swerved twenty years . . . just for a five-minute chat with you, it would seem. That is *serious* energy usage . . . especially as it's accelerating away just as fast. Look at that kid go . . . oh, sorry; you can't. Well, take it from us; we're impressed. Care to tell a humble Hub Mind subsection what it was all about?"

"Any chance of contacting the ship?" Gurgeh said, ignoring the question.

"Dragging away like that? Business end pointed straight back at a mere civilian machine like ourselves . . . ?" The Hub Mind sounded amused. "Yeah . . . we suppose so."

"I want a drone on it called Loash Armasco-Iap Wu-Handrahen Xato Koum."

"Holy shit, Gurgeh, what *are* you tangling with here? Handrahen? Xato? That's equiv-tech espionage-level SC nomenclature. Heavy messing. . . . Shit. . . . We'll try. . . . Just a moment."

Gurgeh waited in silence for a few seconds.

"Nothing," the voice from the terminal said. "Gurgeh, this is Hub Entire speaking here; not a subsection; all of me. That ship's acknowledging but it's claiming there is no drone of that name or anything like it aboard."

Gurgeh slumped back in the seat. His neck was stiff. He looked down from the stars, down at the table. "You don't say," he said.

"Shall I try again?"

"Think it'll do any good?"

"No."

"Then don't."

"Gurgeh. This disturbs me. What is going on?"

"I wish," Gurgeh said, "I knew." He looked up at the stars again. The little drone's ghostly vapor-trail had almost disappeared. "Get me Chamlis Amalk-ney, will you?"

"On line. . . . Jernau?"

"What, Hub?"

"Be careful."

"Oh. Thanks. Thanks a lot."

"You must have annoyed it," Chamlis said through the terminal.

"Very likely," Gurgeh said. "But what do you think?"

"They were sizing you up for something."

"You think so?"

"Yes. But you just refused the deal."

"Did I?"

"Yes, and think yourself lucky you did, too."

"What do you mean? This was your idea."

"Look, you're out of it. It's over. But obviously my request went further and quicker than I thought it would. We triggered something. But you've put them off. They aren't interested anymore."

"Hmm. I suppose you're right."

"Gurgeh; I'm sorry."

"Never mind," Gurgeh told the old machine. He looked up at the stars. "Hub?"

"Hey; we're interested. If it had been purely personal we wouldn't have listened to a word, we swear, and besides, it'd be notified on your daily communication statement we were listening."

"Never mind all that." Gurgeh smiled, oddly relieved the

Orbital's Mind had been eavesdropping. "Just tell me how far away that ROU is."

"On the word 'is,' it was a minute and forty-nine seconds away; a light month distant, already clear of the system, and well out of our jurisdiction, we're *very* glad to say. Hightailing it in a direction a little up-spin of Galactic Core. Looks like it's heading for the GSV *Unfortunate Conflict of Evidence,* unless one of them's trying to fool somebody."

"Thank you, Hub. Good night."

"To you too. And you're on your own this time, we promise."

"Thank you, Hub. Chamlis?"

"You might just have missed the chance of a lifetime, Gurgeh . . . but it was more likely a narrow escape. I'm sorry for suggesting Contact. They came too fast and too hard to be casual."

"Don't worry so much, Chamlis," he told the drone. He looked back at the stars again, and sat back, swinging his foot up onto the table. "I handled it. We managed. Will I see you at Tronze tomorrow?"

"Maybe. I don't know. I'll think about it. Good luck—I mean against this wonderchild, at Stricken—if I don't see you tomorrow."

He grinned ruefully into the darkness. "Thanks. Good night, Chamlis."

"Good night, Gurgeh."

The train emerged from the tunnel into bright sunlight. It banked round the remainder of the curve, then set out across the slender bridge. Gurgeh looked over the handrail and saw the lush green pastures and brightly winding river half a kilometer below on the valley floor. Shadows of mountains lay across the narrow meadows; shadows of clouds freckled the tree-covered hills themselves. The wind of the train's slipstream ruffled his hair as he drank in the sweet, scented mountain air and waited for his opponent to return. Birds circled in the distance over the valley, almost level with the bridge. Their cries sounded through the still air, just audible over the windrush sound of the train's passing.

Normally he'd have waited until he was due in Tronze that evening and go there underground, but that morning he'd felt like getting away from Ikroh. He'd put on boots, a pair of conservatively styled pants and a short open jacket, then taken to the hill paths, hiking over the mountain and down the other side.

He'd sat by the side of the old railway line, glanding a mild buzz and amusing himself by chucking little bits of lodestone into the track's magnetic field and watching them bounce out again. He'd thought about Yay's floating islands.

He'd also thought about the mysterious visitation from the Contact drone, on the previous evening, but somehow that just would not come clear; it was as though it had been a dream. He had checked the house communication and systems statement: as far as the house was concerned, there had been no visit; but his conversation with Chiark Hub was logged, timed and witnessed by other subsections of the Hub, and by the Hub Entire for a short while. So it had happened all right.

He'd flagged down the antique train when it appeared, and even as he'd climbed on had been recognized by a middle-aged man called Dreltram, also making his way to Tronze. Mr. Dreltram would treasure a defeat at the hands of the great Jernau Gurgeh more than victory over anybody else; would he play? Gurgeh was well used to such flattery—it usually masked an unrealistic but slightly feral ambition—but had suggested they play Possession. It shared enough rule-concepts with Stricken to make it a decent limbering-up exercise.

They'd found a Possession set in one of the bars and taken it out onto the roof-deck, sitting behind a windbreak so that the cards wouldn't blow away. They ought to have enough time to complete the game; the train would take most of the day to get to Tronze, a journey an underground car could accomplish in ten minutes.

The train left the bridge and entered a deep, narrow ravine, its slipstream producing an eerie, echoing noise off the naked rocks on either side. Gurgeh looked at the game-board. He was playing straight, without the help of any glanded substances; his opponent was using a potent mixture suggested by Gurgeh himself. In addition, Gurgeh had given Mr. Dreltram a seven-piece lead at the start, which was the maximum allowed. The fellow wasn't a bad player, and had come near to overwhelming Gurgeh at the start, when his advantage in pieces had the greatest effect, but Gurgeh had defended well and the man's chance had probably gone, though there was still the possibility he might have a few mines left in awkward places.

Thinking of such unpleasant surprises, Gurgeh realized he hadn't looked at where his own hidden piece was. This had been another, unofficial, way of making the game more even. Possession is played on a forty-square grid; the two players' pieces are distributed in one major group and two minor groups each. Up to three pieces can be hidden on different initially unoccupied intersections. Their locations are dialed—and locked—into three circular cards; thin ceramic wafers which are turned over only when the player wishes to bring those pieces into play. Mr. Dreltram had already revealed all three of his hidden pieces (one had happened to be on the intersection Gurgeh had, sportingly, sown all nine of his mines on, which really was bad luck).

Gurgeh had spun the dials on his single hidden-piece wafer and put it face down on the table without looking at it; he had no more idea where that piece was than Mr. Dreltram. It might turn out to be in an illegal position, which could well lose him the game, or (less likely) it might turn up in a strategically useful place deep inside his opponent's territory. Gurgeh liked playing this way, if it wasn't a serious game; as well as giving his opponent a probably needed extra advantage, it made the match as a whole more interesting and less predictable; added an extra spice to the proceedings.

He supposed he ought to find out where the piece was; the eighty-move point was fast approaching when the piece had to be revealed anyway.

He couldn't see his hidden-piece wafer. He looked over the card and wafer-strewn table. Mr. Dreltram was not the most tidy of players; his cards and wafers and unused or removed pieces were scattered over most of the table, including the part supposed to be Gurgeh's. A gust of wind when they'd entered a tunnel an hour earlier had almost blown some of the lighter cards away, and they'd weighed them down with goblets and lead-glass paperweights; these added to the impression of confusion, as did Mr. Dreltram's quaint, if rather affected, custom of noting down all the moves by hand on a scratch tablet (he claimed the built-in memory on a board had broken down on him once, and lost him all record of one of the best games he'd ever played). Gurgeh started lifting bits and pieces up, humming to himself and looking for the flat wafer.

He heard a sudden intake of breath, then what sounded like a rather embarrassed cough, just behind him. He turned round to see Mr. Dreltram behind him, looking oddly awkward. Gurgeh frowned as Mr. Dreltram, just returned from the bathroom, his eyes wide with the mixture of drugs he was glanding, and followed by a tray bearing drinks, sat down again, staring at Gurgeh's hands.

It was only then, as the tray set the glasses on the table, that Gurgeh realized the cards he happened to be holding, which he had lifted up to look for his hidden-piece wafer, were Mr. Dreltram's remaining mine-cards. Gurgeh looked at them—they were still face down; he hadn't seen where the mines were—and understood what Mr. Dreltram must be thinking.

He put the cards back where he'd found them. "I'm very sorry," he laughed, "I was looking for my hidden piece."

He saw it, even as he spoke the words. The circular wafer was lying, uncovered, almost right in front of him on the table. "Ah," he said, and only then felt the blood rise to his face. "Here it is. Hmm. Couldn't see it for looking at it."

He laughed again, and as he did so felt a strange, clutching sensation coursing through him, seeming to squeeze his guts in something between terror and ecstasy. He had never experienced anything like it. The closest any sensation had ever come, he thought (suddenly, clearly), had been when he was still a boy and he'd experienced his first orgasm, at the hands of a girl a few years older than him. Crude, purely human-basic, like a single instrument picking out a simple theme a note at a time (compared to the drug-gland-boosted symphonies sex would later become), that first time had nevertheless been one of his most memorable experiences; not just because it was then novel, but because it seemed to open up a whole new fascinating world, an entirely different type of sensation and being. It had been the same when he'd played his first competition game, as a child, representing Chiark against another Orbital's junior team, and it would be the same again when his drug-glands matured, a few years after puberty.

Mr. Dreltram laughed too, and wiped his face with a handkerchief.

Gurgeh played furiously for the next few moves, and had to be reminded by his opponent when the eighty-move deadline came up. Gurgeh turned over his hidden piece without having checked it first, risking it occupying the same square as one of his revealed pieces.

The hidden piece, on a sixteen-hundred-to-one chance, turned up in the same position as the Heart; the piece the whole game was about; the piece one's opponent was trying to take possession of.

Gurgeh stared at the intersection where his well-defended Heart piece sat, then again at the coordinates he'd dialed at random onto the wafer, two hours earlier. They were the same, there was no doubt. If he'd looked a move earlier, he could have moved the Heart out of danger, but he hadn't. He'd lost both pieces; and with the Heart lost, the game was lost; he'd lost.

"Oh, bad luck," Mr. Dreltram said, clearing his throat.

Gurgeh nodded. "I believe it's customary, at such moments of disaster, for the defeated player to be given the Heart as a keepsake," he said, fingering the lost piece.

"Um . . . so I understand," Mr. Dreltram said, obviously at once embarrassed on Gurgeh's behalf, and delighted at his good fortune.

Gurgeh nodded. He put the Heart down, lifted the ceramic wafer which had betrayed him. "I'd rather have this, I think." He held it up to Mr. Dreltram, who nodded.

"Well, of course. I mean, why not; I certainly wouldn't object."

The train rolled quietly into a tunnel, slowing for a station set in the caverns inside the mountain.

* * *

"All reality is a game. Physics at its most fundamental, the very fabric of our universe, results directly from the interaction of certain fairly simple rules, and chance; the same description may be applied to the best, most elegant and both intellectually and aesthetically satisfying games. By being unknowable, by resulting from events which, at the sub-atomic level, cannot be fully predicted, the future remains malleable, and retains the possibility of change, the hope of coming to prevail; victory, to use an unfashionable word. In this, the future is a game; time is one of the rules. Generally, all the best mechanistic games—those which can be played in any sense 'perfectly,' such as grid, Prallian scope, 'nkraytle, chess, Farnic dimensions—can be traced to civilizations lacking a relativistic view of the universe (let alone the reality). They are also, I might add, invariably pre-machine-sentience societies.

"The very first-rank games acknowledge the element of chance, even if they rightly restrict raw luck. To attempt to construct a game on any other lines, no matter how complicated and subtle the rules are, and regardless of the scale and differentiation of the playing volume and the variety of the powers and attributes of the pieces, is inevitably to shackle oneself to a conspectus which is not merely socially but techno-philosophically lagging several ages behind our own. As a historical exercise it might have some value. As a work of the intellect, it's just a waste of time. If you want to make something old-fashioned, why not build a wooden sailing boat, or a steam engine? They're just as complicated and demanding as a mechanistic game, and you'll keep fit at the same time."

Gurgeh gave an ironic bow to the young man who'd approached him with an idea for a game. The fellow looked nonplussed. He took a breath and opened his mouth to speak.

Gurgeh was waiting for this; as he had on the last five or six occasions when the young man had tried to say something, Gurgeh interrupted him before he'd even started.

"I'm quite serious, you know; there is nothing intellectually inferior about using your hands to build something as opposed to using only your brain. The same lessons can be learned, the same skills acquired, at the only levels that really matter." He paused again. He could see the drone Mawhrin-Skel floating toward him over the heads of the people thronging the broad plaza.

The main concert was over. The mountain summits around Tronze echoed to the sounds of various smaller bands as people gravitated toward the specific musical forms they preferred; some formal, some improvised, some for dancing, some for experiencing under a specific drug-trance. It was a warm, cloudy night; a little farside light shone a milky halo directly overhead on the high overcast. Tronze, the largest town on both the Plate and the Orbital, had been built on the edge of the Gevant Plate's great central massif, at the point where the kilometer-high Lake Tronze flowed over the lip of the plateau and tumbled its waters toward the plain below, where they fell as a permanent downpour into the rain forest.

Tronze was the home of fewer than a hundred thousand people, but to Gurgeh it still felt too crowded, despite its spacious houses and squares, its sweeping galleries and plazas and terraces, its thousands of houseboats and its elegant, bridge-linked towers. Tronze, for all the fact that Chiark was a fairly recent Orbital, only a thousand or so years old, was already almost as big as any Orbital community ever grew; the Culture's real cities were its great ships, the General Systems Vehicles. Orbitals were its rustic hinterland, where people liked to spread themselves out with plenty of elbow room. In terms of scale, when compared to one of the larger GSVs containing billions of people, Tronze was barely a village.

Gurgeh usually attended the Tronze Sixty-fourth Day concert. And he was usually buttonholed by enthusiasts. Normally Gurgeh was civil, if occasionally abrupt. Tonight, after the fiasco on the train, and that strange, exciting, shaming pulse of emotion he'd experienced as a result of being thought to cheat, not to mention the slight nervousness he felt because he'd heard the girl off the GSV *Cargo Cult* was indeed here in Tronze this evening and looking forward to meeting him, he was in no mood to suffer fools gladly.

Not that the unlucky young male was necessarily a complete idiot; all he'd done was sketch out what had been, after all, not a bad idea for a game; but Gurgeh had fallen on him like an avalanche. The conversation—if you could call it that—had become a game.

The object was to keep talking; not to talk continuously, which any idiot could do, but to pause only when the young man was not signaling—through bodily or facial language, or actually starting to speak—that he wanted to cut in. Instead, Gurgeh would stop unexpectedly in the middle of a point, or after having just said something mildly insulting, but while still giving the impression he was going to keep talking. Also, Gurgeh was quoting almost verbatim from one of his own more famous papers on game-theory; an added insult, as the young man probably knew the text as well as he did.

"To imply," Gurgeh continued, as the young man's mouth started to open again, "that one can remove the element of luck, chance, happenstance in life by—"

"Jernau Gurgeh, not interrupting anything, am I?" Mawhrin-Skel said.

"Nothing of note," Gurgeh said, turning to face the small machine. "How are you, Mawhrin-Skel? Been up to any fresh mischief?"

"Nothing of note," the tiny drone echoed, as the young man Gurgeh had been talking to sidled off. Gurgeh sat in a creeper-covered pergola positioned close to one edge of the plaza, near the observation platforms which reached out over the broad curtain of the falls, where spray rose from the rapids lying between the lip of the lake and the vertical drop to the forest a kilometer below. The roaring falls provided a background wash of white noise.

"I've found your young adversary," the small drone announced. It extended one softly glowing blue field and plucked a nightflower from a growing vine.

"Hmm?" Gurgeh said. "Oh, the young, ah . . . Stricken player?"

"That's right," Mawhrin-Skel said evenly, "the young, ah . . . Stricken player." It folded some of the nightflower's petals back, straining them on the plucked stem.

"I heard she was here," Gurgeh said.

"She's at Hafflis's table. Shall we go and meet her?"

"Why not?" Gurgeh stood; the machine floated away.

"Nervous?" Mawhrin-Skel asked as they headed through the crowds toward one of the raised terraces level with the lake, where Hafflis's apartments were.

"Nervous?" Gurgeh said. "Of a child?"

Mawhrin-Skel floated silently for a moment or two as Gurgeh climbed some steps—Gurgeh nodded and said hello to a few people—then the machine came close to him and said quietly, as it slowly stripped the petals from the dying blossom, "Want me to tell you your heart rate, skin receptivity level, pheromone signature, neuron function-state . . . ?" Its voice trailed off as Gurgeh came to a halt, halfway up the flight of broad steps.

He turned to face the drone, looking through half-hooded eyes at the tiny machine. Music drifted over the lake, and the air was full of the nightflowers' musky scent. The lighting set into the stone balustrades lit the game-player's face from underneath. People flooding down the steps from the terrace above, laughing and joking, parted round the man like waters round a rock, and—Mawhrin-Skel noticed—went oddly quiet as they did so. After a few seconds, as Gurgeh stood there, silent, breathing evenly, the little drone made a chuckling noise.

"Not bad," it said. "Not bad at all. I can't tell just yet what you're glanding, but that's a very impressive degree of control. Everything parameter-centered, near as damn. Except your neuron function-state; that's even less like normal than usual, but then your average civilian drone probably couldn't spot that. Well done."

"Don't let me detain you, Mawhrin-Skel," Gurgeh said coldly. "I'm sure you can find something else to amuse you besides watching me play a game." He continued up the broad steps.

"Nothing currently on this Orbital is capable of detaining me, dear Mr. Gurgeh," the drone said matter-of-factly, tearing the last of the petals from the nightflower. It dropped the husk in the water channel which ran along the top of the balustrade.

"Gurgeh, good to see you. Come; sit down."

Estray Hafflis's party of thirty or so people sat round a huge, rectangular stone table set on a balcony jutting out over the falls and covered by stone arches strung with nightflower vines and softly shining paper lanterns; there were music-players at one end, sitting on the edge of the great slab with drums and strings and air instruments; they were laughing and playing mostly for themselves, each trying to play too fast for the others to follow.

Set into the center of the table was a long narrow pit full of glowing coals; a kind of miniaturized bucket-line trundled above the fire, carrying little meat and vegetable pieces from one end of the table to the other; they were skewered onto the line at one end by one of Hafflis's children, and removed at the other end, wrapped in edible paper and thrown with a fair degree of accuracy to anybody who wanted them, by Hafflis's youngest, who was only six. Hafflis was unusual in having had seven children; normally people bore one and fathered one. The Culture frowned on such profligacy, but Hafflis just liked being pregnant. He was in a male stage at the moment, however, having changed a few years earlier.

He and Gurgeh exchanged pleasantries, then Hafflis showed the game-player to a seat beside Professor Boruelal, who was grinning happily and swaying in her seat. She wore a long black and white robe, and when she saw Gurgeh kissed him noisily on the lips. She attempted to kiss Mawhrin-Skel too, but it flicked away.

She laughed, and speared a half-done piece of meat from the line over the center of the table with a long fork. "Gurgeh! Meet the lovely Olz Hap! Olz; Jernau Gurgeh. Come on; shake hands!"

Gurgeh sat down, taking the small, pale hand of the frightened-looking girl on Boruelal's right. She was wearing something dark and shapeless, and was in her early teens, at most. He smiled with a slight frown, glancing at the professor, trying to share the joke of her inebria with the young blonde girl, but Olz Hap was looking at his hand, not his face. She let her hand be touched but then withdrew it almost immediately. She sat on her hands and stared at her plate.

Boruelal breathed deeply, seeming to gather herself together. She took a drink from a tall glass in front of her.

"Well," she said, looking at Gurgeh as though he'd only just appeared. "How are you, Jernau?"

"Well enough." He watched Mawhrin-Skel maneuver itself beside Olz Hap, floating over the table beside her plate, fields all formal blue and green friendliness.

"Good evening," he heard the drone say in its most avuncular voice. The girl brought her head up to look at the machine, and Gurgeh listened to their conversation at the same time as he and Boruelal talked.

"Hello."

"Well enough to play a game of Stricken?"

"Mawhrin-Skel's the name. Olz Hap, am I right?"

"I think so, Professor. Are you well enough to invigilate?"

"Yes. How do you do."

"Fuck me, no; drunk as a desert spring. Have to get somebody else. Suppose I could come down in time but . . . naa . . ."

"Oh, ah, shake fields with me, eh? That's very sweet of you; so few people bother. How nice to meet you. We've all heard so much."

"How about the young lady herself?"

"Oh. Oh dear."

"What?"

"What's wrong? Have I said something wrong?"

"Is she ready to play?"

"No, it's just—"

"Play what?"

"Ah; you're shy. You needn't be. Nobody'll force you to play. Least of all Gurgeh, believe me."

"The game, Boruelal."

"Well, I—"

"What, do you mean now?"

"I wouldn't worry, if I were you. Really."

"Now; or any time."

"Well *I* don't know. Let's ask her! Hey, kid . . ."

"Bor—" Gurgeh began, but the professor had already turned to the girl.

"Olz; want to play this game, then?"

The young girl looked straight at Gurgeh. Her eyes were bright in the glare of the line of fire running down the center of the table. "If Mr. Gurgeh would like to, yes."

Mawhrin-Skel's fields glowed red with pleasure, momentarily brighter than the coals. "Oh *good,*" it said. "A fight."

Hafflis had loaned his own ancient Stricken set out; it took a few minutes for a supply drone to bring one from a town store. They set it up at one end of the balcony, by the edge overlooking the roaring white falls. Professor Boruelal fumbled with her terminal and put in a request for some adjudicating drones to oversee the game; Stricken was susceptible to high-tech cheating, and a serious game required that steps be taken to ensure nothing underhand went on. A drone visiting from Chiark Hub volunteered, as did a Manufactury drone from the shipyard under the massif. One of the university's own machines would represent Olz Hap.

Gurgeh turned to Mawhrin-Skel, to ask it to be his representative, but it said, "Jernau Gurgeh; I thought you might like Chamlis Amalk-ney to represent you."

"Is Chamlis here?"

"Arrived a while ago. Been avoiding me. I'll ask it."

Gurgeh's button terminal beeped. "Yes?" he said.

Chamlis's voice spoke from the button. "The fly-dropping just asked me to represent you in a Stricken adjudication. Do you want me to?"

"Yes, I'd like you to," Gurgeh said, watching Mawhrin-Skel's fields flicker white with anger in front of him.

"I'll be there in twenty seconds," Chamlis said, closing the channel.

"Twenty-one point two," Mawhrin-Skel said acidly, exactly twenty-one point two seconds later, as Chamlis appeared over the edge of the balcony, its casing dark against the cataract beyond. Chamlis turned its sensing band to the smaller machine.

"Thank you," Chamlis said warmly. "I had a bet on with myself that I'd have you counting the seconds to my arrival."

Mawhrin-Skel's fields blazed brightly, painfully white, lighting up the entire balcony for a second; people stopped talking and turned; the music hesitated. The tiny drone seemed almost literally to shake with dumb rage.

"Fuck you!" it screeched at last, and seemed to disappear, leaving only an after-image of sun-bright blindness behind it in the night. The coals blazed bright, a wind whipped at clothes and hair, several of the paper lanterns bucked and shook and fell from the arches overhead; leaves and nightflowers drifted down from the two arches immediately over where Mawhrin-Skel had been floating.

Chamlis Amalk-ney, red with happiness, tipped to look up into the dark sky, where a small hole appeared briefly in the cloud cover. "Oh dear," it said. "Do you think I said something to upset it?"

Gurgeh smiled and sat down at the game-set. "Did you plan that, Chamlis?"

Amalk-ney bowed in midair to the other drones, and to

Boruelal. "Not exactly." It turned to face Olz Hap, sitting on the far side of the game-web from Gurgeh. "Ah . . . by way of contrast: a fair human."

The girl blushed, looked down. Boruelal made the introductions.

Stricken is played in a three-dimensional web stretched inside a meter cube. The traditional materials are taken from a certain animal on the planet of origin; cured tendon for the web, tusk ivory for the frame. The set Gurgeh and Olz Hap used was synthetic. They each put up their hinged screens, took the bags of hollow globes and colored beads (nutshells and stones in the original) and selected the beads they wanted, locking them in the globes. The adjudicating drones ensured there was no possibility of anyone seeing which beads went into which shells. Then the man and the girl each took a handful of the little spheres and placed them in various places inside the web. The game had begun.

She was good. Gurgeh was impressed. Olz Hap was impetuous but canny, brave but not stupid. She was also very lucky. But there was luck and luck. Sometimes you could sniff it out, recognize things were going well and would probably continue to go well, and play to that. If things did keep going right, you profited extravagantly. If the luck didn't persist, well, you just played the percentages.

The girl had that sort of luck, that night. She made the right guesses about Gurgeh's pieces, capturing several strong beads in weak disguises; she anticipated moves he'd sealed in the Foretell shells; and she ignored the tempting traps and feints he set up.

Somehow he struggled on, coming up with desperate, improvised defenses against each attack, but it was all too seat-of-the-pants, too extemporary and tactical. He wasn't being allowed the time to develop his pieces or plan a strategy. He was responding, following, replying. He preferred to have the initiative.

It was some time before he realized just how audacious the girl was being. She was going for a Full Web; the simultaneous capture of every remaining point in the game-space. She wasn't just trying to win, she was trying to pull off a coup which only a handful of the game's greatest players had ever accomplished, and which nobody in the Culture—to Gurgeh's knowledge—had yet achieved. Gurgeh could hardly believe it, but it was what she was doing. She was sapping pieces but not obliterating them, then falling back; she was striking out through his own avenues of weakness, then holding there.

She was inviting him to come back, of course, giving him a better chance of winning, and indeed of achieving the same momentous result, though with far less hope of doing so. But the self-confidence of it! The experience and even arrogance such a course implied!

He looked at the slight, calm-faced girl through the web of thin wires and little suspended spheres, and could not help but admire her ambition, her vaulting ability and self-belief. She was playing for the grand gesture, and to the gallery, not settling for a reasonable win, despite the fact that the reasonable win would be over a famous, respected game-player. And Boruelal had thought she might feel intimidated by him! Well, good for her.

Gurgeh sat forward, rubbing his beard, oblivious of the people now packing the balcony, silently watching the game.

He struggled back into it somehow. Partly luck, partly more skill than even he thought he possessed. The game was still poised for a Full Web victory, and she was still the most likely to achieve it, but at least his position looked less hopeless. Somebody brought him a glass of water and something to eat. He vaguely recalled being grateful.

The game went on. People came and went around him. The web held all his fortune; the little spheres, holding their secret treasures and threats, became like discrete parcels of life and death, single points of probability which could be guessed at but never known until they were challenged, opened, looked at. All reality seemed to hinge on those infinitesimal bundles of meaning.

He no longer knew what body-made drugs washed through him, nor could he guess what the girl was using. He had lost all sense of self and time.

The game drifted for a few moves, as they both lost concentration, then came alive again. He became aware, very slowly, very gradually, that he held some impossibly complex model of the contest in his head, unknowably dense, multifariously planed.

He looked at that model, twisted it.

The game changed.

He saw a way to win. The Full Web remained a possibility. His, now. It all depended. Another *twist.* Yes; he would win. Almost certainly. But that was no longer enough. The Full Web beckoned, tantalizingly, seductively, entrancingly . . .

"Gurgeh?" Boruelal shook him. He looked up. There was a hint of dawn over the mountains. Boruelal's face looked gray and sober. "Gurgeh; a break. It's been six hours. Do you agree? A break, yes?"

He looked through the web at the pale, waxen face of the young girl. He gazed round in a sort of daze. Most of the people had gone. The paper lanterns had disappeared, too; he felt vaguely sorry to have missed the little ritual of throwing the glowing lamps over the terrace edge and watching them drift down to the forest.

Boruelal shook him once more. "Gurgeh?"

"Yes; a break. Yes, of course," he croaked. He got up, stiff and sore, muscles protesting and joints creaking.

Chamlis had to stay with the game-set, to ensure the adjudication. Gray dawn spread across the sky. Somebody gave him some hot soup, which he sipped while he ate a few crackers and wandered through the quiet arcades for a while, where a few people slept or still sat and talked, or danced to quiet, recorded music. He leaned on the balustrade above the kilometer drop, sipping and munching, dazed and vacant from the game, still playing and replaying it somewhere inside his head.

The lights of the towns and villages on the mist-strewn plain below, beyond the semicircle of dark rain forest, looked pale and uncertain. Distant mountaintops shone pink and naked.

"Jernau Gurgeh?" a soft voice said.

He looked over the plain. The drone Mawhrin-Skel floated a meter from his face. "Mawhrin-Skel," he said quietly.

"Good morning."

"Good morning."

"How goes the game?"

"Fine, thank you. I think I'll win now . . . pretty sure in fact. But there's just a chance I might win . . ." He felt himself smiling. ". . . famously."

"Really?" Mawhrin-Skel continued to float there, over the drop in front of him. It kept its voice soft, though there was nobody nearby. Its fields were off. Its surface was an odd, mottled mixture of gray tones.

"Yes," Gurgeh said, and briefly explained about a Full Web victory.

The drone seemed to understand. "So, you have won, but you could win the Full Web, which no one in the Culture has ever done save for exhibition purposes, to prove its possibility."

"That's right!" He nodded, looked over the light-speckled plain. "That's right." He finished the crackers, brushed his hands slowly free of crumbs. He left the soup bowl balanced on the balustrade.

"Does it really," Mawhrin-Skel said thoughtfully, "matter who first wins a Full Web?"

"Hmm?" Gurgeh said.

Mawhrin-Skel drifted closer. "Does it really matter who first wins one? Somebody will, but does it count for much who does? It would appear to be a very unlikely eventuality in any given game . . . has it really much to do with skill?"

"Not beyond a certain point," Gurgeh admitted. "It requires a lucky genius."

"But that could be you."

"Maybe." Gurgeh smiled across the gulf of chill morning air. He drew his jacket closer about him. "It depends entirely on the disposition of certain colored beads in certain metal spheres." He laughed. "A victory that would echo round the game-playing galaxy, and it depends on where a child placed . . ." his voice trailed off. He looked at the tiny drone again, frowning. "Sorry; getting a bit melodramatic." He shrugged, leaned on the stone edge. "It would be . . . pleasant to win, but it's unlikely, I'm afraid. Somebody else will do it, some time."

"But it *might as well be you,*" Mawhrin-Skel hissed, floating still closer.

Gurgeh had to draw away to focus on the device. "Well—"

"Why leave it to chance, Jernau Gurgeh?" Mawhrin-Skel said, pulling back a little. "Why abandon it to mere, stupid luck?"

"What are you talking about?" Gurgeh said slowly, eyes narrowing. The drug-trance was dissipating, the spell breaking. He felt keen, keyed-up; nervous and excited at once.

"I can tell you which beads are in which globes," Mawhrin-Skel said.

Gurgeh laughed gently. "Nonsense."

The drone floated closer. "I can. They didn't tear everything out of me when they turned me away from SC. I have more senses than cretins like Amalk-ney have even heard of." It closed in. "Let me use them; let me tell you what is where in your bead-game. Let me help you to the Full Web."

Gurgeh stood back from the balustrade, shaking his head. "You can't. The other drones—"

"—are weak simpletons, Gurgeh," Mawhrin-Skel insisted. "I have the measure of them, believe me. Trust me. Another SC machine, definitely not; a Contact drone, probably not . . . but this gang of obsoletes? I could find out where every bead that girl has placed is. Every single one!"

"You wouldn't need them all," Gurgeh said, looking troubled, waving his hand.

"Well then! Better yet! Let me do it! Just to prove to you! To myself!"

"You're talking about *cheating*, Mawhrin-Skel," Gurgeh said, looking round the plaza. There was nobody nearby. The paper lanterns and the stone ribs they hung from were invisible from where he stood.

"You're going to win; what difference does it make?"

"It's still cheating."

"You said yourself it's all luck. You've won—"

"Not definitely."

"Almost certainly; a thousand to one you don't."

"Probably longer odds than that," Gurgeh conceded.

"So the game is over. The girl can't lose any more than she has already. Let her be part of a game that will go down in history. Give her that!"

"It," Gurgeh said, slapping his hand on the stonework, "is," another slap, "still," slap, "cheating!"

"Keep your voice down," Mawhrin-Skel murmured. It backed away a little. It spoke so low he had to lean out over the drop to hear it. "It's luck. All is luck when skill's played out. It was luck left me with a face that didn't fit in Contact, it's luck that's made you a great game-player, it's luck that's put you here tonight. Neither of us were fully planned, Jernau Gurgeh; your genes determined you and your mother's genofixing made certain you would not be a cripple or mentally subnormal. The rest is chance. I was brought into being with the freedom to be myself; if what that general plan and that particular luck produced is something a majority—a *majority,* mark you; not all—of one SC admissions board decides is not what they just happen to want, is it my *fault?* Is it?"

"No," Gurgeh sighed, looking down.

"Oh, it's all so wonderful in the Culture, isn't it, Gurgeh; nobody starves and nobody dies of disease or natural disasters and nobody and nothing's exploited, but there's still luck and heartache and joy, there's still chance and advantage and disadvantage."

The drone hung above the drop and the waking plain. Gurgeh watched the Orbital dawn come up, swinging from the edge of the world. "Take hold of your luck, Gurgeh. Accept what I'm offering you. Just this once let's both make our own chances. You already know you're one of the best in the Culture; I'm not trying to flatter you; you know that. But this win would seal that fame forever."

"If it's possible . . ." Gurgeh said, then went silent. His jaw clenched. The drone sensed him trying to control himself the way he had done on the steps up to Hafflis's house, seven hours ago.

"If it isn't, at least have the courage to *know,*" Mawhrin-Skel said, voice pitched at an extremity of pleading.

The man raised his eyes to the clear blue-pinks of dawn. The ruffled, misty plain looked like a vast and tousled bed. "You're crazy, drone. You could never do it."

"I know what *I* can do, Jernau Gurgeh," the drone said. It pulled away again, sat in the air, regarding him.

He thought of that morning, sitting on the train; the rush of that delicious fear. Like an omen, now.

Luck; simple chance.

He knew the drone was right. He knew it was wrong, but he knew it was right, too. It all depended on him.

He leaned against the balustrade. Something in his pocket dug into his chest. He felt in, pulled out the hidden-piece wafer he'd taken as a memento after the disastrous Possession game. He turned the wafer over in his hands a few times. He looked at the drone, and suddenly felt very old and very childlike at the same time.

"If," he said slowly, "anything goes wrong, if you're found out—I'm dead. I'll kill myself. Brain death; complete and utter. No remains."

"Nothing is going to go wrong. For me, it is the simplest thing in the world to find out what's inside those shells."

"What if you are discovered, though? What if there is an SC drone around here somewhere, or the Hub is watching?"

The drone said nothing for a moment. "They'd have noticed by now. It is already done."

Gurgeh opened his mouth to speak, but the drone quickly floated closer, calmly continuing. "For my own sake, Gurgeh . . . for my own peace of mind. I wanted to know, too. I came back long ago; I've been watching for the past five hours, quite fascinated. I couldn't resist finding out if it was possible. . . . To be honest, I still don't know; the game is beyond me, just over-complicated for the way my poor target-tracking mind is configured . . . but I had to try to find out. I had to. So, you see; the risk is run, Gurgeh; the deed is done. I can tell you what you need to know. . . . And I ask nothing in return; that's up to you. Maybe you can do something for me some day, but no obligation; believe me, please believe me. No obligation at all. I'm doing this because I want to see you—somebody; anybody—do it."

Gurgeh looked at the drone. His mouth was dry. He could hear somebody shouting in the distance. The terminal button on his jacket shoulder beeped. He drew breath to speak to it, but then heard his own voice say, "Yes?"

"Ready to resume, Jernau?" Chamlis said from the button.

And he heard his own voice say, "I'm on my way."

He stared at the drone as the terminal beeped off.

Mawhrin-Skel floated closer. "As I said, Jernau Gurgeh; I can fool these adding machines, no problem at all. Quickly now. Do you want to know or not? The Full Web; yes or no?"

Gurgeh glanced round in the direction of Hafflis's apartments. He turned back, leaned out over the drop, toward the drone.

"All right," he said, whispering, "just the five prime points and the four verticals nearest topside center. No more."

* * *

Mawhrin-Skel told him.

It was almost enough. The girl struggled brilliantly to the very end, and deprived him on the final move.

The Full Web fell apart, and he won by thirty-one points, two short of the Culture's existing record.

One of Estray Hafflis's house drones was dimly confused to discover, while cleaning up under the great stone table much later that morning, a crushed and shattered ceramic wafer with warped and twisted numbered dials set into its crazed and distorted surface.

It wasn't part of the house Possession set.

The machine's non-sentient, mechanistic, entirely predictable brain thought about it for a while, then finally decided to junk the mysterious remnant along with the rest of the debris.

When he woke up that afternoon, it was with the memory of defeat. It was some time before he recalled that he had in fact won the Stricken match. Victory had never been so bitter.

He breakfasted alone on the terrace, watching a fleet of sailboats cut down the narrow fjord, bright sails in a fresh breeze. His right hand hurt a little as he held his bowl and cup; he'd come close to drawing blood when he'd crushed the Possession wafer at the end of the Stricken match.

He dressed in a long coat, trous and short kilt, and went on a long walk, down to the shore of the fjord and then along it, toward the sea coast and the windswept dunes where Hassease lay, the house he'd been born in, where a few of his extended family still lived. He tramped along the coast path toward the house, through the blasted, twisted shapes of wind-misshapen trees. The grass made sighing noises around him, and seabirds cried. The breeze was cold and freshening under ragged clouds. Out to sea, beyond Hassease village, where the weather was coming from, he could see tall veils of rain under a dark front of storm-clouds. He drew his coat tighter about him and hurried toward the distant silhouette of the sprawling, ramshackle house, thinking he should have taken an underground car. The wind whipped up sand from the distant beach and threw it inland; he blinked, eyes watering.

"Gurgeh."

The voice was quite loud; louder than the sound of sighing grass and wind-troubled tree branches. He shielded his eyes, looked to one side. "Gurgeh," the voice said again. He peered into the shade of a stunted, slanting tree.

"Mawhrin-Skel? Is that you?"

"The same," the small drone said, floating forward over the path.

Gurgeh looked out to sea. He started down the path to the house again, but the drone did not follow him. "Well," he told it, looking back from a few paces away, "I must keep going. I'll get wet if I—"

"No," Mawhrin-Skel said. "Don't go. I have to talk to you. This is important."

"Then tell me as I walk," he said, suddenly annoyed. He strode away. The drone flashed round in front of him, at face level, so that he had to stop or he'd have bumped into it.

"It's about the game; Stricken; last night and this morning."

"I believe I already said thank you," he told the machine. He looked beyond it. The leading edge of the squall was hitting the far end of the village harbor beyond Hassease. The dark clouds were almost above him, casting a great shadow.

"And I believe I said you might be able to help me one day."

"Oh," Gurgeh said, with an expression more sneer than smile. "And what am *I* supposed to be able to do for *you?*"

"Help me," Mawhrin-Skel said quietly, voice almost lost in the noise of the wind. "Help me to get back into Contact."

"Don't be absurd," Gurgeh said, and put out one hand to swipe the machine out of his path. He forced his way past it.

The next thing he knew he'd been shoved down into the grass at the path-side, as though shoulder-charged by someone invisible. He stared up in amazement at the tiny machine floating above him, while his hands felt the damp ground under him and the grass hissed on each side.

"You little—" he said, trying to stand up. He was shoved back down again, and sat there incredulous, simply unbelieving. No machine had ever used force on him. It was unheard of. He tried to rise again, a shout of anger and frustration forming in his throat.

He went limp. The shout died in his mouth.

He felt himself flop back into the grass.

He lay there, looking up into the dark clouds overhead. He could move his eyes. Nothing else.

He remembered the missile shoot and the immobility the suit had imposed on him when it had been hit once too often. This was worse.

This was paralysis. He could do nothing.

He worried about his breathing stopping, his heart stopping, his tongue blocking his throat, his bowels relaxing.

Mawhrin-Skel floated into his field of view. "Listen to me, Jernau Gurgeh." Some cold drops of rain started to patter into the grass and onto his face. "Listen to me. . . . You shall help me. I have our entire conversation, your every word and gesture from this morning, recorded. If you don't help me, I'll release that recording. Everyone will know you cheated in the game against

Olz Hap." The machine paused. "Do you understand, Jernau Gurgeh? Have I made myself clear? Do you realize what I am saying? There is a name—an old name—for what I am doing, in case you haven't already guessed. It is called blackmail."

The machine was mad. Anybody could make up anything they wanted; sound, moving pictures, smell, touch . . . there were machines that did just that. You could order them from a store and effectively paint whatever pictures—still or moving—you wanted, and with sufficient time and patience you could make it look as realistic as the real thing, recorded with an ordinary camera. You could simply make up any film sequence you wanted.

Some people used such machines just for fun or revenge, making up stories where appalling or just funny things happened to their enemies or their friends. Where nothing could be authenticated, blackmail became both pointless and impossible; in a society like the Culture, where next to nothing was forbidden, and both money and individual power had virtually ceased to exist, it was doubly irrelevant.

The machine really must be mad. Gurgeh wondered if it intended to kill him. He turned the idea over in his mind, trying to believe it could happen.

"I know what's going through your mind, Gurgeh," the drone went on. "You're thinking that I can't prove it; I could have made it up; nobody will believe me. Well, wrong. I had a real-time link with a friend of mine; an SC Mind sympathetic to my cause, who's always known I would have made a perfectly good operative and has worked on my appeal. What passed between us this morning is recorded in perfect detail in a Mind of unimpeachable moral credentials, and at a level of perceived fidelity unapproachable with the sort of facilities generally available.

"What I have on you could not have been falsified, Gurgeh.

If you don't believe me, ask your friend Amalk-ney. It'll confirm all I say. It may be stupid, and ignorant too, but it ought to know where to find out the truth."

Rain struck Gurgeh's helpless, relaxed face. His jaw was slack and his mouth open, and he wondered if perhaps he would drown eventually; drowned by the falling rain.

The drone's small body splashed and dripped above him as the drops grew larger and fell harder. "You're wondering what I want from you?" the drone said. He tried to move his eyes to say "no," just to annoy it, but it didn't seem to notice. "Help," it said. "I need your help; I need you to speak for me. I need you to go to Contact and add your voice to those demanding my return to active duty." The machine darted down toward his face; he felt his coat collar pulled. His head and upper torso were lifted with a jerk from the damp ground until he stared helplessly at the gray-blue casing of the small machine. Pocket-size, he thought, wishing he could blink, and glad of the rain because he could not. Pocket-size; it would fit into one of the big pockets in this coat.

He wanted to laugh.

"Don't you understand what they've done to me, *man?*" the machine said, shaking him. "I've been castrated, spayed, paralyzed! How you feel now; helpless, knowing the limbs are there but unable to make them work! Like that, but knowing that they *aren't* there! Can you understand that? Can you? Did you know that in our history people used to lose whole limbs, forever? Do you remember your social history, little Jernau Gurgeh? Eh?" It shook him. He felt and heard his teeth rattle. "Do you remember seeing cripples, from before arms and legs just grew back? Back then, humans lost limbs—blown off or cut off or amputated—but still thought they had them, still thought they could feel them; 'ghost limbs' they called them.

Those unreal arms and legs could itch and they could ache but they could not be used; can you imagine? Can you imagine *that,* Culture man with your genofixed regrowth and your over-designed heart and your doctored glands and clot-filtered brain and flawless teeth and perfect immune system? *Can you?*"

It let him fall back to the ground. His jaw jerked and he felt his teeth nip the end of his tongue. A salt taste filled his mouth. Now he really would drown, he thought; in his own blood. He waited for real fear. The rain filled his eyes but he could not cry.

"Well, imagine that, times eight, times more; imagine what I feel, all set up to be the good soldier fighting for all that we hold dear, to seek out and smite the barbarians around us! Gone, Jernau Gurgeh; razed; gone. My sensory systems, my weapons, my very memory-capacity; all reduced, laid waste: crippled. I peek into shells in a Stricken game, I push you down with an eight-strength field and hold you there with an excuse for an electro-magnetic effector . . . but this is nothing, Jernau Gurgeh; nothing. An echo; a shadow . . . nothing . . ."

It floated higher, away from him.

It gave him back the use of his body. He struggled off the damp ground, and felt his tongue with one hand; the blood had stopped flowing, closed off. He sat up, a little groggy, feeling the back of his head where it had hit the ground. It was not sore. He looked at the small, dripping body of the machine, floating over the path.

"I have nothing to lose, Gurgeh," it said. "Help me or I'll destroy your reputation. Don't think I wouldn't. Whether it would mean almost nothing to you—which I doubt—I'd do it just for the fun of causing you even the smallest amount of embarrassment. And if it means everything, and you really would kill yourself—which I also very much doubt—then I would still. I've never killed a human before. It's possible I might have been given the chance, somewhere, some time, if I'd been allowed to join SC . . . but I'd settle for causing a suicide."

He held up one hand to it. His coat felt heavy. The trous were soaked. "I believe you," he said. "All right. But what can I do?"

"I've told you," the drone said, over the noise of the wind howling in the trees and the rain beating against the swaying stalks of grass. "Speak for me. You have more influence than you realize. Use it."

"But I *don't,* I—"

"I've seen your mail, Gurgeh," the drone said tiredly. "Don't you know what a guest-invitation from a GSV means? It's the closest Contact ever comes to offering a post directly. Didn't anybody ever teach you anything besides games? Contact wants you. Officially Contact never head-hunts; you have to apply, then once you're in it's the other way round; to join SC you have to wait to be invited. But they want you, all right. . . . Gods, man, can't you take a *hint?*"

"Even if you're right, what am I supposed to do, just go to Contact and say 'Take this drone back'? Don't be stupid. I wouldn't even know how to start going about it." He didn't want to say anything about the visit from the Contact drone the other evening.

He didn't have to.

"Haven't they already been in touch with you?" Mawhrin-Skel asked. "The night before last?"

Gurgeh got shakily to his feet. He brushed some sandy earth from his coat. The rain gusted on the wind. The village on the coast and the sprawling house of his childhood were almost invisible under the dark sheets of driving rain.

"Yes, I've been watching you, Jernau Gurgeh," Mawhrin-Skel said. "I know Contact are interested in you. I have no idea just what it is Contact might *want* from you, but I suggest that you find out. Even if you don't want to play, you'd better make a damn good plea on my behalf; I'll be watching, so I'll know whether you do or not. . . . I'll prove it to you. Watch."

A screen unfolded from the front of the drone's body like a strange flat flower, expanding to a square a quarter-meter or so to a side. It lit up in the rainy gloom to show Mawhrin-Skel itself, suddenly glowing a blinding, flashing white, above the stone table at Hafflis's house. The scene was shot from above, probably near one of the stone ribs over the terrace. Gurgeh watched again as the line of coals glowed bright, and the lanterns and flowers fell. He heard Chamlis say, "Oh dear. Do you think I said something to upset it?" He saw himself smile as he sat down by the Stricken game-set.

The scene faded. It was replaced by another dim scene viewed from above; a bed; his bed, in the principal chamber at Ikroh. He recognized the small, ringed hands of Ren Myglan kneading his back from beneath. There was sound, too:

". . . ah, Ren, my baby, my child, my love . . ."

". . . Jernau . . ."

"You piece of shit," he told the drone.

The scene faded and the sound cut off. The screen collapsed, sucked back inside the body of the drone.

"Just so, and don't you forget it, Jernau Gurgeh," Mawhrin-Skel said. "Those bits were quite fakeable; but you and I know they were real, don't we? Like I said; I'm watching you."

He sucked on the blood in his mouth, spat. "You can't do this. Nobody's allowed to behave like this. You won't get—"

"—away with it? Well, maybe not. But the thing is, if I don't get away with it, I don't care. I'm no worse off. I'm still going to try." It paused, physically shook itself free of water, then produced a spherical field about itself, clearing the moisture from its casing, leaving it spotless and clean, and sheltering it from the rain.

"Can't you understand what they've done to me, man? Better I had never been brought into being than forced to wander the Culture forever, knowing what I've lost. They call it compassion to draw my talons and remove my eyes and cast me adrift in a paradise made for others; I call it torture. It's obscene, Gurgeh, it's barbaric, *diabolic;* recognize that old word? I see you do. Well, try to imagine how I might feel, and what I might do. . . . Think about it, Gurgeh. Think about what you can do for me, and what I can do to you."

The machine drew away from him again, retreating through the pouring rain. The cold drops splashed on top of its invisible globe of fields, and little rivulets of water ran round the transparent surface of that sphere to dribble underneath, falling in a steady stream into the grass. "I'll be in touch. Goodbye, Gurgeh," Mawhrin-Skel said.

The drone flicked away, tearing over the grass and into the sky in a gray cone of slipstream. Gurgeh lost sight of it within seconds.

He stood for a while, brushing sand and bits of grass from his sodden clothes, then turned to walk back in the direction he'd come from, through the falling rain and the beating wind.

He looked back, once, to gaze again upon the house where he'd grown up, but the squall, billowing round the low summits of the rolling dunes, had all but obscured the rambling chaotic structure.

"But Gurgeh, what *is* the problem?"

"I can't tell you!" He walked up to the rear wall of the main room of Chamlis's apartment, turned and paced back again, before going to stand by the window. He looked out over the square.

People walked, or sat at tables under the awnings and archways of the pale, green-stone galleries which lined the village's main square. Fountains played, birds flew from tree to tree, and on the tiled roof of the square's central bandstand/stage/holoscreen housing, a jet black tzile, almost the size of a full-grown human, lay sprawled, one leg hanging over the edge of the tiles. Its trunk, tail and ears all twitched as it dreamed; its rings and bracelets and earrings glinted in the sunlight. Even as Gurgeh watched, the creature's thin trunk articulated lazily, stretching back over its head to scratch indolently at the back of its neck, near its terminal collar. Then the black proboscis fell back as though exhausted, to swing to and fro for a few seconds. Laughter drifted up through the warm air from some nearby tables. A red-colored dirigible floated over distant hills, like a vast blob of blood in the blue sky.

He turned back into the room again. Something about the square, the whole village, disgusted and angered him. Yay was right; it was all too safe and twee and ordinary. They might as well be on a planet. He walked over to where Chamlis floated, near the long fishtank. Chamlis's aura was tinged with gray frustration. The old drone gave an exasperated shudder and picked up a little container of fish-food; the tank lid lifted and Chamlis sprinkled some of the food grains onto the top of the water; the glittering mirrorfish moved silkily up to the surface, mouths working rhythmically.

"Gurgeh," Chamlis said reasonably, "how can I help you if you won't tell me what's wrong?"

"Just tell me; is there any way you can find out more about what Contact wanted to talk about? Can I get in touch with them again? Without everybody else knowing? Or . . ." He shook his head, put his hands to his head. "No; I suppose people will know, but it doesn't matter . . ." He stopped at the wall, stood looking at the warm sandstone blocks between the paintings. The apartments had been built in an old-fashioned style; the pointing between the sandstone blocks was dark, inlaid with little white pearls. He gazed at the richly beaded lines and tried to think, tried to know what it was he could ask and what there was he could do.

"I can get in touch with the two ships I know," Chamlis said. "The ones I contacted originally, I can ask them; they might know what Contact was going to suggest." Chamlis watched the silvery fish silently feeding. "I'll do that now, if you like."

"Please. Yes," he said, and turned away from the manufactured sandstone and the cultivated pearls. His shoes clacked across the patterned tiles of the room. The sunlit square again. The tzile, still sleeping. He could see its jaws moving, and wondered what alien words the creature was mouthing in its sleep.

"It'll be a few hours before I hear anything," Chamlis said. The fishtank lid closed; the drone put the fish-food container into a drawer in a tiny, delicate table near the tank. "Both ships are fairly distant." Chamlis tapped the side of the tank with a silvered field; the mirrorfish floated over to investigate. "But why?" the drone said, looking at him. "What's changed? What sort of trouble are you . . . *can* you be in? Gurgeh; please tell me. I want to help."

The machine floated closer to the tall human, who was standing staring down to the square, his hands clasped and unconsciously kneading each other. The old drone had never seen the man so distressed.

"Nothing," Gurgeh said hopelessly, shaking his head, not

looking at the drone. "Nothing's changed. There's no trouble. I just need to know a few things."

He had gone straight back to Ikroh the day before. He'd stood in the main room, where the house had lit the fire a couple of hours earlier after hearing the weather forecast, and he'd taken off the wet, dirty clothes and thrown them all onto the fire. He'd had a hot bath and a steam bath, sweating and panting and trying to feel clean. The plunge bath had been so cold there had been a thin covering of ice on it; he'd dived in, half expecting his heart to stop with the shock.

He'd sat in the main room, watching the logs burn. He'd tried to pull himself together, and once he'd felt capable of thinking clearly he'd raised Chiark Hub.

"Gurgeh; Makil Stra-bey again, at your service. How's tricks? Not another visitation from Contact, surely?"

"No. But I have a feeling they left something behind when they were here; something to watch me."

"What . . . you mean a bug or a microsystem or something?"

"Yes," he said, sitting back in the broad couch. He wore a simple robe. His skin felt scrubbed and shiny clean after his bathe. Somehow, the friendly, understanding voice of Hub made him feel better; it would be all right, he'd work something out. He was probably frightened over nothing; Mawhrin-Skel was just a demented, insane machine with delusions of power and grandeur. It wouldn't be able to prove anything, and nobody would believe it if it simply made unsubstantiated claims.

"What makes you think you're being bugged?"

"I can't tell you," Gurgeh said. "Sorry. But I have seen some evidence. Can you send something—drones or whatever—to

Ikroh, to sweep the place? Would you be able to find something if they did leave anything?"

"If it's ordinary tech stuff, yes. But it depends on the soph level. A warship can passive-bug using its electro-magnetic effector; they can watch you under a hundred klicks of rock-cover from the next stellar system and tell you what your last meal was. Hyper-space tech; there are defenses against it, but no way of detecting it's going on."

"Nothing that complicated; just a bug or a camera or something."

"Should be possible. We'll displace a drone team to you in a minute or so. Want us to harden this comm channel? Can't make it totally eavesdrop-proof, but we can make it difficult."

"Please."

"No problem. Detach the terminal speaker pip and shove it in your ear. We'll soundfield the outside."

Gurgeh did just that. He felt better already. The Hub seemed to know what it was doing. "Thanks, Hub," he said. "I appreciate all this."

"Hey, no thanks required, Gurgeh. That's what we're here for. Besides; this is fun!"

Gurgeh smiled. There was a distant thump somewhere above the house as the Hub's drone team arrived.

The drones swept the house for sensory equipment and secured the buildings and grounds; they polarized the windows and drew the drapes; they put some sort of special mat under the couch he sat on; they even installed a kind of filter or valve inside the chimney of the fire.

Gurgeh felt grateful and cosseted, and both important and foolish, all at once.

He set to work. He used his terminal to probe the Hub's information banks. They contained as a matter of course almost every even moderately important or significant or useful piece of information the Culture had ever accumulated; a near infinite ocean of fact and sensation and theory and artwork which the Culture's information net was adding to at a torrential rate every second of the day.

You could find out most things, if you knew the right questions to ask. Even if you didn't, you could still find out a lot. The Culture had theoretical total freedom of information; the catch was that consciousness was private, and information held in a Mind—as opposed to an unconscious system, like the Hub's memory-banks—was regarded as part of the Mind's being, and so as sacrosanct as the contents of a human brain; a Mind could hold any set of facts and opinions it wanted without having to tell anybody what it knew or thought, or why.

And so, while Hub protected his privacy, Gurgeh found out, without having to ask Chamlis, that what Mawhrin-Skel had said might be true; there were indeed levels of event-recording which could not be easily faked, and which drones of above-average specification were potentially capable of using. Such recordings, especially if they had been witnessed by a Mind in a real-time link, would be accepted as genuine. His mood of renewed optimism started to sink away from him again.

Also, there was an SC Mind, that of the Limited Offensive Unit *Gunboat Diplomat,* which had supported Mawhrin-Skel's appeal against the decision which had removed the drone from Special Circumstances.

The feeling of dazed sickness started to fill him again.

He wasn't able to find out when Mawhrin-Skel and the LOU had last been in touch; that, again, counted as private information. Privacy; that brought a bitter laugh to his mouth, thinking of the privacy he'd had over the last few days and nights.

But he did discover that a drone like Mawhrin-Skel, even in civilianized form, was capable of sustaining a one-way real-time link with such a ship over millennia distances, so long as the ship was watching out for the signal and knew where to look. He could not find out there and then where the *Gunboat Diplomat* was in the galaxy—SC ships routinely kept their locations secret—but put in a request that the ship release its position to him.

From what he could tell from the information he'd discovered, Mawhrin-Skel's claim that the Mind had recorded their conversation would not hold up if the ship was more than about twenty millennia away; if it turned out, say, that the craft was on the other side of the galaxy, then the drone had definitely lied, and he would be safe.

He hoped the vessel was on the other side of the galaxy; he hoped it was a hundred thousand light-years away or more, or it had gone crazy and run into a black hole or decided to head for another galaxy, or stumbled across a hostile alien ship powerful enough to blow it out of the skies . . . anything, so long as it wasn't nearby and able to make that real-time link.

Otherwise, everything Mawhrin-Skel had said checked out. It could be done. He could be blackmailed. He sat in the couch, while the fire burned down and the Hub drones floated through the house humming and clicking to themselves, and he stared into the graying ashes, wishing that it was all unreal, wishing it hadn't happened, cursing himself for letting the little drone talk him into cheating.

Why? he asked himself. Why did I do it? How could I have been so stupid? It had seemed a glamorous, enticingly dangerous thing at the time; a little crazy, but then, was he not different from other people? Was he not the great game-player and so allowed his eccentricities, granted the freedom to make his own rules? He hadn't wanted self-glorification, not really. And he had already won the game; he just wanted *somebody* in the Culture to have completed a Full Web; hadn't he? It wasn't like him to cheat; he had never done it before; he would never do it again . . . how could Mawhrin-Skel do this to him? *Why had he done it?* Why couldn't it just not have happened? Why didn't they have time-travel, why couldn't he go back and stop it happening? Ships that could circumnavigate the galaxy in a few years, and count every cell in your body from light-years off, but he wasn't able to go back one miserable day and alter one tiny, stupid, idiotic, shameful decision . . .

He clenched his fists, trying to break the terminal he held in his right hand, but it wouldn't break. His hand hurt again.

He tried to think calmly. What if the worst did happen? The Culture was generally rather disdainful of individual fame, and therefore equally uninterested in scandal—there was, anyway, little that *was* scandalous—but Gurgeh had no doubt that if Mawhrin-Skel did release the recordings it claimed to have made, they would be propagated; people would know.

There were plenty of news and current affairs indices and networks in the multiplicity of communications which linked every Culture habitat, be it ship, rock, Orbital or planet. Somebody somewhere would be only too pleased to broadcast Mawhrin-Skel's recordings. Gurgeh knew of a couple of recently established games indices whose editors, writers and correspondents regarded him and most of the other well-known players and authorities as some sort of constricting, over-privileged hierarchy; they thought too much attention was paid to too few players, and sought to discredit what they called the old guard (which included him, much to his amusement). They would love what Mawhrin-Skel had on him. He could deny it all, once it was out, and some people would doubtless believe him despite the hardness of the evidence, but the other top players, and the responsible, well-established and authoritative indices, would know the truth of it, and that was what he would not be able to bear.

He would still be able to play, and he would still be allowed to publish, to register his papers as open for dissemination, and probably many of them would be taken up; not quite so often as before, perhaps, but he would not be frozen out completely. It would be worse than that; he would be treated with compassion, understanding, tolerance. But he would never be forgiven.

Could he come to terms with that, ever? Could he weather the storm of abuse and knowing looks, the gloating sympathy of his rivals? Would it all die down enough eventually, would a few years pass and it be sufficiently forgotten? He thought not. Not for him. It would always be there. He could not face down Mawhrin-Skel with that; publish and be damned. The drone had been right; it would destroy his reputation, destroy him.

He watched the logs in the wide grate glow duller red and then go soft and gray. He told Hub he was finished; it quietly returned the house to normal and left him alone with his thoughts.

He woke the next morning, and it was still the same universe; it had not been a nightmare and time had not gone backward. It had all still happened.

He took the underground to Celleck, the village where Chamlis Amalk-ney lived by itself, in an old-fashioned and odd approximation of human domesticity, surrounded by wall paintings, antique furniture, inlaid walls, fishtanks and insect vivaria.

* * *

"I'll find out all I can, Gurgeh," Chamlis sighed, floating beside him, looking out to the square. "But I can't guarantee that I can do it without whoever was behind your last visit from Contact finding out about it. They may think you're interested."

"Maybe I am," Gurgeh said. "Maybe I do want to talk to them again, I don't know."

"Well, I've sent the message to my friends, but—"

He had a sudden, paranoid idea. He turned to Chamlis urgently. "These friends of yours are ships."

"Yes," Chamlis said. "Both of them."

"What are they called?"

"The *Of Course I Still Love You* and the *Just Read the Instructions.*"

"They're not warships?"

"With names like that? They're GCUs; what else?"

"Good," Gurgeh said, relaxing a little, looking out to the square again. "Good. That's all right." He took a deep breath.

"Gurgeh, can't you—please—tell me what's wrong?" Chamlis's voice was soft, even sad. "You know it'll go no further. Let me help. It hurts me to see you like this. If there's anything I can—"

"Nothing," Gurgeh said, looking at the machine again. He shook his head. "There's nothing, nothing else you can do. I'll let you know if there is." He started across the room. Chamlis watched him. "I have to go now. I'll see you again, Chamlis."

He went down to the underground. He sat in the car, staring at the floor. On about the fourth request, he realized the car was talking to him, asking where he wanted to go. He told it.

He was staring at one of the wall-screens, watching the steady stars, when the terminal beeped.

"Gurgeh? Makil Stra-bey, yet again one more time once more."

"What?" he snapped, annoyed at the Mind's glib chumminess.

"That ship just replied with the information you asked for."

He frowned. "What ship? What information?"

"The *Gunboat Diplomat,* our game-player. Its location."

His heart pounded and his throat seemed to close up. "Yes," he said, struggling to get the word out. "And?"

"Well, it didn't reply direct; it sent via its home GSV *Youthful Indiscretion* and got it to confirm its location."

"Yes, well? Where is it?"

"In the Altabien-North cluster. Sent coordinates, though they're only accurate to—"

"Never mind the coordinates!" Gurgeh shouted. "Where is that cluster? How far *away* is it from here?"

"Hey; calm down. It's about two and a half millennia away."

He sat back, closing his eyes. The car started to slow down.

Two thousand five hundred light-years. It was, as the urbanely well-traveled people on a GSV would say, a long walk. But close enough—by quite a long way—for a warship to minutely target an effector, throw a sensing field a light-second in diameter across the sky, and pick up the weak but indisputable flicker of coherent HS light coming from a machine small enough to fit into a pocket.

He tried to tell himself it was still no proof, that Mawhrin-Skel might still have been lying, but even as he thought that, he saw something ominous in the fact the warship had not replied direct. It had used its GSV, an even more reliable source of information, to confirm its whereabouts.

"Want the rest of the LOU's message?" Hub said. "Or are you going to bite my head off again?"

Gurgeh was puzzled. "What rest of the message?" he said. The underground car swung round, slowed further. He could see Ikroh's transit gallery, hanging under the Plate surface like an upside-down building.

"Mysteriouser and mysteriouser," Hub said. "You been communicating with this ship behind my back, Gurgeh? The message is: 'Nice to hear from you again.'"

Three days passed. He couldn't settle to anything. He tried to read—papers, old books, the material of his own he'd been working on—but on every occasion he found himself reading and re-reading the same piece or page or screen, time and time again, trying hard to take it in but finding his thoughts constantly veering away from the words and diagrams and illustrations in front of him, refusing to absorb anything, going back time and time again to the same treadmill, the same looping, tail-swallowing, eternally pointless round of questioning and regret. Why had he done it? What way out was there?

He tried glanding soothing drugs, but it took so much to have any effect he just felt groggy. He used *Sharp Blue* and *Edge* and *Focal* to force himself to concentrate, but it gave him a jarring feeling at the back of his skull somewhere, and exhausted him. It wasn't worth it. His brain wanted to worry and fret and there was no point in trying to frustrate it.

He refused all calls. He called Chamlis a couple of times, but never found anything to say. All Chamlis could tell him was that the two Contact ships it knew had both been in touch; each said it had passed on Chamlis's message to a few other Minds. Both had been surprised Gurgeh had been contacted so quickly. Both would pass on Gurgeh's request to be told more; neither knew anything else about what was going on.

He heard nothing from Mawhrin-Skel. He asked Hub to find the machine, just to let him know where it was, but Hub couldn't, which obviously annoyed the Orbital Mind a lot. He had it send the drone team down again and they swept the house once more. Hub left one of the machines there in the house, to monitor continuously for surveillance.

Gurgeh spent a lot of time walking in the forests and mountains around Ikroh, walking and hiking and scrambling twenty or thirty kilometers each day just for the natural soporific of being dead, animal-tired at night.

On the fourth day, he was almost starting to feel that if he didn't do anything, didn't talk to anybody or communicate or write, and didn't stir from the house, nothing would happen. Maybe Mawhrin-Skel had disappeared forever. Perhaps Contact had come to take it away, or said it could come back to the fold. Maybe it had gone totally crazy and flown off into space; maybe it had taken seriously the old joke about Styglian enumerators, and had gone off to count all the grains of sand on a beach.

It was a fine day. He sat in the broad lower branches of a sunbread tree in the garden at Ikroh, looking out through the canopy of leaves to where a small herd of feyl had emerged from the forest to crop the wineberry bushes at the bottom of the lower lawn. The pale, shy animals, stick-thin and camouflage-skinned, pulled nervously at the low shrubs, their triangular heads jigging and bobbing, jaws working.

Gurgeh looked back to the house, just visible through the gently moving leaves of the tree.

He saw a tiny drone, small and gray-white, near one of the windows of the house. He froze. It might not be Mawhrin-Skel, he told himself. It was too far away to be certain. It might be Loash and-all-the-rest. Whatever it was, it was a good forty meters away, and he must be almost invisible sitting here in the tree. He couldn't be traced; he'd left his terminal back at the house, something he had taken to doing increasingly often recently, even though it was a dangerous, irresponsible thing to do, to be apart from the Hub's information network, effectively cut off from the rest of the Culture.

He held his breath, sat dead still.

The little machine seemed to hesitate in midair, then point in his direction. It came floating straight toward him.

It wasn't Mawhrin-Skel or Loash the verbose; it wasn't even the same type. It was a little larger and fatter and it had no aura at all. It stopped just below the tree and said in a pleasant voice, "Mr. Gurgeh?"

He jumped out of the tree. The herd of feyl started and disappeared, leaping into the forest in a confusion of green shapes. "Yes?" he said.

"Good afternoon. My name's Worthil; I'm from Contact. Pleased to meet you."

"Hello."

"What a lovely place. Did you have the house built?"

"Yes," Gurgeh said. Irrelevant small-talk; a nano-second interrogation of Hub's memories would have told the machine exactly when Ikroh was built, and by whom.

"Quite beautiful. I couldn't help noticing the roofs all slope at more or less the same mean angle as the surrounding mountain slopes. Your idea?"

"A private aesthetic theory," Gurgeh admitted, a little more impressed; he'd never mentioned that to anybody. The fieldless machine made a show of looking around.

"Hmm. Yes, a fine house and an impressive setting. But now: may I come to the reason for my visit?"

Gurgeh sat down cross-legged by the tree. "Please do."

The drone lowered itself to keep level with his face. "First of all, let me apologize if we put you off earlier. I think the drone who visited you previously may have taken its instructions a little too literally, though, to give it its due, time is rather limited. . . . Anyway; I'm here to tell you all you want to know. We have, as you probably suspected, found something we think might interest you. However . . ." The drone turned away from the man, to look at the house and its garden again. "I wouldn't blame you if you didn't want to leave your beautiful home."

"So it does involve traveling?"

"Yes. For some time."

"How long?" Gurgeh asked.

The drone seemed to hesitate. "May I tell you what it is we've found, first?"

"All right."

"It must be in confidence, I'm afraid," the drone said apologetically. "What I've come to tell you has to remain restricted for the time being. You'll understand why once I've explained. Can you give me your word you won't let this go any further?"

"What would happen if I say No?"

"I leave. That's all."

Gurgeh shrugged, brushed a little bark from the hem of the gathered-up robe he was wearing. "All right. In secret, then."

Worthil floated upward a little, turning its front briefly toward Ikroh. "It'll take a little time to explain. Might we retire to your house?"

"Of course." Gurgeh rose to his feet.

Gurgeh sat in the main screen-room of Ikroh. The windows were blanked out and the wall holoscreen was on; the Contact drone was controlling the room systems. It put the lights out. The screen went blank, then showed the main galaxy, in 2-D, from a considerable distance. The two Clouds were nearest

Gurgeh's point of view, the larger Cloud a semi-spiral with a long tail leading away from the galaxy, and the smaller Cloud vaguely Y-shaped.

"The Greater and Lesser Clouds," the drone Worthil said. "Each about one hundred thousand light-years away from where we are now. No doubt you've admired them from Ikroh in the past; they're quite visible, though you're on the under-edge of the main galaxy relative to them, and so looking at them through it. We've found what you might consider a rather interesting game . . . here." A green dot appeared near the center of the smaller Cloud.

Gurgeh looked at the drone. "Isn't that," he said, "rather far away? I take it you're suggesting I go there."

"It is a long way away, and we do suggest just that. The journey will take nearly two years on the fastest ships, due to the nature of the energy grid; it's more tenuous out there, between the star-clumps. Inside the galaxy such a journey would take less than a year."

"But that means I'd be away four years," Gurgeh said, staring at the screen. His mouth had gone dry.

"More like five," the drone said matter-of-factly.

"That's . . . a long time."

"It is, and I'll certainly understand if you decline our invitation. Though we do think you'll find the game itself interesting. First of all, however, I have to explain a little about the setting, which is what makes the game unique." The green dot expanded, became a rough circle. The screen went suddenly out-holo, filling the room with stars. The rough green circle of suns became an even rougher sphere. Gurgeh experienced the momentary swimming sensation he sometimes felt when surrounded by space or its impression.

"These stars," Worthil said—the green-colored stars, at least a couple of thousand suns, flashed once—"are under the control of what one can only describe as an empire. Now . . ." The drone turned to look at him. The little machine lay in space like some impossibly large ship, stars in front of it as well as behind it. "It is unusual for us to discover an imperial power-system in space. As a rule, such archaic forms of authority wither long before the relevant species drags itself off the home planet, let alone cracks the lightspeed problem, which of course one has to do, to rule effectively over any worthwhile volume.

"Every now and again, however, Contact disturbs some particular ball of rock and discovers something nasty underneath. On every occasion, there is a specific and singular reason, some special circumstance which allows the general rule to go by the board. In the case of the conglomerate you see before you—apart from the obvious factors, such as the fact that we didn't get out there until fairly recently, and the lack of any other powerful influence in the Lesser Cloud—that special circumstance is a game."

It took a while to sink in. Gurgeh looked at the machine. "A *game?*" he said to it.

"That game is called 'Azad' by the natives. It is important enough for the empire itself to take its name from the game. You are looking at the Empire of Azad."

Gurgeh did just that. The drone went on. "The dominant species is humanoid, but, very unusually—and certain analyses claim that this too has been a factor in the survival of the empire as a social system—it is composed of three sexes." Three figures appeared in the center of Gurgeh's field of vision, as though standing in the middle of the ragged sphere of stars. They were rather shorter than Gurgeh if the scale was right. Each of them looked odd in different ways, but they shared what looked to Gurgeh to be rather short legs and slightly bloated, flat and very pale faces. "The one on the left," Worthil said, "is a male, carrying the testes and penis. The middle one is equipped with a kind of reversible vagina, and ovaries. The vagina turns inside-out to implant the fertilized egg in the third sex, on the right, which has a womb. The one in the middle is the dominant sex."

Gurgeh had to think about this. "The what?" he said.

"The dominant sex," Worthil repeated. "Empires are synonymous with centralized—if occasionally schismatized—hierarchical power structures in which influence is restricted to an economically privileged class retaining its advantages through—usually—a judicious use of oppression and skilled manipulation of both the society's information dissemination systems and its lesser—as a rule nominally independent—power systems. In short, it's all about dominance. The intermediate—or apex—sex you see standing in the middle there controls the society and the empire. Generally, the males are used as soldiers and the females as possessions. Of course, it's a little more complicated than that, but you get the idea?"

"Well." Gurgeh shook his head. "I don't understand how it works, but if you say it does . . . all right." He rubbed his beard. "I take it this means these people can't change sex."

"Correct. Genetechnologically, it's been within their grasp for hundreds of years, but it's forbidden. Illegal, if you remember what that means." Gurgeh nodded. The machine went on. "It looks perverse and wasteful to us, but then one thing that empires are not about is the efficient use of resources and the spread of happiness; both are typically accomplished despite the economic short-circuiting—corruption and favoritism, mostly—endemic to the system."

"Okay," Gurgeh said. "I'll have a lot of questions to ask later, but go on. What about this game?"

"Indeed. Here is one of the boards."

". . . You're joking," Gurgeh said eventually. He sat forward, gazing at the holo still picture spread before him.

The starfield and the three humanoids had vanished, and Gurgeh and the drone called Worthil were, seemingly, at one end of a huge room many times larger than the one they in fact occupied. Before them stretched a floor covered with a stunningly complicated and seemingly chaotically abstract and irregular mosaic pattern, which in places rose up like hills and dipped into valleys. Looking closer, it could be seen that the hills were not solid, but rather stacked, tapering levels of the same bewildering meta-pattern, creating linked, multilayered pyramids over the fantastic landscape, which, on still closer inspection, had what looked like bizarrely sculpted game-pieces standing on its riotously colored surface. The whole construction must have measured at least twenty meters to a side.

"That," Gurgeh asked, "is a board?" He swallowed. He had never seen, never heard about, never had the least hint of a game as complicated as this one must surely be, if those were individual pieces and areas.

"One of them."

"How many are there?" It couldn't be real. It had to be a joke. They were making fun of him. No human brain could possibly cope with a game on such a scale. It was impossible. It had to be.

"Three. All that size, plus numerous minor ones, played with cards as well. Let me give you some of the background to the game.

"First, the name; 'Azad' means 'machine,' or perhaps 'system,' in the wide sense which would include any functioning entity, such as an animal or a flower, as well as something like myself, or a water-wheel. The game has been developed over several thousand years, reaching its present form about eight hundred years ago, around the same time as the institutionalization of the species' still extant religion. Since then the game has altered little. It dates in its finalized form, then, from about the time of the hegemonization of the empire's home planet, Eä, and the first, relativistic exploration of nearby space."

Now the view was of a planet, hanging huge in the room in front of Gurgeh; blue-white and brilliant and slowly, slowly, revolving against a background of dark space. "Eä," the drone said. "Now; the game is used as an absolutely integral part of the power-system of the empire. Put in the crudest possible terms, whoever wins the game becomes emperor."

Gurgeh looked round slowly at the drone, which looked back. "I kid you not," it said drily.

"Are you serious?" Gurgeh said, nevertheless.

"Quite entirely," the drone said. "Becoming emperor does constitute a rather unusual . . . prize," the machine said, "and the whole truth, as you might imagine, is much more complicated than that. The game of Azad is used not so much to determine which person will rule, but which tendency within the empire's ruling class will have the upper hand, which branch of economic theory will be followed, which creeds will be recognized within the religious apparat, and which political policies will be followed. The game is also used as an exam for both entry into and promotion within the empire's religious, educational, civil administrational, judicial and military establishments.

"The idea, you see, is that Azad is so complex, so subtle, so flexible and so demanding that it is as precise and comprehensive a model of life as it is possible to construct. Whoever succeeds at the game succeeds in life; the same qualities are required in each to ensure dominance."

"But . . ." Gurgeh looked at the drone beside him, and seemed to feel the presence of the planet before them as an almost physical force, something he felt drawn to, pulled toward, "is that *true?*"

The planet disappeared and they were back looking at the vast game-board again. The holo was in motion now, though silently, and he could see the alien people moving around, shifting pieces and standing around the edges of the board.

"It doesn't have to be totally true," the drone said, "but cause and effect are not perfectly polarized here; the set-up assumes that the game and life are the same thing, and such is the pervasive nature of the *idea* of the game within the society that just by believing that, they make it so. It becomes true; it is willed into actuality. Anyway; they can't be too far wrong, or the empire would not exist at all. It is by definition a volatile and unstable system; Azad—the game—would appear to be the force that holds it together."

"Wait a moment now," Gurgeh said, looking at the machine. "We both know Contact's got a reputation for being devious; you wouldn't be expecting me to go out there and become emperor or anything, would you?"

For the first time, the drone showed an aura, flashing briefly red. There was a laugh in its voice, too. "I wouldn't expect you'd get very far trying that. No; the empire falls under the general definition of a 'state,' and the one thing states always try to do is to ensure their own existence in perpetuity. The idea of anybody from outside coming in and trying to take the empire over would fill them with horror. *If* you decide you want to go, and *if* you are able to learn the game sufficiently well during the voyage, then there might be a chance, we think, going on your past performance as a game-player, of you qualifying as a clerk in the civil service, or as an army lieutenant. Don't forget; these people are surrounded by this game from birth. They have anti-agatic drugs, and the best players are about twice your own age. Even they, of course, are still learning.

"The point is not what you would be able to achieve in terms of the semi-barbarous social conditions the game is set up to support, but whether you can master the theory and practice of the game at all. Opinions in Contact differ over whether it is possible for even a game-player of your stature to compete successfully, just on general game-playing principles and a crash-course in the rules and practice."

Gurgeh watched the silent, alien figures move across the artificial landscape of the huge board. He couldn't do this. Five years? That was insane. He might as well let Mawhrin-Skel broadcast his shame; in five years he might have made a new life, leaving Chiark, finding something else to interest him besides games, changing his appearance . . . maybe changing his name; he had never heard of anybody doing that, but it must be possible.

Certainly, the game of Azad, if it really existed, was quite fascinating. But why had he heard nothing of it until now? How could Contact keep something like this secret; and why? He rubbed his beard, still watching the silent aliens as they stalked the broad board, stopping to move pieces or have others move them for them.

They were alien, but they were people; humanoid. *They* had mastered this bizarre, outrageous game. "They're not super-intelligent, are they?" he asked the drone.

"Hardly, retaining such a social system at this stage of technological development, game or no game. On average, the intermediate or apex sex is probably a little less bright than the average Culture human."

Gurgeh was mystified. "That implies there's a difference between the sexes."

"There is now," Worthil said.

Gurgeh didn't quite see what that meant, but the drone went on before he could ask any further questions. "In fact, we are reasonably hopeful that you will be able to play an above-average game of Azad if you study for the two years your outward journey would take. It would require continued and comprehensive use of memory and learning-enhancing secretions, of course, and I might point out that possession of drug-glands alone would disqualify you from actually gaining any post within the empire through your game performance, even if you weren't an alien anyway. There is a strict ban on any 'unnatural' influence being used during the game; all the game-rooms are electronically shielded to prevent the use of a computer link, and drug tests are carried out after every game. Your own body chemistry, as well as your alien nature and the fact that to them you are a heathen, means that you would—if you did decide to go—only be taking part in an honorary capacity."

"Drone . . . Worthil . . ." Gurgeh said, turning to face it. "I don't think I'll be going all that way, not so far, for so long . . . but I'd love to know more about this game; I want to discuss it, analyze it along with other—"

"Not possible," the drone said. "I'm allowed to tell you all that I am telling you, but none of this can go any further. You have given your word, Jernau Gurgeh."

"And if I break it?"

"Everybody would think you'd made it up; there's nothing on accessible record to show any different."

"Why is it all so secret, anyway? What are you frightened of?"

"The truth is, we don't know what to do, Jernau Gurgeh. This is a larger problem than Contact usually has to deal with; as a rule it's possible to go by the book; we've built up enough experience with every sort of barbarian society to know what does and does not work with each type; we monitor, we use controls, we cross-evaluate and Mind-model and generally take every possible precaution to make sure we're doing the right thing . . . but something like Azad is unique; there are no templates, no reliable precedents. We have to play it by ear, and that's something of a responsibility, dealing with an entire stellar empire. Which is why Special Circumstances has become involved; we're used to dealing with tricky situations. And frankly, with this one, we're sitting on it. If we let everybody know about Azad we may be pressured into making a decision just by the weight of public opinion . . . which may not sound like a bad thing, but might prove disastrous."

"For whom?" Gurgeh said skeptically.

"The people of the empire, and the Culture. We might be forced into a high-profile intervention against the empire; it would hardly be war as such because we're way ahead of them technologically, but we'd have to become an occupying force to control them, and that would mean a huge drain on our resources as well as morale; in the end such an adventure would almost certainly be seen as a mistake, no matter the popular enthusiasm for it at the time. The people of the empire would lose by uniting against us instead of the corrupt regime which controls them, so putting the clock back a century or two, and the Culture would lose by emulating those we despise; invaders, occupiers, hegemonists."

"You seem very sure there would be a wave of popular opinion."

"Let me explain something to you, Jernau Gurgeh," the drone said. "The game of Azad is a gambling game, frequently even at the highest levels. The form these wagers take is occasionally macabre. I very much doubt that you'd be involved on the sort of levels you'd be playing at if you did agree to take part, but it is quite usual for them to wager prestige, honors, possessions, slaves, favors, land and even physical license on the outcome of games."

Gurgeh waited, but eventually sighed and said, "All right . . . what's 'physical license'?"

"The players wager tortures and mutilations against each other."

"You mean, if you lose a game . . . you have . . . these things done to you?"

"Exactly. One might bet, say, the loss of a finger against aggravated male-to-apex rectal rape."

Gurgeh looked levelly at the machine for a few seconds, then said slowly, nodding, "Well . . . that *is* barbaric."

"Actually it's a later development in the game, and seen as a rather liberal concession by the ruling class, as in theory it allows a poor person to keep up in the bidding with a rich person. Before the introduction of the physical license option, the latter could always outbid the former."

"Oh." Gurgeh could see the logic, just not the morality.

"Azad is not the sort of place it's easy to think about coldly, Jernau Gurgeh. They have done things the average Culture person would find . . . unspeakable. A program of eugenic manipulation has lowered the average male and female intelligence; selective birth-control sterilization, area starvation, mass deportation and racially based taxation systems produced the equivalent of genocide, with the result that almost everybody on the home planet is the same color and build. Their treatment of alien captives, their societies and works is equally—"

"Look, is all this serious?" Gurgeh got up from the seat and walked into the field of the hologram, gazing down at the fabulously complicated game-floor, which appeared to be under his feet but was in fact, he knew, a terrible gulf of space away. "Are you telling me the truth? Does this empire really exist?"

"Very much so, Jernau Gurgeh. If you want to confirm all I've said, I can arrange for special access rights to be granted to you, direct from the GSVs and other Minds who've taken charge of this. You can have all you want on the empire of Azad, from the first sniff of contact to the latest real-time news reports. It's all true."

"And when did you first get that sniff of contact?" Gurgeh said, turning to the drone. "How long have you been sitting on this?"

The drone hesitated. "Not long," it said eventually. "Seventy-three years."

"You people certainly don't rush into things, do you?"

"Only when we've no choice," the drone agreed.

"And how does the empire feel about us?" Gurgeh asked. "Let me guess; you haven't told them all about the Culture."

"Very good, Jernau Gurgeh," the drone said, with what was almost a laugh in its voice. "No, we haven't told them everything. That's something the drone we'd be sending with you would have to keep you straight on; right from the start we've misled the empire about our distribution, numbers, resources, technological level and ultimate intentions . . . though of course only the relative paucity of advanced societies in the relevant region of the Lesser Cloud has made this possible. The

Azadians do not, for example, know that the Culture is based in the main galaxy; they believe we come from the Greater Cloud, and that our numbers are only about twice theirs. They have little inkling of the level of genofixing in Culture humans, or of the sophistication of our machine intelligences; they've never heard of a ship Mind, or seen a GSV.

"They've been trying to find out about us ever since first contact, of course, but without any success. They probably think we have a home planet or something; they themselves are still very much planet-oriented, using planeforming techniques to create usable ecospheres, or more usually just taking over already occupied globes; ecologically and morally, they're catastrophically bad. The reason they're trying to find out about us is they want to invade us; they want to conquer the Culture. The problem is that, as with all playground-bully mentalities, they're quite profoundly *frightened;* xenophobic and paranoid at once. We daren't let them know the extent and power of the Culture yet, in case the whole empire self-destructs . . . such things have happened before, though of course that was long before Contact itself was formed. Our technique's better these days. Still tempting, all the same," the drone said, as though thinking aloud, not talking to him.

"They do," Gurgeh said, "sound fairly . . ."—he'd been going to say "barbaric," but that didn't seem strong enough—". . . animalistic."

"Hmm," the drone said. "Be careful, now; that is how they term the species they subjugate; animals. Of course they are animals, just as you are, just as I am a machine. But they are fully conscious, and they have a society at least as complicated as our own; more so, in some ways. It is pure chance that we've met them when their civilization looks primitive to us; one less ice age on Eä and it could conceivably have been the other way round."

Gurgeh nodded thoughtfully, and watched the silent aliens move across the game-floor, in the reproduced light of a distant, alien sun.

"But," Worthil added brightly, "it didn't happen that way, so not to worry. Now then," it said, and suddenly they were back in the room at Ikroh, the holoscreen off and the windows clear; Gurgeh blinked in the sudden wash of daylight. "I'm sure you realize there's still a vast amount left to tell you, but you have our proposal now, in its barest outline. I'm not asking you to say 'Yes' unequivocally at this stage, but is there any point in my going on, or have you already decided that you definitely don't want to go?"

Gurgeh rubbed his beard, looking out of the window toward the forest above Ikroh. It was too much to take in. If it really was genuine, then Azad was the single most significant game he'd ever encountered in his life . . . possibly more significant than all the rest put together. As an ultimate challenge, it excited and appalled him in equal measure; he felt instinctively, almost sexually drawn to it, even now, knowing so little . . . but he wasn't sure he possessed the self-discipline to study that intensely for two years solid, or that he was capable of holding a mental model of a game so bewilderingly complex in his head. He kept coming back to the fact that the Azadians themselves managed it, but, as the machine said, they were submerged in the game from birth; perhaps it could only be mastered by somebody who'd had their cognitive processes shaped by the game itself . . .

But five years! All that time; not just away from here, but at least half, probably more, of that stretch spent with no time for keeping abreast of developments in other games, no time to read papers or write them, no time for anything except this one, absurd, obsessive game. He would change; he would be a different person at the end of it; he could not help but change, take on something of the game itself; that would be inevitable. And would he ever catch up again, once he came back? He would be forgotten; he would be away so long the rest of the game-playing Culture would just disregard him; he'd be a historical figure. And when he came back, would he be allowed to talk about it? Or would Contact's seven-decade-long embargo continue?

But if he went, he might be able to buy Mawhrin-Skel off. He could make its price his price. Let it back in to SC. Or—it occurred to him there and then—have them silence it, somehow.

A flock of birds flew across the sky, white scraps against the dark greens of the mountain forest; they landed on the garden outside the window, strutting back and forth and pecking at the ground. He turned to the drone again, crossed his arms. "When would you need to know?" he said. He still hadn't decided. He had to stall, find out all he could first.

"It would have to be within the next three or four days. The GSV *Little Rascal* is heading out in this direction from the middle-galaxy at the moment, and will be leaving for the Clouds within the next hundred days. If you were to miss it, your journey would last a lot longer; your own ship will have to sustain maximum velocity right up to the rendezvous point, even as things stand."

"My own *ship?*" Gurgeh said.

"You'll need your own craft, firstly to get you to the *Little Rascal* in time, and then again at the other end, to travel from the GSV's closest approach to the Lesser Cloud into the empire itself."

He watched the snow-white birds peck on the lawn for a while. He wondered whether he ought to mention Mawhrin-Skel now. Part of him wanted to, just to get it over with, just in case they would say Yes immediately and he could stop worrying about the machine's threat (and start worrying about that insanely complicated game). But he knew he mustn't. Wisdom is patience, as the saying said. Keep that back; if he was going to go (though of course he wouldn't, couldn't, it was madness even to think of going), then make them think he had nothing he wanted in return; let it all be arranged and then make his condition clear . . . if Mawhrin-Skel waited that long before getting pushy.

"All right," he said to the Contact drone. "I'm not saying I will go, but I will think about it. Tell me more about Azad."

Stories set in the Culture in which Things Went Wrong tended to start with humans losing or forgetting or deliberately leaving behind their terminal. It was a conventional opening, the equivalent of straying off the path in the wild woods in one age, or a car breaking down at night on a lonely road in another. A terminal, in the shape of a ring, button, bracelet or pen or whatever, was your link with everybody and everything else in the Culture. With a terminal, you were never more than a question or a shout away from almost anything you wanted to know, or almost any help you could possibly need.

There were (true) stories of people falling off cliffs and the terminal relaying their scream in time for a Hub unit to switch to that terminal's camera, realize what was happening and displace a drone to catch the faller in midair; there were other stories about terminals recording the severing of their owner's head from their body in an accident, and summoning a medical drone in time to save the brain, leaving the de-bodied person with no more a problem than finding ways to pass the months it took to grow a new body.

A terminal was safety.

So Gurgeh took his on the longer walks.

He sat, a couple of days after the drone Worthil's visit, on a small stone bench near the tree-line a few kilometers from Ikroh. He was breathing hard from the climb up the path. It was a bright, sunny day and the earth smelled sweet. He used the terminal to take a few photographs of the view from the little clearing. There was a rusting piece of ironware beside the bench; a present from an old lover he'd almost forgotten about. He took a few photographs of that, too. Then the terminal beeped.

"House here, Gurgeh. You said to give you the choice on Yay's calls. She says this is moderately urgent."

He hadn't been accepting calls from Yay. She'd tried to get in touch several times over the last few days. He shrugged. "Go ahead," he said, leaving the terminal to float in midair in front of him.

The screen unrolled to reveal Yay's smiling face. "Ah, the recluse. How are you, Gurgeh?"

"I'm all right."

Yay peered forward at her own screen. "What is that you're sitting beside?"

Gurgeh looked at the piece of ironware by the side of the bench. "That's a cannon," he told her.

"That's what I thought."

"It was a present from a lady friend," Gurgeh explained. "She was very keen on forging and casting. She graduated from pokers and fire grates to cannons. She thought I might find it amusing to fire large metal spheres at the fjord."

"I see."

"You need a fast-burning powder to make it work, though, and I never did get round to acquiring any."

"Just as well; the thing would probably have exploded and blown your brains out."

"That did occur to me as well."

"Good for you." Yay's smile widened. "Hey, guess what?"

"What?"

"I'm going on a cruise; I persuaded Shuro he needs his horizons broadened. You remember Shuro; at the shoot?"

"Oh. Yes, I remember. When do you go?"

"I've gone. We just undocked from Tronze port; the clipper *Screw Loose.* This is the last chance I had to call you real-time. The delay'll mean letters in future."

"Ah." He wished he hadn't accepted this call, too, now. "How long are you going for?"

"A month or two." Yay's bright, smiling face crinkled. "We'll see. Shuro might get tired of me before then. Kid's mostly into other men, but I'm trying to persuade him otherwise. Sorry I couldn't say goodbye before I left, but it's not for long; I'll s—"

The terminal screen went blank. The screen snapped back into the casing as it fell to the ground and lay, silent and dead, on the tree-needled ground of the clearing. Gurgeh stared at the terminal. He leaned forward and picked it up. Some needles and bits of grass had been caught in the screen as it rolled back into the casing. He pulled them out. The machine was lifeless; the little tell-tale light on the base was off.

"Well, Jernau Gurgeh?" Mawhrin-Skel said, floating in from the side of the clearing.

He clutched the terminal with both hands. He stood up, staring at the drone as it sidled through the air, bright in the sunlight. He made himself relax, putting the terminal in a jacket pocket and sitting down, legs crossed, on the bench. "Well what, Mawhrin-Skel?"

"A decision." The machine floated level with his face. Its fields were formal blue. "Will you speak for me?"

"What if I do and nothing happens?"

"You'll just have to try harder. They'll listen, if you're persuasive enough."

"But if you're wrong, and they don't?"

"Then I'd have to think about whether to release your little entertainment or not; it would be fun, certainly . . . but I might save it, in case you could be useful to me in some other way; one never knows."

"No, indeed."

"I saw you had a visitor, the other day."

"I thought you might have noticed."

"Looked like a Contact drone."

"It was."

"I'd like to pretend I knew what it said to you, but once you went into the house, I had to stop eavesdropping. Something about traveling, I believe I heard you say?"

"A cruise, of sorts."

"Is that all?"

"No."

"Hmm. My guess was they might want you to join Contact, become a Referrer, one of their planners; something like that. Not so?"

Gurgeh shook his head. The drone wobbled from side to side in the air, a gesture Gurgeh was not sure he understood. "I see. And have you mentioned me yet?"

"No."

"I think you ought to, don't you?"

"I don't know whether I'm going to do what they ask. I haven't decided yet."

"Why not? What are they asking you to do? Can it compare to the shame—"

"I'll do what *I* want to do," he told it, standing up. "I might as well, after all, drone, mightn't I? Even if I can persuade Contact to take you back, you and your friend *Gunboat Diplomat* would still have the recording; what's to prevent you doing all this again?"

"Ah, so you know its name. I wondered what you and Chiark Hub were up to. Well, Gurgeh; just ask yourself this: what else could I possibly want from you? This is all I want; to be allowed to be what I was meant to be. When I am restored to that state, I'll have all I could possibly desire. There would be nothing else you could possibly have any control over. I want to fight, Gurgeh; that's what I was designed for; to use skill and cunning and *force* to win battles for our dear, beloved Culture. I'm not interested in controlling others, or in making the strategic decisions; that sort of power doesn't interest me. The only destiny I want to control is my own."

"Fine words," Gurgeh said.

He took the dead terminal out of his pocket, turned it over in his hands. Mawhrin-Skel plucked the terminal out of his hands from a couple of meters away, held it underneath its casing, and folded it neatly in half. It bent it again, into quarters; the pen-shaped machine snapped and broke. Mawhrin-Skel crumpled the remains into a little jagged ball.

"I'm getting impatient, Jernau Gurgeh. Time goes slower the faster you think, and I think very fast indeed. Let's say another four days, shall we? You have one hundred and twenty-eight hours before I tell *Gunboat* to make you even more famous than you are already." It tossed the wrecked terminal back to him; he caught it.

The little drone drifted off toward the edge of the clearing. "I'll be waiting for your call," it said. "Better get a new terminal, though. And do be careful on the walk back to Ikroh; dangerous to be out in the wilds with no way of summoning help."

"Five years?" Chamlis said thoughtfully. "Well, it's some game, I agree, but won't you lose touch over that sort of period? Have you thought this through properly, Gurgeh? Don't let them rush you into anything you might regret later."

They were in the lowest cellar in Ikroh. Gurgeh had taken Chamlis down there to tell it about Azad. He'd sworn the old drone to secrecy first. They'd left Hub's resident anti-surveillance drone guarding the cellar entrance and Chamlis had done its best to check there was nobody and nothing listening in, as well as producing a reasonable impression of a quietfield around them. They talked against a background of pipes and service ducts rumbling and hissing around them in the darkness; the naked walls' rock sweated, darkly glistening.

Gurgeh shook his head. There was nowhere to sit down in the cellar, and its roof was just a little too low for him to stand fully upright. So he stood, head bowed. "I think I'm going to do it," he said, not looking at Chamlis. "I can always come back, if it's too difficult, if I change my mind."

"Too difficult?" Chamlis echoed, surprised. "That's not like you. I agree it's a tough game, but—"

"Anyway, I can come back," he said.

Chamlis was silent for a moment. "Yes. Yes, of course you can."

He still didn't know if he was doing the right thing. He had tried to think it through, to apply the same sort of cold, logical analysis to his own plight that he would normally bring to bear in a tricky situation in a game, but he just didn't seem to be able to do so; it was as though that ability could look calmly only on distant, abstract problems, and was incapable of focusing on anything so intricately enmeshed with his own emotional state.

He wanted to go to get away from Mawhrin-Skel, but—he had to admit to himself—he was attracted by Azad. Not just the game. That was still slightly unreal, too complicated to be taken seriously yet. The empire itself interested him.

And yet of course he wanted to stay. He had enjoyed his life, until that night in Tronze. He had never been totally satisfied, but then, who was? Looking back, the life he'd led seemed idyllic. He might lose the occasional game, feel that another game-player was unjustifiably lauded over himself, lust after Yay Meristinoux and feel piqued she preferred others, but these were small, small hurts indeed, compared both with what Mawhrin-Skel held on him, and with the five years' exile which now faced him.

"No," he said, nodding at the floor, "I think I will go."

"All right . . . but this just doesn't seem like you, Gurgeh. You've always been so . . . measured. In control."

"You make me sound like a machine," Gurgeh said tiredly.

"No, but more . . . predictable than this; more comprehensible."

He shrugged, looked at the rough rock floor. "Chamlis," he said, "I'm only human."

"That, my dear old friend, has never been an excuse."

He sat in the underground car. He'd been to the university to see Professor Boruelal; he'd taken with him a sealed, handwritten letter for her to keep, to be opened only if he died, explaining all that had happened, apologizing to Olz Hap, trying to make clear how he'd felt, what had made him do such a terrible, stupid thing . . . but in the end he hadn't handed the letter over. He'd been terrified at the thought of Boruelal opening it, accidentally perhaps, and reading it while he was still alive.

The underground car raced across the base of the Plate, heading for Ikroh again. He used his new terminal to call the drone named Worthil. It had left after their last meeting to go exploring in one of the system's gas-giant planets, but on receiving his call had itself displaced by Chiark Hub to the base underside. It came in through the speeding car's lock. "Jernau Gurgeh," it said, condensation frosting on its casing, its presence entering the car's warm interior like a cold draft, "you've reached a decision?"

"Yes," he said. "I'll go."

"Good!" the drone said. It placed a small container about half its own size down on one of the padded car seats. "Gas-giant flora," it explained.

"I hope I didn't unduly curtail your expedition."

"Not at all. Let me offer you my congratulations; I think you've made a wise, even brave choice. It did cross my mind that Contact was only offering you this opportunity to make you more content with your present life. If that's what the big Minds were expecting, I'm glad to see you confounding them. Well done."

"Thank you." Gurgeh attempted a smile.

"Your ship will be prepared immediately. It should be on its way within the day."

"What kind of ship is it?"

"An old 'Murderer' class GOU left over from the Idiran war; been in deep storage about six decades from here for the last seven hundred years. Called the *Limiting Factor.* It's still in battle-trim at the moment, but they'll strip out the weaponry and emplace a set of game-boards and a module hangar. I understand the Mind isn't anything special; these warship forms can't afford to be sparkling wits or brilliant artists, but I believe it's a likeable enough device. It'll be your opponent during the journey. If you want, you're free to take somebody else along with you, but we'll send a drone with you anyway. There's a human envoy at Groasnachek, the capital of Eä, and he'll be your guide as well . . . were you thinking of taking a companion?"

"No," Gurgeh said. In fact he had thought of asking Chamlis, but knew the old drone felt it had already had enough excitement—and boredom—in its life. He didn't want to put the machine in the position of having to say no. If it actually wanted to go, he was sure it wouldn't be afraid to ask.

"Probably wise. What about personal possessions? It could be awkward if you want to take anything larger than a small module, say, or livestock larger than human size."

Gurgeh shook his head. "Nothing remotely that large. A few cases of clothes . . . perhaps one or two ornaments . . . nothing more. What sort of drone were you thinking of sending?"

"Basically a diplomat-cum-translator and general gofer; probably an old-timer with some experience of the empire. It'll have to have a comprehensive knowledge of all the empire's social mannerisms and forms of address and so on; you wouldn't believe how easy it is to make gaffes in a society like that. The drone will keep you clear as far as etiquette goes. It'll have a library too, of course, and probably a limited degree of offensive capability."

"I don't want a gun-drone, Worthil," Gurgeh said.

"It is advisable, for your own protection. You'll be under the protection of the imperial authorities, of course, but they aren't infallible. Physical attack isn't unknown during a game, and there are groups within the society which might want to harm you. I ought to point out the *Limiting Factor* won't be able to stay nearby once it's dropped you on Eä; the empire's military have insisted they will not allow a warship to be stationed over their home planet. The only reason they're letting it approach Eä at all is because we're removing all the armament. Once the ship has departed, that drone will be the only totally reliable protection you have."

"It won't make me invulnerable, though, will it?"

"No."

"Then I'll take my chances with the empire. Give me a mild-mannered drone; positively nothing armed, nothing . . . target-oriented."

"I really do strongly advise—"

"Drone," Gurgeh said, "to play this game properly I'll need to feel as much as possible like one of the locals, with the same vulnerability and worries. I don't want your device bodyguarding me. There won't be any point in my going if I know I don't have to take the game as seriously as everybody else."

The drone said nothing for some time. "Well, if you're sure," it said eventually, sounding unhappy.

"I am."

"Very well. If you insist." The drone made a sighing sound. "I think that settles everything. The ship ought to be here in a—"

"There is a condition," Gurgeh said.

"A . . . *condition?*" the drone said. Its fields became briefly visible, a glittering mixture of blue and brown and gray.

"There is a drone here, called Mawhrin-Skel," Gurgeh said.

"Yes," Worthil said carefully. "I was briefed that that device lives here now. What about it?"

"It was exiled from Special Circumstances; thrown out. We've become . . . friends since it came here. I promised if I ever had any influence with Contact, I'd do what I could to help it. I'm afraid I can only play Azad on condition that the drone's returned to SC."

Worthil said nothing for a moment. "That was rather a foolish promise to have made, Mr. Gurgeh."

"I admit I didn't ever think I would be in a position to have to fulfill it. But I am, so I have to make that a condition."

"You don't want to take this machine *with* you, do you?" Worthil sounded puzzled.

"No!" he said. "I just promised I'd try to get it back into service."

"Uh-huh. Well, I'm not really in a position to make that sort of deal, Jernau Gurgeh. That machine was civilianized because it was dangerous and refused to undergo reconstruction therapy; its case is not something that I can decide on. It's a matter for the admissions board concerned."

"All the same; I have to insist."

Worthil made a sighing noise, lifted the spherical container it had placed on the seat and seemed to study its blank surface. "I'll do what I can," it said, a trace of annoyance in its tone, "but I can't promise anything. Admissions and appeal boards hate being leaned on; they go terribly moralistic."

"I need my obligation to Mawhrin-Skel discharged somehow," Gurgeh said quietly. "I can't leave here with it able to claim I didn't try to help it."

The Contact drone seemed not to hear. Then it said, "Hmm. Well, we'll see what we can do."

The underground car flew across the base of the world, silent and swift.

"To Gurgeh; a great game-player, a great man!" Hafflis stood on the parapet at one end of the terrace, the kilometer drop behind him, a bottle in one hand, a fuming drug-bowl in the other. The stone table was crowded with people who'd come to wish Gurgeh goodbye. It had been announced that he was leaving tomorrow morning, to journey to the Clouds on the GSV *Little Rascal,* to be one of the Culture's representatives at the Pardethillisian Games, the great ludic convocation held every twenty-two years or so by the Meritocracy Pardethillisi, in the Lesser Cloud.

Gurgeh had, indeed, been invited to this tournament, as he had been invited to the Games before that, just as he was to several thousand competitions and convocations of various sizes and complexions every year, either within the Culture or outside it. He'd refused that invitation as he refused them all, but the story now was that he'd changed his mind and would go there and play for the Culture. The next Games were to be held in three and a half years, which made the need to leave at such short notice somewhat tricky to explain, but Contact had done a little creative timetabling and some bare-faced lying and made it appear to the casual inquirer that only the *Little Rascal* could get Gurgeh there in time for the lengthy formal registration and qualifying period required.

"Cheers!" Hafflis put his head back and the bottle to his lips. Everybody round the great table joined in, drinking from a dozen different types of bowl, glass, goblet and tankard. Hafflis rocked further and further back on his heels as he drained the bottle; a few people shouted out warnings or threw bits of food at him; he just had time to put the bottle down and smack his wine-wet lips before he overbalanced and disappeared over the edge of the parapet.

"Oops," came his muffled voice. Two of his younger children, sitting playing three-cups with a thoroughly mystified Styglian enumerator, went to the parapet and dragged their drunken parent back over from the safety field. He tumbled onto the terrace and staggered back to his seat, laughing.

Gurgeh sat between Professor Boruelal and one of his old flames; Vossle Chu, the woman whose hobbies had in the past included iron-foundry. She had crossed from Rombree, on Chiark's farside from Gevant, to come and see Gurgeh off. There were at least ten of his former lovers among the crowd squeezed around the table. He wondered fuzzily what the significance might be that out of that ten, six had chosen to change sex and become—and remain—men over the past few years.

Gurgeh, along with everybody else, was getting drunk, as was traditional on such occasions. Hafflis had promised that they would not do to Gurgeh what they had done to a mutual friend a few years earlier; the young man had been accepted into Contact and Hafflis had held a party to celebrate. At the end of the evening they'd stripped the fellow naked and thrown him over the parapet . . . but the safety field had been turned off; the new Contact recruit had fallen nine hundred meters—six hundred of them with empty bowels—before three of Hafflis's pre-positioned house drones rose calmly out of the forest beneath to catch him and take him back up.

The (Demilitarized) General Offensive Unit *Limiting Factor* had arrived under Ikroh that afternoon. Gurgeh had gone down to the transit gallery to inspect it. The craft was a third of a kilometer long, very sleek and simple looking; a pointed nose, three long blisters like vast aircraft cockpits leading to the nose, and another five fat blisters circling the vessel's waist; its rear was blunt and flat. The ship had said hello, told him it was there to take him to the GSV *Little Rascal,* and asked him if he had any special dietary requirements.

Boruelal slapped him on the back. "We're going to miss you, Gurgeh."

"Likewise," Gurgeh said, swaying, and felt quite emotional. He wondered when it would be time to throw the paper lanterns over the parapet to float down to the rain forest. They'd turned the lights on behind the waterfall, all the way down the cliff, and an itinerant dirigible, seemingly crewed largely by game-fans, had anchored above the plain level with Tronze, promising a firework display later. Gurgeh had been quite touched by such shows of respect and affection.

"Gurgeh," Chamlis said. He turned, still holding his glass, to look at the old machine. It put a small package into his hand. "A present," it said. Gurgeh looked at the small parcel; paper tied up with ribbon. "Just an old tradition," Chamlis explained. "You open it when you're under way."

"Thank you," Gurgeh said, nodding slowly. He put the present into his jacket, then did something he rarely did with drones, and hugged the old machine, putting his arms round its aura fields. "Thank you, very very much."

The night darkened; a brief shower almost extinguished the coals in the center of the table, but Hafflis got supply drones to bring crates of spirits and they all had fun squirting the drink onto the coals to keep them alight in pools of blue flame which burned down half the paper lanterns and scorched the night-flower vines and made many holes in clothes and singed the Styglian enumerator's pelt. Lightning flashed in the mountains above the lake, the falls glowed, backlit and fabulous, and the dirigible's fireworks drew applause and answering fireworks and cloud-lasers from all over Tronze. Gurgeh was dumped naked into the lake, but hauled out spluttering by Hafflis's children.

He woke up in Boruelal's bed, at the university, a little after dawn. He sneaked away early.

He looked around the room. Early morning sunlight flooded the landscape outside Ikroh and lanced through the lounge, streaming in from the fjord-side windows, across the room and out through the windows opening onto the uphill lawns. Birds filled the cool, still air with song.

There was nothing else to take, nothing more to pack. He'd sent the house drones down with a chest of clothes the night before, but now wondered why he'd bothered; he wouldn't need many changes on the warship, and when they got to the GSV he could order anything he wanted. He'd packed a few personal ornaments, and had the house copy his stock of still and moving pictures to the *Limiting Factor*'s memory. The last thing he'd done was burn the letter he'd written to leave with Boruelal, and stir the ashes in the fireplace until they were fine as dust. Nothing more remained.

"Ready?" Worthil said.

"Yes," he said. His head was clear and no longer sore, but he felt tired, and knew he'd sleep well that night. "Is it here yet?"

"On its way."

They were waiting for Mawhrin-Skel. It had been told its appeal had been re-opened; as a favor to Gurgeh, it was likely to be given a role in Special Circumstances. It had acknowledged, but not appeared. It would meet them when Gurgeh left.

Gurgeh sat down to wait.

A few minutes before he was due to leave, the tiny drone appeared, floating down the chimney to hover over the empty fire grate.

"Mawhrin-Skel," Worthil said. "Just in time."

"I believe I'm being recalled to duty," the smaller drone said.

"You are indeed," Worthil said heartily.

"Good. I'm sure my friend the LOU *Gunboat Diplomat* will follow my future career with great interest."

"Of course," Worthil said. "I would hope it would."

Mawhrin-Skel's fields glowed orange-red. It floated over to Gurgeh, its gray body shining brightly, fields all but extinguished in the bright sunshine. "Thank you," it said to him. "I wish you a good journey, and much luck."

Gurgeh sat on the couch and looked at the tiny machine. He thought of several things to say, but said none of them. Instead, he stood up, straightened his jacket, looked at Worthil and said, "I think I'm ready to go now."

Mawhrin-Skel watched him leave the room, but did not try to follow.

He boarded the *Limiting Factor.*

Worthil showed him the three great game-boards, set in three of the effector bulges round the vessel's waist, pointed out the module hangar housed in the fourth blister and the swimming pool which the dockyard had installed in the fifth because they couldn't think of anything else at such short notice and they didn't like to leave the blister just empty. The three effectors in the nose had been left in but disconnected, to be removed once the *Limiting Factor* docked with the *Little Rascal.* Worthil guided him round the living quarters, which seemed perfectly acceptable.

Surprisingly quickly, it was time to leave, and Gurgeh said goodbye to the Contact drone. He sat in the accommodation section, watching the small drone float down the corridor to the warship's lock, and then told the screen in front of him to switch to exterior view. The temporary corridor joining the ship to Ikroh's transit gallery retracted, and the long tube of the ship's innard-hull slotted back into place from outside.

Then, with no notice or noise at all, the view of the Plate base withdrew, shrinking. As the ship pulled away, the Plate merged into the other three on that side of the Orbital, to become part of a single thick line, and then that line dwindled rapidly to a point, and the star of Chiark's system flashed brilliantly from behind it, before the star too quickly dulled and shrank, and Gurgeh realized he was on his way to the Empire of Azad.

# 2

## *Imperium*

Still with me?

Little textual note for you here (bear with me).

Those of you unfortunate enough not to be reading or hearing this in Marain may well be using a language without the requisite number or type of personal pronouns, so I'd better explain that bit of the translation.

Marain, the Culture's quintessentially wonderful language (so the Culture will tell you), has, as any schoolkid knows, one personal pronoun to cover females, males, in-betweens, neuters, children, drones, Minds, other sentient machines, and every life-form capable of scraping together anything remotely resembling a nervous system and the rudiments of language (or a good excuse for not having either). Naturally, there *are* ways of specifying a person's sex in Marain, but they're not used in everyday conversation; in the archetypal language-as-moral-weapon-and-proud-of-it, the message is that it's brains that matter, kids; gonads are hardly worth making a distinction over.

So, in what follows, Gurgeh is quite happily thinking about the Azadians just as he'd think about any other (see list above) . . . But what of you, O unlucky, possibly brutish, probably ephemeral and undoubtedly disadvantaged citizen of some unCultured society, especially those unfairly (and the Azadians would say under-) endowed with only the mean number of genders?!

How shall we refer to the triumvirate of Azadian sexes without resorting to funny-looking alien terms or gratingly awkward phrases-not-words?

. . . . Rest at ease; I have chosen to use the natural and obvious pronouns for male and female, and to represent the intermediates—or apices—with whatever pronominal term best indicates their place in their society, relative to the existing sexual power-balance of yours. In other words, the precise translation depends on whether your own civilization (for let us err on the side of terminological generosity) is male or female dominated.

(Those which can fairly claim to be neither will of course have their own suitable term.)

Anyway, enough of that.

Let's see now: we've finally got old Gurgeh off Gevant Plate, Chiark Orbital, and we have him fizzing away at quite a clip in a stripped-down military ship heading for a rendezvous with the Cloudbound General Systems Vehicle *Little Rascal.*

Points to Ponder:

Does Gurgeh really understand what he's done, and what might happen to him? Has it even begun to occur to him that he might have been tricked? And does he really know what he's let himself in for?

Of course not!

That's part of the fun!

Gurgeh had been on cruises many times in his life and—on that longest one, thirty years earlier—traveled some thousands of light-years from Chiark, but within a few hours of his departure aboard the *Limiting Factor* he was feeling the gap of light-years the still accelerating ship was putting between him and his home with an immediacy he had not anticipated. He spent some time watching the screen, where Chiark's star shone yellow-white and gradually diminishing, but nevertheless he felt further away from it than even the screen showed.

He had never felt the falseness of such representations before, but sitting there, in the old accommodation social area, looking at the rectangle of screen on the wall, he couldn't help feeling like an actor, or a component in the ship's circuitry: like part of, and therefore as false as, the pretend-view of Real Space hung in front of him.

Maybe it was the silence. He had expected noise, for some reason. The *Limiting Factor* was tearing through something it called ultraspace with increasing acceleration; the craft's velocity was hurtling toward its maximum with a rapidity which, when displayed in numbers on the wall-screen, numbed Gurgeh's brain. He didn't even know what ultraspace was. Was it the same as hyperspace? At least he had heard of that, even if he didn't know much about it . . . whatever; for all its apparent speed, the ship was almost perfectly silent, and he experienced an enervating, eerie feeling, as though the ancient warship, mothballed all those centuries, had somehow not yet fully woken up, and events within its sleek hull still moved to another, slower tempo, made half of dreams.

The ship didn't seem to want to start any conversations, either, which normally wouldn't have bothered Gurgeh, but now did. He left his cabin and went for a walk, going down the narrow, hundred-meter-long corridor which led to the waist of the craft. In the bare corridor, hardly a meter wide, and so low he could touch the ceiling without having to stretch, he thought he could hear a very faint hum, coming from all around him. At the end of that passage he turned down another, apparently sloping at an angle of at least thirty degrees, but seemingly level as soon as he stepped (with a moment of dizziness) into it. That corridor ended at an effector blister, where one of the great game-boards had been set up.

The board stretched out in front of him, a swirl of geometric shapes and varying colors; a landscape spreading out over five hundred square meters, with the low pyramid-ranges of stacked, three-dimensional territory increasing even that total. He walked over to the edge of the huge board wondering if he had, after all, taken on too much.

He looked around the old effector blister. The board took up a little more than half the floor space, lying on top of the light foammetal planking the dockyard had installed. Half the volume of the space was beneath Gurgeh's feet; the cross-section of the effector housing was circular, and the planking and board described a diameter across it, more or less flush with the hull of the ship beyond the blister. The housing roof curved, gunmetal dull, arcing twelve meters overhead.

Gurgeh dropped under the planking on a float-hatch into the dimly lit bowl under the foammetal floor. The echoing space was even more empty than that above; save for a few hatches and shallow holes on the surface of the bowl, the removal of the mass of weaponry had been accomplished without leaving a trace. Gurgeh remembered Mawhrin-Skel, and wondered how the *Limiting Factor* felt about having its talons drawn.

"Jernau Gurgeh." He turned as his name was pronounced and saw a cube of skeletal components floating near him.

"Yes?"

"We have now reached our Terminal Aggregation Point and are sustaining a velocity of approximately eight point five kilolights in ultraspace one positive."

"Really?" Gurgeh said. He looked at the half-meter cube and wondered which bits were its eyes.

"Yes," the remote-drone said. "We are due to rendezvous with the GSV *Little Rascal* in approximately one hundred and two days from now. We are currently receiving instructions from the *Little Rascal* on how to play Azad, and the ship has instructed me to tell you it will shortly be able to commence playing. When do you wish to start?"

"Well, not right now," Gurgeh said. He touched the float-hatch controls, rising through the floor into the light. The remote-drone drifted up above him. "I want to settle in first," he told it. "I need more theoretical work before I start playing."

"Very well." The drone started to drift away. It stopped. "The ship wishes to advise you that its normal operating mode includes full internal monitoring, removing the need for your terminal. Is this satisfactory, or would you prefer the internal observation systems to be switched off, and to use your terminal to contact the ship?"

"The terminal," Gurgeh said, immediately.

"Internal monitoring has been reduced to emergency-only status."

"Thanks," Gurgeh said.

"You're welcome," the drone said, floating off.

Gurgeh watched it disappear into the corridor, then turned back to look at the vast board, shaking his head once more.

Over the next thirty days, Gurgeh didn't touch a single Azad piece; the whole time was spent learning the theory of the game, studying its history where it was useful for a better understanding of the play, memorizing the moves each piece could make, as well as their values, handedness, potential and actual morale-strength, their varied intersecting time/power-curves, and their specific skill harmonics as related to different areas of the boards; he pored over tables and grids setting out the qualities inherent in the suits, numbers, levels and sets of the associated cards and puzzled over the place in the greater play the lesser boards occupied, and how the elemental imagery in the later stages fitted in with the more mechanistic workings of the pieces, boards and die-matching in the earlier rounds, while at the same time trying to find some way of linking in his mind the tactics and strategy of the game as it was usually played, both in its single-game mode—one person against another—and in the multiple-game versions, when up to ten contestants might compete in the same match, with all the potential for alliances, intrigue, concerted action, pacts and treachery that such a game-form made possible.

Gurgeh found the days slipping by almost unnoticed. He would sleep only two or three hours each night, and the rest of the time he was in front of the screen, or sometimes standing in the middle of one of the game-boards as the ship talked to him, drew holo diagrams in the air, and moved pieces about. He was glanding the whole time, his bloodstream full of secreted drugs, his brain pickled in their genofixed chemistry as his much-worked maingland—five times the human-basic size it had been in his primitive ancestors—pumped, or instructed other glands to pump, the coded chemicals into his body.

Chamlis sent a couple of messages. Gossip about the Plate, mostly. Mawhrin-Skel had disappeared; Hafflis was talking about changing back to a woman so he could have another child; Hub and the Plate landscapers had set a date for the opening of Tepharne, the latest, farside, Plate to be constructed, which had still been undergoing its weathering when Gurgeh had left. It would be opened to people in a couple of years. Chamlis suspected Yay would not be pleased she hadn't been consulted before the announcement was made. Chamlis wished Gurgeh well, and asked him how he was.

Yay's communication was barely more than a moving-picture postcard. She lay sprawled in a G-web, before a vast screen or a huge observation port showing a blue and red gas-giant planet, and told him she was enjoying her cruise with Shuro and a couple of his friends. She didn't seem entirely sober. She wagged one finger at him, telling him he was bad for leaving so soon and for so long, without waiting until she got back . . . then she seemed to see somebody outside the terminal's field of view, and closed, saying she'd be in touch later.

Gurgeh told the *Limiting Factor* to acknowledge the communications, but did not reply directly. The calls left him feeling a little alone but he threw himself back into the game each time, and everything else was washed from his mind but that.

He talked to the ship. It was more approachable than its remote-drone had been; as Worthil had said, it was likeable, but not in any way brilliant, except at Azad. In fact it occurred to Gurgeh that the old warship was getting more out of the game than he was; it had learned it perfectly, and seemed to enjoy teaching him as well as simply glorying in the game itself as a complex and beautiful system. The ship admitted it had never fired its effectors in anger, and that perhaps it was finding something in Azad that it had missed in real fighting.

The *Limiting Factor* was "Murderer" class General Offensive Unit number 50017, and as such was one of the last built, constructed seven hundred and sixteen years earlier in the closing stages of the Idiran war, when the conflict in space was almost over. In theory the craft had seen active service, but at no point had it ever been in any danger.

After thirty days, Gurgeh started to handle the pieces.

A proportion of Azad game-pieces were biotechs: sculpted artifacts of genetically engineered cells which changed character from the moment they were first unwrapped and placed on the board; part vegetable, part animal, they indicated their values and abilities by color, shape and size. The *Limiting Factor* claimed the pieces it had produced were indistinguishable from the real things, though Gurgeh thought this was probably a little optimistic.

It was only when he started to try to gauge the pieces, to feel and smell what they were and what they might become—weaker or more powerful, faster or slower, shorter or longer lived—that he realized just how hard the whole game was going to be.

He simply could not work the biotechs out; they were just like lumps of carved, colored vegetables, and they lay in his hands like dead things. He rubbed them until his hands stained, he sniffed them and stared at them, but once they were on the board they did quite unexpected things; changing to become cannon-fodder when he'd thought they were battleships, altering from the equivalent of philosophical premises stationed well back in his own territories to become observation pieces best suited for the high ground or a front line.

After four days he was in despair, and seriously thinking of demanding to be returned to Chiark, admitting everything to Contact and just hoping they would take pity on him and either keep Mawhrin-Skel on, or keep it silenced. Anything rather than go on with this demoralizing, appallingly frustrating charade.

The *Limiting Factor* suggested he forgot about the biotechs for the moment and concentrated on the subsidiary games, which, if he won them, would give him a degree of choice over the extent to which biotechs had to be used in the following stages. Gurgeh did as the ship suggested, and got on reasonably well, but he still felt depressed and pessimistic, and sometimes he would find that the *Limiting Factor* had been talking to him for some minutes while he had been thinking about some quite different aspect of the game, and he had to ask the ship to repeat itself.

The days went by, and now and again the ship would suggest Gurgeh handled a biotech, and would advise him which secretions to build up beforehand. It even suggested he take some of the more important pieces into bed with him, so that he would lie asleep, hands clutched or arms cradled round a biotech, as though it was a tiny baby. He always felt rather foolish when he woke up, and he was glad there was nobody there to see him in the morning (but then he wondered if that was true; his experience with Mawhrin-Skel might have made him over-sensitive, but he doubted he would ever be certain again that he wasn't being watched. Perhaps the *Limiting Factor* was spying on him, perhaps Contact was observing him, evaluating him . . . but—he decided—he no longer cared if they were or not).

He took every tenth day off, again at the ship's suggestion; he explored the vessel more fully, though there was little enough to see. Gurgeh was used to civilian craft, which could be compared in density and design to ordinary, human-habitable buildings, with comparatively thin walls enclosing large volumes of space, but the warship was more like a single solid chunk of rock or metal; like an asteroid, with only a few small hollowed-out tubes and tiny caves fit for humans to wander about in. He walked along or clambered through or floated up and down what corridors and passageways it did have though, and stood in one of the three nose blisters for a while, gazing at the congealed-looking clutter of still-unremoved machinery and equipment.

The primary effector, surrounded by its associated shield-disruptors, scanners, trackers, illuminators, displacers and secondary weaponry systems, bulked large in the dim light, and looked like some gigantic cone-lensed eyeball encrusted with gnarled metallic growths. The whole, massy assemblage was easily twenty meters in diameter, but the ship told him—he thought with some pride—that when it was all connected up, it could spin and stop the whole installation so fast that to a human it would appear only to flicker momentarily; blink, and you'd miss it.

He inspected the empty hangar in one of the waist blisters; it would eventually house a Contact module which was being converted on the GSV they were on their way to meet. That module would be Gurgeh's home when he arrived on Eä. He'd seen holos of how the interior would look; it was passably spacious, if hardly up to the standards of Ikroh.

He learned more about the Empire itself, its history and politics, philosophy and religion, its beliefs and mores, and its mixtures of subspecies and sexes.

It seemed to him to be an unbearably vivid tangle of contradictions; at the same time pathologically violent and lugubriously sentimental, startlingly barbaric and surprisingly sophisticated, fabulously rich and grindingly poor (but also, undeniably, unequivocally fascinating).

And it was true that, as he'd been told, there was one constant in all the numbing variety of Azadian life; the game of Azad permeated every level of society, like a single steady theme nearly buried in a cacophony of noise, and Gurgeh started to see what the drone Worthil had meant when it said Contact suspected it was the game that held the Empire together. Nothing else seemed to.

He swam in the pool most days. The effector housing had been converted to include a holo projector, and the *Limiting Factor* started out by showing a blue sky and white clouds on the inside surface of the twenty-five meter broad blister, but he grew tired of looking at that, and told the ship to produce the view he would see if they were traveling in real space; the adjusted equivalent view, as the ship called it.

So he swam beneath the unreal blackness of space and the hard little lightmotes of the slowly moving stars, pulling himself through and diving beneath the gently underlit surface of the warm water like a soft, inverted image of a ship himself.

By about the ninetieth day he felt he was just starting to develop a feel for the biotechs; he could play a limited game against the ship on all the minor boards and one of the major boards, and, when he went to sleep, he spent the whole three hours each night dreaming about people and his life, reliving his childhood and his adolescence and his years since then in a strange mixture of memory and fantasy and unrealized desire. He always meant to write to—or record something for—Chamlis or Yay or any of the other people back at Chiark who'd sent messages, but the time never seemed quite right, and the longer he delayed the harder the task became. Gradually people stopped sending to him, which made Gurgeh feel guilty and relieved at once.

One hundred and one days after leaving Chiark, and well over two thousand light-years from the Orbital, the *Limiting Factor* made its rendezvous with the River class Superlifter *Kiss My Ass.* The tandemed craft, now enclosed within one ellipsoid field, began to increase their speed to match that of the GSV. This was going to take a few hours, apparently, so Gurgeh went to bed as normal.

The *Limiting Factor* woke him halfway into his sleep. It switched his cabin screen on.

"What's happening?" Gurgeh said sleepily, just starting to worry. The screen which made up one wall of the cabin was in-holoed, so that it acted like a window. Before he had switched it off and gone to sleep, it had shown the rear end of the Superlifter against the starfield.

Now it showed a landscape; a slowly moving panorama of lakes and hills, streams and forests, all seen from directly overhead.

An aircraft flew slowly over the view like a lazy insect.

"I thought you might like to see this," the ship said.

"Where's that?" Gurgeh asked, rubbing his eyes. He didn't understand. He'd thought the whole idea of meeting the Superlifter was so that the GSV which they were due to meet soon didn't have to slow down; the Superlifter was supposed to haul them along even faster so they could catch up with the giant craft. Instead, they must have stopped, over an orbital or a planet, or something even bigger.

"We have now rendezvoused with the GSV *Little Rascal,*" the ship told him.

"Have we? Where is it?" Gurgeh said, swinging his feet out of bed.

"You're looking at its topside rear park."

The view, which must have been magnified earlier, retreated, and Gurgeh realized that he was looking down at a huge craft over which the *Limiting Factor* was moving slowly. The park seemed to be roughly square; he couldn't guess how many kilometers to a side. In the hazy distance forward there was the hint of immense, regular canyons; ribs on that vast surface stepping down to further levels. The whole sweep of air and ground and water was lit from directly above, and he realized that he couldn't even see the *Limiting Factor*'s shadow.

He asked a few questions, still staring at the screen.

Although it was only four kilometers in height, the Plate class General Systems Vehicle *Little Rascal* was fully fifty-three in length, and twenty-two across the beam. The topside rear park covered an area of four hundred square kilometers, and the craft's overall length, from end-to-end of its outermost field, was a little over ninety kilometers. It was ship-construction rather than accommodation biased, so there were only two hundred and fifty million people on it.

In the five hundred days it took the *Little Rascal* to cross from the main galaxy to the region of the Clouds, Gurgeh gradually learned the game of Azad, and even found sufficient spare time to meet and casually befriend a few people.

These were Contact people. Half of them formed the crew of the GSV itself, there not so much to run the craft—any one of its triumvirate of Minds was quite capable of doing that—as to manage their own human society on board. And to witness; to study the never-ending torrent of data delivered on new discoveries by distant Contact units and other GSVs; to learn, and be the Culture's human representatives among the systems of stars and the systems of sentient societies Contact was there to discover, investigate and—occasionally—change.

The other half was composed of the crews of smaller craft; some were there for recreation and refit stops, others were hitching a ride just as Gurgeh and the *Limiting Factor* were, some left en route to survey more of the clusters and clumps of stars which existed between the galaxy and the Clouds, while other people were waiting for their vessels to be built, the ships and smaller Systems Vehicles they would one day crew existing only as another number on a list of craft to be built on board at some point in the future.

The *Little Rascal* was what Contact termed a throughput GSV; it acted as a kind of marshaling point for humans and material, picking people up and assembling them into crews for the units, LSVs, MSVs and smaller classes of GSVs which it constructed. Other types of large GSVs were accommodation biased, and effectively self-sufficient in human crews for their offspring craft.

Gurgeh spent some days in the park on top of the vessel, walking through it or flying over it in one of the real-winged, propellor-driven aircraft which were the fashion on the GSV at the time. He even became a proficient enough flyer to enter himself in a race, during which several thousand of the flimsy planes flew figures-of-eight over the top of the Vehicle, through one of the cavernous accessways that ran the length of the craft, out the other end and underneath.

The *Limiting Factor,* housed in one of the Mainbays just off a Way, encouraged him in this, saying it provided Gurgeh with much needed relaxation. Gurgeh accepted none of the offers to play people at games, but did take up a trickle from the flood of invitations to parties, events and other gatherings; he spent some days and nights off the *Limiting Factor,* and the old warship was in turn host to a select number of young female guests.

Most of the time, though, Gurgeh spent alone inside the ship, poring over tables of figures and the records of past games, rubbing the biotechs in his hands, and striding over the three great boards, gaze flickering over the lay of land and pieces, his mind racing, searching for patterns and opportunities, strengths and weaknesses.

He spent twenty days or so taking a crash course in Eächic, the imperial language. He had originally envisaged speaking Marain as usual and using an interpreter, but he suspected there were subtle links between the language and the game, and for that reason alone learned the tongue. The ship told him later it would have been desirable anyway; the Culture was trying to keep even the intricacies of its language secret from the Empire of Azad.

Not long after he'd arrived, he'd been sent a drone, a machine even smaller than Mawhrin-Skel. It was circular in plan and composed of separate revolving sections; rotating rings around a stationary core. It said it was a library drone with diplomatic training and it was called Trebel Flere-Imsaho Ep-handra Lorgin Estral. Gurgeh said hello and made sure his terminal was switched on. As soon as the machine had gone again he sent a message to Chamlis Amalk-ney, along with a recording of his meeting with the tiny drone. Chamlis signaled back later that the device appeared to be what it claimed; one of a fairly new model of library drone. Not the old-timer they might have expected, but probably harmless enough. Chamlis had never heard of an offensive version of that type.

The old drone closed with some Gevant gossip. Yay Meristinoux was talking about leaving Chiark to pursue her landscaping career elsewhere. She'd developed an interest in things called volcanoes; had Gurgeh heard of those? Hafflis was changing sex again. Professor Boruelal sent her regards but no more messages until he wrote back. Mawhrin-Skel still thankfully absent. Hub was piqued it appeared to have lost the ghastly machine; technically the wretch was still within the Orbital Mind's jurisdiction and it would have to account for it somehow at the next inventory and census.

For a few days after that first meeting with Flere-Imsaho, Gurgeh wondered what it was that he found disturbing about the tiny library drone. Flere-Imsaho was almost pathetically small—it could have hidden inside a pair of cupped hands—but there was something about it which made Gurgeh feel oddly uncomfortable in its presence.

He worked it out, or rather he woke up knowing, one morning, after a nightmare in which he'd been trapped inside a metal sphere and rolled around in some bizarre and cruel game. . . . Flere-Imsaho, with its spinning outer sections and its disc-like white casing, looked rather like a hidden-piece wafer from a Possession game.

Gurgeh lounged in an envelopingly comfortable chair set underneath some lushly canopied trees and watched people skating in the rink below. He was dressed only in a waistcoat and shorts, but there was a leakfield between the observation area and the icerink itself, keeping the air around Gurgeh warm. He divided his time between his terminal screen, from which he was memorizing some probability equations, and the rink, where a few people he knew were sweeping about the sculpted pastel surfaces.

"Good day, Jernau Gurgeh," said the drone Flere-Imsaho in its squeaky little voice, settling delicately on the plump arm of the chair. As usual, its aura field was yellow-green; mellow approachability.

"Hello," Gurgeh said, glancing at it briefly. "And what have you been up to?" He touched the terminal screen to inspect another set of tables and equations.

"Oh, well, actually I've been studying some of the species of birds which live here within the interior of the vessel. I do find birds interesting, don't you?"

"Hmm." Gurgeh nodded vaguely, watching the tables change. "What I haven't been able to work out," he said, "is when you go for a walk in the topside park you find droppings, as you'd expect to, but inside here everything's spotless. Does the GSV have drones to clean up after the birds, or what? I know I could just ask it, but I wanted to work it out for myself. There must be some answer."

"Oh, that's easy," the little machine said. "You just use birds and trees with a symbiotic relationship; the birds soil only in the bolls of certain trees, otherwise the fruit they depend on doesn't grow."

Gurgeh looked down at the drone. "I see," he said coldly. "Well, I was growing tired of the problem anyway." He turned back to the equations, adjusting the floating terminal so that its screen hid Flere-Imsaho from his sight. The drone stayed silent, went a confused medley of contrite purple and do-not-disturb silver, and flew away.

Flere-Imsaho kept itself to itself most of the time, only calling on Gurgeh once a day or so, and not staying on board the *Limiting Factor.* Gurgeh was glad of that; the young machine—it said it was only thirteen—could be trying at times. The ship reassured Gurgeh that the little drone would be up to the task of preventing social gaffes and keeping him informed on the finer linguistic points by the time they arrived at the Empire, and—it told Gurgeh later—reassured Flere-Imsaho that the man didn't really despise it.

There was more news from Gevant. Gurgeh had actually written back to a few people, or recorded messages for them, now that he felt he was finally coming to grips with Azad and could spare the time. He and Chamlis corresponded every fifty days or so, though Gurgeh found he had little to say, and most of the news came from the other direction. Hafflis was fully changed; broody but not pregnant. Chamlis was compiling a definitive history of some primitive planet it had once visited. Professor Boruelal was taking a half-year sabbatical, living in a mountain retreat on Osmolon Plate, terminalless. Olz Hap the wunderkind had come out of her shell; she was already lecturing on games at the university and had become a brilliant regular on the best party circuits. She had spent some days staying at Ikroh, just to be better able to relate to Gurgeh; she'd gone on record as claiming he was the best player in the Culture. Hap's analysis of the famous Stricken game at Hafflis's that night was the best-received first work anybody could remember.

Yay sent to say she was fed up with Chiark; she was off, away; she'd had offers from other Plate building collectives and she was going to take up at least one of them, just to show what she could do. She spent most of the communication explaining her theories on artificial volcanoes for Plates, describing in gesticulatory detail how you could lens sunlight to focus it on the undersurface of the Plate, melting the rock on the other side, or just use generators to provide the heat. She enclosed some film of eruptions on planets, with explanations of the effects and notes on how they could be improved.

Gurgeh thought the idea of sharing a world with volcanoes made floating islands look like not such a bad idea after all.

* * *

"Have you *seen* this!" Flere-Imsaho yelped one day, floating quickly up to him in the pool's airstream cabinet, where Gurgeh was drying off. Behind the little machine, attached to it by a thin strand of field still colored yellow-green (but speckled with angry white), there floated a large, rather old-fashioned and complicated-looking drone.

Gurgeh squinted at it. "What about it?"

"I've got to wear the damn thing!" Flere-Imsaho wailed. The field strand joining it to the other drone flicked, and the old-looking drone's casing hinged open. The old body-shell appeared to be completely empty, but as Gurgeh—puzzled—looked closer, he saw that in the center of the casing there was a little mesh cradle, just the right size to hold Flere-Imsaho.

"Oh," Gurgeh said, and turned away, rubbing the water from his armpits, and grinning.

"They didn't tell me this when they offered me the job!" Flere-Imsaho protested, slamming the body-shell shut again. "They say it's because the Empire isn't supposed to know how small us drones are! Why couldn't they just have got a big drone then? Why saddle me with this . . . this . . ."

"Fancy dress?" Gurgeh suggested, rubbing a hand through his hair and stepping out of the airstream.

"*Fancy?*" the library drone screamed. "*Fancy? Dowdy's* what it is; rags! Worse than that, I'm supposed to make a 'humming' noise and produce lots of *static electricity,* just to convince these barbarian dingbats we can't build *drones* properly!" The small machine's voice rose to a screech. "A 'humming' noise! I ask you!"

"Perhaps you could ask for a transfer," Gurgeh said calmly, slipping into his robe.

"Oh yes," Flere-Imsaho said bitterly, with a trace of what might almost have been sarcasm, "and get all the shit jobs from now on because I haven't been cooperative." It lashed a field out and thumped the antique casing. "I'm stuck with this heap of junk."

"Drone," Gurgeh said, "I can't tell you how sorry I am."

The *Limiting Factor* nosed its way out of the Mainbay. Two Lifters nudged the craft round until it faced down the twenty-kilometer length of corridor. The ship and its little tugs eased their way forward, exiting from the body of the GSV at its nose. Other ships and craft and pieces of equipment moved inside the shell of air surrounding the *Little Rascal;* GCUs and Superlifters, planes and hot-air balloons, vacuum dirigibles and gliders, people floating in modules or cars or harnesses.

Some watched the old warship go. The Lifter tugs dropped away.

The ship went up, passing level upon level of bay doors, blank hull, hanging gardens, and whole jumbled arrays of opened accommodation sections, where people walked or danced or sat eating or just gazing out, watching the fuss of airborne activity, or played sports and games. Some waved. Gurgeh watched on the lounge screen, and even recognized a few people he'd known, flying past in an aircraft, shouting goodbye.

Officially, he was going on a solo cruising holiday before traveling to the Pardethillisian Games. He had already dropped hints he might forgo the tournament. Some of the theoretical and news journals had been interested enough in his sudden departure from Chiark—and the equally abrupt cessation of his publications—to have representatives on the *Little Rascal* interview him. In a strategy he'd already agreed with Contact, he'd given the impression he was growing bored with games in general, and that the journey—and his entry in the great tournament—were attempts to restore his flagging interest.

People seemed to have fallen for this.

The ship cleared the top of the GSV, rising beside the cloud-speckled topside park. It rose on into the thinner air above, met with the Superlifter *Prime Mover,* and together they gradually dropped back and to the side of the GSV's inner atmospheric envelope. They went slowly through the many layers of fields; the bumpfield, the insulating, the sensory, the signaling and receptor, the energy and traction, the hullfield, the outer sensory and, finally, the horizon, until they were free in hyperspace once more. After a few hours of deceleration to speeds the *Limiting Factor*'s engines could cope with, the disarmed warship was on its own, and the *Prime Mover* was powering away again, chasing its GSV.

". . . so you'd be well advised to stay celibate; they'll find it difficult enough taking a male seriously even if you do look bizarre to them, but if you tried to form any sexual relationships they'd almost certainly take it as a gross insult."

"Any more good news, drone?"

"Don't say anything about sexual alterations either. They do know about drug-glands, even if they don't know about their precise effects, but they don't know about most of the major physical improvements. I mean, you can mention blister-free callousing and that sort of thing, that isn't important; but even the gross re-plumbing involved in your own genital design would cause something of a furor if they found out about it."

"Really," Gurgeh said. He was sitting in the *Limiting Factor*'s main lounge. Flere-Imsaho and the ship were giving him a briefing on what he could and couldn't say and do in the Empire. They were a few days' travel from the frontier.

"Yes; they'd be jealous," the tiny drone said in its high, slightly grating voice. "And probably quite disgusted too."

"Especially jealous though," the ship said through its remote-drone, making a sighing noise.

"Well, yes," Flere-Imsaho said, "but definitely disg—"

"The thing to remember, Gurgeh," the ship interrupted quickly, "is that their society is based on *ownership.* Everything that you see and touch, everything you come into contact with, will *belong* to somebody or to an institution; it will be theirs, they will own it. In the same way, everyone you meet will be conscious of both their position in society and their relationship to others around them.

"It is especially important to remember that the ownership of humans is possible too; not in terms of actual slavery, which they are proud to have abolished, but in the sense that, according to which sex and class one belongs to, one may be partially owned by another or others by having to sell one's labor or talents to somebody with the means to buy them. In the case of males, they give themselves most totally when they become soldiers; the personnel in their armed forces are like slaves, with little personal freedom, and under threat of death if they disobey. Females sell their bodies, usually, entering into the legal contract of 'marriage' to Intermediates, who then pay them for their sexual favors by—"

"Oh, ship, come on!" He laughed. He had done his own research into the Empire, reading its own histories and watching its explanatory recordings. The ship's view of the Empire's customs and institutions sounded biased and unfair and terribly Culture-prim.

Flere-Imsaho and the ship remote made a show of looking at each other, then the small library drone flushed gray yellow with resignation, and said in its high voice, "All right, let's go back to the beginning . . ."

* * *

The *Limiting Factor* lay in space above Eä, the beautiful blue-white planet Gurgeh had seen for the first time almost two years earlier in the screen-room at Ikroh. On either side of the ship lay an imperial battlecruiser, each twice the length of the Culture craft.

The two warships had met the smaller vessel at the limits of the star clump Eä's system lay in, and the *Limiting Factor,* already on a slow warp drive rather than its normal hyperspace propulsion—something else the Empire was being kept in the dark about—had stopped. Its eight effector blisters were transparent, showing the three game-boards, module hangar and pool in the waist housings, and the empty spaces in the three long nose emplacements, the weaponry having been removed on the *Little Rascal.* Nevertheless, the Azadians sent a smallcraft over to the ship with three officers in it. Two stayed with Gurgeh while the third checked each of the blisters in turn, then took a general look round the entire ship.

Those or other officers stayed on board for the five days it took to get to Eä itself. They were much as Gurgeh had expected, with flat, broad faces and the shaven, almost white skin. They were smaller than he was, he realized when they stood in front of him, but somehow their uniforms made them look much larger. These were the first real uniforms Gurgeh had ever seen, and he felt a strange, dizzying sensation when he saw them; a sense of displacement and foreignness as well as an odd mixture of dread and awe.

Knowing what he did, he wasn't surprised at the way they acted toward him. They seemed to try to ignore him, rarely speaking to him, and never looking him in the eyes when they did; he had never felt quite so dismissed in life.

The officers did appear to be interested in the ship, but not in either Flere-Imsaho—which was keeping well out of their way anyway—or in the ship's remote-drone. Flere-Imsaho had, only minutes before the officers arrived on board, finally and with extreme and voluble reluctance, enclosed itself in the fake carapace of the old drone casing. It had fumed quietly for a few minutes while Gurgeh told it how attractive and valuably antique the ancient, aura-less casing looked, then it had floated quickly off when the officers came aboard.

So much, thought Gurgeh, for its helping with awkward linguistic points and the intricacies of etiquette.

The ship's remote-drone was no better. It followed Gurgeh round, but it was playing dumb, and made a show of bumping into things now and again. Twice Gurgeh had turned round and almost fallen over the slow and clumsy cube. He was very tempted to kick it.

It was left to Gurgeh to try to explain that there was no bridge or flight-deck or control-room that he knew of in the ship, but he got the impression the Azadian officers didn't believe him.

When they arrived over Eä, the officers contacted their battle-cruiser and talked too fast for Gurgeh to understand, but the *Limiting Factor* broke in and started speaking too; there was a heated discussion. Gurgeh looked round for Flere-Imsaho to translate, but it had disappeared again. He listened to the jabbering exchange for some minutes with increasing frustration; he decided to let them argue it out and turned to go and sit down. He stumbled over the remote-drone, which was floating near the floor just behind him; he fell into rather than sat on the couch. The officers looked round at him briefly, and he felt himself blush. The remote-drone drifted hesitantly away before he could aim a foot at it.

So much, he thought, for Flere-Imsaho; so much for Contact's supposedly flawless planning and stupendous cunning.

Their juvenile representative didn't even bother to hang around and do its job properly; it preferred to hide, nursing its pathetic self-esteem.

Gurgeh knew enough about the way the Empire worked to realize that it wouldn't let such things happen; its people knew what duties and orders meant, and they took their responsibilities seriously, or, if they didn't, they suffered for it.

They did as they were told; they had discipline.

Eventually, after the three officers had talked among themselves for a while, and then to their ship again, they left him and went to inspect the module hangar. When they'd gone, Gurgeh used his terminal to ask the ship what they'd been arguing about.

"They wanted to bring some more personnel and equipment over," the *Limiting Factor* told him. "I told them they couldn't. Nothing to worry about. You'd better get your stuff together and go to the module hangar; I'll be heading out of imperial space within the hour."

Gurgeh turned to head toward his cabin. "Wouldn't it be terrible," he said, "if you forgot to tell Flere-Imsaho you were going, and I had to visit Eä all by myself." He was only half joking.

"It would be unthinkable," the ship said.

Gurgeh passed the remote-drone in the corridor, spinning slowly in midair and bobbing erratically up and down. "And is this really necessary?" he asked it.

"Just doing what I'm told," the drone replied testily.

"Just overdoing it," Gurgeh muttered, and went to pack his things.

As he packed, a small parcel fell out of a cloak he hadn't worn since he'd left Ikroh; it bounced on the soft floor of the cabin.

He picked it up and opened the ribbon-tied packet, wondering who it might be from; any one of several ladies on the *Little Rascal,* he imagined.

It was a thin bracelet, a model of a very broad, fully completed Orbital, its inner surface half light and half dark. Bringing it up to his eyes, he could see tiny, barely discernible pinpricks of light on the nighttime half; the daylight side showed bright blue sea and scraps of land under minute cloud systems. The whole interior scene shone with its own light, powered by some source inside the narrow band.

Gurgeh slipped it over his hand; it glowed against his wrist. A strange present for somebody on a GSV to give, he thought.

Then he saw the note in the package, picked it out and read, "Just to remind you, when you're on that planet. Chamlis."

He frowned at the name, then—distantly at first, but with a growing and annoying sense of shame—remembered the night before he'd left Gevant, two years earlier.

Of course.

Chamlis had given him a present.

He'd forgotten.

"What's that?" Gurgeh said. He sat in the front section of the converted module the *Limiting Factor* had picked up from the GSV. He and Flere-Imsaho had boarded the little craft and said their au revoirs to the old warship, which was to stand off the Empire, waiting to be recalled. The hangar blister had rotated and the module, escorted by a couple of frigates, had fallen toward the planet while the *Limiting Factor* made a show of moving very slowly and hesitantly away from the gravity well with the two battlecruisers.

"What's what?" Flere-Imsaho said, floating beside him, disguise discarded and lying on the floor.

"That," Gurgeh said, pointing at the screen, which displayed the view looking straight down. The module was flying overland toward Groasnachek, Eä's capital city; the Empire didn't like vessels entering the atmosphere directly above its cities, so they'd come in over the ocean.

"Oh," Flere-Imsaho said. "That. That's the Labyrinth Prison."

"A prison?" Gurgeh said. The complex of walls and long, geometrically contorted buildings slid away beneath them as the outskirts of the sprawling capital invaded the screen.

"Yes. The idea is that people who've broken laws are put into the labyrinth, the precise place being determined by the nature of the offense. As well as being a physical maze, it is constructed to be what one might call a moral and behavioristic labyrinth as well (its external appearance offers no clues to the internal lay-out, by the way; that's just for show); the prisoner must make correct responses, act in certain approved ways, or he will get no further, and may even be put further back. In theory a perfectly good person can walk free of the labyrinth in a matter of days, while a totally bad person will never get out. To prevent overcrowding, there's a time-limit which, if exceeded, results in the prisoner being transferred for life to a penal colony."

The prison had disappeared from beneath them by the time the drone finished; the city swamped the screen instead, its swirling patterns of streets, buildings and domes like another sort of maze.

"Sounds ingenious," Gurgeh said. "Does it work?"

"So they'd have us believe. In fact it's used as an excuse for not giving people a proper trial, and anyway the rich just bribe their way out. So yes, as far as the rulers are concerned, it works."

* * *

The module and the two frigates touched down at a huge shuttle-port on the banks of a broad, muddy, much bridged river, still some distance from the center of the city but surrounded by medium-rise buildings and low geodesic domes. Gurgeh walked out of the craft with Flere-Imsaho—in its fake antique guise, humming loudly and crackling with static—at his side; he found himself standing on a huge square of synthetic grass which had been unrolled up to the rear of the module. Standing on the grass were perhaps forty or fifty Azadians in various styles of uniform and clothing. Gurgeh, who'd been trying hard to work out how to recognize the various sexes, reckoned they were mostly of the intermediate or apex sex, with only a smattering of males and females; beyond them stood several lines of identically uniformed males, carrying weapons. Behind them, another group played rather strident and brash-sounding music.

"The guys with the guns are just the honor guard," Flere-Imsaho said through its disguise. "Don't be alarmed."

"I'm not," Gurgeh said. He knew this was how things were done in the Empire; formally, with official welcoming parties composed of imperial bureaucrats, security guards, officials from the games organizations, associated wives and concubines, and people representing news-agencies. One of the apices strode forward toward him.

"This one is addressed as 'sir' in Eächic," Flere-Imsaho whispered.

"What?" Gurgeh said. He could hardly hear the machine's voice over the humming noise it was making. It was buzzing and crackling loud enough to all but drown the sound of the ceremonial band, and the static the drone was producing made Gurgeh's hair stick out on one side.

"I said, he's called *sir,* in Eächic," Flere-Imsaho hissed over the hum. "Don't touch him, but when he holds up one hand, you hold up two and say your bit. Remember; don't touch him."

The apex stopped just in front of Gurgeh, held up one hand and said, "Welcome to Groasnachek, Eä, in the Empire of Azad, Murat Gurgee."

Gurgeh controlled a grimace, held up both hands (to show they were empty of weapons, the old books explained) and said, "I am honored to set foot upon the holy ground of Eä," in careful Eächic. ("Great start," muttered the drone.)

The rest of the welcoming passed in something of a daze. Gurgeh's head swam; he sweated under the heat of the bright binary overhead while he was outside (he was expected to inspect the honor guard, he knew, though quite what he was supposed to be looking for had never been explained), and the alien smells of the shuttleport buildings once they passed inside to the reception made him feel more strongly than he'd expected that he really was somewhere quite foreign. He was introduced to lots of people, again mostly apices, and sensed they were delighted to be addressed in what was apparently quite passable Eächic. Flere-Imsaho told him to do and say certain things, and he heard himself mouth the correct words and felt himself perform the acceptable gestures, but his overall impression was of chaotic movement and noisy, unlistening people—rather smelly people, too, though he was sure they thought the same of him. He also had an odd feeling that they were laughing at him, somewhere behind their faces.

Apart from the obvious physical differences, the Azadians all seemed very compact and hard and determined compared to Culture people; more energetic and even—if he was going to be critical—neurotic. The apices were, anyway. From the little he saw of the males, they seemed somehow duller, less fraught and more stolid as well as being physically bulkier, while the females appeared to be quieter—somehow deeper—and more delicate-looking.

He wondered how he looked to them. He was aware he stared a little, at the oddly alien architecture and confusing interiors, as well as at the people . . . but on the other hand he found a lot of people—mostly apices, again—staring at him. On a couple of occasions Flere-Imsaho had to repeat what it said to him, before he realized it was talking to him. Its monotonous hum and crackling static, never far away from him that afternoon, seemed only to add to the air of dazed, dreamlike unreality.

They served food and drink in his honor; Culture and Azadian biology was close enough for a few foods and several drinks to be mutually digestible, including alcohol. He drank all they gave him, but bypassed it. They sat in a long, low shuttleport building, simply styled outside but ostentatiously furnished inside, around a long table loaded with food and drink. Uniformed males served them; he remembered not to speak to them. He found that most of the people he spoke to either talked too fast or painstakingly slowly, but struggled through several conversations nevertheless. Many people asked why he had come alone, and after several misunderstandings he stopped trying to explain he was accompanied by the drone and simply said he liked traveling by himself.

Some asked him how good he was at Azad. He replied truthfully he had no idea; the ship had never told him. He said he hoped he would be able to play well enough not to make his hosts regret they had invited him to take part. A few seemed impressed by this, but, Gurgeh thought, only in the way that adults are impressed by a respectful child.

One apex, sitting on his right and dressed in a tight, uncomfortable-looking uniform similar to those worn by the three officers who'd boarded the *Limiting Factor,* kept asking him about his journey, and the ship he'd made it on. Gurgeh stuck to the agreed story. The apex continually refilled Gurgeh's ornate crystal goblet with wine; Gurgeh was obliged to drink on each occasion a toast was proposed. Bypassing the liquor to avoid getting drunk meant he had to go to the toilet rather often (for a drink of water, as much as to urinate). He knew this was a subject of some delicacy with the Azadians, but he seemed to be using the correct form of words each time; nobody looked shocked, and Flere-Imsaho seemed calm.

Eventually, the apex on Gurgeh's left, whose name was Lo Pequil Monenine senior, and who was a liaison official with the Alien Affairs Bureau, asked Gurgeh if he was ready to leave for his hotel. Gurgeh said he thought that he was supposed to be staying on board the module. Pequil began to talk rather fast, and seemed surprised when Flere-Imsaho cut in, talking equally quickly. The resulting conversation went a little too rapidly for Gurgeh to follow perfectly, but the drone eventually explained that a compromise had been reached; Gurgeh would stay in the module, but the module would be parked on the roof of the hotel. Guards and security would be provided for his protection, and the catering services of the hotel, which was one of the very best, would be at his disposal.

Gurgeh thought this all sounded reasonable. He invited Pequil to come along in the module to the hotel, and the apex accepted gladly.

"Before you ask our friend what we're passing over now," Flere-Imsaho said, hovering and buzzing at Gurgeh's elbow, "that's called a shantytown, and it's where the city draws its surplus unskilled labor from."

Gurgeh frowned at the bulkily disguised drone. Lo Pequil

was standing beside Gurgeh on the rear ramp of the module, which had opened to make a sort of balcony. The city unrolled beneath them. “I thought we weren’t to use Marain in front of these people,” Gurgeh said to the machine.

“Oh, we’re safe enough here; this guy’s bugged, but the module can neutralize that.”

Gurgeh pointed at the shantytown. “What’s that?” he asked Pequil.

“That is where people who have left the countryside for the bright lights of the big city often end up. Unfortunately, many of them are just loafers.”

“Driven off the land,” Flere-Imsaho added in Marain, “by an ingeniously unfair property-tax system and the opportunistic top-down reorganization of the agricultural production apparatus.”

Gurgeh wondered if the drone’s last phrase meant “farms,” but he turned to Pequil and said, “I see.”

“What does your machine say?” Pequil inquired.

“It was quoting some . . . poetry,” Gurgeh told the apex. “About a great and beautiful city.”

“Ah.” Pequil nodded; a series of upward jerks of the head. “Your people like poetry, do they?”

Gurgeh paused, then said, “Well, some do and some don’t, you know?”

Pequil nodded wisely.

The wind above the city drifted in over the restraining field around the balcony, and brought with it a vague smell of burning. Gurgeh leaned on the haze of field and looked down at the huge city slipping by underneath. Pequil seemed reluctant to come too near the edge of the balcony.

“Oh; I have some good news for you,” Pequil said, with a smile (rolling both lips back).

“What’s that?”

"My office," Pequil said, seriously and slowly, "has succeeded in obtaining permission for you to follow the progress of the Main Series games all the way to Echronedal."

"Ah; where the last few games are played."

"Why yes. It is the culmination of the full six-year Grand Cycle, on the Fire Planet itself. I assure you, you are most privileged to be allowed to attend. Guest players are rarely granted such an honor."

"I see. I am indeed honored. I offer my sincere thanks to you and your office. When I return to my home I shall tell my people that the Azadians are a most generous folk. You have made me feel very welcome. Thank you. I am in your debt."

Pequil seemed satisfied with this. He nodded, smiled. Gurgeh nodded too, though he thought the better of attempting the smile.

"Well?"

"Well what, Jernau Gurgeh?" Flere-Imsaho said, its yellow-green fields extending from its tiny casing like the wings of some exotic insect. It laid a ceremonial robe on Gurgeh's bed. They were in the module, which now rested on the roof-garden of Groasnachek's Grand Hotel.

"How did I do?"

"You did very well. You didn't call the minister 'Sir' when I told you to, and you were a bit vague at times, but on the whole you did all right. You haven't caused any catastrophic diplomatic incidents or grievously insulted anybody. . . . I'd say that's not too bad for the first day. Would you turn round and face the reverser? I want to make sure this thing fits properly."

Gurgeh turned round and held out his arms as the drone smoothed the robe against his back. He looked at himself in the reverser field.

"It's too long and it doesn't suit me," he said.

"You're right, but it's what you have to wear for the grand

ball in the palace tonight. It'll do. I might take the hem up. The module tells me it's bugged, incidentally, so watch what you say once you're outside the module's fields."

"Bugged?" Gurgeh looked at the image of the drone in the reverser.

"Position monitor and mike. Don't worry; they do this to everybody. Stand still. Yes, I think that hem needs to come up. Turn round."

Gurgeh turned round. "You like ordering me around, don't you, machine?" he said to the tiny drone.

"Don't be silly. Right. Try it on."

Gurgeh put the robe on, looked at his image in the reverser. "What's this blank patch on the shoulder for?"

"That's where your insignia would go, if you had one."

Gurgeh fingered the bare area on the heavily embroidered robe. "Couldn't we have made one up? It looks a bit bare."

"I suppose we could," Flere-Imsaho said, tugging at the robe to adjust it. "You have to be careful doing that sort of thing though. Our Azadian friends are always rather nonplussed by our lack of a flag or a symbol, and the Culture rep here—you'll meet him tonight if he remembers to turn up—thought it was a pity there was no Culture anthem for bands to play when our people come here, so he whistled them the first song that came into his head, and they've been playing that at receptions and ceremonies for the last eight years."

"I thought I recognized one of the tunes they played," Gurgeh admitted.

The drone pushed his arms up and made some more adjustments. "Yes, but the first song that came into the guy's head was 'Lick Me Out'; have you heard the lyrics?"

"Ah." Gurgeh grinned. "*That* song. Yes, that could be awkward."

"Damn right. If they find out they'll probably declare war. Usual Contact snafu."

Gurgeh laughed. "And I used to think Contact was so organized and efficient." He shook his head.

"Nice to know something works," the drone muttered.

"Well, you've kept this whole Empire secret seven decades; that's worked too."

"More luck than skill," Flere-Imsaho said. It floated round in front of him, inspecting the robe. "Do you really want an insignia? We could rustle something up if it'd make you feel happier."

"Don't bother."

"Right. We'll use your full name when they announce you at the ball tonight; sounds reasonably impressive. They can't grasp we don't have any real ranks, either, so you may find they use 'Morat' as a kind of title." The little drone dipped to fix a stray gold-thread near the hem. "It's all to the good in the end; they're a bit blind to the Culture, just because they can't comprehend it in their own hierarchical terms. Can't take us seriously."

"What a surprise."

"Hmm. I've got a feeling it's all part of a plan; even this delinquent rep—ambassador, sorry—is part of it. You too, I think."

"You think?" Gurgeh said.

"They've built you up, Gurgeh," the drone told him, rising to head height and brushing his hair back a little. Gurgeh in turn brushed the meddlesome field away from his brow. "Contact's told the Empire you're one hot-shot game-player; they've said they reckon you can get to colonel/bishop/junior ministerial level."

"What?" Gurgeh said, looking horrified. "That's not what they told me!"

"Or me," the drone said. "I only found out myself looking

at a news roundup an hour ago. They're setting you up, man; they want to keep the Empire happy and they're using you to do it. First they get them good and worried telling them you can beat some of their finest players, then, when—as is probably going to happen—you get knocked out in the first round, they thereby reassure the Empire the Culture's just a joke; we get things wrong, we're easily humiliated."

Gurgeh looked levelly at the drone, eyes narrowed. "First round, you think, do you?" he said calmly.

"Oh. I'm sorry." The little drone wavered back a little in the air, looking embarrassed. "Are you offended? I was just assuming . . . well, I've watched you play . . . I mean . . ." The machine's voice trailed off.

Gurgeh removed the heavy robe and dropped it onto the floor. "I think I'll take a bath," he told the drone. The machine hesitated, then picked up the robe and quickly left the cabin. Gurgeh sat on the bed and rubbed his beard.

In fact, the drone hadn't offended him. He had his own secrets. He was sure he could do better in the game than Contact expected. For the last hundred days on the *Limiting Factor* he knew he hadn't been extending himself; while he hadn't been trying to lose or make any deliberate mistakes, he also hadn't been concentrating as much as he intended to in the coming games.

He wasn't sure himself why he was pulling his punches in this way, but somehow it seemed important not to let Contact know everything, to keep something back. It was a small victory against them, a little-game, a gesture on a lesser board; a blow against the elements and the gods.

The Great Palace of Groasnachek lay by the broad and murky river which had given the city its name. That night there was a grand ball for the more important people who would be playing the game of Azad over the next half-year.

They were taken there in a groundcar, along broad, tree-lined boulevards lit by tall floodlights. Gurgeh sat in the back of the vehicle with Pequil, who'd been in the car when it arrived at the hotel. A uniformed male drove the car, apparently in sole control of the machine. Gurgeh tried not to think about crashes. Flere-Imsaho sat on the floor in its bulky disguise, humming quietly and attracting small fibers from the limousine's furry floor covering.

The palace wasn't as immense as Gurgeh had expected, though still impressive enough; it was ornately decorated and brightly illuminated, and from each of its many spires and towers, long, richly decorated banners waved sinuously, slow brilliant waves of heraldry against the orange-black sky.

In the awning-covered courtyard where the car stopped there was a huge array of gilded scaffolding on which burned twelve thousand candles of various sizes and colors; one for every person entered in the games. The ball itself was for over a thousand people, about half of them game-players; the rest were mostly partners of the players, or officials, priests, officers and bureaucrats who were sufficiently content with their present position—and who had earned the security of tenure which meant they could not be displaced, no matter how well their underlings might do in the games—not to want to compete.

The mentors and administrators of the Azad colleges—the game's teaching institutions—formed the remainder of the gathering, and were similarly exempt from the need to take part in the tournament.

The night was too warm for Gurgeh's taste; a thick heat filled with the city-smell, and stagnant. The robe was heavy and surprisingly uncomfortable; Gurgeh wondered how soon he could politely leave the ball. They entered the palace through a huge doorway flanked by massive opened gates of polished, jewel-studded metal. The vestibules and halls they passed through glittered with sumptuous decorations standing on tables or hanging from walls and ceilings.

The people were as fabulous as their surroundings. The females, of whom there seemed to be a great number, were ablaze with jewelry and extravagantly ornamented dresses. Gurgeh guessed that, measuring from the bottom of their bell-shaped gowns, the women must have been as broad as they were tall. They rustled as they went by, and smelled strongly of heavy, obtrusive perfumes. Many of the people he passed glanced or looked or actually stopped and stared at Gurgeh and the floating, humming, crackling Flere-Imsaho.

Every few meters along the walls, and on both sides of every doorway, gaudily uniformed males stood stock still, their trousered legs slightly apart, gloved hands clasped behind their rod-straight backs, their gaze fixed firmly on the high, painted ceilings.

"What are they standing there for?" Gurgeh whispered to the drone in Eächic, low enough so that Pequil couldn't hear.

"Show," the machine said.

Gurgeh thought about this. "Show?"

"Yes; to show that the Emperor is rich and important enough to have hundreds of flunkeys standing around doing nothing."

"Doesn't everybody know that already?"

The drone didn't answer for a moment. Then it sighed. "You haven't really cracked the psychology of wealth and power yet, have you, Jernau Gurgeh?"

Gurgeh walked on, smiling on the side of his face Flere-Imsaho couldn't see.

The apices they passed were all dressed in the same heavy robes Gurgeh was wearing; ornate without being ostentatious. What struck Gurgeh most strongly, though, was that the whole place and everybody in it seemed to be stuck in another age. He could see nothing in the palace or worn by the people that could not have been produced at least a thousand years earlier; he had watched recordings of ancient imperial ceremonies when he'd done his own research into the society, and thought he had a reasonable grasp of ancient dress and forms. It struck him as strange that despite the Empire's obvious, if limited, technological sophistication, its formal side remained so entrenched in the past. Ancient customs, fashions and architectural forms were all common in the Culture too, but they were used freely, even haphazardly, as only parts of a whole range of styles, not adhered to rigidly and consistently to the exclusion of all else.

"Just wait here; you'll be announced," the drone said, tugging at Gurgeh's sleeve so that he stopped beside the smiling Lo Pequil at a doorway leading down a huge flight of broad steps into the main ballroom. Pequil handed a card to a uniformed apex standing at the top of the steps, whose amplified voice rang round the vast hall.

"The honorable Lo Pequil Monenine, AAB, Level Two Main, Empire Medal, Order of Merit and bar . . . with Chark Gavant-sha Gernow Morat Gurgee Dam Hazeze."

They walked down the grand staircase. The scene below them was an order of magnitude brighter and more impressive than any social event Gurgeh had ever witnessed. The Culture simply didn't do things on such a scale. The ballroom looked like a vast and glittering pool into which somebody had thrown a thousand fabulous flowers, and then stirred.

"That announcer murdered my name," Gurgeh said to the

drone. He glanced at Pequil. "But why does our friend look so unhappy?"

"I think because the 'senior' in his name was missed out," Flere-Imsaho said.

"Is that important?"

"Gurgeh, in this society *everything* is important," the drone said, then added glumly, "At least you both got announced."

"Hello there!" a voice shouted out as they got to the bottom of the stairs. A tall, male-looking person pushed between a couple of Azadians to get beside Gurgeh. He wore garish, flowing robes. He had a beard, bunned brown hair, bright staring green eyes, and he looked as though he might come from the Culture. He stuck one long-fingered, many-ringed hand out, took Gurgeh's hand and clasped it. "Shohobohaum Za; pleased to meet you. I used to know your name too until that delinquent at the top of the stairs got his tongue round it. Gurgeh, isn't it? Oh, Pequil; you here too, eh?" He pushed a glass into Pequil's hands. "Here; you drink this muck, don't you? Hi, drone. Hey; Gurgeh," he put his arm round Gurgeh's shoulders, "you want a proper drink, yeah?"

"Jernow Morat Gurgee," Pequil began, looking awkward, "Let me introduce . . ."

But Shohobohaum Za was already steering Gurgeh away through the crowds at the bottom of the staircase. "How's things anyway, Pequil?" he shouted over his shoulder at the dazed-looking apex. "Okay? Yeah? Good. Talk to you later. Just taking this other exile for a little drink!"

A pale-looking Pequil waved back weakly. Flere-Imsaho hesitated, then stayed with the Azadian.

Shohobohaum Za turned back to Gurgeh, removed his arm from the other man's shoulders and, in a less strident voice, said, "Boring bladder, old Pequil. Hope you didn't mind being dragged away."

"I'll cope with the remorse," Gurgeh said, looking the other Culture man up and down. "I take it you're the . . . ambassador?"

"The same," Za said, and belched. "This way," he nodded, guiding Gurgeh through the crowds. "I spotted some *grif* bottles behind one of the drink tables and I want to dock with a couple before the Emp and his cronies snaffle the lot." They passed a low stage where a band played loudly. "Crazy place, isn't it?" Za shouted at Gurgeh as they headed for the rear of the hall.

Gurgeh wondered exactly what the other man was referring to.

"Here we is," Za said, coming to a stop by a long line of tables. Behind the tables, liveried males served drinks and food to the guests. Above them, on a huge arched wall, a dark tapestry sewn with diamonds and gold-thread depicted an ancient space battle.

Za gave a whistle and leaned over to whisper to the tall, stern-looking male who approached. Gurgeh saw a piece of paper being exchanged, then Za slapped his hand over Gurgeh's wrist and breezed away from the tables, hauling Gurgeh over to a large circular couch set round the bottom of a fluted pillar of marble inlaid with precious metals.

"Wait till you taste this stuff," Za said, leaning toward Gurgeh and winking. Shohobohaum Za was a little lighter in color than Gurgeh, but still much darker than the average Azadian. It was notoriously difficult to judge the age of Culture people, but Gurgeh guessed the man was a decade or so younger than he. "You do drink?" Za said, looking suddenly alarmed.

"I've been bypassing the stuff," Gurgeh told him.

Za shook his head emphatically. "Don't do that with *grif,*" he said, patting Gurgeh's hand. "Would be tragic. Ought to be a treasonable offense, in fact. Gland *Crystal Fugue State* instead. Brilliant combination; blows your neurons out your ass. *Grif* is stunning stuff. Comes from Echronedal, you know; shipped over for the games. Only make it during the Oxygen Season; stuff we're getting should be two Great Years old. Costs a fortune. Opened more legs than a cosmetic laser. Anyway." Za sat back, clasping his hands and looking seriously at Gurgeh. "What do you think of the Empire? Isn't it wonderful? Isn't it? I mean, vicious but sexy, right?" He jumped forward as a male servant carrying a tray with a couple of small, stoppered jugs came up to them. "Ah-ha!" He took the tray with its jugs in exchange for another scrap of paper. He unstoppered both jugs and handed one to Gurgeh. He raised his jug to his lips, closed his eyes and breathed deeply. He muttered something under his breath that sounded like a chant. Finally he drank, keeping his eyes tightly closed.

When he opened his eyes, Gurgeh was sitting with one elbow on his knee, his chin in his hand, looking quizzically at him. "Did they recruit you like this?" he asked. "Or is it an effect the Empire has?"

Za laughed throatily, gazing up to the ceiling where a vast painting showed ancient seaships fighting some millennia-old engagement. "Both!" Za said, still chuckling. He nodded at Gurgeh's jug, an amused but—so it seemed to Gurgeh—more intelligent look on his face now; a look which made Gurgeh revise his estimation of the other man's age upward by several decades. "You going to drink that stuff?" Za said. "I just spent an unskilled worker's yearly wage getting it for you."

Gurgeh looked into the other man's bright green eyes for a moment, then raised the jug to his lips. "To the unskilled workers, Mr. Za," he said, and drank.

Za laughed uproariously again, head back. "I think we're going to get along just fine, game-player Gurgeh."

The *grif* was sweet, scented, subtle and smoky. Za drained his own jug, holding the thin spout over his opened mouth to savor the last few drops. He looked at Gurgeh and smacked his lips. "Slips down like liquid silk," he said. He put the jug on the floor. "So; you're going to play the great game, eh, Jernau Gurgeh?"

"That's what I'm here for." Gurgeh sipped a little more of the heady liquor.

"Let me give you some advice," Za said, briefly touching his arm. "Don't bet on *anything.* And watch the women—or men, or both, or whatever you're into. You could get into some very nasty situations if you aren't careful. Even if you mean to stay celibate you might find some of them—women especially—just can't wait to see what's between your legs. And they take that sort of stuff ri-*diculously* seriously. You want any body-games; tell me. I've got contacts; I can set it up nice and discreet. Utter discretion and complete secrecy totally guaranteed; ask anybody." He laughed, then touched Gurgeh's arm again and looked serious. "I'm serious," he said. "I can fix you up."

"I'll bear that in mind," Gurgeh said, drinking. "Thanks for the warning."

"My pleasure; no problem. I've been here eight . . . nine years now; envoy before me only lasted twenty days; got chucked out for consorting with a minister's wife." Za shook his head and chuckled. "I mean, I like her style, but *shit;* a minister! Crazy bitch was lucky she was only thrown out; if she'd been one of their own they'd have been up her orifices with acid leeches before the prison gate had shut. Makes me cross my legs just thinking about it."

Before Gurgeh could reply, or Za could continue, there was a terrific crashing noise from the top of the great staircase, like the sound of thousands of breaking bottles. It echoed through the ballroom. "Damn, the Emperor," Za said, standing. He nodded at Gurgeh's jug. "Drink up, man!"

Gurgeh stood up slowly; he pushed the jug into Za's hands. "You have it. I think you appreciate it more." Za restoppered the jug and shoved it into a fold in his robe.

There was a lot of activity at the top of the stairs. People in the ballroom were milling about too, apparently forming a sort of human corridor which led from the bottom of the staircase to a large, glittering seat set on a low dais covered with gold-cloth.

"Better get you into your place," Za said; he went to grab Gurgeh's wrist again, but Gurgeh raised his hand suddenly, smoothing his beard; Za missed.

Gurgeh nodded forward. "After you," he said. Za winked and strode off. They came up behind the group of people in front of the throne.

"Here's your boy, Pequil," Za announced to the worried-looking apex, then went to stand further away. Gurgeh found himself standing beside Pequil, with Flere-Imsaho floating behind him at waist level, humming assiduously.

"Mr. Gurgee, we were starting to worry about you," Pequil whispered, glancing nervously up at the staircase.

"Were you?" Gurgeh said. "How comforting." Pequil didn't look very pleased. Gurgeh wondered if the apex had been addressed wrongly again.

"I have good news, Gurgee," Pequil whispered. He looked up at Gurgeh, who tried hard to look inquisitive. "I have succeeded in obtaining for you a *personal* introduction to Their Royal Highness the Emperor-Regent Nicosar!"

"I am greatly honored." Gurgeh smiled.

"Indeed! Indeed! A most singular and exceptional honor!" Pequil gulped.

"So don't fuck up," Flere-Imsaho muttered from behind. Gurgeh looked at the machine.

The crashing noise sounded again, and suddenly, sweeping down the staircase, quickly filling its breadth, a great gaudy wave of people flowed down toward the floor. Gurgeh assumed the one in the lead carrying a long staff was the Emperor—or Emperor-Regent as Pequil had called him—but at the bottom of the stairs that apex stood aside and shouted, "Their Imperial Highness of the College of Candsev, Prince of Space, Defender of the Faith, Duke of Groasnachek, Master of the Fires of Echronedal, the Emperor-Regent Nicosar the first!"

The Emperor was dressed all in black; a medium-sized, serious-looking apex, quite unornamented. He was surrounded by fabulously dressed Azadians of all sexes, including comparatively conservatively uniformed male and apex guards toting big swords and small guns; preceding the Emperor was a variety of large animals, four- and six-legged, variously colored, collared and muzzled, and held on the end of emerald- and ruby-chained leads by fat, almost naked males whose oiled skins glowed like frosted gold in the ballroom lights.

The Emperor stopped and talked to some people (who knelt when he approached), further down the line on the far side, then he crossed with his entourage to the side Gurgeh was on.

The ballroom was almost totally silent. Gurgeh could hear the throaty breathing of several of the tamed carnivores. Pequil was sweating. A pulse beat quickly in the hollow of his cheek.

Nicosar came closer. Gurgeh thought the Emperor looked, if anything, a little less impressively hard and determined than the average Azadian. He was slightly stooped, and even when he was talking to somebody only a couple of meters away, Gurgeh could hear only the guest's side of the conversation. Nicosar looked a little younger than Gurgeh had expected.

Despite having been advised about his personal introduction by Pequil, Gurgeh nevertheless felt mildly surprised when the black-clothed apex stopped in front of him.

"Kneel," Flere-Imsaho hissed.

Gurgeh knelt on one knee. The silence seemed to deepen. "Oh shit," the humming machine muttered. Pequil moaned.

The Emperor looked down at Gurgeh, then gave a small smile. "Sir one-knee; you must be our foreign guest. We wish you a good game."

Gurgeh realized what he'd done wrong, and went down on the other knee too, but the Emperor gave a small wave with one ringed hand and said, "No, no; we admire originality. You shall greet us on one knee in future."

"Thank you, Your Highness," Gurgeh said, with a small bow. The Emperor nodded, and turned to walk further up the line.

Pequil gave a quivering sigh.

The Emperor reached the throne on the dais, and music started; people suddenly started talking, and the twin lines of people broke up; everybody chattered and gesticulated at once. Pequil looked as though he was about to collapse. He seemed to be speechless.

Flere-Imsaho floated up to Gurgeh. "Please," it said, "don't *ever* do something like that again." Gurgeh ignored the machine.

"At least you could talk, eh?" Pequil said suddenly, taking a glass from a tray with a shaking hand. "At least he could talk, eh, machine?" He was talking almost too fast for Gurgeh to follow. He sank the drink. "Most people freeze. I think I might have. Many people do. What does one knee matter, eh? What does that matter?" Pequil looked round for the male with the drinks tray, then gazed at the throne, where the Emperor was sitting talking to some of his retinue. "What a majestic presence!" Pequil said.

"Why's he 'Emperor-Regent'?" Gurgeh asked the sweating apex.

"Their Royal Highness had to take up the Royal Chain after the Emperor Molsce sadly died two years ago. As second-best player during the last games, Our Worship Nicosar was elevated to the throne. But I have no doubt they will remain there!"

Gurgeh, who'd read about Molsce dying but hadn't realized Nicosar wasn't regarded as a full Emperor in his own right, nodded and, looking at the extravagantly accoutred people and beasts surrounding the imperial dais, wondered what additional splendors Nicosar could possibly merit if he did win the games.

"I'd offer to dance with you but they don't approve of men dancing together," Shohobohaum Za said, coming up to where Gurgeh stood by a pillar. Za took a plate of paper-wrapped sweetmeats from a small table and held it out to Gurgeh, who shook his head. Za popped a couple of the little pastries into his mouth while Gurgeh watched the elaborate, patterned dances surge in eddies of flesh and colored cloth across the ballroom floor. Flere-Imsaho floated nearby. There were some bits of paper sticking to its static-charged casing.

"Don't worry," Gurgeh told Za. "I shan't feel insulted."

"Good. Enjoying yourself?" Za leaned against the pillar. "Thought you looked a bit lonely standing here. Where's Pequil?"

"He's talking to some imperial officials, trying to arrange a private audience."

"Ho, he'll be lucky," snorted Za. "What d'you think of our wonderful Emperor, anyway?"

"He seems . . . very imperious," Gurgeh said, and made a frowning gesture at the robes he was wearing, and tapped one ear.

Za looked amused, then mystified, then he laughed. "Oh; the microphone!" He shook his head, unwrapped another couple of pastries and ate them. "Don't worry about that. Just say what you want. You won't be assassinated or anything. They don't mind. Diplomatic protocol. We pretend the robes aren't bugged, and they pretend they haven't heard anything. It's a little game we play."

"If you say so," Gurgeh said, looking over at the imperial dais.

"Not much to look at at the moment, young Nicosar," Za said, following Gurgeh's gaze. "He gets his full regalia after the game; theoretically in mourning for Molsce at the moment. Black's their color for mourning; something to do with space, I think." He looked at the Emperor for a while. "Odd set-up, don't you think? All that power belonging to one person."

"Seems a rather . . . potentially unstable way to run a society," Gurgeh agreed.

"Hmm. Of course, it's all relative, isn't it? Really, you know, that old guy the Emp's talking to at the moment probably has more real power than Nicosar himself."

"Really?" Gurgeh looked at Za.

"Yes; that's Hamin, rector of Candsev College. Nicosar's mentor."

"You don't mean he tells the Emperor what to do?"

"Not officially, but"—Za belched—"Nicosar was brought up in the college; spent sixty years, child and apex, learning the game from Hamin. Hamin raised him, groomed him, taught him all he knew, about the game and everything else. So when old Molsce gets his one-way ticket to the land of nod—not before time—and Nicosar takes over, who's the first person he's going to turn to for advice?"

"I see," Gurgeh nodded. He was starting to regret not having studied more on Azad the political system rather than just Azad the game. "I thought the colleges just taught people how to play."

"That's all they do in theory, but in fact they're more like surrogate noble families. Where the Empire gains over the usual bloodline set-up is they use the game to recruit the cleverest, most ruthless and manipulative apices from the whole population to run the show, rather than have to marry new blood into some stagnant aristocracy and hope for the best when the genes shake out. Actually quite a neat system; the game solves a lot. I can see it lasting; Contact seems to think it's all going to fall apart at the seams one day, but I doubt it myself. This lot could outlast us. They *are* impressive, don't you think? Come on; you have to admit you're impressed, aren't you?"

"Unspeakably," Gurgeh said. "But I'd like to see more before I come to any final judgment."

"You'll end up impressed; you'll appreciate its savage beauty. No; I'm serious. You will. You'll probably end up wanting to stay. Oh, and don't pay any attention to that dingbat drone they've sent to nursemaid you. They're all the same, those machines; want everything to be like the Culture; peace and love and all that same bland crap. They haven't got the"—Za belched—"the sensuality to appreciate the"—he belched again—"Empire. Believe me. Ignore the machine."

Gurgeh was wondering what to say to that when a brightly dressed group of apices and females came up to surround him and Shohobohaum Za. An apex stepped out of the smiling, shining group, and, with a bow Gurgeh thought looked exaggerated, said to Za, "Would our esteemed envoy amuse our wives with his eyes?"

"I'd be delighted!" Za said. He handed the sweetmeat tray to Gurgeh, and while the women giggled and the apices smirked at each other, he went close to the females and flicked the nictitating membranes in his eyes up and down. "There!" He laughed, dancing back. One of the apices thanked him, then the group of people walked away, talking and laughing.

"They're like big kids," Za told Gurgeh, then patted him on the shoulder and wandered off, a vacant look in his eyes.

Flere-Imsaho floated over, making a noise like rustling paper. "I heard what that asshole said about ignoring machines," it said.

"Hmm?" Gurgeh said.

"I said—oh, it doesn't matter. Not feeling left out because you can't dance, are you?"

"No. I don't enjoy dancing."

"Just as well. It would be socially demeaning for anybody here even to touch you."

"What a way with words you have, machine," Gurgeh said. He put the plate of savories in front of the drone and then let go and walked off. Flere-Imsaho yelped, and just managed to grab the falling plate before all the paper-wrapped pastries fell off.

Gurgeh wandered around for a while, feeling a little angry and more than a little uncomfortable. He was consumed with the idea that he was surrounded by people who were in some way failed, as though they were all the unpassed components from some high-quality system which would have been polluted by their inclusion. Not only did those around him strike him as foolish and boorish, but he felt also that he was not much different himself. Everybody he met seemed to feel he'd come here just to make a fool of himself.

Contact sent him out here with a geriatric warship hardly worthy of the name, gave him a vain, hopelessly gauche young drone, forgot to tell him things which they ought to have known would make a considerable difference to the way the game was played—the college system, which the *Limiting Factor* had glossed over, was a good example—and put him at least partly in the charge of a drunken, loud-mouthed fool childishly infatuated with a few imperialist tricks and a resourcefully inhumane social system.

During the journey here, the whole adventure had seemed so romantic; a great and brave commitment, a noble thing to do. That sense of the epic had left him now. All he felt at this moment was that he, like Shohobohaum Za or Flere-Imsaho, was just another social misfit and this whole, spectacularly seedy Empire had been thrown to him like a scrap. Somewhere, he was sure, Minds were loafing in hyperspace within the field-fabric of some great ship, laughing.

He looked about the ballroom. Reedy music sounded, the paired apices and luxuriously dressed females moved about the shining marquetry floor in pre-set arrangements, their looks of pride and humility equally distasteful, while the servant males moved carefully around like machines, making sure each glass was kept full, each plate covered. He hardly thought it mattered what their social system was; it simply looked so crassly, rigidly over-organized.

"Ah, Gurgee," Pequil said. He came through the space between a large potted plant and a marble pillar, holding a young-looking female by one elbow. "There you are. Gurgee;

please meet Trinev Dutleysdaughter." The apex smiled from the girl to the man, and guided her forward. She bowed slowly. "Trinev is a game-player too," Pequil told Gurgeh. "Isn't that interesting?"

"I'm honored to meet you, young lady," Gurgeh said to the girl, bowing a little too. She stood still in front of him, her gaze directed at the floor. Her dress was less ornate than most of those he'd seen, and the woman inside it looked less glamorous.

"Well, I'll leave you two odd-ones-out to talk, shall I?" Pequil said, taking a step back, hands clasped. "Miss Dutleysdaughter's father is over by the rear bandstand, Gurgee; if you wouldn't mind returning the young lady when you've finished talking . . . ?"

Gurgeh watched Pequil go, then smiled at the top of the young woman's head. He cleared his throat. The girl remained silent. Gurgeh said, "I, ah . . . I'd thought that only intermediates—apices—played Azad."

The girl looked up as far as his chest. "No, sir. There are some capable female players, of minor rank, of course." She had a soft, tired-sounding voice. She still did not raise her face to him, so he had to address the crown of her head, where he could see the white scalp through the black, tied hair.

"Ah," he said. "I thought it might have been . . . forbidden. I'm glad it isn't. Do males play too?"

"They do, sir. Nobody is forbidden to play. That is embodied in the Constitution. It is simply made—it is only that it is more difficult for either—" The woman broke off and brought her head up with a sudden, startling look. "—for either of the *lesser* sexes to learn, because all the great colleges must take only apex scholars." She looked back down again. "Of course, this is to prevent the distraction of those who study."

Gurgeh wasn't sure what to say. "I see," was all he could come up with at first. "Do you . . . hope to do well in the games?"

"If I can do well—if I can reach the second game in the main series—then I hope to be able to join the civil service, and travel."

"Well, I hope you succeed."

"Thank you. Unfortunately, it is not very likely. The first game, as you know, is played by groups of ten, and to be the only woman playing nine apices is to be regarded as a nuisance. One is usually put out of the game first, to clear the field."

"Hmm. I was warned something similar might happen to me," Gurgeh said, smiling at the woman's head and wishing she would look up at him again.

"Oh no." The woman did look up then, and Gurgeh found the directness of her flat-faced gaze oddly disconcerting. "They won't do that to you; it wouldn't be polite. They don't *know* how weak or strong you are. They . . ." She looked down again. "They know that I am, so it is no disrespect to remove me from the board so that they may get on with the game."

Gurgeh looked round the huge, noisy, crowded ballroom, where the people talked and danced and the music sounded loud. "Is there nothing you can do?" he asked. "Wouldn't it be possible to arrange that ten women play each other in the first round?"

She was still looking down, but something about the curve of her cheek told him she might have been smiling. "Indeed, sir. But I believe there has never been an occasion in the great-game series when two lesser-sexes have played in the same group. The draw has never worked out that way, in all these years."

"Ah," Gurgeh said. "And single games, one-against-one?"

"They do not count unless one has gone through the earlier

rounds. When I do practice single games, I am told . . . that I'm very lucky. I suppose I must be. But then, I know I am, for my father has chosen me a fine master and husband, and even if I do not succeed in the game, I shall marry well. What more can a woman ask for, sir?"

Gurgeh didn't know what to say. There was a strange tingling feeling at the back of his neck. He cleared his throat a couple of times. In the end all he could find to say was, "I hope you do win. I really hope you do."

The woman looked briefly up at him, then down again. She shook her head.

After a while, Gurgeh suggested that he take her back to her father, and she assented. She said one more thing.

They were walking down the great hall, threading their way through the clumps of people to where her father waited, and at one point they passed between a great carved pillar and a wall of battle-murals. During the instant they were quite hidden from the rest of the room, the woman reached out one hand and touched him on the top of his wrist; with the other hand she pressed a finger over a particular point on the shoulder of his robe, and with that one finger pressing, and the others lightly brushing his arm, in the same moment whispered, "You win. *You* win!"

Then they were with her father, and after repeating how welcome he felt, Gurgeh left the family group. The woman didn't look at him again. He had had no time to reply to her.

"Are you all right, Jernau Gurgeh?" Flere-Imsaho said, finding the man leaning against a wall and seemingly just staring into space, as though he was one of the liveried male servants.

Gurgeh looked at the drone. He put his finger to the point on the robe's shoulder the girl had pressed. "Is this where the bug is on this thing?"

"Yes," the machine said. "That's right. Did Shohobohaum Za tell you that?"

"Hmm, thought so," Gurgeh said. He pushed himself away from the wall. "Would it be polite to leave now?"

"Now?" The drone started back a little, humming loudly. "Well, I suppose so . . . are you sure you're all right?"

"Never felt better. Let's go." Gurgeh walked away.

"You seem agitated. Are you really all right? Aren't you enjoying yourself? What did Za give you to drink? Are you nervous about the game? Has Za said something? Is it because nobody'll touch you?"

Gurgeh walked through the people, ignoring the humming, crackling drone at his shoulder.

As they left the great ballroom, he realized that apart from remembering that she was called somebody's-daughter, he had forgotten the woman's name.

Gurgeh was due to play his first game of Azad two days after the ball. He spent the time working out a few set-piece maneuvers with the *Limiting Factor.* He could have used the module's brain, but the old warship had a more interesting game-style. The fact that the *Limiting Factor* was several decades away by real space light meant there was a significant delay involved—the ship itself always replied instantly to a move—but the effect was still of playing an extraordinarily quick and gifted player.

Gurgeh didn't take up any more invitations to formal functions; he'd told Pequil his digestive system was taking time to adjust to the Empire's rich food, and that appeared to be an acceptable excuse. He even refused the chance to go on a sightseeing trip of the capital.

He saw nobody during those days except Flere-Imsaho,

which spent most of its time, in its disguise, sitting on the hotel parapet, humming quietly and watching birds, which it attracted with crumbs scattered on the roof-garden lawn.

Now and again, Gurgeh would walk out onto the grassed roof and stand looking out over the city.

The streets and the sky were both full of traffic. Groasnachek was like a great, flattened, spiky animal, awash with lights at night and hazy with its own heaped breath during the day. It spoke with a great, garbled choir of voices; an encompassing background roar of engines and machines that never ceased, and the sporadic tearing sounds of passing aircraft. The continual wails, whoops, warbles and screams of sirens and alarms were strewn across the fabric of the city like shrapnel holes.

Architecturally, Gurgeh thought, the place was a hopeless mix of styles, and far too big. Some buildings soared, some sprawled, but each seemed to have been designed without any regard to any other, and the whole effect—which might have been interestingly varied—was in fact gruesome. He kept thinking of the *Little Rascal,* holding ten times as many people as the city in a smaller area, and far more elegantly, even though most of the craft's volume was taken up with ship-building space, engines, and other equipment.

Groasnachek had all the planning of a bird-dropping, Gurgeh thought, and the city was its own maze.

When the day came for the game to start he woke feeling elated, as though he'd just won a game, rather than being about to embark on the first real, serious match of his life. He ate very little for breakfast, and dressed slowly in the ceremonial garments the game required; rather ridiculous gathered-up clothes, with soft slippers and hose beneath a bulky jacket with rolled, gartered sleeves. At least, as a novice, Gurgeh's robes were relatively unornamented, and restrained in color.

Pequil arrived to take him to the game in an official groundcar. The apex chattered during the journey, enthusing about some recent conquest the Empire had made in a distant region of space; a glorious victory.

The car sped along the broad streets, heading for the outskirts of the city where the public hall Gurgeh would play in had been converted into a game-room.

All over the city that morning, people were going to their first game of the new series; from the most optimistic young player lucky enough to win a place in the games in a state lottery, right up to Nicosar himself, those twelve thousand people faced that day knowing that their lives might change utterly and forever, for better or worse, starting from right now.

The whole city was alive with the game-fever which infected it every six years; Groasnachek was packed with the players, their retinues, advisors, college mentors, relations and friends, the Empire's press and news-services, and visiting delegations from colonies and dominions there to watch the future course of imperial history being decided.

Despite his earlier euphoria, Gurgeh discovered that his hands were shaking by the time they arrived at the hall, and as he was led into the place with its high white walls and its echoing wooden floor, an unpleasant sensation of churning seemed to emanate from his belly. It felt quite different from the normal feeling of being keyed-up which he experienced before most games; this was something else; keener, and more thrilling and unsettling than anything he'd known before.

All that lightened this mood of tension was discovering that Flere-Imsaho had been refused permission to remain in the game-hall when the match was in progress; it would have to stay outside. Its display of clicking, humming, crackling crudity had not been sufficient to convince the imperial authorities that it was incapable of somehow assisting Gurgeh during the game. It was shown to a small pavilion in the grounds of the hall, to wait there with the imperial guards on security duty.

It complained, loudly.

Gurgeh was introduced to the other nine people in his game. In theory, they had all been chosen at random. They greeted him cordially enough, though one of them, a junior imperial priest, nodded rather than spoke to him.

They played the lesser game of strategy-cards first. Gurgeh started very cautiously, surrendering cards and points to discover what the others held. When it finally became obvious, he began playing properly, hoping he would not be made to look too silly in the rush, but over the next few turns he realized the others were still unsure exactly who held what, and he was the only one playing the game as though it was in its final stages.

Thinking that perhaps he'd missed something, he played a couple of more exploratory cards, and only then did the priest start to play for the end. Gurgeh resumed, and when the game finished before midday he held more points than anybody else.

"So far so good, eh, drone?" he said to Flere-Imsaho. He was sitting at the table where the players, game-officials and some of the more important spectators were at lunch.

"If you say so," the machine said grumpily. "I don't get to see much, stuck in the outhouse with the jolly soldier boys."

"Well, take it from me; it's looking all right."

"Early days yet, Jernau Gurgeh. You won't catch them that easily again."

"I knew I could rely on your support."

In the afternoon they played on a couple of the smaller boards in a series of single games to decide order of precedence. Gurgeh knew he was good at both these games, and easily beat the others. Only the priest seemed upset by this. There was another break, for dinner, during which Pequil arrived unofficially, on his way home from the office. He expressed his pleased surprise at how well Gurgeh was doing, and even patted him on the arm before he left.

The early-evening session was a formality; all that happened was that they were told by the game-officials—amateurs from a local club, with one imperial official in charge—the exact configuration and order of play for the following day, on the Board of Origin. As had now become obvious, Gurgeh was going to start with a considerable advantage.

Sitting in the back of the car with only Flere-Imsaho for company, and feeling quite pleased with himself, Gurgeh watched the city go by in the violet light of dusk.

"Not too bad, I suppose," the drone said, humming only a little as it lay on the seat by Gurgeh. "I'd contact the ship tonight if I were you, to discuss what you're going to do tomorrow."

"Would you really?"

"Yes. You're going to need all the help you can get. They'll gang up on you tomorrow; bound to. This is where you lose out, of course; if any of them were in this situation they'd be getting in touch with one or more of the less well-placed players and doing a deal with them to go for—"

"Yes, but as you never seem to tire of telling me, they would all demean themselves doing anything of the sort with me. On the other hand though, with your encouragement and the *Limiting Factor*'s help, how can I lose?"

The drone was silent.

Gurgeh got in touch with the ship that night. Flere-Imsaho had declared itself bored; it had discarded its casing, gone black-body, and floated off unseen into the night to visit a city park where there were some nocturnal birds.

Gurgeh talked over his plans with the *Limiting Factor,* but the time-delay of almost a minute made the conversation with the distant warship a slow business. The ship had some good suggestions, though. Gurgeh was certain that at this level at least he must be getting far better advice from the ship than any of his immediate opponents were receiving from their advisors, aides and mentors. Probably only the top hundred or so players, those directly sponsored and supported by the leading colleges, would have access to such informed help. This thought cheered him further, and he went to bed happy.

Three days later, just as play was closing after the early-evening session, Gurgeh looked at the Board of Origin and realized he was going to be put out of the game.

Everything had gone well at first. He'd been pleased with his handling of the pieces, and sure he'd had a more subtle appreciation of the game's strategic balance. With his superiority in position and forces resulting from his successes during the early stages, he'd been confident he was going to win, and so stay in the Main Series to play in the second round, of single games.

Then, on the third morning, he realized he had been over-confident, and his concentration had lapsed. What had looked like a series of unconnected moves by most of the other players suddenly became a coordinated mass attack, with the priest at its head. He'd panicked and they'd trounced him. Now he was a dead man.

The priest came up to Gurgeh when the session's play was over and Gurgeh was still sitting in his high stoolseat, looking down at the shambles on the board and wondering what had gone wrong. The apex asked the man if he was willing to concede; it was the conventional course when somebody was so far behind in pieces and territory, and there was less shame attached to an honorable admission of defeat than to a stubborn refusal to face reality which only dragged the game out longer for one's opponents. Gurgeh looked at the priest, then at Flere-Imsaho, who'd been allowed into the hall once the play had ended. The machine wobbled a little in front of him, humming mightily and fairly buzzing with static.

"What do you think, drone?" he said tiredly.

"I think the sooner you get out of those ridiculous clothes, the better," the machine said. The priest, whose own robes were a more gaudy version of Gurgeh's, glanced angrily at the humming machine, but said nothing.

Gurgeh looked at the board again, then at the priest. He took a long, sighing breath and opened his mouth, but before he could speak Flere-Imsaho said, "So I think you should go back to the hotel and get changed and relax and give yourself an opportunity to think."

Gurgeh nodded his head slowly, rubbing his beard and looking at the mess of tangled fortunes on the Board of Origin. He told the priest he'd see him tomorrow.

"There's nothing I can do; they've won," he told the drone once they were back in the module.

"If you say so. Why not ask the ship?"

Gurgeh contacted the *Limiting Factor* to give it the bad news. It commiserated, and, rather than come up with any helpful ideas, told him exactly where he'd gone wrong, going into considerable detail. Gurgeh thanked it with little good grace, and went to bed dispirited, wishing he'd resigned when the priest had asked him.

Flere-Imsaho had gone off exploring the city again. Gurgeh lay in the darkness, the module quiet around him.

He wondered what they'd really sent him here for. What did Contact actually expect him to do? Had he been sent to be humiliated, and so reassure the Empire the Culture was unlikely to be any threat to it? It seemed as likely as anything else. He could imagine Chiark Hub rattling off figures about the colossal amount of energy expended in sending him all this way . . . and even the Culture, even Contact, would think twice about doing all it had just to provide one citizen with a glorified adventure holiday. The Culture didn't use money as such, but it also didn't want to be *too* conspicuously extravagant with matter and energy, either (so inelegant to be wasteful). But to keep the Empire satisfied that the Culture was just a joke, no threat . . . how much was that worth?

He turned over in the bed, switched on the floatfield, adjusted its resistance, tried to sleep, turned this way and that, adjusted the field again but still could not get comfortable, and so, eventually, turned it off.

He saw the slight glow from the bracelet Chamlis had given him, shining by the bedside. He picked the thin band up, turning it over in his hands. The tiny Orbital was bright in the darkness, lighting up his fingers and the covers on the bed. He gazed at its daylight surface and the microscopic whorls of weather systems over blue sea and dun-colored land. He really ought to write to Chamlis, say thank you.

It was only then he realized quite how clever the little piece of jewelry was. He'd assumed it was just an illuminated still picture, but it wasn't; he could remember how it had looked when he'd first seen it, and now the scene was different; the island continents on the daylight side were mostly different shapes to those he remembered, though he recognized a couple of them, near the dawn terminator. The bracelet was a moving representation of an Orbital; possibly even a crude clock.

He smiled in the darkness, turned away.

They all expected him to lose. Only he knew—or had known—he was a better player than they thought. But now he'd thrown away the chance of proving he was right and they were wrong.

"Fool, fool," he whispered to himself in the darkness.

He couldn't sleep. He got up, switched on the module-screen and told the machine to display his game. The Board of Origin appeared, thru-holoed in front of him. He sat there and stared at it, then he told the module to contact the ship.

It was a slow, dreamlike conversation, during which he gazed as though transfixed at the bright game-board seemingly stretching away from him, while waiting for his words to reach the distant warship, and then for its reply to come back.

"Jernau Gurgeh?"

"I want to know something, ship. Is there any way out of this?"

Stupid question. He could see the answer. His position was an inchoate mess; the only certain thing about it was that it was hopeless.

"Out of your present situation in the game?"

He sighed. What a waste of time. "Yes. Can you see a way?"

The frozen holo on the screen in front of him, his displayed position, was like some trapped moment of falling; the instant when the foot slips, the fingers lose their last strength, and the fatal, accelerating descent begins. He thought of satellites, forever falling, and the controlled stumble that bipeds call walking.

"You are more points behind than anybody who has ever come back to win in any Main Series game. You have already been defeated, they believe."

Gurgeh waited for more. Silence. "Answer the question," he told the ship. "You didn't answer the question. Answer me."

What was the ship playing at? Mess, mess, a total mess. His position was a swirling, amorphous, nebulous, almost barbaric welter of pieces and areas, battered and crumbling and falling away. Why was he even bothering to ask? Didn't he trust his own judgment? Did he need a Mind to tell him? Would only that make it real?

"Yes, of course there is a way," the ship said. "Many ways, in fact, though they are all unlikely, near impossible. But it can be done. There isn't nearly enough time to—"

"Good night, ship," he said, as the signal continued.

"—explain any of them in detail, but I think I can give you a general idea what to do, though of course just because it has to be such a synoptic appraisal, such a—"

"Sorry, ship; good night." Gurgeh turned the channel off. It clicked once. After a little while the closing chime announced the ship had signed off too. Gurgeh looked at the holo image of the board again, then closed his eyes.

By morning he still had no idea what he was going to do. He hadn't slept at all that night, just sat in front of the screen, staring at its displayed panorama of the game until the view was seemingly etched into his brain, and his eyes hurt with the strain. Later he'd eaten lightly and watched some of the broadcast entertainments the Empire fed the population with. It was a suitably mindless diversion.

Pequil arrived, smiling, and said how well Gurgeh had done to stay in contention at all, and how, personally, Pequil was sure that Gurgeh would do well in the second-series games for those knocked out of the Main Series, if he wished to take part. Of course, they were mostly of interest to those seeking promotion in their careers, and led no further, but Gurgeh might do better against other . . . ah, unfortunates. Anyway; he was still going to Echronedal to see the end of the games, and that was a great privilege, wasn't it?

Gurgeh hardly spoke, just nodded now and again. They rode out to the hall, while Pequil went on and on about the great victory Nicosar had achieved in his first game the previous day; the Emperor-Regent was already on to the second board, the Board of Form.

The priest again asked Gurgeh to resign, and again Gurgeh said he wished to play. They all sat down around the great spread of board, and either dictated their moves to the club players, or made them themselves. Gurgeh sat for a long time before placing his first piece that morning; he rubbed the biotech between his hands for minutes, looking down, wide-eyed, at the board for so long the others thought he'd forgotten it was his turn, and asked the Adjudicator to remind him.

Gurgeh placed the piece. It was as though he saw two boards; one here in front of him and one engraved into his mind from the night before. The other players made their moves, gradually forcing Gurgeh back into one small area of the board, with only a couple of free pieces outside it, hunted and fleeing.

When it came, as he'd known it would without wanting to admit to himself that he did know, the . . . he could only think of it as a revelation . . . made him want to laugh. In fact he did rock back in his seat, head nodding. The priest looked at him expectantly, as though waiting for the stupid human to finally give up, but Gurgeh smiled over at the apex, selected the strongest cards from his dwindling supply, deposited them with the Adjudicator, and made his next move.

All he was banking on, it turned out, was the rest being too concerned with winning the game quickly. It was obvious that some sort of deal had been arranged which would let the priest win, and Gurgeh guessed that the others wouldn't be playing at their best when they were competing for somebody else; it would not be *their* victory. They would not own it. Certainly, they didn't have to play well; sheer weight of numbers could compensate for indifferent play.

But the moves could become a language, and Gurgeh thought he could speak that language now, well enough (tellingly) to lie in it . . . so he made his moves, and at one moment, with one move, seemed to be suggesting that he had given up . . . then with his next move he appeared to indicate he was determined to take one of several players down with him . . . or two of them . . . or a different one . . . the lies went on. There was no single message, but rather a succession of contradictory signals, pulling the syntax of the game to and fro and to and fro until the common understanding the other players had reached began to fatigue and tear and split.

In the midst of this, Gurgeh made some at first sight inconsequential, purposeless moves which—seemingly suddenly, apparently without any warning—threatened first a few, then several, then most of the troop-pieces of one player, but at the cost of making Gurgeh's own forces more vulnerable. While that player panicked, the priest did what Gurgeh was relying on him doing, rushing into the attack. Over the next few moves, Gurgeh asked for the cards he'd deposited with the game official to be revealed. They acted rather like mines in a Possession game. The priest's forces were variously destroyed, demoralized, random-move blinded, hopelessly weakened or turned over to Gurgeh or—in only a few cases—to some of the other players. The priest was left with almost nothing, forces scattering over the board like dead leaves.

In the confusion, Gurgeh watched the others, devoid of their leader, squabble over the scraps of power. One got into serious trouble; Gurgeh attacked, annihilated most of his forces and captured the rest, and then kept on attacking without even waiting to regroup.

He realized later he'd still been behind in points at that time, but the sheer momentum of his own resurrection from oblivion carried him on, spreading an unreasoning, hysterical, almost superstitiously intense panic among the others.

From that point on he made no more errors; his progress across the board became a combination of rout and triumphal procession. Perfectly adequate players were made to look like idiots as Gurgeh's forces rampaged across their territories, consuming ground and material as though nothing could be easier or more natural.

Gurgeh finished the game on the Board of Origin before the evening session. He'd saved himself; he wasn't just through to the next board, he was in the lead. The priest, who'd sat looking at the game-surface with an expression Gurgeh thought he'd have recognized as "stunned" even without his lessons in Azadian facial language, walked out of the hall without the customary end-of-game pleasantries, while the other players either said very little or were embarrassingly effusive about his performance.

A crowd of people clustered round Gurgeh; the club members, some press people and other players, some observing guests. Gurgeh felt oddly untouched by the surrounding, chattering apices. Crowding up to him, but still trying not to touch him, somehow their very numbers lent an air of unreality to the scene. Gurgeh was buried in questions, but he couldn't answer any of them. He could hardly make them out as individual inquiries anyway; the apices all talked too fast. Flere-Imsaho floated in above the heads of the crowd, but despite trying to shout people down to gain their attention, all it succeeded in attracting was their hair, with its static. Gurgeh saw one apex try to push the machine out of his way, and receive an obviously unexpected and painful electric shock.

Pequil shoved his way through the crowd and bustled up to Gurgeh, but instead of coming to rescue the man, he told him he'd brought another twenty reporters with him. He touched Gurgeh without seeming to think about it, turning him to face some cameras.

More questions followed, but Gurgeh ignored them. He had to ask Pequil several times if he could leave before the apex had a path cleared to the door and the waiting car.

"Mr. Gurgee; let me add my congratulations," Pequil said in the car. "I heard while I was in the office and came straight away. A famous victory."

"Thank you," Gurgeh said, slowly calming himself. He sat in the car's plushly upholstered seat, looking out at the sunlit city. The car was air-conditioned, unlike the game-hall, but it was only now Gurgeh found himself sweating. He shivered.

"Me too," Flere-Imsaho said. "You raised your game just in time."

"Thank you, drone."

"You were lucky as hell, too, mind you."

"I trust you'll let me arrange a proper press-conference, Mr. Gurgee," Pequil said eagerly. "I'm sure you're going to be quite famous after this, no matter what happens during the rest of the match. Heavens, you'll be sharing leaders with the Emperor himself tonight!"

"No thanks," Gurgeh said. "Don't arrange anything." He couldn't think that he'd have anything useful to tell people. What was there to say? He'd won the game; he'd every chance of taking the match itself. He was anyway a little uncomfortable at the thought of his image and voice being broadcast all over the Empire, and his story, undoubtedly sensationalized, being told and retold and distorted by these people.

"Oh, but you must!" Pequil protested. "Everybody will want to see you! You don't seem to realize what you've done; even if you lose the match you've established a new record! *Nobody* has ever come back from being so far behind! It was quite brilliant!"

"All the same," Gurgeh said, suddenly feeling very tired, "I don't want to be distracted. I have to concentrate. I have to rest."

"Well," Pequil said, looking crestfallen, "I see your point, but I warn you; you're making a mistake. People will want to hear what you've got to say, and our press always gives the people what they want, no matter what the difficulties. They'll just make it up. You'd be better off saying something yourself."

Gurgeh shook his head, looked out at the traffic on the boulevard. "If people want to lie about me that's a matter for their consciences. At least I don't have to talk to them. I really could not care less what they say."

Pequil looked at Gurgeh with an expression of astonishment, but said nothing. Flere-Imsaho made a chuckling noise over its constant hum.

* * *

Gurgeh talked it over with the ship. The *Limiting Factor* said that the game could probably have been won more elegantly, but what Gurgeh had done did represent one end of the spectrum of unlikely possibilities it had been going to sketch out the previous night. It congratulated him. He had played better than it had thought possible. It also asked him why he hadn't listened after it had told him it could see a way out.

"All I wanted to know was that there *was* a way out."

(Again the delay, the weight of time while his beamed words lanced beneath the matter-dimpled surface that was real space.)

"But I could have helped you," said the ship. "I thought it was a bad sign when you refused my aid. I began to think you had given up in your mind, if not on the board."

"I didn't want help, ship." He played with the Orbital bracelet, wondering absently if it portrayed any particular world, and if so, which. "I wanted hope."

"I see," the ship said, eventually.

"I wouldn't accept it," the drone said.

"You wouldn't accept what?" Gurgeh asked, looking up from a holo-displayed board.

"Za's invitation." The tiny machine floated closer; it had discarded its bulky disguise now they were back inside the module.

Gurgeh looked coldly at it. "I didn't notice it was addressed to you too." Shohobohaum Za had sent a message congratulating Gurgeh and inviting him out for an evening's entertainment.

"Well, it wasn't; but I'm supposed to monitor everything—"

"Are you really?" Gurgeh turned back to the holospread before him. "Well you can stay here and monitor whatever you like while I go out on the town with Shohobohaum Za tonight."

"You'll regret it," the drone told him. "You've been very sensible, staying in and not getting involved, but you'll suffer for it if you do start gallivanting."

"'Gallivanting'?" Gurgeh stared at the drone, realizing only then how difficult it was to look something up and down when it was just a few centimeters high. "What are you, drone; my mother?"

"I'm just trying to be sensible about this," the machine said, voice rising. "You're in a strange society, you're not the most worldly-wise of people, and Za certainly isn't my idea of—"

"You opinionated box of junk!" Gurgeh said loudly, rising and switching off the holoscreen.

The drone jumped in midair; it backed off hastily. "Now, now, Jernau Gurgeh . . ."

"Don't you 'Now, now' me, you patronizing adding machine. If I want to take an evening off, I will. And quite frankly the thought of some human company for a change is looking more attractive all the time." He jabbed a finger at the machine. "*Don't* read any more of my mail, and *don't* bother about escorting Za and me this evening." He walked quickly past it, heading for his cabin. "Now, I'm going to take a shower; why don't you go watch some birds?"

The man left the module's lounge. The little drone hovered steadily in midair for a while. "Oops," it said to itself, eventually, then, with a shrug-like wobble, swooped away, fields vaguely rosy.

"Have some of this," Za said. The car swept along the city streets beneath the erubescent skies of dusk.

Gurgeh took the flask and drank.

"Not quite *grif,*" Za told him, "but it does the job." He took the flask back while Gurgeh coughed a little. "Did you let that *grif* get to you at the ball?"

"No," Gurgeh admitted. "I bypassed it; wanted a clear head."

"Aw *heck,*" Za said, looking downcast. "You mean I could have had more?" He shrugged, brightened, tapped Gurgeh on the elbow. "Hey; I never said; congratulations. On winning the game."

"Thanks."

"That showed them. Wow, did you give them a shock." Za shook his head in admiration; his long brown hair swung across his loose tunic top like heavy smoke. "I had you filed as a prime-time loser, J-G, but you're some kind of showman." He winked one bright green eye at Gurgeh, and grinned.

Gurgeh looked uncertainly at Za's beaming face for a moment, then burst out laughing. He took the flask from Za's hand and put it to his lips.

"To the showmen," he said, and drank.

"Amen to that, my maestro."

The Hole had been on the outskirts of the city once, but now it was just another part of one more urban district. The Hole was a set of vast artificial caverns burrowed out of the chalk centuries ago to store natural gas in; the gas had long since run out, the city ran on other forms of energy, and the set of huge, linked caves had been colonized, first by Groasnachek's poor, then (by a slow process of osmosis and displacement, as though—gas or human—nothing ever really changed) by its criminals and outlaws, and finally, though not completely, by its effectively ghettoized aliens and their supporting cast of locals.

Gurgeh and Za's car drove into what had once been a massive above-ground gas-storage cylinder; it had become the housing for a pair of spiraling ramps taking cars and other vehicles down into and up out of the Hole. In the center of the still mostly empty, ringingly echoing cylinder, a cluster of variously sized lifts slid up and down inside ramshackle frameworks of girders, tubing and beams.

The outer and inner surfaces of the ancient gasometer sparkled slatily under rainbow lights and the flickeringly unreal, grotesquely oversize images of advertizing holos. People milled about the surface level of the cavernous tower, and the air was full of shouting, screaming, haggling voices and the sound of laboring engines. Gurgeh watched the crowds and the stalls and stands slide by as the car dipped and started its long descent. A strange, half-sweet, half-acrid smell seeped through the car's conditioning, like a sweaty breath from the place.

They quit the car in a long, low, crowded tunnel where the air was heavy with fumes and shouts. The gallery was choked with multifariously shaped and sized vehicles which rumbled and hissed and edged about among the swarmingly varied people like massive, clumsy animals wading in an insect sea. Za took Gurgeh by the hand as their car trundled toward the ascending ramp. They went bustling through the buffeting crowds of Azadians and other humanoids toward a limily-glowing tunnel mouth.

"What d'you think so far?" Za shouted back to Gurgeh.

"Crowded, isn't it?"

"You should see it on a holiday!"

Gurgeh looked round at the people. He felt ghostlike, invisible. Until now he'd been the center of attention; a freak, stared and gawped and peered at, and kept entirely at arm's length. Now suddenly nobody gave a damn, hardly sparing him a second glance. They bumped into him, jostled him, shoved past him, brushed against him, all quite careless.

And so varied, even in this sickly, sea-green tunnel light. So many different types of people mixed in with the Azadians he was becoming used to seeing; a few aliens that looked vaguely familiar from his memory of pan-human types, but mostly quite wildly different; he lost count of the variations in limbs, height, bulk, physiognomy and sensory apparatus he was confronted with during that short walk.

They went down the warm tunnel and into a huge, brightly lit cavern, at least eighty meters tall and half as broad again; lengthwise, its cream-colored walls stretched away in both directions for half a kilometer or more, ending in great side-lit arches leading to further galleries. Its flat floor was chock-a-block with shack-like buildings and tents, partitions and covered walkways, stalls and kiosks and small squares with dribbling fountains and gaily striped awnings. Lamps danced from wires strung on thin poles, and overhead brighter lights burned, high in the vaulted roof; a color between ivory and pewter. Structures of stepped buildings and wall- or roof-hung gantries lined the sides of the gallery, and whole areas of grimy gray wall were punctured by the irregular holes of windows, balconies, terraces and doors. Lifts and pulleys creaked and rattled, taking people to higher levels, or lowering them to the bustling floor.

"This way," Za said. They wove their way through the narrow streets of the gallery surface until they came to the far wall, climbed some broad but rickety wooden steps, and approached a heavy wooden door guarded by a metal portcullis and a pair of lumberingly large figures; one Azadian male and another whose species Gurgeh couldn't identify. Za waved and, without either guard appearing to do anything, the portcullis rose, the door swung ponderously open, and he and Za left the echoing cave behind for the relative quietness of a dim, wood-lined, heavily carpeted tunnel.

The cavern light closed off behind them; a hazy, cerise glow came through an arched ceiling of wafer-thin plaster. The polished wooden walls looked thick, were char-dark, and felt warm. Muffled music came from ahead.

Another door; a desk set into an alcove where two apices eyed them both sullenly, then consented to smile at Za, who passed over a small hide pouch to them. The door opened. He and Gurgeh went through to the light and music and noise beyond.

It was a jumble of a space; impossible to decide whether it was one confusingly subdivided, chaotically split-leveled hall, or a profusion of smaller rooms and galleries all knocked into one. The place was packed, and loud with high-pitched atonal music. It could have been on fire, judging from the thick haze of smoke filling it, but the fumes smelled sweet, almost perfumed.

Za guided Gurgeh through crowds to a wooden cupola raised a meter off a small covered walkway and looking out from the rear onto a sort of staggered stage beneath. The stage was surrounded by similar circular boxes as well as various stepped areas of seats and benches, all of which were crowded, mostly with Azadians.

On the small, roughly circular stage below, some dwarfish alien—only vaguely pan-human—was wrestling, or perhaps copulating, with an Azadian female in a quivering tub full of gently steaming red mud, all seemingly held in a low-G field. The spectators shouted and clapped and threw drinks.

"Oh good," Za said, sitting down. "The fun's started."

"Are they fucking or fighting?" Gurgeh said, leaning over

the rail and peering down at the struggling, heaving bodies of the alien and the female.

Za shrugged. "Does it matter?"

A waitress, an Azadian female wearing only a little cloth around her waist, took Za's drink order. The woman's puff-balled hair appeared to be on fire, surrounded by a flickering hologram of yellow-blue flames.

Gurgeh turned away from the stage. The audience behind him yelled appreciatively as the woman threw the alien off and jumped on top of him, throwing him under the steaming mud. "You come here often?" he asked Za.

The tall male laughed loudly. "No." The great green eyes flashed. "But I leave quite a lot."

"This where you relax?"

Za shook his head emphatically. "Absolutely not. Common misconception that; that fun is relaxing. If it is, you're not doing it right. That's what the Hole's for; fun. Fun and games. Cools down a bit during the day, but it can get pretty wild, too. The drink festivals are usually the worst. Shouldn't be any trouble tonight though. Fairly quiet."

The crowd shrieked; the woman was holding the dwarfish alien's face under the mud; it struggled desperately.

Gurgeh turned round to watch. The alien's movements weakened slowly as the naked, mud-slicked woman forced its head into the bubbling red liquid. Gurgeh glanced at Za. "So they were fighting."

Za shrugged again. "We may never know." He looked down too, as the woman forced the now limp alien's body further into the ochre mud.

"Has she killed it?" Gurgeh asked. He had to raise his voice as the crowd screamed, stamping feet and beating fists on tables.

"Na," Shohobohaum Za said, shaking his head. "The little

guy's a Uhnyrchal." Za nodded down, as the woman used one hand to keep the alien's head submerged, and raised the other in triumph in the air, glaring bright-eyed at the baying audience. "See that little black thing sticking up?"

Gurgeh looked. There was a little black bulb poking up through the surface of the red mud. "Yes."

"That's his dick."

Gurgeh looked suspiciously at the other man. "How exactly is that going to help him?"

"The Uhnyrchal can breathe through their dicks," Za said. "That guy's fine; he'll be fighting in another club tomorrow night; maybe even later this evening."

Za watched the waitress place their drinks on the table. He leaned forward to whisper something to her; she nodded and walked off. "Try glanding *Expand* with this stuff," Za suggested. Gurgeh nodded. They both drank.

"Wonder why the Culture's never genofixed that," Za said, staring into his glass.

"What?"

"Being able to breathe through your dick."

Gurgeh thought. "Sneezing at certain moments could be messy."

Za laughed. "There might be compensations."

The audience behind them went "Oooo." Za and Gurgeh turned round to see the victorious woman pulling her opponent's body up out of the mud by its penis; the alien being's head and feet were still under the glutinous, slowly slopping liquid. "Ouch," Za muttered, drinking.

Somebody in the crowd tossed the woman a dagger; she caught it, stooped, and sliced off the alien genitals. She brandished the dripping flesh aloft while the crowd went wild with delight and the alien sank slowly beneath the cloying red liquid, the woman's foot on its chest. The mud gradually turned black where the blood oozed, and a few bubbles surfaced.

Za sat back, looking mystified. "Must have been some sub-species I haven't heard of."

The low-G mud-tub was trundled away, the woman still shaking her trophy at the baying crowd.

Shohobohaum Za rose to greet a party of four dramatically beautiful and stunningly dressed Azadian females who were approaching the cupola. Gurgeh had glanded the body-drug Za had suggested, and was just beginning to feel the effects of both that and the liquor.

The women looked, he thought, quite the equals of any he'd seen the night of the welcoming ball, and much more friendly.

The acts went on; sex acts, mostly. Acts which, outside the Hole, Gurgeh was told by Za and two of the Azadian females (Inclate and At-sen, sitting on either side of him), would mean death for both participants; death by radiation or death by chemicals.

Gurgeh didn't pay too much attention. This was his night out and the staged obscenities were the least important part of it. He was away from the game; that was what mattered. Living by another set of rules. He knew why Za had had the women come to the table, and it amused him. He felt no particular desire for the two exquisite creatures he sat between—certainly nothing uncontrollable—but they made good company. Za was no fool, and the two charming females—Gurgeh knew they would have been males, or even apices had Za discovered Gurgeh's preferences lay in that direction—were both intelligent and witty.

They knew a little about the Culture, had heard rumors about the sexual alterations Culture people possessed, and made discreetly roguish jokes about Gurgeh's proclivities and abilities compared to their own, and to both the other Azadian genders. They were flattering, enticing and friendly; they drank from small glasses, they sipped smoke from tiny, slender pipes—Gurgeh had tried a pipe too, but only coughed, much to everyone's amusement—and they both had long, sinuously curling blue-black hair, silkily membraned with near-invisibly fine platinum nets and beaded with minute, glinting AG studs, which made their hair move in slow motion and gave each graceful movement of their delicately structured heads a dizzyingly unreal quality.

Inclate's slim dress was the ever-shifting color of oil on water, speckled with jewels which twinkled like stars; At-sen's was a video-dress, glowing fuzzy red with its own concealed power. A choker round her neck acted as a small television monitor, displaying a hazy, distorted image of the view around her—Gurgeh to one side, the stage behind, one of Za's ladies on the other side, the other directly across the table. Gurgeh showed her the Orbital bracelet, but she was not especially impressed.

Za, on the other side of the table, was playing small games of forfeit with his two giggling ladies, handling tiny, almost transparent slice-jewel-cards and laughing a lot. One of the ladies noted the forfeits down in a little notebook, with much giggling and feigned embarrassment.

"But Jernow!" At-sen said, from Gurgeh's left. "You must have a scar-portrait! So that we may remember you when you have gone back to the Culture and its decadent, many-orificed ladies!" Inclate, on his right, giggled.

"Certainly not," Gurgeh said, mock-serious. "It sounds quite barbaric."

"Oh yes, yes, it is!" At-sen and Inclate laughed into their

glasses. At-sen pulled herself together, put her hand on his wrist. "Wouldn't you like to think there was some poor person walking around on Eä with your face on their skin?"

"Yes, but on which bit?" Gurgeh asked.

They thought this hilariously funny.

Za stood; one of his ladies packed the tiny slivers of the game-cards away in a little chain purse. "Gurgeh," Za said, knocking back the last of his drink. "We're off for a more private chat; you three too?" Za grinned wickedly at Inclate and At-sen, producing gales of laughter and small shrieks. At-sen dipped her fingers in her drink and flicked some liquor at Za, who dodged.

"Yes, come, Jernow," Inclate said, taking hold of Gurgeh's arm with both hands. "Let's all go; the air is so stuffy here, and the noise so loud."

Gurgeh smiled, shook his head. "No; I'd only disappoint you."

"Oh no! No!" Slim fingers tugged at his sleeves, curled round his arms.

The politely mocking argument went on for some minutes, while Za stood, grinning, ladies draped on either side, looking on, and Inclate and At-sen tried their hardest either to physically lift Gurgeh to his feet, or, by pouting protestations, persuade him to move.

All failed. Za shrugged—his ladies imitated the alien gesture, before dissolving into laughter—and said, "Okay; just stay there, all right, game-player?"

Za looked at Inclate and At-sen, who were temporarily subdued and petulant. "You two look after him, right?" Za told them. "Don't let him talk to any strangers."

At-sen sniffed imperiously. "Your friend declines all; strange or familiar."

Inclate snorted despite herself. "Or both in one," she blurted.

Whereupon she and At-sen started laughing again and reaching behind Gurgeh to slap and pinch each other's shoulders.

Za shook his head. "Jernau; try and control those two as well as you control yourself."

Gurgeh ducked a few flicked drops of drink while the females squealed on either side of him. "I'll try," he told Za.

"Well," Za said, "I'll try not to be too long. Sure you won't join in? Could be quite an experience."

"I'm sure. But I'm fine here."

"Okay. Don't wander. See you soon." Za grinned at the giggling girls on either side of him, and then they turned together, walked away. "Ish!" Za shouted back over his shoulder. "Soon-*ish,* game-player!"

Gurgeh waved goodbye. Inclate and At-sen quietened fractionally and set about telling him what a naughty boy he was for not being more naughty. Gurgeh ordered more drinks and pipes to keep them quiet.

They showed him how to play the game of elements, chanting, "Blade cuts cloth, cloth wraps stone, stone dams water, water quenches fire, fire melts blade . . ." like serious schoolgirls, and showing him the appropriate hand-shapes, so that he could learn.

It was a truncated, two-dimensional version of the elemental die-matching from the Board of Becoming, minus Air and Life. Gurgeh found it amusing that even in the Hole he could not escape the influence of Azad. He played the simple game because the ladies wanted to, and he took care not to win too many hands . . . something, he realized, he had never done before in his life.

Still puzzling over this anomaly, he went to the toilets, of which there were four different types. He used the Aliens, but took some time to find the right piece of equipment. He was still chortling over this when he came out, to find Inclate standing outside the sphincter-like doorway. She looked worried; the oil-film dress rippled dully.

"What's wrong?" he asked her.

"At-sen," she said, kneading her little hands together. "Her ex-master came; took her away. He wants to have her again or it will be a tenth-year since they are one, and she will be free." She looked up at Gurgeh, small face contorted, distressed. The blue-black hair washed round her face like a slow and fluid shadow. "I know Sho-Za said you must not move, but will you? This is not your concern, but she's my friend . . ."

"What can I do?" Gurgeh said.

"Come; we two may distract him. I think I know where he's taken her. I shall not endanger you, Jernow." She took his hand.

They half walked, half ran down twisting wooden corridors, past many rooms and doors. He was lost in a maze of sensation; a welter of sounds (music, laughter, screams), sights (servants, erotic pictures, glimpsed galleries of packed, swaying bodies) and smells (food, perfume, alien sweats).

Suddenly, Inclate stopped. They were in a deep, bowled room like a theater, where a naked human male stood on stage, turning slowly, this way and that, in front of a giant screen showing a close-up of his skin. Deep, booming music played. Inclate stood looking round the packed auditorium, still holding Gurgeh's hand.

Gurgeh glanced at the man on stage. The lights were bright, sunlight spectraed. The slightly plump, pale-skinned male had several enormous, multicolored bruises—like huge prints—on his body. Those on his back and chest were largest, and showed Azadian faces. The mixture of blacks, blues, purples, greens, yellows and reds combined to form portraits of uncanny accuracy and subtlety, which the flexings of the man's muscles seemed to make live, exactly as though those faces took on new expressions with each moment. Gurgeh looked, and felt his breath draw in.

"There!" Inclate shouted over the pulsing music, and tugged at his hand. They set off through the crowding people, toward where At-sen stood, near the front of the stage. She was being held by an apex who was pointing at the man on the stage and shouting at her, shaking her. At-sen's head was down, her shoulders quivered as if she was crying. The video-dress was turned off; it hung on her, gray and drab and lifeless. The apex hit At-sen across the head (the slow black hair twisted languidly), and shouted at her again. She fell to her knees; the beaded hair followed her as if she was sinking slowly under water. Nobody around the couple took any notice. Inclate strode toward them, pulling Gurgeh after her.

The apex saw them coming, tried to drag At-sen away. Inclate started to shout at the apex; she held up Gurgeh's hand as they pushed people aside, drew closer. The apex looked suddenly fearful; he stumbled away, dragging At-sen with him to an exit beneath the raised stage.

Inclate started forward, but her way was blocked by a cluster of large Azadian males, standing staring open-mouthed at the man on the stage. Inclate beat at their backs with her fists. Gurgeh watched At-sen disappear, dragged through the door beneath the stage. He pulled Inclate to one side and used his greater mass and strength to force a way between two of the protesting males; he and the girl ran to the swinging door.

The corridor curved sharply. They followed the sounds of screams, down some narrow stairs, over a step where the broken monitor-collar lay, snapped and dead, down to a quiet corridor where the light was jade and there were many doors. At-sen was lying on the floor, the apex above her, screaming at her. He saw Gurgeh and Inclate, shook his fist at them. Inclate screamed incoherently at him.

Gurgeh started forward; the apex took a gun from a pocket.

Gurgeh stopped. Inclate went quiet. At-sen whimpered on the floor. The apex started talking, far too fast for Gurgeh to follow; he pointed at the woman on the floor, then gestured at the ceiling. He began to cry, and the gun shook in his hand (and part of Gurgeh, sitting back calmly analyzing, thought, *Am I frightened? Is this fear yet? I'm looking death in the face, staring at it through that little black hole, the little twisted tunnel in this alien's hand [like another element the hand can show], and I'm waiting to feel fear . . .*

*. . . and it hasn't happened yet. I'm still waiting. Does this mean that I shan't die now, or that I shall?*

*Life or death in a finger's twitch, a single nerve-pulse, just one perhaps not fully willed decision by some jealous irrelevant one-credit sick-head, a hundred millennia from home . . .*).

The apex backed away, gesturing imploringly, pathetically to At-sen, and at Gurgeh and Inclate. He came forward and kicked At-sen, once, in the back, with no great force, making her cry out, then turned and ran, shouting incoherently and throwing the gun down to the floor. Gurgeh ran after him, vaulting over At-sen. The apex disappeared down a dark spiral staircase at the far end of the curved passage. Gurgeh started to follow, then stopped. The sound of clattering footsteps died away. He went back to the jade-lit corridor.

A door was open; soft citrine light spilled out.

There was a short hall, a bathroom off, then the room. It was small, and mirrored everywhere; even the soft floor rippled with unsteady reflections the color of honey. He walked in, at the center of a vanishing army of reflected Gurgehs.

At-sen sat on a translucent bed, forlorn in her wrecked gray dress, head down and sobbing while Inclate, kneeling by her, arm round the crying woman's shoulders, whispered gently. Their images proliferated about the shining walls of the room. He hesitated, glanced back at the door. At-sen looked up at him, tears streaming.

"Oh, Jernow!" She held out one shaking hand. He squatted by the bedside, his arm round her as she quivered, while both women cried.

He stroked At-sen's back.

She put her head on his shoulder, and her lips were warm and strange on his neck; Inclate left the bed, padded to the door and closed it, then joined the man and the woman, dropping the oil-film dress to the mirror-floor in a glistening pool of iridescence.

Shohobohaum Za arrived a minute later, kicking the door in, walking smartly into the middle of the mirrored room (so that an infinitude of Zas repeated and repeated their way across that cheating space), and glared round, ignoring the three people on the bed.

Inclate and At-sen froze, hands at Gurgeh's clothing-ties and buttons. Gurgeh was momentarily shocked, then tried to assume an urbane expression. Za looked at the wall behind Gurgeh, who followed his gaze; he found himself looking at his own reflection; face dark, hair mussed, clothes half undone. Za leapt across the bed, kicking into the image.

The wall shattered in a chorus of screams; the mirror-glass cascaded to reveal a dark and shallow room behind, and a small machine on a tripod, pointing into the mirror-room. Inclate and At-sen sprang off the bed and raced out; Inclate grabbed her dress on the way.

Za took the tiny camera off its tripod and looked at it. "Record only, thank goodness; no transmitter." He stuffed the machine into a pocket, then turned and grinned at Gurgeh. "Put it back in the holster, game-player. We got to run!"

They ran. Down the jade passage toward the same spiral steps At-sen's abductor had taken. Za stooped as he ran, scooping up the gun the apex had dropped and Gurgeh had forgotten about. It was inspected, tried and discarded within a couple of seconds. They got to the spiral steps and leapt up them.

Another corridor, darkly russet. Music boomed above. Za skidded to a stop as two large apices ran toward them. "Oops," Za said, doing an about-turn. He shoved Gurgeh back to the stairs and they ran up again, coming out in a dark space full of the beating, pulsing music; light blazed to one side. Footsteps hammered up the stairs. Za turned and kicked down into the stairwell with one foot, producing an explosive yelp and a sudden clatter.

A thin blue beam freckled the darkness, lancing from the stairwell and bursting yellow flame and orange sparks somewhere overhead. Za dodged away. "Fucking artillery indeed." He nodded past Gurgeh toward the light. "Exit stage center, maestro."

They ran out onto the stage, flooded with sunlight brilliance. A bulky male in the center of the stage turned resentfully as they thundered out from the wings; the audience yelled abuse. Then the expression on the near-naked bruise artiste's face switched from vexation to stunned surprise.

Gurgeh almost fell; he did stop, dead still.

. . . to gaze, again, at his own face.

It was printed, twice life-size, in a bloody rainbow of contusions, on the torso of the dumbstruck performer. Gurgeh stared, expression mirroring the amazement on the tubby artiste's face.

"No time for art now, Jernau." Za pulled him away, dragged him to the front of the stage and threw him off. He dived after him.

They landed on top of a group of protesting Azadian males, tumbling them to the ground. Za hauled Gurgeh to his feet, then nearly fell again as a blow struck the back of his head. He turned and lashed out with one foot, fending off another punch with one arm. Gurgeh felt himself twirled round; he found himself facing a large, angry male with blood on his face. The man drew his arm back, made a fist of his hand (so that Gurgeh thought; *stone!* from the game of elements).

The man seemed to move very slowly.

Gurgeh had time to think what to do.

He brought his knee up into the male's groin and heel-palmed his face. He shook the falling man's grip free, ducked a blow from another male, and saw Za elbow yet another Azadian in the face.

Then they were sprinting away again. Za roared and waved his hands as he ran for an exit. Gurgeh fought a strange urge to laugh at this, but the tactic seemed to work; people parted for them like water round the bows of a boat.

They sat in a small, open-ceilinged bar, deep in the maze-like clutter of the main gallery, under a solid sky of chalky pearl. Shohobohaum Za was dismantling the camera he'd discovered behind the false mirror, teasing its delicate components apart with a humming, toothpick-size instrument. Gurgeh dabbed at a graze on his cheek, incurred when Za had thrown him from the stage.

"Na, my fault, game-player. I should have known. Inclate's brother's in Security, and At-sen's got an expensive habit. Nice kids, but a bad combination, and not exactly what I asked for. Damn lucky for your ass one of my sweeties dropped a slice-jewel-card and wouldn't play anything else without it. Ah well; half a fuck's better than none at all."

He prized another piece out of the camera body; there was a crackle and a little flash. Za poked dubiously at the smoking casing.

"How did you know where to find us?" Gurgeh asked. He felt like a fool, but less embarrassed than he'd have expected.

"Knowledge, guesswork and luck, game-player. There are places in that club you go when you want to roll somebody, other places where you can question them, or kill them, or hook them on something . . . or take their picture. I was just hoping it was lights-action time and not something worse." He shook his head, peered at the camera. "I should have known though. Ought to have guessed. Getting too damn trusting."

Gurgeh shrugged, sipped at his hot liquor and studied the guttering candle on the counter in front of them. "I was the one who was suckered. But who?" He looked at Za. "Why?"

"The state, Gurgeh," Za said, prodding at the camera again. "Because they want to have something on you, just in case."

"Just in case what?"

"Just in case you keep surprising them and winning games. It's insurance. You heard of that? No? Never mind. It's like gambling in reverse." Za held the camera with one hand, straining at part of it with the thin instrument. A hatch popped open. Za looked happy, and extracted a coin-sized disk from the guts of the machine. He held it up to the light, where it glinted nacreously. "Your holiday snaps," Za told Gurgeh.

He adjusted something at the end of the toothpick, so that the little disk stuck to the instrument's point as though glued there, then held the tiny polychromatic coin over the candle flame until it sizzled and smoked and hissed, and finally fell in dull flakes onto the wax.

"Sorry you couldn't have that as a souvenir," Za said.

Gurgeh shook his head. "Something I'd rather forget."

"Ah, never mind. I'll get those two bitches though," Za grinned. "They owe me one for free. Several, in fact." Za looked happy at the thought.

"Is that all?" Gurgeh asked.

"Hey; they were just playing their parts. No malice involved. Worth a spanking at most." Za waggled his eyebrows lasciviously.

Gurgeh sighed.

When they went back to the transit gallery to order their car, Za waved at some bulky, severely casual males and apices waiting in the lime-lit tunnel, and tossed one of them what was left of the camera. The apex caught it, and turned away along with the others.

The car arrived minutes later.

"And what time do you call this? Do you know how long I've been waiting for you? You've got a game to play tomorrow, you know. Just *look* at the state of your clothes! And *where* did you pick up that graze? What have you—"

"Machine." Gurgeh yawned, throwing his jacket down onto a seat in the lounge. "Go fuck yourself."

The following morning, Flere-Imsaho wasn't talking to him. It joined him in the module lounge just as the call came through that Pequil had arrived with the car, but when Gurgeh said hello, it ignored him, and traveled down in the hotel elevator studiously humming and crackling even louder than usual. It was similarly uncommunicative in the car. Gurgeh decided he could live with this.

"Gurgee, you have hurt yourself." Pequil looked with concern at the graze over Gurgeh's cheek.

"Yes," Gurgeh smiled, stroking his beard. "I cut myself shaving."

It was attrition time on the Board of Form.

Gurgeh was up against the other nine players from the start, until it became too obvious that was what was happening. He'd used the advantage accrued on the previous board to set up a small, dense and almost impregnable enclave; he just sat in there for two days, letting the others beat up against it. Done properly, this would have broken him, but his opponents were trying not to look too concerted in their actions, so attacked a few at a time. They were anyway each fearful of weakening themselves over-much in case they were pounced upon by the others.

By the end of those two days, a couple of the news-agencies were saying it was unfair and discourteous to the stranger to gang up on him.

Flere-Imsaho—over its huff by then and talking to him again—reckoned this reaction might be genuine and unprompted, but was more likely to be the result of imperial pressure. Certainly it thought the Church—which had doubtless been instructing the priest as well as financing the deals he'd been making with the other players—had been leaned on by the Imperial Office. Whatever, on the third day the massed attacks against Gurgeh fell away and the game resumed a more normal course.

The game-hall was crowded with people. There were many more paying spectators, numerous invited guests had changed venue to come and see the alien play, and the press-agencies had sent extra reporters and cameras. The club players, under the stewardship of the Adjudicator, succeeded in keeping the crowd quiet, so Gurgeh didn't find the extra people caused any great distraction during the game. It was difficult to move around the hall during the breaks though; people were constantly accosting him, asking him questions, or just wanting to look at him.

Pequil was there most of the time, but seemed more taken up with going in front of the cameras himself than shielding Gurgeh from all the people wanting to talk to him. At least he helped to divert the attentions of the news-people and let Gurgeh concentrate on the game.

Over the next couple of days, Gurgeh noticed a subtle change in the way the priest was playing, and, to a lesser degree, in the game-style of another two players.

Gurgeh had taken three players right out of the game; another three had been taken by the priest, without much of a fight. The remaining two apices had established their own small enclaves on the board and were taking comparatively little part in the wider game. Gurgeh was playing well, if not at quite the pitch he had when he'd won on the Board of Origin. He ought to be defeating the priest and the other two fairly easily. He was, indeed, gradually prevailing, but very slowly. The priest was playing better than he had before, especially at the beginning of each session, which made Gurgeh think that the apex was getting some high-grade help during the breaks. The same applied to the other two players, though they were presumably being less extensively briefed.

When the end came, though, on the fifth day of the game,

it was sudden, and the priest's play simply collapsed. The other two players resigned. More adulation followed, and the news-agencies began to run editorials worrying that somebody from Outside could do so well. Some of the more sensational releases even carried stories that the alien from the Culture was using some sort of supernatural sense or illegal technical device. They'd found out Flere-Imsaho's name and mentioned it as the possible source of Gurgeh's illicit skill.

"They're calling me a *computer,*" the drone wailed.

"And they're calling me a cheat," Gurgeh said, thoughtfully. "Life is cruel, as they keep saying here."

"*Here* they are correct."

The last game, on the Board of Becoming, the one Gurgeh felt most at home on, was a romp. The priest had filed a special objective plan with the Adjudicator before the game commenced, something he was entitled to do as the player with the second largest number of points. He was effectively playing for second place; although he would be out of the Main Series, he would have a chance to re-enter it if he won his next two games in the second series.

Gurgeh suspected this was a ruse, and played very cautiously at first, waiting for either the mass attack or some cunning individual set-piece. But the others seemed to be playing almost aimlessly, and even the priest seemed to be making the sort of slightly mechanical moves he'd been making in the first game. When Gurgeh made a few light, exploratory attacks, he found little opposition. He divided his forces in half and went on a full-scale raid into the territory of the priest, just for the sheer hell of it. The priest panicked and hardly made one good move after that; by the end of the session he was in danger of being wiped out.

After the break Gurgeh was attacked by all the others, while the priest struggled, pinned against one edge of the board. Gurgeh took the hint. He gave the priest room to maneuver and let him attack two of the weaker players to regain his position on the board. The game finished with Gurgeh established over most of the board and the others either eradicated or confined to small, strategically irrelevant areas. Gurgeh had no particular interest in fighting the game out to the bitter end, and anyway guessed that if he tried to do so the others would form a united opposition, no matter how obvious it was they were working together; Gurgeh was being offered victory, but he would suffer if he tried to be greedy, or vindictive. The status quo was agreed; the game ended. The priest came second on points, just.

Pequil congratulated him again, outside the hall. He'd reached the second round of the Main Series; he was one of only twelve hundred First Winners and twice that number of Qualifiers. He would now play against one person in the second round. Again, the apex begged Gurgeh to give a news-conference, and again Gurgeh refused.

"But you must! What are you trying to do? If you don't say something soon you'll turn them against you; this enigmatic stuff won't do forever, you know. You're the underdog at the moment; don't lose that!"

"Pequil," Gurgeh said, fully aware he was insulting the apex by addressing him so, "I have no intention of speaking to anybody about my game, and what they choose to say or think about me is irrelevant. I am here to play the game and nothing else."

"You are our guest," Pequil said coldly.

"And you are my hosts." Gurgeh turned and walked away from the official, and the ride back in the car was completed in silence, save for Flere-Imsaho's humming, which occasionally sounded to Gurgeh as if it barely concealed a chuckling laugh.

"Now the trouble starts."

"Why do you say that, ship?" It was night. The rear doors of the module lay open. Gurgeh could hear the distant buzz of the police hoverplane stationed over the hotel to keep news-agency craft away; the smell of the city, warm and spicy and smoky, drifted in too. Gurgeh was studying a set-piece problem in a single game, and taking notes. This seemed to be the best way of talking to the *Limiting Factor* with the time-delay; talk, then switch off and consider the problem while the HS light flashed to and fro; then, when the reply came, switch back to speech mode; it was almost like having a real conversation.

"Because now you have to show your moral cards. It's the single match, so you have to define your first principles, register your philosophical premises. Therefore you'll have to give them some of the things you believe in. I believe this could prove troublesome."

"Ship," Gurgeh said, writing some notes on a scratch tablet as he studied the holo in front of him, "I'm not sure I have any beliefs."

"I think you do, Jernau Gurgeh, and the Imperial Game Bureau will want to know what they are, for the record; I'm afraid you'll have to think of something."

"Why should I? What does it matter? I can't win any posts or ranks, I'm not going to gain any power out of this, so what difference does it make what I believe in? I know they need to find out what people in power think, but I just want to play the game."

"Yes, but they will need to know for their statistics. Your

views may not matter a jot in terms of the elective properties of the game, but they do need to keep a record of what sort of player wins what sort of match . . . besides which, they will be interested in what sort of extremist politics you give credence to."

Gurgeh looked at the screen camera. "Extremist politics? What are you talking about?"

"Jernau Gurgeh," the machine said, making a sighing noise, "a guilty system recognizes no innocents. As with any power apparatus which thinks everybody's either for it or against it, we're against it. You would be too, if you thought about it. The very way you think places you among its enemies. This might not be your fault, because every society imposes some of its values on those raised within it, but the point is that some societies try to maximize that effect, and some try to minimize it. You come from one of the latter and you're being asked to explain yourself to one of the former. Prevarication will be more difficult than you might imagine; neutrality is probably impossible. You cannot choose not to have the politics you do; they are not some separate set of entities somehow detachable from the rest of your being; they are a function of your existence. I know that and they know that; you had better accept it."

Gurgeh thought about this. "Can I lie?"

"I shall take it you mean, would you be advised to register false premises, rather than, are you capable of telling untruths." (Gurgeh shook his head.) "This would probably be the wisest course. Though you may find it difficult to come up with something acceptable to them which you didn't find morally repugnant yourself."

Gurgeh looked back to the holo display. "Oh, you'd be surprised," he muttered. "Anyway, if I'm lying about it, how can I find it repugnant?"

"An interesting point; if one assumes that one is not morally opposed to lying in the first place, especially when it is largely or significantly what we term self-interested rather than disinterested or compassionate lying, then—"

Gurgeh stopped listening and studied the holo. He really must look up some of his opponent's previous games, once he knew who it would be.

He heard the ship stop talking. "Tell you what, ship," he said. "Why don't you think about it? You seem more engrossed in the whole idea than I do, and I'm busy enough anyway, so why don't you work out a compromise between truth and expediency we'll all be happy with, hmm? I'll agree to whatever you suggest, probably."

"Very well, Jernau Gurgeh. I'll be happy to do that."

Gurgeh bade the ship good night. He completed his study of the single-game problem, then switched the screen off. He stood and stretched, yawning. He strolled out of the module, into the orange-brown darkness of the hotel roof-garden. He almost bumped into a large, uniformed male.

The guard saluted—a gesture Gurgeh never did know how to reply to—and handed him a piece of paper. Gurgeh took it and thanked him; the guard went back to his station at the top of the roof-stairs.

Gurgeh walked back into the module, trying to read the note.

"Flere-Imsaho?" he called, uncertain whether the little machine was still around or not. It came floating through from another part of the module in its undisguised, quiet form, carrying a large, richly illustrated book on the avian fauna of Eä.

"Yes?"

"What does this say?" Gurgeh flourished the note.

The drone floated up to the piece of paper. "Minus the imperial embroidery, it says they'd like you to go to the palace tomorrow so they can add their congratulations. What it means is, they want to take a look at you."

"I suppose I have to go?"

"I would say so."

"Does it mention you?"

"No, but I'll come along anyway; they can only throw me out. What were you talking to the ship about?"

"It's going to register my Premises for me. It was also giving me a lecture on sociological conditioning."

"It means well," said the drone. "It just doesn't want to leave such a delicate task to someone like you."

"Just going out, were you, drone?" Gurgeh said, switching on the screen again and sitting down to watch it. He brought up the game-player's channel on the imperial waveband and flicked through to the draw for the single matches in the second round. Still no decision; the draw was still being decided; expected any minute.

"Well," Flere-Imsaho said, "There *is* a very interesting species of nocturnal fish-hunter that inhabits an estuary just a hundred kilometers from here, and I was thinking—"

"Don't let me keep you," Gurgeh said, just as the draw started to come through on the imperial game-channel; the screen started to fill with numbers and names.

"Right. I'll say good night, then." The drone floated away.

Gurgeh waved without looking round. "Good night," he said. He didn't hear whether the drone replied or not.

He found his place in the draw; his name appeared on the screen beside that of Lo Wescekibold Ram, governing director of the Imperial Monopolies Board. He was ranked as Level Five Main, which meant he was one of the sixty best game-players in the Empire.

* * *

The following day was Pequil's day off. An imperial aircraft was sent for Gurgeh and landed beside the module. Gurgeh and Flere-Imsaho—which had been rather late returning from its estuarial expedition—were taken out over the city to the palace. They landed on the roof of an impressive set of office buildings overlooking one of the small parks set within the palace grounds, and were led down wide, richly carpeted stairs to a high-ceilinged office where a male servant asked Gurgeh if he wanted anything to eat or drink. Gurgeh said no, and he and the drone were left alone.

Flere-Imsaho drifted over to the tall windows. Gurgeh looked at some portrait paintings hanging on the walls. After a short while, a youngish apex entered the room. He was tall, dressed in a relatively unfussy and businesslike version of the uniform of the Imperial Bureaucracy.

"Mr. Gurgeh; good day. I'm Lo Shav Olos."

"Hello," Gurgeh said. They exchanged polite nods, then the apex walked quickly to a large desk in front of the windows and set a bulky sheaf of papers down on it before sitting down.

Lo Shav Olos looked round at Flere-Imsaho, buzzing and hissing away nearby. "And this must be your little machine."

"Its name is Flere-Imsaho. It helps me with your language."

"Of course." The apex gestured to an ornate seat on the other side of his desk. "Please; sit down."

Gurgeh sat, and Flere-Imsaho came to float near him. The male servant returned with a crystal goblet and placed it on the desk near Olos, who drank before saying, "Not that you must need much help, Mr. Gurgeh." The young apex smiled. "Your Eächic is very good."

"Thank you."

"Let me add my personal congratulations to those of the Imperial Office, Mr. Gurgeh. You have done far better than many of us expected you to do. I understand you were learning the game only for about a third of one of our Great Years."

"Yes, but I found Azad so interesting I did little else during that time. And it does share concepts with other games I've studied in the past."

"Nevertheless, you've beaten people who've been learning the game all their lives. The priest Lin Goforiev Tounse was expected to do well in these games."

"So I saw," Gurgeh smiled. "Perhaps I was lucky."

The apex gave a little laugh, and sat back in his chair. "Perhaps you were, Mr. Gurgeh. I'm sorry to see your luck didn't extend to cover the draw for the next round. Lo Wescekibold Ram is a formidable player, and many expect him to better his previous performance."

"I hope I can give him a good game."

"So do we all." The apex drank from his goblet again, then got up and went to the windows behind him, looking out over the park. He scratched at the thick glass, as though there was a speck on it. "While not, strictly speaking, my province, I confess I'd be interested if you could tell me a little about your plans for the registration of Premises." He turned and looked at Gurgeh.

"I haven't decided quite how to express them yet," Gurgeh said. "I'll register them tomorrow, probably."

The apex nodded thoughtfully. He pulled at one sleeve of the imperial uniform. "I wonder if I might advise you to be . . . somewhat circumspect, Mr. Gurgeh?" (Gurgeh asked the drone to translate "circumspect." Olos waited, then continued.) "Of course you must register with the Bureau, but as you know, your participation in these games is in a purely honorary capacity, and so exactly what you say in your Premises has only . . . statistical value, shall we say?"

Gurgeh asked the drone to translate "capacity."

"Garbleness, game-playeroid," Flere-Imsaho muttered darkly in Marain. "Twiddly-dee; you that word *capacity* beforely usedish Eächic in. Placey-wacey's buggy-wuggied. Stoppy-toppy deez guys spladdiblledey-dey-da more cluettes on da lingo offering, righty?"

Gurgeh suppressed a smile. Olos went on. "As a rule, contestants must be prepared to defend their views with arguments, should the Bureau find it necessary to challenge any of them, but I hope you will understand that this will hardly be likely to happen to you. The Imperial Bureau is not blind to the fact that the . . . values of your society may be quite different from our own. We have no wish to embarrass you by forcing you to reveal things the press and the majority of our citizens might find . . . offensive." He smiled. "Personally, off the record, I would imagine that you could be quite . . . oh, one might almost say 'vague' . . . and nobody would be especially bothered."

" 'Especially'?" Gurgeh said innocently to the humming, crackling drone at his side.

"More gibberish biltrivnik ner plin ferds, you're quontstipilish trying nomonomo wertsishi my zozlik zibbidik dik fucking patience, Gurgeh."

Gurgeh coughed loudly. "Excuse me," he said to Olos. "Yes. I see. I'll bear that in mind when I draw up my Premises."

"I'm glad, Mr. Gurgeh," Olos said, coming back to his chair and sitting again. "What I've said is my personal view, of course, and I have no links with the Imperial Bureau; this office is quite independent of that body. Nevertheless, one of the great strengths of the Empire is its cohesion, its . . . unity, and I doubt that I could be very wide of the mark in judging what the attitude of another imperial department might be." Lo Shav Olos smiled indulgently. "We really do all pull together."

"I understand," Gurgeh said.

"I'm sure you do. Tell me; are you looking forward to your trip to Echronedal?"

"Very much so, especially as the honor is extended so rarely to guest players."

"Indeed." Olos looked amused. "Few guests are ever allowed onto the Fire Planet. It is a holy place, as well as being itself a symbol of the everlasting nature of the Empire and the Game."

"My gratitude extends beyond the limits of my capacity to express it," Gurgeh purred, with the hint of a bow. Flere-Imsaho made a spluttering noise.

Olos smiled broadly. "I feel quite certain that having established yourself as being so proficient—indeed gifted—at our game, you will prove yourself to be more than worthy of your place in the game-castle on Echronedal. Now," the apex said, glancing at his desk-screen, "I see it is time for me to attend yet another doubtless insufferably tedious meeting of the Trade Council. I'd far prefer to continue our own exchange, Mr. Gurgeh, but unhappily it must be curtailed in the interests of the efficiently regulated exchange of goods between our many worlds."

"I fully understand," Gurgeh said, standing at the same time as the apex.

"I'm pleased to have met you, Mr. Gurgeh," Olos smiled.

"And I you."

"Let me wish you luck in your game against Lo Wescekibold

Ram," the apex said as he walked to the door with Gurgeh. "I'm afraid you will need it. I'm sure it will be an interesting game."

"I hope so," Gurgeh said. They left the room. Olos offered his hand; Gurgeh clasped it, allowing himself to look a little surprised.

"Good day, Mr. Gurgeh."

"Goodbye."

Then Gurgeh and Flere-Imsaho were escorted back to the aircraft on the roof while Lo Shav Olos strode off down another corridor to his meeting.

"You asshole, Gurgeh!" the drone said in Marain as soon as they were back in the module. "First you ask me two words you already know, and then you use *both* of them and the—"

Gurgeh was shaking his head by this time, and interrupted. "You really don't understand very much about game-playing, do you, drone?"

"I know when people are playing the fool."

"Better than playing a household pet, machine."

The machine made a noise like an indrawn breath, then seemed to hesitate and said, "Well, anyway . . . at least you don't have to worry about your Premises now." It gave a rather forced-sounding chuckle. "They're as frightened of you telling the truth as you are!"

Gurgeh's game against Lo Wescekibold Ram attracted great attention. The press, fascinated by this odd alien who refused to speak to them, sent their most acerbic reporters, and the camera operators best able to catch any fleeting facial expression which would make the subject look ugly, stupid or cruel (and preferably all three at once). Gurgeh's off-world physiognomy was regarded as a challenge by some camera people, and as a large fish in a small barrel by others.

Numerous paying game-fans had traded tickets for other games so they could watch this one, and the guests' gallery could have been filled many times over, even though the venue had been changed from the original hall Gurgeh had played in before to a large marquee erected in a park only a couple of kilometers from both the Grand Hotel and the Imperial Palace. The marquee held three times as many people as the old hall, and was still crowded.

Pequil had arrived as usual in the Alien Affairs Bureau car in the morning, and taken Gurgeh to the park. The apex no longer tried to put himself in front of the cameras, but busily hurried them out of the way to clear a path for Gurgeh.

Gurgeh was introduced to Lo Wescekibold Ram. He was a short, bulky apex with a more rugged face than Gurgeh had expected and a military bearing.

Ram played quick, incisive lesser games, and they finished two on the first day, ending about even. Gurgeh only realized how hard he'd been concentrating that evening when he fell asleep watching the screen. He slept for almost six hours.

The next day they played another two of the lesser games, but the play extended, by agreement, into the evening session; Gurgeh felt the apex was testing him, trying to wear him out, or at least see what the limits of his endurance were; they would be playing all six of the lesser games before the three main boards, and Gurgeh already knew he was under much more strain playing Ram alone than he'd been competing against nine others.

After a great struggle, almost to midnight, Gurgeh finished fractionally ahead. He slept seven hours and woke up just in time to get ready for the next day's play. He forced himself awake, glanding the Culture's favorite breakfast drug, *Snap,* and was a little disappointed to see Ram looked just as fresh and energetic as he felt.

That game became another war of attrition, dragging through the afternoon, and Ram didn't suggest playing into the evening. Gurgeh spent a couple of hours discussing the game with the ship during the evening, then, to wash it from his mind, watched the Empire's broadcast channels for a while.

There were adventure programs and quizzes and comedies, news-stations and documentaries. He looked for reports on his own game. He was mentioned, but the day's rather dull play didn't merit much space. He could see that the agencies were becoming less and less well-disposed to him, and he wondered if they now regretted standing up for him when he'd been ganged up on during the first match.

Over the next five days the news-stations became even less happy with "Alien Gurgey" (Eächic was phonetically less subtle than Marain, so his name was always going to be spelled incorrectly). He finished the lesser games about level with Ram, then beat him on the Board of Origin after being well down at one stage, and lost on the Board of Form only by the most slender of margins.

The news-agencies at once decided that Gurgeh was a menace to the Empire and the common good, and began a campaign to have him thrown off Eä. They claimed he was in telepathic touch with the *Limiting Factor,* or with the robot called Flere-Imsaho, that he used all manner of disgusting drugs which were kept in the vice den and drug emporium he lived in on the roof of the Grand Hotel, then—as though just discovering the fact—that he could make the drugs inside his own body (which was true) using glands ripped out of little children in appalling and fatal operations (which was not). The effect of these drugs seemed to be to turn him into either a super-computer or an alien sex-maniac (even both, in some reports).

One agency discovered Gurgeh's Premises, which the ship had drawn up and registered with the Games Bureau. These were held to be typically shifty and mealy-mouthed Culture double-talk; a recipe for anarchy and revolution. The agencies adopted hushed and reverent tones as they appealed loyally to the Emperor to "do something" about the Culture, and blamed the Admiralty for having known about this gang of slimy perverts for decades without, apparently, showing them who was boss, or just crushing them completely (one daring agency even went so far as to claim the Admiralty wasn't totally certain where the Culture's home planet was). They offered up prayers that Lo Wescekibold Ram would wipe the Alien Gurgey off the Board of Becoming as decisively as the Navy would one day dispose of the corrupt and socialistic Culture. They urged Ram to use the physical option if he had to; that would show what the namby-pamby Alien was made of (perhaps literally!).

"Is all this serious?" Gurgeh said, turning, amused, from the screen to the drone.

"Deadly serious," Flere-Imsaho told him.

Gurgeh laughed and shook his head. He thought the common people must be remarkably stupid if they believed all this nonsense.

After four days of the game on the Board of Becoming, Gurgeh was poised to win. He saw Ram talking worriedly with some of his advisors afterward, and half expected the apex to offer his resignation then, after the afternoon session. But Ram decided to fight on; they agreed to forgo the evening session and resume the next morning.

The big tent ruffled slightly in a warm breeze as Flere-Imsaho joined Gurgeh at the exit. Pequil supervised the way being cleared through the crowds outside to where the car was waiting. The crowd was composed mostly of people who just wanted to see the alien, though there were a few demonstrating noisily against Gurgeh, and an even smaller number who were cheering him. Ram and his advisors left the tent first.

"I think I see Shohobohaum Za in the crowd," the drone said as they waited at the exit. Ram's entourage was still cluttering the far end of the ribbon of path held clear by the two lines of policemen.

Gurgeh glanced at the machine, then down the line of arm-linked police. He was still tensed from the game, bloodstream suffused with multifarious chemicals. As happened every now and again, everything he saw around him seemed to be part of the game; the way people stood like pieces, grouped according to who could take or affect whom; the way the pattern on the marquee was like a simple grid-area on the board, and the poles like planted power-sources waiting to replenish some exhausted minor piece and supporting a crux-point in the game; the way the people and police stood like the suddenly closed jaws of some nightmarish pincer-movement . . . all was the game, everything was seen in its light, translated into the combative imagery of its language, evaluated in the context its structure imposed upon the mind.

"Za?" Gurgeh said. He looked in the direction the drone's field was pointing, but couldn't see the man.

The last of Ram's group cleared the pavement where the official cars waited. Pequil gestured for Gurgeh to proceed. They walked between the lines of uniformed males. Cameras pointed, questions were shouted. Some ragged chanting began and Gurgeh saw a banner waving over the heads of the crowd; "GO HOME ALIEN."

"Seems I'm not too popular," he said.

"You aren't," Flere-Imsaho told him.

In two steps (Gurgeh realized in a distant, game-sense way even as he was speaking and the drone was replying), he was going to be adjacent to . . . it took one more step to analyze the problem . . . something bad, something jarring and discordant . . . there was something . . . different; wrong about the three-group he was about to pass on his left; like unplaced ghost-pieces hiding in forest territory. . . . He had no idea exactly what was wrong with the group, but he knew immediately—as the protagonizing structures of the game-sense claimed precedence in his thoughts—that he wasn't going to risk putting a piece in *there.*

. . . Another half-step . . .

. . . to realize that the piece he didn't want to risk was himself.

He saw the three-group start to move and split up. He turned and ducked automatically; it was the obvious replying move of a threatened piece with too much momentum to stop or bound back from such an attacking force.

There were several loud bangs. The three-group of people burst toward him through the arms of two policemen, like a composite piece suddenly fragmenting. He converted his ducking motion into a dive and roll which he realized with some delight was the almost perfect physical equivalent to a trip-piece tying up a light-attacker. He felt a pair of legs thud into his side, not hard, then there was a weight on top of him and more loud noises. Something else fell on top of his legs.

It was like waking up.

He'd been attacked. There had been flashes, explosions, people launching themselves at him.

He struggled under the warm, animal weight on top of him, the one he'd tripped up. People were shouting; police moved quickly. He saw Pequil lying on the ground. Za was there too, standing looking rather confused. Somebody was screaming. No sign of Flere-Imsaho. Something warm was seeping into the hose he wore on his legs.

He struggled out from under the body lying on top of him, suddenly revolted by the thought that the person—apex or male, he couldn't tell—might be dead. Shohobohaum Za and a policeman helped him up. There was a lot of shouting still; people were moving or being moved back, clearing a space around whatever had happened; bodies lay on the ground, some covered in bright red-orange blood. Gurgeh got dizzily to his feet.

"All right, game-player?" Za asked, grinning.

"Yes, I think so," Gurgeh nodded. There was blood on his legs, but it was the wrong color to be his.

Flere-Imsaho descended from the sky. "Jernau Gurgeh! Are you all right?"

"Yes." Gurgeh looked around. "What happened?" he asked Shohobohaum Za. "Did you see what happened?" The police had drawn their guns and were clustered around the area; the people were moving away, the press-cameras were being forced back by shouting police. Five policemen were pinning somebody down on the grass. Two apices in civilian clothes lay on the path; the one Gurgeh had tripped was covered in blood. A policeman stood over each body; another two were tending to Pequil.

"Those three attacked you," Za said, eyes flicking around as he nodded at the two bodies and the figure under the pile of police. Gurgeh could hear somebody sobbing loudly, in what was left of the crowd. Reporters were still shouting questions.

Za guided Gurgeh over to where Pequil lay, while Flere-Imsaho fussed and hummed overhead. Pequil lay on his back, eyes open, blinking, while a policeman cut away the blood-soaked sleeve of his uniform jacket. "Old Pequil here got in the way of a bullet," Za said. "You all right, Pequil?" he shouted jovially.

Pequil smiled weakly and nodded.

"Meanwhile," Za said, putting his arm round Gurgeh's shoulders and looking round all the time, gaze darting everywhere, "your brave and resourceful drone here exceeded the speed of sound to get about twenty meters out of the way, upward."

"I was merely gaining height the better to ascertain wh—"

"You dropped," Za told Gurgeh, still without looking at him, "and rolled; I thought they'd got you, actually. I managed to knock one of these bods on the head and I think the police burned the other one." Za's gaze settled momentarily on the knot of people beyond the cordon of police, where the sobbing was coming from. "Somebody in the crowd got hit too; the bullets meant for you."

Gurgeh looked down at one of the dead apices; his head lay at right angles to his body, across his shoulder; it would have looked wrong on almost any humanoid. "Yeah, that's the one I hit," Za said, glancing briefly at the apex. "Bit too hard, I think."

"I repeat," Flere-Imsaho said, moving round in front of Gurgeh and Za, "I was merely gaining height in order to—"

"Yes, we're glad you're safe, drone," Za said, waving the buzzing bulk of the machine away like a large and cumbersome insect and guiding Gurgeh forward to where an apex in police uniform was gesturing toward the cars. Whooping noises sounded in the sky and the surrounding streets.

"Ah, here's the boys," Za said, as a wailing noise dopplered its way over the park, and a large orange-red airvan rushed out of the sky to land in a storm of dust on the grass nearby; the marquee fabric flapped and banged and rippled in the blast of air. More heavily armed police jumped out of the van.

There was some confusion about whether they ought to go to the cars or not; finally they were taken back into the marquee and statements were taken from them and some other witnesses; two cameras were confiscated from protesting news-people.

Outside, the two dead bodies and the wounded attacker were loaded onto the airvan. An air-ambulance arrived for Pequil, who was lightly wounded in the arm.

As Gurgeh, Za and the drone finally left the marquee to be taken back to the hotel in a police aircraft, a groundcar-ambulance was pulling in through the park gates to pick up the two males and a female also injured in the attack.

"Nice little module," Shohobohaum Za said, throwing himself into a formseat. Gurgeh sat down too. The noise of the departing policecraft echoed through the interior. Flere-Imsaho went quiet as soon as they got in and disappeared through to another part of the module.

Gurgeh ordered a drink from the module and asked Za if he would like anything. "Module," Za said, sprawling out over the seat and looking thoughtful, "I'd like a double standard measure of *staol* and chilled Shungusteriaung warp-wing liver wine bottoming a mouth of white Eflyre-Spin cruchen-spirit in a slush of medium cascalo, topped with roasted weirdberries and served in a number three strength Tipprawlic osmosis-bowl, or your best approximation thereof."

"Male or female warp-wing?" the module said.

"In this place?" Za laughed. "Hell; both."

"It will take some minutes."

"That is perfectly all right." Za rubbed his hands together and then looked at Gurgeh. "So, you survived; well done."

Gurgeh looked uncertain for an instant, then said, "Yes. Thanks."

"Think comparatively little of it." Za flapped one hand. "Quite enjoyed myself, actually. Just sorry I killed the guy."

"I wish I could take such a magnanimous view," Gurgeh said. "He was trying to kill me. And with bullets." Gurgeh found the idea of being hit by a bullet particularly horrible.

"Well," Za shrugged, "I'm not sure it makes much difference whether you're killed by a projectile or a CREW; you're just as dead. Anyway, I still feel sorry for those guys. Poor bastards were probably just doing their jobs."

"Their jobs?" Gurgeh said, mystified.

Za yawned and nodded, stretching out in the folds of the accommodating formseat. "Yeah; they'll be imperial secret police or Bureau Nine or something like that." He yawned again. "Oh, the story'll be they're disaffected civilians . . . though they *might* try to hang it on the revs . . . but that'd be a bit unlikely . . ." Za grinned, shrugged. "Na; they might try it anyway; just for a laugh."

Gurgeh thought. "No," he said finally. "I don't understand. You said these people were police. How—"

"*Secret* police, Jernau."

". . . But how can you have a secret policeman? I thought one of the points of having a uniform for the police was so that they could be easily identified and act as a deterrent."

"Good grief," Za said, covering his face with his hands. He put them down and gazed at Gurgeh. He took a deep breath.

"Right . . . well; the secret police are people who go about listening to what people say when they *aren't* being deterred by the sight of a uniform. Then if the person hasn't actually said anything illegal, but has said something they think is dangerous to the security of the Empire, they kidnap them and interrogate them and—as a rule—kill them. Sometimes they send them to a penal colony but usually they incinerate them or throw them down an old mineshaft; the atmosphere here's rich with revolutionary fervor, Jernau Gurgeh, and there are some rich seams of loose tongues beneath the city streets. They do other things as well, these secret police. What happened to you today was one of those other things."

Za sat back and made an expansive, shrugging gesture. "Or, on the other hand, I suppose it isn't impossible they really were revs, or disaffected citizens. Except that they moved all wrong. . . . But that's what secret police do, take it from me. Ah!"

A tray approached bearing a large bowl in a holder; vapor rose dramatically from the frothing, multicolored surface of the liquid. Za took the bowl.

"To the Empire!" he shouted, and drained it in one go. He slammed the bowl back onto the tray. "Haaa!" he exclaimed, sniffing and coughing and wiping his eyes with the sleeves of his tunic. He blinked at Gurgeh.

"Sorry if I'm being slow," Gurgeh said, "but if these people were imperial police, mustn't they have been acting on orders? What's going on? Does the Empire want me dead because I'm winning the game against Ram?"

"Hmm," Za said, coughing a little. "You're learning, Jernau Gurgeh. Shit, I thought a game-player would have a bit more . . . natural deviousness about him . . . you're a babe among the carnivores out here . . . anyway, yes, somebody in a position of power wants you dead."

"Think they'll try it again?"

Za shook his head. "Too obvious; they'd have to be pretty desperate to try something like that again . . . in the short term at least. I think they'll wait and see what happens in your next ten game, then if they can't ditch you in that they'll get your next single opponent to use the physical option on you and hope you'll scare off. If you get that far."

"Am I really such a threat to them?"

"Hey, Gurgeh; they realize now they've made a mistake. You didn't see the 'casts before you got here. They were saying you were *the* best player in the whole Culture and you were some sort of decadent slob, a hedonist who'd never worked a day in your life, that you were arrogant and totally convinced you were going to win the game, that you had all sorts of new glands sewn into your body, that you'd fucked your mother, men . . . animals for all I know, that you were half computer . . . then the Bureau saw some of your games you'd been playing on the way here, and announced—"

"What?" Gurgeh said, sitting forward. "What do you mean they'd seen some of the games I'd been playing?"

"They asked me for some recent games you'd played; I got in touch with the *Limiting Factor*—isn't that thing a bore?—and had it send me the moves in a couple of your recent games against it. The Bureau said on the strength of those they were more than happy to let you play using your drug-glands and everything else. . . . I'm sorry; I'd assumed the ship asked your permission first. Didn't it?"

"No," Gurgeh said.

"Well, anyway, they said you could play without restrictions. I don't think they really wanted to—purity of the game, you know?—but the orders must have been handed down. The Empire wanted to prove that even with your unfair advantages you still weren't capable of staying in the Main Series. Your first couple of days' play against that priest and his squaddies must have had them rubbing their little hands with glee, but then that out-of-the-hat stunt-win dropped their chins in their soup. Having you drawn against Ram in the single game probably seemed like a really good wheeze too, but now you're about to kick his latrine boards out from under him and they've panicked." Za hiccuped. "Hence the bungled splat-job today."

"So the draw against Ram wasn't really random, either?"

"God's balls, Gurgeh," Za laughed. "No, man! Holy shit! Are you really this naïve?" He sat shaking his head and looking at the floor and hiccuping every now and again.

Gurgeh stood up and went to the opened module doors. He looked out at the city, shimmering in the late evening haze. Long tower-shadows lay on it like widely spaced hairs on some near-bald pelt. Aircraft glinted sunset-red above it.

Gurgeh didn't think he'd ever felt so angry and frustrated in his life. Another uncomfortable feeling to add to those he'd been experiencing lately, feelings he'd put down to the game, and to really playing seriously for the first time.

Everybody seemed to be treating him like a child. They happily decided what he need and need not be told, they kept things back from him that he ought to have been told, and when they did tell him they acted as if he should have known all the time.

He looked back at Za, but the man was sitting rubbing his belly and looking distracted. He belched loudly, then smiled happily and shouted, "Hey, module! Put up channel ten! . . . yeah, on the screen; yo." He got up and trotted forward to stand right in front of the screen, and stood there, arms folded, whistling tunelessly and grinning vacantly at the moving pictures. Gurgeh watched from the side.

The news showed film of imperial troopers landing on a distant planet. Towns and cities burned, refugee lines snaked, bodies were shown. There were interviews with the tearful families of slain troopers. The just invaded locals—hairy quadrupeds with prehensile lips—were shown lying down tied up in the mud, or on their knees before a portrait of Nicosar. One was shorn, so the people back home could see what they looked like under all that fur. Their lips had become prized trophies.

The following story was about Nicosar demolishing his opponent in the single game. The Emperor was shown walking from one part of the board to another, signing some documents in an office, then from a distance, standing on the board again while a commentator enthused over the way he'd played.

The attack on Gurgeh was next. He was amazed when he saw the incident on film. It was over in an instant; a sudden leap, him falling, the drone disappearing upward, some flashes, Za springing forward out of the crowd, confusion and movement, then his face in close-up, a shot of Pequil on the ground, and another of the dead attackers. He was described as being dazed but unharmed, thanks to the prompt action of the police. Pequil was not seriously wounded; he was interviewed in hospital, explaining how he felt. The attackers were described as extremists.

"That means they might decide to call them revs later on," Za said. He told the screen to turn off, then turned to Gurgeh. "Didn't you think I was *quick* there, though?" he said, grinning widely and throwing his arms wide. "Did you see the way I moved? It was *beautiful!*" He laughed and spun round, then half walked, half danced to the formseat again, and fell into it. "Shit, I was only there to see what sort of loonies they had out protesting against you, but *wow* am I glad I went! What speed! Fucking animal grace, maestro!"

Gurgeh agreed Za had moved very quickly.

"Let's see it again, module!" Za shouted. The module-screen obliged, and Shohobohaum Za laughed and giggled as he watched the few seconds of action. He replayed it a few more times, in slow motion, clapping his hands, then called for another drink. The frothing bowl came quicker this time, the module's synthesizers having wisely kept the previous coding. Gurgeh sat down again, seeing that Za wasn't thinking of leaving just yet. Gurgeh ordered some snacks; Za snorted in derision when offered food, and crunched the roasted weirdberries that came with his foaming cocktail.

They watched imperial broadcasts while Za slurped slowly at his drink. Outside, one sun went down and the city lights sparkled in the half-light. Flere-Imsaho appeared without its disguise—Za took no notice of it—and announced it was on its way out, making yet another foray into the avian population of the planet.

"Don't think that thing fucks *birds,* d'you?" Za said after it had disappeared.

"No," Gurgeh said, drinking his light wine.

Za snorted. "Hey; you want to come out again some time? That visit to the Hole was a real hoot. I really enjoyed it in a weird sort of way. How about it? Except let's go totally wild this time; show these constipated bonebrains what Culture guys are like when they *really* put their minds to it."

"I don't think so," Gurgeh said. "Not after that last time."

"You mean you didn't *enjoy* it?" Za said, astonished.

"Not that much."

"But we had a great time! We got drunk, we got stoned, we got—well, *one* of us got laid, and you nearly did—we had a fight, which we *won,* dammit, and then we ran away . . . holy shit; what more do you want?"

"Not more, less. Anyway; I have other games to play."

"You're crazy; that was . . . a wonderful night out. Wonderful." He rested his head on the seat-back and breathed deeply.

"Za," Gurgeh said, sitting forward, chin in hand, elbow on knee, "why do you drink so much? You don't need to; you've got all the usual glands. Why?"

"Why?" Za said, his head coming upright again; he looked round as though startled to see where he was for a moment. "Why?" he repeated. He hiccuped. "You ask me 'Why?'" he said.

Gurgeh nodded.

Za scratched under one armpit, shook his head and looked apologetic. "What was the question again?"

"Why do you drink so much?" Gurgeh smiled tolerantly.

"Why not?" Za's arms flapped once. "I mean, have you never done something just . . . just *because?* I mean . . . it's um . . . empathy. This is what the locals do, y'know. This is their way out; this is how they escape their place in the glorious imperial machine . . . and a fucking grand position it is to appreciate its finer points from too . . . it all makes sense, y'know, Gurgeh; I worked it out." Za nodded wisely, tapped the side of his head very slowly with one limp finger. "Worked it out," he repeated. "Think about it; the Culture's all its . . ." The same finger made a twirling motion in the air. ". . . built-in glands; hundreds of secretions and thousands of effects, any combination you like and all for free . . . but the Empire, ah ha!" The finger pointed upward. "In the Empire you got to pay; escape is a commodity like anything else. And it's this stuff; drink. Lowers the reaction time, makes the tears come easier . . ." Za put two swaying fingers to his cheeks. ". . . makes the fists come easier . . ." Now his hands were clenched, and he pretended to box; jabbing. ". . . and . . ." He shrugged.

". . . it eventually kills you." He looked more or less at Gurgeh. "See?" He spread his arms wide again and then let them fall back limply on the seat. "Besides," he said, in a suddenly weary voice. "I *don't* have all the usual glands."

Gurgeh looked up in surprise. "You don't?"

"Nup. Too dangerous. The Empire would disappear me and do the most thorough PM you ever seen. Want to find out what a *Culturnik*'s like inside, see?" Za closed his eyes. "Had to have almost everything taken out, and then . . . when I got here, let the Empire do all sorts of tests and take all sorts of samples . . . let them find out what they wanted without causing a diplomatic incident, disappearing an ambassador . . ."

"I see. I'm sorry." Gurgeh didn't know what else to say. He honestly hadn't realized. "So all those drugs you were advising me to gland . . ."

"Guesswork, and memory," Za said, eyes still shut. "Just trying to be friendly."

Gurgeh felt embarrassed, almost ashamed.

Za's head went back and he started to snore.

Then suddenly his eyes opened and he jumped up. "Well, must be toddling," he said, making what looked like a supreme effort to pull himself together. He stood swaying in front of Gurgeh. "D'you think you could call me an aircab?"

Gurgeh did that. A few minutes later, after receiving clearance from Gurgeh via the guards on the roof, the machine arrived and took Shohobohaum Za away, singing.

Gurgeh sat for a little while as the evening wore on and the second sun set, then he finally dictated a letter to Chamlis Amalk-ney, thanking the old drone for the Orbital bracelet, which he still wore. He copied most of the letter to Yay, too, and told them both what had happened to him since he'd arrived. He didn't bother to disguise the game he was playing or the Empire itself, and wondered how much of this truth would actually get through to his friends. Then he studied some problems on the screen and talked over the next day's play with the ship.

He picked up Shohobohaum Za's discarded bowl at one point, discovering there were still a few mouthfuls of drink left inside. He sniffed it, then shook his head, and told a tray to tidy the debris up.

Gurgeh finished Lo Wescekibold Ram off the next day with what the press described as "contempt." Pequil was there, looking little the worse for wear save for a sling bandage on his arm. He said he was glad Gurgeh had escaped injury. Gurgeh told him how sorry he was Pequil had been hurt at all.

They went to and returned from the game-tent in an aircraft; the Imperial Office had decided Gurgeh was at too much risk traveling on the ground.

When he got back to the module again, Gurgeh discovered he was to have no interval between that game and the next; the Games Bureau had couriered a letter to say his next ten game would start the following morning.

"I'd have preferred a break," Gurgeh confessed to the drone. He was having a float-shower, hanging in the middle of the AG chamber while the water sprayed from various directions and was sucked away through tiny holes all over the semi-spherical interior. Membrane plugs prevented the water from going into his nose, but speaking was still a little spluttery.

"No doubt you would," Flere-Imsaho said in its squeaky voice. "But they're trying to wear you out. And of course it also means you'll be playing against some of the best players, the ones who've also managed to finish their games quickly."

"That had occurred to me," Gurgeh said. He could only just

see the drone through the spray and steam. He wondered what would happen if somehow the machine hadn't been made quite perfectly and some water got into it. He turned lazily head over heels in the shifting currents of air and water.

"You could always appeal to the Bureau. I think it's obvious you're being discriminated against."

"So do I. So do they. So what?"

"It might do some good to make an appeal."

"You make it then."

"Don't be stupid; you know they ignore me."

Gurgeh started humming to himself, eyes closed.

One of his opponents in the ten game was the same priest he'd beaten in the first one, Lin Goforiev Tounse; he'd won through his second-string games to rejoin the Main Series. Gurgeh looked at the priest when the apex entered the hall of the entertainment complex where they'd be playing, and smiled. It was an Azadian facial gesture he'd found himself practicing occasionally, unconsciously, rather like a baby attempts to imitate the expressions on the faces of the adults around it. Suddenly it seemed like the right time to use it. He would never get it quite right, he knew—his face simply wasn't built quite the same as an Azadian's—but he could imitate the signal well enough for it to be unambiguous.

Translated or not, though, Gurgeh knew it was a smile that said, "Remember me? I've beaten you once and I'm looking forward to doing it again"; a smile of self-satisfaction, of victory, of superiority. The priest tried to smile back with the same signal, but it was unconvincing, and soon turned to a scowl. He looked away.

Gurgeh's spirits soared. Elation filled him, burning bright inside. He had to force himself to calm down.

The other eight players had all, like Gurgeh, won their matches. Three were Admiralty or Navy men, one was an Army colonel, one a judge and the other three were bureaucrats. All were very good players.

At this third stage in the Main Series the contestants played a mini-tournament of one-against-one lesser games, and Gurgeh thought this would provide his best chance of surviving the match; on the main boards he was likely to face some sort of concerted action, but in the single games he had a chance of building up enough of an advantage to weather such storms.

He found himself taking great pleasure in beating Tounse, the priest. The apex swept his arm across the board after Gurgeh's winning move, and stood up and started shouting and waving his fist at him, raving about drugs and heathens. Once, Gurgeh was aware, such a reaction would have brought him out in a cold sweat, or at the very least left him dreadfully embarrassed. But now he found himself just sitting back and smiling coldly.

Still, as the priest ranted at him, he thought the apex might be about to hit him, and his heart did beat a little faster . . . but Tounse stopped in mid-flow, looked round the hushed, shocked people in the room, seemed to realize where he was, and fled.

Gurgeh let out a breath, relaxed his face. The imperial Adjudicator came over and apologized on the priest's behalf.

Flere-Imsaho was still popularly thought to be providing some sort of in-game aid to Gurgeh. The Bureau said that, to allay uninformed suspicions of this sort, they would like the machine to be held in the offices of an imperial computer company on the other side of the city during each session. The drone had protested noisily, but Gurgeh readily agreed.

He was still attracting large crowds to his games. A few came to glare and hiss, until they were escorted off the premises by game-officials, but mostly they just wanted to see the play. The entertainment complex had facilities for diagrammatic representations of the main boards so that people outside the main hall could follow the proceedings, and some of Gurgeh's sessions were even shown in live broadcasts, when they didn't clash with the Emperor's.

After the priest, Gurgeh played two of the bureaucrats and the colonel, winning all his games, though by a slender margin against the Army man. These games took a total of five days to play, and Gurgeh concentrated hard for all that time. He'd expected to feel worn out at the end; he did feel slightly drained, but the primary sensation was one of jubilation. He'd done well enough to have at least a chance of beating the nine people the Empire had set against him, and far from appreciating the rest, he found he was actually impatient for the others to finish their minor games so that the contest on the main boards could begin.

"It's all very well for you, but I'm being kept in a monitoring chamber all day! A monitoring chamber; I ask you! These meatbrains are trying to *probe* me! Beautiful weather outside and a major migratory season just starting, but I'm locked up with a shower of heinous sentientophiles trying to *violate* me!"

"Sorry, drone, but what can I do? You know they're just looking for an excuse to throw me out. If you want, I'll make a request you're allowed to stay here in the module instead, but I doubt they'll let you."

"I don't have to do this you know, Jernau Gurgeh; I can do what I like. If I wanted to I could just refuse to go. I'm not yours—or theirs—to be ordered around."

"I know that but they don't. Of course you can do as you please . . . whatever you see fit."

Gurgeh turned away from the drone and back to the module-screen, where he was studying some classic ten games. Flere-Imsaho was gray with frustration. The normal green-yellow aura it displayed when out of its disguise had been growing increasingly pale over the past few days. Gurgeh almost felt sorry for it.

"Well . . ." Flere-Imsaho whined—and Gurgeh got the impression that had it had a real mouth it would have spluttered, too—"it's just not good enough!" And with that rather lame remark, the drone whirled out of the lounge.

Gurgeh wondered just how badly the drone felt about being imprisoned all day. It had occurred to him recently that the machine might even have been instructed to stop him from getting too far in the games. If so, then refusing to be detained would be an acceptable way of doing it; Contact could justifiably claim that asking the drone to give up its freedom was an unreasonable request, and one it had every right to turn down. Gurgeh shrugged to himself; there was nothing he could do about it.

He switched to another old game.

Ten days later it was over, and Gurgeh was through to the fourth round; he had only one more opponent to beat and then he would be going to Echronedal for the final matches, not as an observer or guest, but as a contestant.

He'd built up the lead he'd hoped for in the lesser games, and in the main boards had not even tried to mount any great offensives. He'd waited for the others to come to him, and they had, but he was counting on them not being so willing to cooperate with each other as the players in the first match. These were important people; they had their own careers to think about, and however loyal they might be to the Empire, they had to look after their own interests as well. Only the priest had relatively little to lose, and so might be prepared to sacrifice himself for the imperial good and whatever not game-keyed post the Church could find for him.

In the game outside the game, Gurgeh thought the Games Bureau had made a mistake in pitching him against the first ten people to qualify. It appeared to make sense because it gave him no respite, but, as it turned out, he didn't need any, and the tactic meant that his opponents were from different branches of the imperial tree, and thus harder to tempt with departmental inducements, as well as being less likely to know each other's game-styles.

He'd also discovered something called inter-service rivalry—he'd found records of some old games that didn't seem to make sense until the ship described this odd phenomenon—and made special efforts to get the Admiralty men and the colonel at each other's throats. They'd needed little prompting.

It was a workmanlike match; uninspiring but functional, and he simply played better than any of the others. His winning margin wasn't great, but it was a win. One of the Fleet vice-admirals came second. Tounse, the priest, finished last.

Again, the Bureau's supposedly random scheduling gave him as little time as possible between matches, but Gurgeh was secretly pleased at this; it meant he could keep the same high pitch of concentration going from day to day, and it gave him no time to worry or stop too long to think. Somewhere, at the back of his mind, a part of him was sitting back as stunned and amazed as anybody else was at how well he was doing. If that part ever came forward, ever took center-stage and was allowed to say, "Now wait a minute here . . ." he suspected his nerve would fail, the spell would break, and the walk that was a fall would become a plunge into defeat. As the adage said; falling never killed anybody; it was when you stopped . . .

Anyway, he was awash with a bittersweet flood of new and enhanced emotions; the terror of risk and possible defeat, the sheer exultation of the gamble that paid off and the campaign which triumphed; the horror of suddenly seeing a weakness in his position which could lose him the game; the surge of relief when nobody else noticed and there was time to plug the gap; the pulse of furious, gloating glee when he saw such a weakness in another's game; and the sheer unbridled joy of victory.

And outside, the additional satisfaction of knowing that he was doing so much better than anybody had expected. All their predictions—the Culture's, the Empire's, the ship's, the drone's—had been wrong; apparently strong fortifications which had fallen to him. Even his own expectations had been exceeded, and if he worried at all, he worried that some subconscious mechanism would now let him relax a little, having proved so much, come so far, defeated so many. He didn't want that; he wanted to keep going; he was enjoying all this. He wanted to find the measure of himself through this infinitely exploitable, indefinitely demanding game, and he didn't want some weak, frightened part of himself to let him down. He didn't want the Empire to use some unfair way of getting rid of him, either. But even that was only half a worry. Let them try to kill him; he had a reckless feeling of invincibility now. Just don't let them try to disqualify him on some technicality. That would hurt.

But there was another way they might try to stop him. He knew that in the single game they would be likely to use the physical option. It was how they'd think; this Culture man would not accept the bet, he'd be too frightened. Even if he did accept, and fought on, the terror of knowing what might happen to him would paralyze him, devour and defeat him from inside.

He talked it over with the ship. The *Limiting Factor* had consulted with the *Little Rascal* then—tens of millennia distant, in the greater Cloud—and felt able to guarantee his survival. The old warship would stay outside the Empire but power up to a maximum velocity, minimum radius holding circle as soon as the game started. If Gurgeh was forced to bet against a physical option, and lost, the ship would drive in at full speed for Eä. It was certain it could evade any imperial craft on the way, get to Eä within a few hours and use its heavy-duty displacer to snap Gurgeh and Flere-Imsaho off the place without even slowing down.

"What's this?" Gurgeh looked dubiously at the tiny spherical pellet Flere-Imsaho had produced.

"Beacon and one-off communicator," the drone told him. It dropped the tiny pellet into his hand, where it rolled around. "You put it under your tongue; it'll implant; you'll never know it's there. The ship homes in on that as it comes in, if it can't find you any other way. When you feel a series of sharp pains under your tongue—four stabs in two seconds—you've got two seconds to assume a fetal position before everything within a three-quarter-meter radius of that pellet gets slung aboard the ship; so get your head between knees and don't swing your arms about."

Gurgeh looked at the pellet. It was about two millimeters across. "Are you serious, drone?"

"Profoundly. That ship'll probably be on sprint boost; it could be dragging past here at anything up to one-twenty kilolights. At that speed even its heavy-duty displacer will only be within range for about a fifth of a millisecond, so we're going to need all the help we can get. This is a very dubious situation you're putting me and yourself in, Gurgeh. I want you to know I'm not very happy about it."

"Don't worry, drone; I'll make sure they don't include you in the physical bet."

"No; I mean the possibility of being displaced. It's risky. I wasn't told about this. Displacement fields in hyperspace are singularities, subject to the Uncertainty Principle—"

"Yeah; you might end up getting zapped into another dimension or something—"

"Or smeared over the wrong bit of this one, more to the point."

"And how often does that happen?"

"Well, about once in eighty-three million displacements, but that's not—"

"So it still compares pretty favorably with the risk you take getting into one of this gang's groundcars, or even an aircraft. Be a rascal, Flere-Imsaho; risk it."

"That's all very well for you to say, but even if—"

Gurgeh let the machine witter on.

He'd risk it. The ship, if it did have to come in, would take a few hours to make the journey, but death-bets were never carried out until the next dawn, and Gurgeh was perfectly capable of switching off the pain of any tortures involved. The *Limiting Factor* had full medical facilities; it would be able to patch him up, if the worst happened.

He popped the pellet under his tongue; there was a sensation of numbness for a second, then it was gone, as though dissolved. He could just feel it with his finger, under the floor of his mouth.

He woke on the morning of the first day's play with an almost sexual thrill of anticipation.

Another venue; this time it was a conference-center near the shuttleport he'd first arrived at. There he faced Lo Prinest Bermoiya, a judge in the Supreme Court of Eä, and one of the most impressive apices Gurgeh had yet seen. He was tall, silver-haired, and he moved with a grace Gurgeh found oddly, even disturbingly familiar, without at first being able to explain why. Then he realized the elderly judge walked like somebody from the Culture; there was a slow ease about the apex's movements which lately Gurgeh had stopped taking for granted and so, for the first time in a way, seen.

Bermoiya sat very still between moves in the lesser games, staring at the board continually and only ever moving to shift a piece. His card-playing was equally studied and deliberate, and Gurgeh found himself reacting in the opposite manner, becoming nervous and fidgety. He fought back against this with body-drugs, deliberately calming himself, and over the seven full days the lesser games lasted gradually got to grips with the steady, considered pace of the apex's style. The judge finished a little ahead after the games were totaled up. There had been no mention of bets of any sort.

They started play on the Board of Origin, and at first Gurgeh thought the Empire was going to be content to rely on Bermoiya's obvious skill at Azad . . . but then, an hour into the game, the silver-haired apex raised his hand for the Adjudicator to approach.

Together they came to Gurgeh, standing at one corner of the board. Bermoiya bowed. "Jernow Gurgey," he said; the voice was deep, and Gurgeh seemed to hear a whole tome of authority within each bass syllable. "I must request that we engage in a wager of the body. Are you willing to consider this?"

Gurgeh looked into the large, calm eyes. He felt his own gaze falter; he looked down. He was reminded momentarily of the girl at the ball. He looked back up . . . to the same steady pressure from that wise and learned face.

This was someone used to sentencing his fellow creatures to execution, disfigurement, pain and prison; an apex who dealt in torture and mutilation and the power to command their use and even that of death itself to preserve the Empire and its values.

*And I could just say "No,"* Gurgeh thought. *I've done enough. Nobody would blame me. Why not? Why not accept they're better at this than I am? Why put yourself through the worry and the torment? Psychological torment at least, physical perhaps. You've proved all you had to, all you wanted, more than they expected.*

*Give in. Don't be a fool. You're not the heroic sort. Apply a bit of game-sense: you've won all you ever needed to. Back out now and show them what you think of their stupid "physical option," their squalid, bullying threats . . . show them how little it really means.*

But he wasn't going to. He looked levelly into the apex's eyes and he knew he was going to keep playing. He suspected he was going slightly mad, but he wasn't going to give this up. He would take this fabulous, maniacal game by the scruff of the neck, jump up onto it and hold on.

And see how far it would take him before it threw him off, or turned and consumed him.

"I'm willing," he said, eyes wide.

"I believe you are a male."

"Yes," Gurgeh said. His palms started to sweat.

"My bet is castration. Removal of the male member and testes against apicial gelding, on this one game on the Board of Origin. Do you accept?"

"I—" Gurgeh swallowed, but his mouth stayed dry. It was absurd; he was in no real danger. The *Limiting Factor* would rescue him; or he could just go through with it; he would feel no pain, and genitalia were some of the faster regrowing parts of the body . . . but still the room seemed to warp and distort in front of him, and he had a sudden, sickening vision of cloying red liquid, slowly staining black, bubbling. . . . "Yes!" he blurted, forcing it out. "Yes," he said to the Adjudicator.

The two apices bowed and retreated.

"You could call the ship now if you want," Flere-Imsaho said. Gurgeh stared at the screen. In fact he was going to call the *Limiting Factor,* but only to discuss his present rather poor position in the game, not to scream for rescue. He ignored the drone.

It was night, and the day had gone badly for him. Bermoiya had played brilliantly and the news-services were full of the game. It was being hailed as a classic, and once again Gurgeh—with Bermoiya—was sharing news-leaders with Nicosar, who was still trampling all over the opposition, good though it was acknowledged to be.

Pequil, his arm still pinned up, approached Gurgeh in a subdued, almost reverent way after the evening session and told him there was a special watch being kept on the module which would last until the game was over. Pequil was sure Gurgeh was an honorable person, but those engaging in physical bets were always discreetly watched, and in Gurgeh's case this was being done by a high-atmosphere AG cruiser, one of a squadron which constantly patrolled the not-quite-space above Groasnachek. The module would not be allowed to move from its position on the hotel roof-garden.

Gurgeh wondered how Bermoiya was feeling now. He had noticed that the apex had said "must" when he stated his intention of using the physical option. Gurgeh had come to respect the apex's style of play, and, therefore, Bermoiya himself. He doubted the judge had any great desire to use the option, but the situation had grown serious for the Empire; it had assumed he'd be beaten by now, and based its strategy of exaggerating the threat he posed to them on that assumption. This supposedly winning play was turning into a small disaster. Rumors were that heads had already rolled in the Imperial Office over the affair. Bermoiya would have been given his orders; Gurgeh had to be stopped.

Gurgeh had checked on the fate the apex would suffer in the now unlikely event it was he and not Gurgeh who lost. Apicial gelding meant the full and permanent removal of the reversible apex vagina and ovaries. Thinking about that, considering what would be done to the steady, stately judge if he lost, Gurgeh realized he hadn't properly thought through the implications of the physical option. Even if he did win, how could he let another being be mutilated? If Bermoiya lost, it would be the end of him; career, family, everything. The Empire did not allow the regeneration or replacement of any wager-lost body parts; the judge's loss would be permanent and possibly fatal; suicide was not unknown in such cases. Perhaps it would be best if Gurgeh did lose.

The trouble was he didn't *want* to. He didn't feel any personal animosity toward Bermoiya, but he desperately wanted to win this game, and the next one, and the one after that. He hadn't realized how seductive Azad was when played in its home environment. While it was technically the same game he'd played on the *Limiting Factor,* the whole feeling he had about it, playing it where it was meant to be played, was utterly different; now he realized . . . now he *knew* why the Empire had survived because of the game; Azad itself simply produced an insatiable desire for more victories, more power, more territory, more dominance . . .

Flere-Imsaho stayed in the module that evening. Gurgeh contacted the ship and discussed his forlorn position in the game; the ship could, as usual, see some unlikely ways out, but they were ways he'd already seen for himself. Recognizing they were there was one thing though; following them through on the board itself in the midst of play was another matter. So the ship was no great help there.

Gurgeh gave up analyzing the game and asked the *Limiting Factor* what he could do about ameliorating the bet he had with Bermoiya if—unlikely though it was—he won, and it was the judge who had to face the surgeon. The answer was nothing. The bet was on and that was it. Neither of them could do anything; they had to play to a finish. If they both refused to play then they would both suffer the bet-penalties.

"Jernau Gurgeh," the ship said, sounding hesitant. "I need to know what you would like me to do, if things go badly tomorrow."

Gurgeh looked down. He'd been waiting for this. "You mean, do I want you to come in and snatch me off here, or go through with it and be picked up later, with my tail but not much else between my legs, and wait for everything to regrow? But of course having kept the Culture sweet with the Empire in the process." He didn't try to disguise the sarcasm in his voice.

"More or less," the ship said, after the delay. "The problem is, while it would cause less of a fuss if you did go through with it, I'll have to displace or destroy your genitals anyway, if they are removed; the Empire would have access to rather too much information about us, if they did a full analysis."

Gurgeh almost laughed. "You're saying my balls are some sort of state secret?"

"Effectively. So we're going to annoy the Empire anyway, even if you do let them operate on you."

Gurgeh was still thinking, even after the delayed signal arrived. He curled his tongue in his mouth, feeling the tiny lump under the soft tissue. "Ah, fuck it," he said, eventually. "Watch the game; if I've definitely lost, I'll try and hold out for as long as possible; somewhere, anywhere. When I'm obviously doing that, come in; zap us off here and make my apologies to Contact. If I just cave in . . . let it happen. I'll see how I feel tomorrow."

"Very well," the ship said, while Gurgeh sat stroking his beard, thinking that, if nothing else, he'd been given the choice. But if they hadn't been going to remove the evidence and possibly cause a diplomatic incident anyway, would Contact have been so accommodating? It didn't matter. But he knew in his heart, after that conversation, he'd lost the will to win.

The ship had more news. It had just received a signal from Chamlis Amalk-ney, promising a longer message soon, but for the meantime just letting him know that Olz Hap had finally done it; she'd achieved a Full Web. A Culture player had—at last—produced the ultimate Stricken result. The young lady was the toast of Chiark and the Culture game-players. Chamlis had already congratulated her on Gurgeh's behalf, but expected he'd want to send her a signal of his own. It wished him well.

Gurgeh switched the screen off and sat back. He sat and

stared at the blank space for a while, unsure what to know, or think, or remember, or even be. A sad smile touched one side of his face, for a while.

Flere-Imsaho floated over to his shoulder.

"Jernau Gurgeh. Are you tired?"

He turned to it eventually. "What? Yes; a little." He stood up, stretched. "Doubt I'll sleep much, though."

"I thought that might be the case. I wondered if you would like to come with me."

"What, to look at birds? I don't think so, drone. Thanks anyway."

"I wasn't thinking of our feathered friends, actually. I have not always gone to watch them when I've gone out at nights. Sometimes I went to different parts of the city; to look for whatever species of birds might be there, at first, but later because . . . well; because."

Gurgeh frowned. "Why do you want me to come with you?"

"Because we might be leaving here rather quickly tomorrow, and it occurred to me that you've seen very little of the city."

Gurgeh waved one hand. "Za showed me quite enough of that."

"I doubt he showed you what I'm thinking of. There are many different things to see."

"I'm not interested in seeing the sights, drone."

"The sights I'm thinking of will interest you."

"Would they now?"

"I believe so. I think I know you well enough to tell. Please come, Jernau Gurgeh. You'll be glad, I swear. Please come. You did say you wouldn't sleep, didn't you? Well then, what do you have to lose?" The drone's fields were their normal green-yellow color, quiet and controlled. Its voice was low, serious.

The man's eyes narrowed. "What are you up to, drone?"

"Please, please come with me, Gurgeh." The drone floated off toward the nose of the module. Gurgeh stood, watching it. It stopped by the door from the lounge. "Please, Jernau Gurgeh. I swear you won't regret this."

Gurgeh shrugged. "Yeah, yeah, all right." He shook his head. "Let's go out to play," he muttered to himself.

He followed the drone as it moved toward the module nose. There was a compartment there with a couple of AG bikes, a few floater harnesses and some other pieces of equipment.

"Put on a harness, please. I won't be a moment." The drone left Gurgeh to fasten the AG harness on over his shorts and shirt. It reappeared shortly afterward holding a long, black, hooded cloak. "Now put this on, please."

Gurgeh put the cloak on over the harness. Flere-Imsaho shoved the hood up over his head and tied it so that Gurgeh's face was hidden from the sides and in deep shadow from the front. The harness didn't show beneath the thick material. The lights in the compartment dimmed and went out, and Gurgeh heard something move overhead. He looked up to see a square of dim stars directly above him.

"I'll control your harness, if that's all right with you," the drone whispered. Gurgeh nodded.

He was lifted quickly into the darkness. He did not dip again as he'd expected, but kept going up into the fragrant warmth of the city night. The cloak fluttered quietly around him; the city was a swirl of lights, a seemingly never-ending plain of scattered radiance. The drone was a small, still shadow by his shoulder.

They set out over the city. They overflew roads and rivers and great buildings and domes, ribbons and clumps and towers of light, areas of vapor drifting over darkness and fire, rearing towers where reflections burned and lights soared, quivering stretches of dark water and broad dark parks of grass and trees. Finally they started to drop.

They landed in an area where there were relatively few lights, dropping between two darkened, windowless buildings. His feet touched down in the dirt of an alley.

"Excuse me," the drone said, and nudged its way into the hood until it was floating up-ended by Gurgeh's left ear. "Walk down here," it whispered. Gurgeh walked down the alley. He tripped over something soft, and knew before he turned it was a body. He looked closer at the bundle of rags, which moved a little. The person was curled up under tattered blankets, head on a filthy sack. He couldn't tell what sex it was; the rags offered no clue.

"Ssh," the drone said as he opened his mouth to speak. "That is just one of the loafers Pequil was talking about; somebody shifted off the land. He's been drinking; that's part of the smell. The rest is him." It was only then that Gurgeh caught the stench rising from the still sleeping male. He almost gagged.

"Leave him," Flere-Imsaho said.

They left the alley. Gurgeh had to step over another two sleeping people. The street they found themselves on was dim and stank of something Gurgeh suspected was supposed to be food. A few people were walking about. "Stoop a little," the drone said. "You'll pass for a Minan disciple dressed like this, but don't let the hood fall, and don't stand upright."

Gurgeh did as he was told.

As he walked up the street, under the dim, grainy, flickering light of sporadic, monochrome streetlamps, he passed what looked like another drunk, lying against a wall. There was blood between the apex's legs, and a dark, dried stream of it leading from his head. Gurgeh stopped.

"Don't bother," came the little voice. "He's dying. Probably been in a fight. The police don't come here too often. And nobody's likely to call for medical aid; he's obviously been robbed, so they'd have to pay for the treatment themselves."

Gurgeh looked round, but there was nobody else nearby. The apex's eyelids fluttered briefly, as though he was trying to open them.

The fluttering stopped.

"There," Flere-Imsaho said quietly.

Gurgeh continued up the street. Screams came from high up in a grimy housing block on the far side of the street. "Just some apex beating up his woman. You know for millennia females were thought to have no effect on the heredity of the children they bore? They've known for five hundred years that they do; a viral DNA analogue which alters the genes a woman's impregnated with. Nevertheless, under the law females are simply possessions. The penalty for murdering a woman is a year's hard labor, for an apex. A female who kills an apex is tortured to death over a period of days. Death by Chemicals. Said to be one of the worst. Keep walking."

They came to an intersection with a busier street. A male stood on the corner, shouting in a dialect Gurgeh didn't understand. "He's selling tickets for an execution," the drone said. Gurgeh raised his eyebrows, turned his head fractionally. "I'm serious," Flere-Imsaho said. Gurgeh shook his head all the same.

Filling the middle of the street was a crowd of people. The traffic—only about half of it powered, the rest human-driven—was forced to mount the pavements. Gurgeh went to the back of the crowd, thinking that with his greater height he would be able to see what was happening, but he found people making way for him anyway, drawing him closer to the center of the crowd.

Several young apices were attacking an old male lying on the ground. The apices wore some sort of strange uniform, though somehow Gurgeh knew it was not an official uniform. They kicked the old male with a sort of poised savagery, as though the attack was some kind of competitive ballet of pain, and they were being evaluated on artistic impression as well as the raw torment and physical injury inflicted.

"In case you think this is staged in any way," Flere-Imsaho whispered, "it isn't. These people aren't paying anything to watch this, either. This is simply an old guy getting beaten up, probably just for the sake of it, and these people would rather watch than do anything to stop it."

As the drone spoke, Gurgeh realized he was at the front of the crowd. Two of the young apices looked up at him.

In a detached way, Gurgeh wondered what would happen now. The two apices shouted at him, then they turned and pointed him out to the others. There were six of them. They all stood—ignoring the whimpering male on the ground behind them—and looked steadily at Gurgeh. One of them, the tallest, undid something in the tight, metallically decorated trousers he wore and hooked out the half-flaccid vagina in its turned-out position, and, with a wide smile, first held it out to Gurgeh, then turned round waving it at the others in the crowd.

Nothing more. The young, identically clad apices grinned at the people for a while, then just walked away; each stepped, as though accidentally, on the head of the crumpled old male on the ground.

The crowd started to drift off. The old man lay on the roadway, covered in blood. A sliver of gray bone poked through the arm of the tattered coat he wore, and there were teeth scattered on the road surface near his head. One leg lay oddly, the foot turned outward, slack looking.

He moaned. Gurgeh started forward and began to stoop.

"Do *not* touch him!"

The drone's voice stopped Gurgeh like a brick wall. "If any of these people see your hands or face, you're dead. You're the wrong color, Gurgeh. Listen; a few hundred dark-skinned babies are still born each year, as the genes work themselves out. They're supposed to be strangled and their bodies presented to the Eugenics Council for a bounty, but a few people risk death and bring them up, blanching their skins as they grow older. If anybody thought you were one, especially in a disciple's cloak, they'd skin you alive."

Gurgeh backed off, kept his head down, and stumbled off down the road.

The drone pointed out prostitutes—mostly females—who sold their sexual favors to apices for a few minutes, or hours, or for the night. In some parts of the city, the drone said as they traveled the dark streets, there were apices who had lost limbs and could not afford grafted arms and legs amputated from criminals; these apices hired their bodies to males.

Gurgeh saw many cripples. They sat on street corners, selling trinkets, playing music on scratchy, squeaky instruments, or just begging. Some were blind, some had no arms, some had no legs. Gurgeh looked at the damaged people and felt dizzy; the gritty surface of the street beneath him seemed to tip and heave. For a moment it was as though the city, the planet, the whole Empire swirled around him in a frantic spinning tangle of nightmare shapes; a constellation of suffering and anguish, an infernal dance of agony and mutilation.

They passed garish shops full of brightly colored rubbish, state-run drug and alcohol stores, stalls selling religious statues, books, artifacts and ceremonial paraphernalia, kiosks vending tickets for executions, amputations, tortures and staged rapes—mostly lost Azad body-bets—and hawkers selling lottery tickets, brothel introductions and unlicensed drugs. A groundvan passed full of police; the nightly patrol. A few of the hawkers scuttled into alleyways and a couple of kiosks slammed suddenly shut as the van drove by, but opened again immediately afterward.

In a tiny park, they found an apex with two bedraggled males and a sick-looking female on long leads. He was making them attempt tricks, which they kept getting wrong; a crowd stood round laughing at their antics. The drone told him the trio were almost certainly mad, and had nobody to pay for their stay in mental hospital, so they'd been de-citizenized and sold to the apex. They watched the pathetic, bedraggled creatures trying to climb lampposts or form a pyramid for a while, then Gurgeh turned away. The drone told him one in ten of the people he passed on the street would be treated for mental illness at some point in their lives. The figure was higher for males than for apices, and higher for females than either. The same applied to the rates of suicide, which was illegal.

Flere-Imsaho directed him to a hospital. It was typical, the drone said. Like the whole area, it was about average for the greater city. The hospital was run by a charity, and many of the people working there were unpaid. The drone told him everybody would assume he was a disciple there to see one of his flock, but anyway the staff were too busy to stop and quiz everybody they saw in the place. Gurgeh walked through the hospital in a daze.

There were people with limbs missing, as he'd seen in the streets, and there were people turned odd colors or covered with scabs and sores. Some were stick-thin; gray skin stretched over bone. Others lay gasping for breath, or retching noisily behind thin screens, moaning or mumbling or screaming. He saw people still covered in blood waiting to be attended to, people doubled up coughing blood into little bowls, and others strapped into metal cots, beating their heads on the sides, saliva frothing over their lips.

Everywhere there were people; on bed after bed and cot after cot and mattress after mattress, and everywhere, too, there were the enveloping odors of corrupting flesh, harsh disinfectant and bodily wastes.

It was an average-bad night, the drone informed him. The hospital was a little more crowded than usual because several ships of the Empire's war-wounded had come back recently from famous victories. Also, it was the night when people got paid and didn't have to work the next day, and so by tradition went out to get drunk and into fights. Then the machine started to reel off infant-mortality rates and life-expectancy figures, sex ratios, types of diseases and their prevalence in the various strata of society, average incomes, the incidence of unemployment, per capita income as a ratio of total population in given areas, birth-tax and death-tax and the penalties for abortion and illegitimate birth; it talked about laws governing types of sexual congress, about charitable payments and religious organizations running soup kitchens and night shelters and first-aid clinics; about numbers and figures and statistics and ratios all the time, and Gurgeh didn't think he picked up a word of it. He just wandered round the building for what seemed like hours, then he saw a door and left.

He was standing in a small garden, dark and dusty and deserted, at the back of the hospital, hemmed in on all sides. Yellow light from grimy windows spilled onto the gray grass and cracked paving-stones. The drone said it still had things it wanted to show him. It wanted him to see a place where down-and-outs slept; it thought it could get him into a prison as a visitor—

"I want to go back; *now!*" he shouted, throwing back the hood.

"All right!" the drone said, tugging the hood back up. They lifted off, going straight up for a long time before they started to head for the hotel and the module. The drone said nothing. Gurgeh was silent too, watching the great galaxy of lights that was the city as it passed beneath his feet.

They got back to the module. The roof-door opened for them as they fell, and the lights came on after it closed again. Gurgeh stood for a while as the drone took the cloak from him and unclipped the AG harness. Slipping down off his shoulders, the removal of the harness left him with an odd sensation of nakedness.

"I've one more thing I'd like to show you," the drone said. It moved down the corridor to the module lounge. Gurgeh followed it.

Flere-Imsaho floated in the center of the room. The screen was on, showing an apex and a male copulating. Background music surged; the setting was plush with cushions and thick drapes. "This is an Imperial Select channel," the drone said. "Level One, mildly scrambled." The scene switched, then switched again, each time showing a slightly different mix of sexual activity, from solo masturbation through to groups involving all three Azadian sexes.

"This sort of thing is restricted," the drone said. "Visitors aren't supposed to see it. The unscrambling apparatus is available for a price on the general market, however. Now we'll see some Level Two channels. These are restricted to the Empire's bureaucratic, military, religious and commercial upper echelons."

The screen went briefly hazy with a swirl of random colors, then cleared to show some more Azadians, mostly naked or very scantily clad. Again, the emphasis was on sexuality, but there was another, new element in what was happening; many of the people wore very strange and uncomfortable-looking clothes, and some were being tied up and beaten, or put into various absurd positions in which they were sexually used. Females dressed in uniforms ordered males and apices around. Gurgeh recognized some of the uniforms as those worn by Imperial

Navy officers; others looked like exaggerations of more ordinary uniforms. Some of the apices were dressed in male clothes, some in female dress. Apices were made to eat their own or somebody else's excreta, or drink their urine. The wastes of other pan-human species seemed to be particularly prized for this practice. Mouths and anuses, animals and aliens were penetrated by males and apices; aliens and animals were persuaded to mount the various sexes, and objects—some everyday, some apparently specially made—were used as phallic substitutes. In every scene, there was an element of . . . Gurgeh supposed it was dominance.

He'd been only mildly surprised that the Empire wanted to hide the material shown on the first level; a people so concerned with rank and protocol and clothed dignity might well want to restrict such things, harmless though they might be. The second level was different; he thought it gave the game away a little, and he could understand them being embarrassed about it. It was clear that the delight being taken in Level Two was not the vicarious pleasure of watching people enjoying themselves and identifying with them, but in seeing people being humiliated while others enjoyed themselves at their expense. Level One had been about sex; this was about something the Empire obviously thought more of but could not disentangle from that act.

"Now Level Three," the drone said.

Gurgeh watched the screen.

Flere-Imsaho watched Gurgeh.

The man's eyes glittered in the screen-light, unused photons reflecting from the halo of iris. The pupils widened at first, then shrank, became pinpoints. The dronc waited for the wide, staring eyes to fill with moisture, for the tiny muscles around the eyes to flinch and the eyelids to close and the man to shake his head and turn away, but nothing of the sort happened. The screen held his gaze, as though the infinitesimal pressure of light it spent upon the room had somehow reversed, and so sucked the watching man forward, to hold him, teetering before the fall, fixed and steady and pointed at the flickering surface like some long-stilled moon.

The screams echoed through the lounge, over its formseats and couches and low tables; the screams of apices, men, women, children. Sometimes they were silenced quickly, but usually not. Each instrument, and each part of the tortured people, made its own noise; blood, knives, bones, lasers, flesh, ripsaws, chemicals, leeches, fleshworms, vibraguns, even phalluses, fingers and claws; each made or produced their own distinctive sounds, counterpoints to the theme of screams.

The final scene the man watched featured a psychotic male criminal previously injected with massive doses of sex hormones and hallucinogens, a knife, and a woman described as an enemy of the state, who was pregnant, and just before term.

The eyes closed. His hands went to his ears. He looked down. "Enough," he muttered.

Flere-Imsaho switched the screen off. The man rocked backward on his heels, as though there had indeed been some attraction, some artificial gravity from the screen, and now that it had ceased, he almost over-balanced in reaction.

"That one is live, Jernau Gurgeh. It is taking place now. It is still happening, deep in some cellar under a prison or a police barracks."

Gurgeh looked up at the blank screen, eyes still wide and staring, but dry. He gazed, rocked backward and forward, and breathed deeply. There was sweat on his brow, and he shivered.

"Level Three is for the ruling elite only. Their strategic military signals are given the same encrypting status. I think you can see why.

"This is no special night, Gurgeh, no festival of sado-erotica. These things go out every evening. . . . There is more, but you've seen a representative cross-section."

Gurgeh nodded. His mouth was dry. He swallowed with some difficulty, took a few more deep breaths, rubbed his beard. He opened his mouth to speak, but the drone spoke first.

"One other thing. Something else they kept from you. I didn't know this myself until last night, when the ship mentioned it. Ever since you played Ram your opponents have been on various drugs as well. Cortex-keyed amphetamines at least, but they have far more sophisticated drugs which they use too. They have to inject, or ingest them; they don't have genofixed glands to manufacture drugs in their own bodies, but they certainly use them; most of the people you've been playing have had far more 'artificial' chemicals and compounds in their bloodstream than you've had."

The drone made a sighing noise. The man was still staring at the dead screen. "That's it," the drone said. "I'm sorry if what I've shown you has upset you, Jernau Gurgeh, but I didn't want you to leave here thinking the Empire was just a few venerable game-players, some impressive architecture and a few glorified nightclubs. What you've seen tonight is also what it's about. And there's plenty in between that I can't show you; all the frustrations that affect the poor and the relatively well-off alike, caused simply because they live in a society where one is not free to do as one chooses. There's the journalist who can't write what he knows is the truth, the doctor who can't treat somebody in pain because they're the wrong sex . . . a million things every day, things that aren't as melodramatic and gross as what I've shown you, but which are still part of it, still some of the effects.

"The ship told you a guilty system recognizes no innocents. I'd say it does. It recognizes the innocence of a young child, for example, and you saw how they treated that. In a sense it even recognizes the 'sanctity' of the body . . . but only to violate it. Once again, Gurgeh, it all boils down to ownership, possession; about taking and *having.*" Flere-Imsaho paused, then floated toward Gurgeh, came very close to him. "Ah, but I'm preaching again, amn't I? The excesses of youth. I've kept you up late. Maybe you're ready for some sleep now; it's been a long night, hasn't it? I'll leave you." It turned and floated away. It stopped near the door again. "Good night," it said.

Gurgeh cleared his throat. "Good night," he said, looking away from the dark screen at last. The drone dipped and disappeared.

Gurgeh sat down on a formseat. He stared at his feet for a while, then got up and walked outside the module, into the roof-garden. The dawn was just coming up. The city looked washed-out somehow, and cold. The many lights burned weakly, brilliance sapped by the calm blue vastness of the sky. A guard at the stairwell entrance coughed and stamped his feet, though Gurgeh could not see him.

He went back into the module and lay down on his bed. He lay in the darkness without closing his eyes, then closed his eyes and turned over, trying to sleep. He could not, and neither could he bring himself to secrete something that would make him sleep.

At last he got up and went back to the lounge where the screen was. He had the module access the game-channels, and sat there looking at his own game with Bermoiya for a long time, without moving or speaking, and without a single molecule of glanded drug in his bloodstream.

A prison ambulance stood outside the conference-center. Gurgeh got out of the aircraft and walked straight into the game-hall. Pequil had to run to keep up with the man. The apex didn't understand the alien; he hadn't wanted to talk during the journey from the hotel to the conference-center, whereas usually people in such a situation couldn't stop talking . . . and somehow he didn't seem to be frightened at all, though Pequil couldn't see how that could be. If he hadn't known the awkward, rather innocent alien better, he'd have thought it was anger he could read on that discolored, hairy, pointed face.

Lo Prinest Bermoiya sat in a stoolseat just off the Board of Origin. Gurgeh stood on the board itself. He rubbed his beard with one long finger, then moved a couple of pieces. Bermoiya made his own moves, then when the action spread—as the alien tried desperately to wriggle out of his predicament—the judge had some amateur players make most of his moves for him. The alien remained on the board, making his own moves, scurrying to and fro like a giant, dark insect.

Bermoiya couldn't see what the alien was playing at; his play seemed to be without purpose, and he made some moves which were either stupid mistakes or pointless sacrifices. Bermoiya mopped up some of the alien's tattered forces. After a while, he thought perhaps the male did have a plan, of sorts, but if so it must be a very obscure one. Perhaps there was some kind of odd, face-saving point the male was trying to make, while he still was a male.

Who knew what strange precepts governed an alien's behavior at such a moment? The moves went on; inchoate, unreadable. They broke for lunch. They resumed.

Bermoiya didn't return to the stoolseat after the break; he stood at the side of the board, trying to work out what slippery, ungraspable plan the alien might have. It was like playing a ghost, now; it was as though they were competing on separate boards. He couldn't seem to get to grips with the male at all; his pieces kept slipping away from him, moving as though the man had anticipated his next move before he'd even thought of it.

What had happened to the alien? He'd played quite differently yesterday. Was he really receiving help from outside? Bermoiya felt himself start to sweat. There was no need for it; he was still well ahead, still poised for victory, but suddenly he began to sweat. He told himself it was nothing to worry about; a side-effect of some of the concentration boosters he'd taken over lunch.

Bermoiya made some moves which ought to settle what was going on; expose the alien's real plan, if he had one. No result. Bermoiya tried some more exploratory gestures, committing a little more to the attempt. Gurgeh attacked immediately.

Bermoiya had spent a hundred years learning and playing Azad, and he'd sat in courts of every level for half that time. He'd seen many violent outbursts by just-sentenced criminals, and watched—and even taken part in—games containing moves of great suddenness and ferocity. Nevertheless, the alien's next few moves contrived to be on a level more barbarous and wild than anything Bermoiya had witnessed, in either context. Without the experience of the courts, he felt he might have physically reeled.

Those few moves were like a series of kicks in the belly; they contained all the berserk energy the very best young players spasmodically exhibited; but marshaled, synchronized, sequenced and unleashed with a style and a savage grace no untamed beginner could have hoped to command. With the first move Bermoiya saw what the alien's plan might be. With the next move he saw how good the plan was; with the next that the play might go on into the following day before the alien could finally be vanquished; with the next that he, Bermoiya, wasn't in quite as unassailable a position as he'd thought . . . and with the following two that he still had a lot of work to do, and then that perhaps the play wouldn't last until tomorrow after all.

Bermoiya made his own moves again, trying every ploy and stratagem he'd learned in a century of game-playing; the disguised observation piece, the feint-within-the-feint using attack-pieces and card-stock; the premature use of the Board of Becoming element-pieces, making a swamp on the territories by the conjunction of Earth and Water . . . but nothing worked.

He stood, just before the break, at the end of the afternoon session, and he looked at the alien. The hall was silent. The alien male stood in the middle of the board, staring impassively at some minor piece, rubbing at the hair on his face. He looked calm, unperturbed.

Bermoiya surveyed his own position. Everything was in a mess; there was nothing he could do now. Beyond redemption. It was like some badly prepared, fundamentally flawed case, or some piece of equipment, three-quarters destroyed; there was no saving it; better to throw it out and start again.

But there was no starting again. He was going to be taken out of here and taken to hospital and spayed; he was going to lose that which made him what he was, and he would never be allowed to have it back; gone forever. Forever.

Bermoiya couldn't hear the people in the hall. He couldn't see them, either, or see the board beneath his feet. All he could see was the alien male, standing tall and insect-like with his sharp-featured face and his angular body and stroking his furred face with one long, dark finger, the two-part nails at its tip showing the lighter skin beneath.

How could he look so unconcerned? Bermoiya fought the urge to scream; a great breath surged out of him. He thought how easy this had all looked this morning; how fine it had felt that not only would he be going to the Fire Planet for the final games, but also that he would be doing the Imperial Office a great favor at the same time. Now he thought that perhaps they had always known this might happen and they wanted him humiliated and brought down (for some reason he could not know, because he had always been loyal and conscientious. A mistake; it had to be a mistake . . .).

But *why now?* he thought, why *now?*

Why this time of all times, why this way, for this bet? Why had they wanted him to do this thing and make this wager when he had within him the seed of a child? *Why?*

The alien rubbed his furry face, pursed his strange lips as he looked down at some point on the board. Bermoiya began to stumble toward the male, oblivious of the obstacles in his way, trampling the biotechs and the other pieces under his feet and crashing over the raised pyramids of higher ground.

The male looked round at him, as though seeing him for the first time. Bermoiya felt himself stop. He gazed into the alien eyes.

And saw nothing. No pity, no compassion, no spirit of kindness or sorrow. He looked into those eyes, and at first he thought of the look criminals had sometimes, when they'd been sentenced to a quick death. It was a look of indifference; not despair, not hatred, but something flatter and more terrifying than either; a look of resignation, of all-hope-gone; a flag hoisted by a soul that no longer cared.

Yet although, in that instant of recognition, the doomed convict was the first image Bermoiya clutched at, he knew immediately it was not the fit one. He did not know what the fit one was. Perhaps it was unknowable.

Then he knew. And suddenly, for the first time in his life, he understood what it was for the condemned to look into *his* eyes.

He fell. To his knees at first, thudding down onto the board, cracking raised areas, then forward, onto his face, eyes level with the board, seeing it from the ground at last. He closed his eyes.

The Adjudicator and his helpers came over to him and gently lifted him; paramedics strapped him to the stretcher, sobbing quietly, and carried him outside to the prison ambulance.

Pequil stood amazed. He had never thought he would see an imperial judge break down like that. And in front of the alien! He had to run after the dark man; he was striding back out of the hall as quickly and quietly as he'd arrived, ignoring the hisses and shouts from the public galleries around him. They were in the aircar before even the press could catch up, speeding away from the game-hall.

Gurgeh, Pequil realized, had not said a single word the whole time they'd been in the hall.

Flere-Imsaho watched the man. It had expected more of a reaction, but he did nothing except sit at the screen, watching replays of all the games he'd played since he'd arrived. He wouldn't talk.

He would be going to Echronedal now, along with a hundred and nineteen other fourth-round single-game winners. As was usual after a bet of such severity had been honored, the family of the now mutilated Bermoiya had resigned for him. Without moving a piece on either of the two remaining great boards, Gurgeh had won the match and his place on the Fire Planet.

Some twenty days remained between the end of Gurgeh's game against Bermoiya and the date when the imperial court's fleet departed for the twelve-day journey to Echronedal. Gurgeh had been invited to spend part of that time at an estate owned by Hamin, the rector of the ruling College of Candsev, and mentor to the Emperor. Flere-Imsaho had advised against it, but Gurgeh had accepted. They would leave tomorrow for the estate, a few hundred kilometers distant on an island in an inland sea.

Gurgeh was taking what the drone believed was an unhealthy, even perverse interest in what the news- and press-agencies were saying about him. The man seemed actually to relish the calumnies and invective poured upon him following his win over Bermoiya. Sometimes he smiled when he read or heard what they said about him, especially when the news-readers—in shocked, reverent tones—related what the alien Gurgey had caused to be done to Lo Prinest Bermoiya; a gentle, lenient judge with five wives and two husbands, though no children.

Gurgeh had also started to watch the channels which showed the imperial troops crushing the savages and infidels it was civilizing in distant parts of the Empire. He had the module unscramble the higher-level military broadcasts which the services put out, it seemed, in a spirit of competition with the court's more highly encrypted entertainment channels.

The military broadcasts showed scenes of alien executions and tortures. Some showed the buildings and artworks of the recalcitrant or rebellious species being blown up or burned; things only very rarely shown on the standard news-channels if for no other reason than that all aliens were depicted as a matter of course as being uncivilized monsters, docile simpletons or greedy and treacherous subhumans, all categories incapable of producing high art and genuine civilization. Sometimes, where physically possible, Azadian males—though never apices—were shown raping the savages.

It upset Flere-Imsaho that Gurgeh should enjoy watching such things, especially as it had been instrumental in introducing him to the scrambled broadcasts in the first place, but at least he didn't appear to find the sights sexually stimulating. He didn't dwell on them the way the drone knew Azadians tended to; he looked, registered, then flicked away again.

He still spent the majority of his time staring at the games shown on the screen. But the coded signals, and his own bad press, kept drawing him back, time and again, like a drug.

"But I don't like rings."

"It isn't a question of what you *like,* Jernau Gurgeh. When you go to Hamin's estate you'll be outside this module. I might not always be close by, and anyway I'm not a specialist in toxicology. You'll be eating their food and drinking their drink and they have some very clever chemists and exobiologists. But if you wear one of these on each hand—index finger preferably—you should be safe from poisoning; if you feel a single jab it means a non-lethal drug, such as a hallucinogen. Three jabs means somebody's out to waste you."

"What do two jabs mean?"

"I don't know! A malfunction, probably; now will you put them on?"

"They really don't suit me."

"Would a shroud?"

"They feel funny."

"Never mind, if they work."

"How about a magic amulet to ward off bullets?"

"Are you serious? I mean, if you are there *is* a passive-sensor impact-shield jewelry set on board, but they'd probably use CREWs—"

Gurgeh waved one (ringed) hand. "Oh, never mind." He sat down again, turning on a military-execution channel.

The drone found it difficult to talk to the man; he wouldn't listen. It attempted to explain that despite all the horrors he had seen in the city and on the screen there was still nothing the Culture could do that wouldn't do more harm than good. It tried to tell him that the Contact section, the whole Culture in fact, was like him, dressed in his cloak and standing unable to help the man lying injured in the street, that they had to stick to their disguise and wait until the moment was right . . . but either its arguments weren't getting through to him, or that wasn't what the man was thinking about, because he made no response, and wouldn't enter into a discussion about it.

Flere-Imsaho didn't go out much during the days between the end of the game with Bermoiya and the journey to Hamin's estate. Instead it stayed in, with the man, worrying.

"Mr. Gurgeh; I am pleased to meet you." The old apex put out his hand. Gurgeh grasped it. "I hope you had a pleasant flight here, yes?"

"We did, thank you," Gurgeh said. They stood on the roof of a low building set in luxuriant green vegetation and looking out over the calm waters of the inland sea. The house was almost submerged in the burgeoning greenery; only the roof was fully clear of the swaying treetops. Nearby were paddocks full of riding animals, and from the various levels of the house long sweeping gantries, elegant and slim, soared out through the crowding trunks above the shady forest floor, giving access to the golden beaches and the pavilions and summer-houses of the estate. In the sky, huge sunlit clouds piled sparkling over the distant mainland.

"You say 'we,'" Hamin said, as they walked across the roof and liveried males took Gurgeh's baggage from the aircraft.

"The drone Flere-Imsaho and I," Gurgeh said, nodding to the bulky, buzzing machine at his shoulder.

"Ah yes," the old apex laughed, bald head reflecting the binary light. "The machine some people thought let you play so well." They descended to a long balcony set with many tables, where Hamin introduced Gurgeh—and the drone—to various people, mostly apices plus a few elegant females. There was only one person Gurgeh already knew; the smiling Lo Shav Olos put down a drink and rose from his table, taking Gurgeh's hand.

"Mr. Gurgeh; how good to see you again. Your luck held out and your skill increased. A formidable achievement. Congratulations, once again." The apex's gaze flicked momentarily to Gurgeh's ringed fingers.

"Thank you. It was at a price I'd have willingly forgone."

"Indeed. You never cease to surprise us, Mr. Gurgeh."

"I'm sure I shall, eventually."

"You are too modest." Olos smiled and sat down.

Gurgeh declined the offer to visit his rooms and freshen up; he felt perfectly fresh already. He sat at a table with Hamin, some other directors of Candsev College, and a few court officials. Chilled wines and spiced snacks were served. Flere-Imsaho settled, relatively quietly, on the floor by Gurgeh's feet. Gurgeh's new rings appeared to be happy there was nothing more damaging than alcohol in the fare being served.

The conversation mostly avoided Gurgeh's last game. Everyone pronounced his name correctly. The college directors asked him about his unique game-style; Gurgeh answered as best he could. The court officials inquired politely about his home world, and he told them some nonsense about living on a planet. They asked him about Flere-Imsaho, and Gurgeh expected the machine to answer, but it didn't, so he told them the truth; the machine was a person by the Culture's definition. It could do as it liked and it did not belong to him.

One tall and strikingly beautiful female, a companion of Lo Shav Olos who'd come over to join their table, asked the drone if its master played logically or not.

Flere-Imsaho replied—with a trace of weariness Gurgeh suspected only he could detect—that Gurgeh was not its master, and that it supposed he thought more logically than it did when he was playing games, but that anyway it knew very little about Azad.

They all found this most amusing.

Hamin stood then and suggested that his stomach, with over two and a half centuries of experience behind it, could tell it was approaching time for dinner better than any servant's clock. People laughed, and gradually began to depart the long balcony. Hamin escorted Gurgeh to his room personally and told him a servant would let him know when the meal was to be served.

"I wish I knew why they invited you here," Flere-Imsaho said, quickly unpacking Gurgeh's few cases while the man looked out of the window at the still trees and the calm sea.

"Perhaps they want to recruit me for the Empire. What do you think, drone? Would I make a good general?"

"Don't be facetious, Jernau Gurgeh." The drone switched to Marain. "And not to forget, random domran, here bugged are we, nonsense wonsense."

Gurgeh looked concerned and said in Eächic, "Heavens, drone; are you developing a speech impediment?"

"*Gurgeh . . .*" the drone hissed, setting out some clothes the Empire deemed suitable to be worn when eating.

Gurgeh turned away, smiling. "Maybe they just want to kill me."

"I wonder if they want any help."

Gurgeh laughed and came over to the bed where the drone had laid out the formal clothing. "It'll be all right."

"So you say. But we haven't even got the protection of the module here, let alone anything else. But . . . let's not worry about it."

Gurgeh picked up a couple of the robe-pieces and tried them against his body, holding them under his chin and looking down. "I'm not worried anyway," he said.

The drone shouted at him in exasperation. "Oh *Jernau* Gurgeh! *How* many times do I have to tell you? You can*not* wear red and green together like that!"

"You like music, Mr. Gurgeh?" Hamin asked, leaning over to the man.

Gurgeh nodded. "Well, a little does no harm."

Hamin sat back, apparently satisfied with this answer. They had climbed to the broad roof-garden after dinner, which had been a long, complicated and very filling affair during which naked females had danced in the center of the room and—if Gurgeh's rings were to be believed—nobody had tried to interfere with his food. It was dusk now, and the party was outside in the warm evening air, listening to the wailing music produced by a group of apex musicians. Slender gantries led from the garden into the tall, graceful trees.

Gurgeh sat at a small table with Hamin and Olos. Flere-Imsaho sat near his feet. Lamps shone in the trees around them; the roof-garden was its own island of light in the night, surrounded by the cries of birds and animals, calling out as though in answer to the music.

"I wonder, Mr. Gurgeh," Hamin said, sipping his drink and lighting a long, small-bowled pipe. "Did you find any of our dancing girls attractive?" He pulled on the long-stemmed pipe, then, with the smoke wreathing around his bald head, went on, "I only ask because one of them—she with the silver streak in her hair, remember?—did express rather an interest in you. I'm sorry . . . I hope I'm not shocking you, Mr. Gurgeh, am I?"

"Not in the least."

"Well, I just wanted to say you're among friends here, yes? You've more than proved yourself in the game, and this is a very private place, outside the gaze of the press and the common people, who of course have to depend on certain hard and fast rules . . . whereas we do not, not here. You catch my drift? You may relax in confidence."

"I'm most grateful. I shall certainly try to relax; but I was told before I came here that I would be found ugly, even disfigured, by your people. Your kindness overwhelms me, but I would prefer not to inflict myself on somebody who might not be available through choice alone."

"Too modest, again, Jernau Gurgeh," Olos smiled.

Hamin nodded, puffing on his pipe. "You know, Mr. Gurgeh, I have heard that in your 'Culture' you have no laws. I am sure this is an exaggeration, but there must be a grain of truth in the assertion, and I would guess you must find the number and strictness of our laws . . . to be a great difference between your society and ours.

"Here we have many rules, and try to live according to the

laws of God, Game and Empire. But one of the advantages of having laws is the pleasure one may take in breaking them. We here are not children, Mr. Gurgeh." Hamin waved the pipe-stem round the tables of people. "Rules and laws exist only because we take pleasure in doing what they forbid, but as long as most of the people obey such proscriptions most of the time, they have done their job; blind obedience would imply we are—ha!"—Hamin chuckled and pointed at the drone with the pipe—"no more than robots!"

Flere-Imsaho buzzed a little louder, but only momentarily.

There was silence. Gurgeh drank from his glass.

Olos and Hamin exchanged looks. "Jernau Gurgeh," Olos said at last, rolling his glass round in his hands. "Let's be frank. You're an embarrassment to us. You've done very much better than we expected; we did not think we could be so easily fooled, but somehow you did it. I congratulate you on whatever ruse it was you used, whether it centered on your drug-glands, your machine there, or simply many more years playing Azad than you admitted to. You have bettered us, and we're impressed. I am only sorry that innocent people, such as those bystanders who were shot instead of you, and Lo Prinest Bermoiya, had to be hurt. As you have no doubt guessed, we would like you to go no further in the game. Now, the Imperial Office has nothing to do with the Games Bureau, so there is little we can do directly. We do have a suggestion though."

"What's that?" Gurgeh sipped his drink.

"As I've been saying"—Hamin pointed the stem of the pipe at Gurgeh—"we have many laws. We therefore have many crimes. Some of these are of a sexual nature, yes?" Gurgeh looked down at his drink. "I need hardly point out," Hamin continued, "that the physiology of our race makes us . . . unusual, one might almost say gifted, in that respect. Also, in our society, it is possible to *control* people. It is possible to make somebody, or even several people, do things they might not want to do. We can offer you, here, the sort of experience which by your own admission would be impossible on your own world." The old apex leaned closer, dropping his voice. "Can you imagine what it might be like to have several females, and males—even apices, if you like—who will do your *every* bidding?" Hamin knocked his pipe out on the table leg; the ash drifted over the humming bulk of Flere-Imsaho. The rector of Candsev College smiled in a conspiratorial way and sat back, re-packing his pipe from a small pouch.

Olos leaned forward. "This whole island is yours for as long as you want it, Jernau Gurgeh. You may have as many people of whatever sexual mix as you like, for as long as you desire."

"But I pull out of the game."

"You retire, yes," Olos said.

Hamin nodded. "There are precedents."

"The whole island?" Gurgeh made a show of looking around the gently lit roof-garden. A troupe of dancers appeared; the lithe, skimpily dressed men, women and apices made their way up some steps to a small stage raised behind the musicians.

"Everything," Olos said. "The island, house, servants, dancers; everything and everyone."

Gurgeh nodded but didn't say anything.

Hamin relit his pipe. "Even the band," he said, coughing. He waved at the musicians. "What do you think of their instruments, Mr. Gurgeh? Do they not sound sweet?"

"Very pleasant." Gurgeh drank a little, watching the dancers arrange themselves onstage.

"Even there, though," Hamin said, "you are missing something. You see, we gain a great deal of pleasure from knowing at what cost this music is bought. You see the stringed instrument; the one on the left with the eight strings?"

Gurgeh nodded. Hamin said, "I can tell you that each of those steel strings has strangled a man. You see that white pipe at the back, played by the male?"

"The pipe shaped like a bone?"

Hamin laughed. "A female's femur, removed without anesthetic."

"Naturally," Gurgeh said, and took a few sweet-tasting nuts from a bowl on the table. "Do they come in matched pairs, or are there a lot of one-legged lady music critics?"

Hamin smiled. "You see?" he said to Olos. "He does appreciate." The old apex gestured back at the band, behind whom the dancers were now arranged, ready to start their performance. "The drums are made from human skin; you can see why each set is called a family. The horizontal percussion instrument is constructed from finger bones, and . . . well, there are other instruments, but can you understand now why that music sounds so . . . *precious* to those of us who know what has gone into the making of it?"

"Oh, yes," Gurgeh said. The dancers began. Fluid, practiced, they impressed almost immediately. Some must have worn AG units, floating through the air like huge, diaphanously slow birds.

"Good," Hamin nodded. "You see, Gurgeh, one can be on either side in the Empire. One can be the player, or one can be . . . played upon." Hamin smiled at what was a play on words in Eächic, and to some extent in Marain too.

Gurgeh watched the dancers for a moment. Without looking away from them, he said, "I'll play, rector; on Echronedal." He tapped one ring on the rim of his glass, in time to the music.

Hamin sighed. "Well, I have to tell you, Jernau Gurgeh, that we are worried." He pulled on the pipe again, studied the glowing bowl. "Worried about the effect your getting any further in the game would have on the morale of our people. So many of them are just simple folk; it is our duty to shield them from the harsh realities, sometimes. And what harsher reality can there be than the realization that most of one's kin are gullible, cruel and foolish? They would not understand that a stranger, an alien, can come here and do so well at the holy game. We here—those of us in the court and the colleges—might not be so concerned, but we have to keep the ordinary, decent . . . I would even go as far as to say *innocent* people in mind, Mr. Gurgeh, and what we have to do in that respect, what we sometimes have to take responsibility for, does not always make us happy. But we know our duty, and we will do it; for them, and for our Emperor."

Hamin leaned forward again. "We don't intend to kill you, Mr. Gurgeh, though I'm told there are factions in the court who'd like nothing better, and—they say—people in the security services easily capable of doing so. No; nothing so gross. But . . ." The old apex sucked on the thin pipe, producing a gentle papping noise. Gurgeh waited.

Hamin pointed the stem at him again. "I have to tell you, Gurgeh, that no matter how you do in the first game on Echronedal, it will be announced that you have been defeated. We have unequivocal control of the communications- and news-services on the Fire Planet, and as far as the press and the public will be concerned, you will be knocked out in the first round there. We will do whatever has to be done to make it appear that that is exactly what has in fact happened. You are free to tell people I've told you this, and free to claim whatever you want after the event; you will be ridiculed, though, and what I have described will happen anyway. The truth has already been decided."

Olos's turn: "So, you see, Gurgeh; you may go to Echronedal, but to certain defeat; absolutely certain defeat. Go as a high-class tourist if you want, or stay here and enjoy yourself as our guest; but there is no longer any point in playing."

"Hmm," Gurgeh said. The dancers were slowly losing their clothes as they stripped each other. Some of them, still dancing, were at the same time contriving to stroke and touch each other in an exaggeratedly sexual way. Gurgeh nodded. "I'll think about it." Then he smiled at the two apices. "I'd like to see your Fire Planet, all the same." He drank from the cool glass, and watched the slow build-up of erotic choreography behind the musicians. "Other than that, though . . . I can't imagine I'll be trying too terribly hard."

Hamin was studying his pipe. Olos looked very serious.

Gurgeh held out his hands in a gesture of resigned helplessness. "What more can I say?"

"Would you be prepared to . . . cooperate, though?" Olos said.

Gurgeh looked inquisitive. Olos reached slowly over and tapped the rim of Gurgeh's glass. "Something that would . . . ring true," he said softly.

Gurgeh watched the two apices exchange glances. He waited for them to make their play.

"Documentary evidence," Hamin said after a moment, talking to his pipe. "Film of you looking worried over a bad board-position. Maybe even an interview. We could arrange these things without your cooperation, naturally, but it would be easier, less fraught for all concerned, with your aid." The old apex sucked on his pipe. Olos drank, glancing at the romantic antics of the dance troupe.

Gurgeh looked surprised. "You mean, lie? Participate in the construction of your false reality?"

"Our *real* reality, Gurgeh," Olos said quietly. "The official version; the one that will have documentary evidence to support it . . . the one that will be believed."

Gurgeh grinned broadly. "I'd be delighted to help. Of course; I shall regard it as a challenge to produce a definitively abject interview for popular consumption. I'll even help you work out positions so awful even I can't get out of them." He raised his glass to them. "After all; it's the game that matters, is it not?"

Hamin snorted, his shoulders shook. He sucked on the pipe again and through a veil of smoke said, "No true game-player could say more." He patted Gurgeh on the shoulder. "Mr. Gurgeh, even if you choose not to avail yourself of the facilities my house has to offer, I hope you'll stay with us for a while. I should enjoy talking with you. Will you stay?"

"Why not?" Gurgeh said, and he and Hamin raised their glasses to each other; Olos sat back, laughing silently. Together the three turned to watch the dancers, who had now formed a copulatorily complicated pattern of bodies in a carnal jigsaw, still keeping, Gurgeh was impressed to note, to the beat of the music.

He stayed at the house for the next fifteen days. He talked, guardedly, with the old rector during that time. He still felt they didn't really know each other when he left, but perhaps they knew a little more of each other's societies.

Hamin obviously found it hard to believe the Culture really did do without money. "But what if I *do* want something unreasonable?"

"What?"

"My own planet?" Hamin wheezed with laughter.

"How can you own a planet?" Gurgeh shook his head.

"But supposing I wanted one?"

"I suppose if you found an unoccupied one you could land without anybody becoming annoyed . . . perhaps that would work. But how would you stop other people landing there too?"

"Could I not buy a fleet of warships?"

"All our ships are sentient. You could certainly *try* telling a ship what to do . . . but I don't think you'd get very far."

"Your ships think they're sentient!" Hamin chuckled.

"A common delusion shared by some of our human citizens."

Hamin found the Culture's sexual mores even more fascinating. He was at once delighted and outraged that the Culture regarded homosexuality, incest, sex-changing, hermaphrodicy and sexual characteristic alteration as just something else people did, like going on a cruise or changing their hairstyle.

Hamin thought this must take all the fun out of things. Didn't the Culture forbid *anything?*

Gurgeh attempted to explain there were no written laws, but almost no crime anyway. There was the occasional crime of passion (as Hamin chose to call it), but little else. It was difficult to get away with anything anyway, when everybody had a terminal, but there were very few motives left, too.

"But if someone kills somebody else?"

Gurgeh shrugged. "They're slap-droned."

"Ah! This sounds more like it. What does this drone do?"

"Follows you around and makes sure you never do it again."

"Is that all?"

"What more do you want? Social death, Hamin; you don't get invited to too many parties."

"Ah; but in your Culture, can't you gatecrash?"

"I suppose so," Gurgeh conceded. "But nobody'd talk to you."

As for what Hamin told Gurgeh about the Empire, it only made him appreciate what Shohobohaum Za had said; that it was a gem, however vicious and indiscriminate its cutting edges might be. It was not so difficult to understand the warped view the Azadians had of what they called "human nature"—the phrase they used whenever they had to justify something inhuman and unnatural—when they were surrounded and subsumed by the self-created monster that was the Empire of Azad, and which displayed such a fierce instinct (Gurgeh could think of no other word) for self-preservation.

The Empire *wanted* to survive; it was like an animal, a massive, powerful body that would only let certain cells or viruses survive within it and as a matter of course killed off any and all others, automatically and unthinkingly. Hamin himself used this analogy when he compared revolutionaries to cancer. Gurgeh tried to say that single cells were single cells, while a conscious collection of hundreds of billions of them—or a conscious device made from arrays of pico-circuitry, for that matter—was simply incomparable . . . but Hamin refused to listen. It was Gurgeh, not he, who'd missed the point.

The rest of the time Gurgeh spent walking in the forest, or swimming in the warm, slack sea. The slow rhythm of Hamin's house was built around meals, and Gurgeh learned to take great care in dressing for these, eating them, talking to the guests—old and new, as people came and went—and relaxing afterward, bloated and spacy, continuing to talk, and watching the deliberate entertainment of—usually—erotic dances, and the involuntary cabaret of changing sexual alliances among the guests, dancers, servants and house staff. Gurgeh was enticed many times, but never tempted. He found the Azadian females more and more attractive all the time, and not just physically . . . but used his genofixed glands in a negative, even contrary way, to stay carnally sober in the midst of the subtly exhibited orgy around him.

A pleasant enough few days. The rings did not jab him, and nobody shot at him. He and Flere-Imsaho got back safely to the module on the roof of the Grand Hotel a couple of days before the Imperial Fleet was due to depart for Echronedal. Gurgeh and the drone would have preferred to take the module, which was perfectly capable of making the crossing by itself, but Contact had forbidden that—the effect on the Admiralty of discovering that something no larger than a lifeboat could outstrip their battlecruisers was not something to be contemplated—and the Empire had refused permission for the alien machine to be conveyed inside an imperial craft. So Gurgeh would have to make the journey with the Fleet like everybody else.

"You think *you've* got problems," Flere-Imsaho said bitterly. "They'll be watching us all the time; on the liner during the crossing and then once we're in the castle. That means I've got to stay inside this ridiculous disguise all day and all night until the games are over. Why couldn't you have lost in the first round like you were supposed to? We could have told them where to insert their Fire Planet and been back on a GSV by now."

"Oh, shut up, machine."

As it turned out, they needn't have returned to the module; there was nothing more to take or pack. He stood in the small lounge, fiddling with the Orbital bracelet on his wrist and realizing he was looking forward to the coming games on Echronedal more than he had any of the others. The pressure would be off; he wouldn't have to face the opprobrium of the press and the Empire's ghastly general public, he could cooperate with the Empire to produce a convincing piece of fake news, and the likelihood of more physical option bets had thereby been reduced almost to zero. He was going to enjoy himself . . .

Flere-Imsaho was glad to see the man was getting over the effects of seeing behind the screen the Empire showed its guests; he was much as he'd been before, and the days at Hamin's estate seemed to have relaxed him. It could see a small change in him though; something it could not quite pin down, but which it knew was there.

They didn't see Shohobohaum Za again. He'd left on a tour "up-country," wherever that was. He sent his regards, and a message in Marain to the effect that if Gurgeh could lay his mitts on some fresh *grif* . . .

Before they left, Gurgeh asked the module about the girl he'd met at the grand ball, months earlier. He couldn't remember her name, but if the module could provide a list of the females who'd survived the first round, he was sure he'd recognize hers . . . the module got confused, but Flere-Imsaho told them both to forget it.

No women had made it to the second round.

Pequil came with them to the shuttleport. His arm was fully healed. Gurgeh and Flere-Imsaho bade farewell to the module; it climbed into the sky for a rendezvous with the distant *Limiting Factor.* They said goodbye to Pequil too—he took Gurgeh's hand in both of his—and then the man and the drone boarded the shuttle.

Gurgeh watched Groasnachek as it fell away beneath them. The city tilted as he was thrown back into his seat; the whole view swung and juddered as the shuttlecraft powered into the hazy skies.

Gradually all the patterns and the shapes came out, revealed for a while before the increasing distance, the city's own vapors, dust and grime, and the altering angle of their climb took it all away.

For all the jumble, it looked momentarily peaceful and ordered in its parts. The distance made its individual, local confusions and dislocations disappear, and from a certain height, where little ever dallied, and almost everything just passed through, it looked exactly like a great, mindless, spreading organism.

# 3

## *Machina Ex Machina*

So far so average. Our game-player's lucked out again. I guess you can see he's a changed man, though. These humans!

I'm going to be consistent, however. I haven't told you who I am so far, and I'm not going to tell you now, either. Maybe later.

Maybe.

Does identity matter anyway? I have my doubts. We are what we do, not what we think. Only the interactions count (there is no problem with free will here; that's not incompatible with believing your actions define you). And what is free will anyway? Chance. The random factor. If one is not ultimately predictable, then of course that's all it can be. I get so frustrated with people who can't see this!

Even a human should be able to understand it's obvious.

The result is what matters, not how it's achieved (unless, of course, the process of achieving is itself a series of results). What difference does it make whether a mind's made up of enormous, squidgy, animal cells working at the speed of sound (in air!), or from a glittering nanofoam of reflectors and patterns of holographic coherence, at lightspeed? (Let's not even think about a Mind mind.) Each is a machine, each is an organism, each fulfills the same task.

Just matter, switching energy of one sort or another.

Switches. Memory. The random element that is chance and that is called choice: common denominators, all.

I say again; you is what you done. Dynamic (mis)behaviorism, that's my creed.

Gurgeh? His switches are working funny. He's thinking differently, acting uncharacteristically. He is a different person. He's seen the worst that meatgrinder of a city could provide, and he just took it personally, and took his revenge.

Now he's spaceborne again, head crammed full of Azad rules, his brain adapted and adapting to the swirling, switching patterns of that seductive, encompassing, feral set of rules and possibilities, and being carted through space toward the Empire's most creakily symbolic shrine: Echronedal; the place of the standing wave of flame; the Fire Planet.

But will our hero prevail? *Can* he possibly prevail? And what would constitute winning, anyway?

How much has the man still got to learn? What will he make of such knowledge? More to the point, what will it make of him?

Wait and see. It'll work itself out, in time.

Take it from there, maestro . . .

Echronedal was twenty light-years from Eä. Halfway there the Imperial Fleet left the region of dust that lay between Eä's system and the direction of the main galaxy, and so that vast armed spiral was spread over half the sky like a million jewels caught in a whirlpool.

Gurgeh was impatient to get to the Fire Planet. The journey seemed to take forever, and the liner he was making it on was hopelessly cramped. He spent most of the time in his cabin. The bureaucrats, imperial officials and other game-players on the ship regarded him with undisguised dislike, and apart from a couple of shuttle trips over to the battlecruiser *Invincible*—the imperial flagship—for receptions, Gurgeh didn't socialize.

The crossing was made without incident, and after twelve days they arrived over Echronedal, a planet orbiting a yellow dwarf in a fairly ordinary system and itself a human-habitable world with only one peculiarity.

It was not unusual to find distinct equatorial bulges on once fast-spinning planets, and Echronedal's was comparatively slight, though sufficient to produce a single unbroken continental ribbon of land lying roughly between the planet's tropics, the rest of the globe lying beneath two great oceans, ice-capped at the poles. What was unique, in the experience of the Culture as well as the Empire, was to discover a wave of fire forever moving round the planet on the continental landmass.

Taking about half a standard year to complete its circumnavigation, the fire swept over the land, its fringes brushing the shores of the two oceans, its wave-front a near-straight line, its flames consuming the growth of the plants which had flourished in the ashes of the previous blaze. The whole land-based ecosystem had evolved around this never-ending conflagration; some plants could only sprout from beneath the still-warm cinders, their seeds jolted into development by the passing heat; other plants blossomed just before the fire arrived, bursting into rapid growth just before the flames found them, and using the fire-front's thermals to transport their seeds into the upper atmosphere, to fall back again, somewhere, onto the ash. The land-animals of Echronedal fell into three categories; some kept constantly on the move, maintaining the same steady walking pace as the fire, some swam round its oceanic boundaries, while other species burrowed into the ground, hid in caves, or survived through a variety of mechanisms in lakes or rivers.

Birds circled the world like a jetstream of feathers.

The blaze remained little more than a large, continuous bush-fire for eleven revolutions. On the twelfth, it changed.

The cinderbud was a tall, skinny plant which grew quickly once its seeds had germinated; it developed an armored base and shot up to a height of ten meters or more in the two hundred days it had before the flames came round again. When the fire did arrive, the cinderbud didn't burn; it closed its leafy head until the blaze had passed, then kept on growing in the ashes. After eleven of those Great Months, eleven baptisms in the flames, the cinderbuds were great trees, anything up to seventy meters in height. Their own chemistry then produced first the Oxygen Season, and then the Incandescence.

And in that sudden cycle the fire didn't walk; it sprinted. It was no longer a wide but low and even mild bush-fire; it was an inferno. Lakes disappeared, rivers dried, rocks crumbled in its baking heat; every animal that had evolved its own way of dodging or keeping pace with the fires of the Great Months had had to find another method of surviving; running fast enough to build up a sufficient lead on the Incandescence to still keep ahead of it, swimming far out into the ocean or to the few mostly small islands off the coasts, or hibernating, deep in great cave-systems or on the beds of deep rivers, lakes and fjords. Plants too switched to new survival mechanisms; rooting deeper, growing thicker seed-cases, or equipping their thermal-seeds for higher, longer flight, and the baked ground they would encounter on landing.

For a Great Month thereafter the planet, its atmosphere choked with smoke, soot and ash, wavered on the edge of catastrophe as smoke clouds blocked out the sun and the temperature plummeted. Then slowly, while the diminished small fire continued on its way, the atmosphere cleared, the animals started to breed again, the plants grew once more, and the little cinderbuds started sprouting through the ashes from the old root complexes.

The Empire's castles on Echronedal, extravagantly sprinklered and doused, had been built to survive whatever terrible heat and screaming winds the planet's bizarre ecology could provide, and it was in the greatest of those fortresses, Castle Klaff, that for the last three hundred standard years the final games of Azad had been played; timed to coincide, whenever possible, with the Incandescence.

The Imperial Fleet arrived above Echronedal in the middle of the Oxygen Season. The flagship remained over the planet while the escorting battleships dispersed to the outskirts of the system. The liners stayed until the *Invincible*'s shuttle squadron had ferried the game-players, court officials, guests and observers down to the surface, then left for a nearby system. The shuttles dropped through the clear air of Echronedal to land at Castle Klaff.

The fortress lay on a spur of rock at the foot of a range of soft, well-worn hills overlooking a broad plain. Normally it looked out over a horizon-wide sweep of low scrub punctuated by the thin towers of cinderbuds at whatever stage they'd reached, but now the cinderbuds had branched and blossomed, and their canopy of rippling leaves fluttered over the plain like some rooted yellow overcast, and the tallest trunks rose higher than the castle's curtain wall.

When the Incandescence arrived it would wash around the

fortress like a livid wave; all that ever saved the castle from incineration was a two-kilometer viaduct leading from a reservoir in the low hills to Klaff itself, where giant cisterns and a complicated system of sprinklers ensured the secured and shuttered fortress was drenched with water as the fire passed. If the dousing system ever broke down, there were deep shelters in the rock far underneath the castle which would house the inhabitants until the burning was over. So far, the waters had always saved the fortress, and it had remained an oasis of scorched yellow in a wilderness of fire.

The Emperor—whoever had won the final game—was traditionally meant to be in Klaff when the fire passed, to rise from the fortress after the flames died, ascending through the darkness of the smoke clouds to the darkness of space and thence to his Empire. The timing hadn't always worked out perfectly, and in earlier centuries the Emperor and his court had had to sit out the fire in another castle, or even missed the Incandescence altogether. However, the Empire had this time calculated correctly, and it looked as though the Incandescence—due to start only two hundred kilometers fireward of the castle, where the cinderbuds changed abruptly from their normal size and shape to the huge trees that surrounded Klaff—would arrive more or less on time, to provide a suitable backdrop for the coronation.

Gurgeh felt uncomfortable as soon as they landed. Eä had been of just a little less than what the Culture rather arbitrarily regarded as standard mass, so its gravity had felt roughly the equivalent of the force Chiark Orbital had produced by rotating and the *Limiting Factor* and the *Little Rascal* had created with AG fields. But Echronedal was half as massive again as Eä, and Gurgeh felt heavy.

The castle had long since been equipped with slow-accelerating elevators, and it was unusual to see anybody other than male servants climbing upstairs, but even walking on the level was uncomfortable for the first few of the planet's short days.

Gurgeh's rooms overlooked one of the castle's inner courtyards. He settled in there with Flere-Imsaho—who gave no sign of being affected by the higher gravity—and the male servant every finalist was entitled to. Gurgeh had voiced some uncertainty about having a servant at all ("Yeah," the drone had said, "who needs two?"), but it had been explained it was traditional, and a great honor for the male, so he'd acquiesced.

There was a rather desultory party on the night of their arrival. Everybody sat around talking, tired after the long journey and drained by the fierce gravity; the conversation was mostly about swollen ankles. Gurgeh went briefly, to show his face. It was the first time he'd met Nicosar since the grand ball at the start of the games; the receptions on the *Invincible* during the journey had not been graced by the imperial presence.

"This time, get it right," Flere-Imsaho told him as they entered the main hall of the castle; the Emperor sat on a throne, welcoming the people as they arrived. Gurgeh was about to kneel like everybody else, but Nicosar saw him, shook one ringed finger and pointed at his own knee.

"Our one-kneed friend; you have not forgotten?"

Gurgeh knelt on one knee, bowing his head. Nicosar laughed thinly. Hamin, sitting on the Emperor's right, smiled.

Gurgeh sat, alone, in a chair by a wall, near a large suit of antique armor. He looked unenthusiastically round the room, and ended up gazing, with a frown, at an apex standing in one corner of the hall, talking to a group of uniformed apices perched on stoolseats around him. The apex was unusual not just because he was standing but because he seemed to be encased in a set of gunmetal bones, worn outside his Navy uniform.

"Who's that?" Gurgeh asked Flere-Imsaho, humming and crackling unenthusiastically between his chair and the suit of armor by the wall.

"Who's who?"

"That apex with the . . . exoskeleton? Is that what you call it? Him."

"That is Star Marshal Yomonul. In the last games he made a personal bet, with Nicosar's blessing, that he would go to prison for a Great Year if he lost. He lost, but he expected that Nicosar would use the imperial veto—which he can do, on wagers which aren't body-bets—because the Emperor wouldn't want to lose the services of one of his best commanders for six years. Nicosar did use the veto, but only to have Yomonul incarcerated in that device he's wearing, rather than shut away in a prison cell.

"The portable prison is proto-sentient; it has various independent sensors as well as conventional exoskeleton features such as a micropile and powered limbs. Its job is to leave Yomonul free to carry out his military duties, but otherwise to impose prison discipline on him. It will only let him eat a little of the simplest food, allows him no alcohol, keeps him to a strict regimen of exercise, will not allow him to take part in social activities—his presence here this evening must mark some sort of special dispensation by the Emperor—and won't let him copulate. In addition, he has to listen to sermons by a prison chaplain who visits him for two hours every ten days."

"Poor guy. I see he has to stand, as well."

"Well, one shouldn't try to outsmart the Emperor, I guess," Flere-Imsaho said. "But his sentence is almost over."

"No time off for good behavior?"

"The Imperial Penal Service does not deal in discounts. They do add time on if you behave badly, though."

Gurgeh shook his head, looking at the distant prisoner in his private prison. "It's a mean old Empire, isn't it, drone?"

"Mean enough. . . . But if it ever tries to fuck with the Culture it'll find out what mean really is."

Gurgeh looked round in surprise at the machine. It floated, buzzing there, its bulky gray and brown casing looking hard and even sinister against the dull gleam of the empty suit of armor.

"My, we're in a combative mood this evening."

"I am. You'd better be."

"For the games? I'm ready."

"Are you really going to take part in this piece of propaganda?"

"What piece of propaganda?"

"You know damn well; helping the Bureau to fake your own defeat. Pretending you've lost; giving interviews and lying."

"Yes. Why not? It lets me play the game. They might try to stop me otherwise."

"Kill you?"

Gurgeh shrugged. "Disqualify me."

"Is it worth so much to keep playing?"

"No," Gurgeh lied. "But telling a few white lies isn't much of a price, either."

"Huh," the machine said.

Gurgeh waited for it to say more, but it didn't. They left a little later. Gurgeh got up out of the chair and walked to the door, only remembering to turn and bow toward Nicosar after the drone prompted him.

* * *

His first game on Echronedal, the one he was officially to lose no matter what happened, was another ten game. This time there was no suggestion of anybody ganging up on him, and he was approached by four of the other players to form a side which would oppose the rest. This was the traditional way of playing ten games, though it was the first time Gurgeh had been directly involved, apart from being on the sharp end of other people's alliances.

So he found himself discussing strategy and tactics with a pair of Fleet admirals, a star general and an imperial minister in what the Bureau guaranteed was an electronically and optically sterile room in one wing of the castle. They spent three days talking over how they would play the game, then they swore before God, and Gurgeh gave his word, they would not break the agreement until the other five players had been defeated or they themselves were brought down.

The lesser games ended with the sides about even. Gurgeh found there were advantages and disadvantages in playing as part of an ensemble. He did his best to adapt and play accordingly. More talks followed, then they joined battle on the Board of Origin.

Gurgeh enjoyed it. It added a lot to the game to play as part of a team; he felt genuinely warm toward the apices he played alongside. They came to each other's aid when they were in trouble, they trusted one another during massed attacks, and generally played as though their individual forces were really a single side. As people, he didn't find his comrades desperately engaging, but as playing partners he could not deny the emotion he felt for them, and experienced a growing sense of sadness—as the game progressed and they gradually beat back their opponents—that they would soon all be fighting each other.

When it came to it, and the last of the opposition had surrendered, much of what Gurgeh had felt before disappeared. He'd been at least partially tricked; he'd stuck to what he saw as the spirit of their agreement, while the others stuck to the letter. Nobody actually attacked until the last of the other team's pieces had been captured or taken over, but there was some subtle maneuvering when it became clear they were going to win, playing for positions that would become more important when the team-agreement ended. Gurgeh missed this until it was almost too late, and when the second part of the game began he was by far the weakest of the five.

It also became obvious that the two admirals were, not surprisingly, cooperating unofficially against the others. Jointly the pair were stronger than the other three.

In a way Gurgeh's very weakness saved him; he played so that it was not worth taking him for a long time, letting the other four fight it out. Later he attacked the two admirals when they had grown strong enough to threaten a complete takeover, but were more vulnerable to his small force than to the greater powers of the general and the minister.

The game toed and froed for a long time, but Gurgeh was gaining steadily, and eventually, though he was put out first of the five, he'd accumulated sufficient points to ensure he'd play on the next board. Three of the other original five-side had done so badly they had to resign from the match.

Gurgeh never really fully recovered from his mistake on the first board, and did badly on the Board of Form. It was starting to look as though the Empire would not need to lie about him being thrown out of the first game.

He still talked to the *Limiting Factor,* using Flere-Imsaho as a relay and the game-screen in his own room for the display.

He felt he'd adjusted to the higher gravity. Flere-Imsaho

had to remind him it was a genofixed response; his bones were rapidly thickening and his musculature had expanded without waiting to be otherwise exercised.

"Hadn't you *noticed* you were getting more thick-set?" the drone said in exasperation, while Gurgeh studied his body in the room mirror.

Gurgeh shook his head. "I did think I was eating rather a lot."

"Very observant. I wonder what else you can do you don't know about. Didn't they teach you anything about your own biology?"

The man shrugged. "I forgot."

He adjusted, too, to the planet's short day-night cycle, adapting faster than anybody else, if the numerous complaints were anything to go by. Most people, the drone told him, were using drugs to bring themselves into line with the three-quarters standard day.

"Genofixing again?" Gurgeh asked at breakfast one morning.

"Yes. Of course."

"I didn't know we could do all this."

"Obviously not," the drone said. "Good grief, man; the Culture's been a spacefaring species for eleven thousand years; just because you've mostly settled down in idealized, tailor-made conditions doesn't mean you've lost the capacity for rapid adaptation. Strength in depth; redundancy; over-design. You know the Culture's philosophy."

Gurgeh frowned at the machine. He gestured to the walls, and then to his ear.

Flere-Imsaho wobbled from side to side; drone shrug.

Gurgeh came fifth out of seven on the Board of Form. He started play on the Board of Becoming with no hope of winning, but a remote chance of getting through as the Qualifier.

He played an inspired game, toward the end. He was starting to feel quite thoroughly at home on the last of the three great boards, and enjoyed using the elemental symbolism the play incorporated instead of the die-matching used in the rest of each match. The Board of Becoming was the least well-played of the three great boards, Gurgeh felt, and one the Empire seemed to understand imperfectly, and pay too little attention to.

He made it. One of the admirals won, and he scraped in as Qualifier. The margin between him and the other admiral was one point; 5,523 against 5,522. Only a draw and play-off could have been closer, but when he thought about it later, he realized he hadn't for one moment entertained the slightest doubt he'd get through to the next round.

"You're coming perilously close to talking about destiny, Jernau Gurgeh," Flere-Imsaho said when he tried to explain this. He was sitting in his room, hand on the table in front of him, while the drone removed the Orbital bracelet from his wrist; he couldn't get it over his hand anymore and it was becoming too tight, thanks to his expanding muscles.

"Destiny," Gurgeh said, looking thoughtful. He nodded. "That's what it feels like, I suppose."

"What next?" exclaimed the machine, using a field to cut the bracelet. Gurgeh had expected the bright little image to disappear, but it didn't. "God? Ghosts? Time-travel?" The drone drew the bracelet off his wrist and reconnected the tiny Orbital so that it was a circle again.

Gurgeh smiled. "The Empire." He took the bracelet from the machine, got up easily and walked to the window, turning the Orbital over in his hands and looking out into the stony courtyard.

*The Empire?* thought Flere-Imsaho. It got Gurgeh to let it store the bracelet inside its casing. No sense in leaving it around; somebody might guess what it represented. *I do hope he's joking.*

With his own game over, Gurgeh found time to watch Nicosar's match. The Emperor was playing in the prow-hall of the fortress; a great bowled room ribbed in gray stone and capable of seating over a thousand people. It was here the last game would be played, the game which would decide who became Emperor. The prow-hall lay at the far end of the castle, facing the direction the fire would come from. High windows, still unshuttered, looked out over the sea of yellow cinderbud heads outside.

Gurgeh sat in one of the observation galleries, watching the Emperor play. Nicosar played cautiously, gradually building up advantages, playing the game in a percentage-wary way, setting up profitable exchanges on the Board of Becoming, and orchestrating the moves of the other four players on his side. Gurgeh was impressed; Nicosar played a deceptive game. The slow, steady style he evinced here was only one side of him; every now and again there would come, just when it was needed, exactly when it would have the most devastating effect, a move of startling brilliance and audacity. Equally, the occasional fine move by an opponent was always at least matched, and usually bettered, by the Emperor.

Gurgeh felt some sympathy for those playing against Nicosar. Even playing badly was less demoralizing than playing sporadically excellently but always being crushed.

"You're smiling, Jernau Gurgeh." Gurgeh had been absorbed in the game and hadn't seen Hamin approach. The old apex sat down carefully beside him. Bulges under his robe showed he wore an AG harness to partially counteract Echronedal's gravity.

"Good evening, Hamin."

"I have heard you qualified. Well done."

"Thank you. Only unofficially, of course."

"Ah yes. Officially you came fourth."

"How unexpectedly generous."

"We took into account your willingness to cooperate. You will still help us?"

"Of course. Just show me the camera."

"Perhaps tomorrow." Hamin nodded, looking down to where Nicosar stood, surveying his commanding position on the Board of Becoming. "Your opponent for the single game will be Lo Tenyos Krowo; an excellent player, I warn you. Are you quite sure you don't want to drop out now?"

"Quite. Would you have me cause Bermoiya's mutilation only to give up now because the strain's getting too much?"

"I see your point, Gurgeh." Hamin sighed, still watching the Emperor. He nodded. "Yes, I see your point. And anyway; you only qualified. By the narrowest of margins. And Lo Tenyos Krowo is very, very good." He nodded again. "Yes; perhaps you have found your level, eh?" The wizened face turned to Gurgeh.

"Very possibly, rector."

Hamin nodded absently and looked away again, at his Emperor.

On the following morning, Gurgeh recorded some faked game-board shots; the game he'd just played was set up again, and Gurgeh made some believable but uninspired moves, and one outright mistake. The part of his opponents was taken by Hamin and a couple of other senior Candsev College professors; Gurgeh was impressed by how well they were able to mimic the game-styles of the apices he'd been playing against.

As had, in effect, been foretold, Gurgeh finished fourth. He recorded an interview with the Imperial News Service expressing his sorrow at being knocked out of the Main Series and saying how grateful he was for having had the chance to play the game of Azad. The experience of a lifetime. He was eternally in the debt of the Azadian people. His respect for the Emperor-Regent's genius had increased immeasurably from its already high starting point. He looked forward to observing the rest of the games. He wished the Emperor, his Empire and all its people and subjects the very best for what would undoubtedly be a bright and prosperous future.

The news-team, and Hamin, seemed well pleased. "You should have been an actor, Jernau Gurgeh," Hamin told him.

Gurgeh assumed this was intended as a compliment.

He sat looking out over the forest of cinderbuds. The trees were sixty meters high or more. At their peak rate, the drone had told him, they grew at nearly a quarter-meter per day, sucking such vast quantities of water and matter from the ground that the soil dropped all around them, subsiding far enough to reveal the uppermost levels of their roots, which would burn in the Incandescence and take the full Great Year to regrow.

It was dusk, the short time in a short day when the rapidly spinning planet left the bright yellow dwarf dropping beyond the horizon. Gurgeh breathed deeply. There was no smell of burning. The air seemed quite clear, and a couple of planets in the Echronedal system shone in the sky. Nevertheless, Gurgeh knew there was sufficient dust in the atmosphere to forever block out most of the stars in the sky and leave the huge wheel that was the main galaxy blurred and indistinct; not remotely as breathtaking as it was when viewed from beyond the planet's hazed covering of gas.

He sat in a tiny garden near the top of the fortress, so that he could see over the summits of most of the cinderbuds. He was level with the fruit-bearing heads of the tallest trees. The fruit pods, each about the size of a curled-up child, were full of what was basically ethyl-alcohol. When the Incandescence arrived some would drop and some would stay hanging there; all would burn.

A shiver ran through Gurgeh when he thought about it. Approximately seventy days to go, they said. Anybody sitting where he was now when the fire-front arrived would be roasted alive, water-sprays or not. Radiated heat alone would cook you. The garden he was sitting in would go; the wooden bench he was sitting on would be taken inside, behind the thick stone and the metal and fireglass shutters. Gardens in the deeper courtyards would survive, though they would have to be dug out from some of the wind-blown ash. The people would be safe, in the drenched castle, or the deep shelters . . . unless they had been very foolish, and were caught outside. It had happened, he'd been told.

He saw Flere-Imsaho flying over the trees toward him. The machine had been given permission to fly off by itself, as long as it told the authorities where it was going and agreed to be fitted with a position monitor. Obviously there wasn't anything on Echronedal the Empire considered especially militarily sensitive. The drone hadn't been too happy with the conditions, but reckoned it would go mad cooped up in the castle, so had agreed. This had been its first expedition.

"Jernau Gurgeh."

"Hello, drone. Bird-watching?"

"Flying fish. Thought I'd start with the oceans."

"Going to take a look at the fire?"

"Not yet. I hear you're playing Lo Tenyos Krowo next."

"In four days. They say he's very good."

"He is. He's also one of the people who know all about the Culture."

Gurgeh glared at the machine. "What?"

"There are never fewer than eight people in the Empire who know where the Culture comes from, roughly what size it is, and our level of technological development."

"Really," Gurgeh said through his teeth.

"For the last two hundred years the Emperor, the chief of Naval Intelligence and the six star marshals have been appraised of the power and extent of the Culture. They don't want anybody else to know; their choice, not ours. They're frightened; it's understandable."

"Drone," Gurgeh said loudly, "has it occurred to you I might be getting a little sick of being treated like a child all the time? Why the hell couldn't you just *tell* me that?"

"Jernau, we only wanted to make things easier for you. Why complicate things by telling you that a few people *did* know when there was no real likelihood of your ever coming into any but the most fleeting contact with any of them? Frankly, you'd never have been told at all if you hadn't got to the stage of playing against one of these people; no need for you to know. We're just trying to help you, really. I thought I'd tell you in case Krowo said something during the course of the game which puzzled you and upset your concentration."

"Well, I wish you cared as much about my temper as you do about my concentration," Gurgeh said, getting up and going to lean on the parapet at the end of the garden.

"I'm very sorry," the drone said, without a trace of contrition.

Gurgeh waved one hand. "Never mind. I take it Krowo's in Naval Intelligence then, not the Office of Cultural Exchange?"

"Correct. Officially his post does not exist. But everybody in court knows the highest placed player who's the least bit devious is offered the job."

"I thought Cultural Exchange was a funny place for somebody that good."

"Well, Krowo's had the intelligence job for three Great Years, and some people reckon he could have been Emperor if he'd really wanted, but he prefers to stay where he is. He'll be a difficult opponent."

"So everybody keeps telling me," Gurgeh said, then frowned and looked toward the fading light on the horizon. "What's that?" he said. "Did you hear that?"

It came again; a long, haunting, plaintive cry from far away, almost drowned by the quiet rustling of the cinderbud canopy. The faint sound rose in a still quiet but chilling crescendo; a scream that died away slowly. Gurgeh shivered for the second time that evening.

"What *is* that?" he whispered.

The drone sidled closer. "What? Those calls?" it said.

"Yes!" Gurgeh said, listening to the faint sound as it came and went on the soft, warm wind, wavering out of the darkness over the rustling heads of the giant cinderbuds.

"Animals," Flere-Imsaho said, dimly silhouetted against the last fractions of light in the western sky. "Big carnivores called troshae, mostly. Six-legged. You saw some from the Emperor's personal menagerie on the night of the ball. Remember?"

Gurgeh nodded, still listening, fascinated, to the cries of the distant beasts. "How do they escape the Incandescence?"

"Troshae run ahead, almost up to the fire-line, during the previous Great Month. The ones you're listening to couldn't run fast enough to escape even if they started now. They've been trapped and penned so they can be hunted for sport.

That's why they're howling like that; they know the fire's coming and they want to get away."

Gurgeh said nothing, head turned to catch the faint sound of the doomed animals.

Flere-Imsaho waited for a minute or so, but the man did not move, or ask anything else. The machine backed off, to return to Gurgeh's rooms. Just before it went through the door into the castle, it looked back at the man standing clutching the stone parapet at the far end of the little garden. He was crouched a little, head forward, motionless. It was quite dark now, and ordinary human eyes could not have picked out the quiet figure.

The drone hesitated, then disappeared into the fortress.

Gurgeh hadn't thought Azad was the sort of game you could have an off-day in, certainly not an off-twenty-days. Discovering that it was came as a great disappointment.

He'd studied many of Lo Tenyos Krowo's past games and had looked forward to playing the Intelligence chief. The apex's style was exciting, far more flamboyant—if occasionally more erratic—than that of any of the other top-flight players. It ought to have been a challenging, enjoyable match, but it wasn't. It was hateful, embarrassing, ignominious. Gurgeh annihilated Krowo. The burly, at first rather jovial and unconcerned-seeming apex made some awful, simple errors, and some that resulted from genuinely inspired, even brilliant play, but which in the end were just as disastrous. Sometimes, Gurgeh knew, you came up against somebody who, just by the way they played, caused you a lot more problems than they ought to, and sometimes, too, you found a game in which everything went badly, no matter how hard you tried, and regardless of your most piercing insights and incisive moves. The chief of Naval Intelligence seemed to have both problems at once. Gurgeh's game-style might have been designed to cause Krowo problems, and the apex's luck was almost nonexistent.

Gurgeh felt real sympathy for Krowo, who was obviously more upset at the manner than the fact of the defeat. They were both glad when it was over.

Flere-Imsaho watched the man play during the closing stages of the match. It read each move as they appeared on the screen, and what it saw was something less like a game and more like an operation. Gurgeh the game-player, the *morat,* was taking his opponent apart. The apex was playing badly, true, but Gurgeh was off-handedly brilliant anyway. There was a callousness in his play that was new, too; something the drone had been half expecting but was still surprised to see so soon and so completely. It read the signs the man's body and face held; annoyance, pity, anger, sorrow . . . and it read the play too, and saw nothing remotely similar. All it read was the ordered fury of a player working the boards and the pieces, the cards and the rules, like the familiar controls of some omnipotent machine.

Another change, it thought. The man had altered, slipped deeper into the game and the society. It had been warned this might happen. One reason was that Gurgeh was speaking Eächic all the time. Flere-Imsaho was always a little dubious about trying to be so precise about human behavior, but it had been briefed that when Culture people didn't speak Marain for a long time and did speak another language, they were liable to change; they acted differently, they started to think in that other language, they lost the carefully balanced interpretative structure of the Culture language, left its subtle shifts of cadence, tone and rhythm behind for, in virtually every case, something much cruder.

Marain was a synthetic language, designed to be phonetically and philosophically as expressive as the pan-human speech apparatus and the pan-human brain would allow. Flere-Imsaho suspected it was over-rated, but smarter minds than it had dreamed Marain up, and ten millennia later even the most rarefied and superior Minds still thought highly of the language, so it supposed it had to defer to their superior understanding. One of the Minds who'd briefed it had even compared Marain to Azad. That really was fanciful, but Flere-Imsaho had taken the point behind the hyperbole.

Eächic was an ordinary, evolved language, with rooted assumptions which substituted sentimentality for compassion and aggression for cooperation. A comparatively innocent and sensitive soul like Gurgeh was bound to pick up some of its underlying ethical framework if he spoke it all the time.

So now the man played like one of those carnivores he'd been listening to, stalking across the board, setting up traps and diversions and killing grounds; pouncing, pursuing, bringing down, consuming, absorbing . . .

Flere-Imsaho shifted inside its disguise as though uncomfortable, then switched the screen off.

The day after Gurgeh's game with Krowo ended, he received a long letter from Chamlis Amalk-ney. He sat in his room and watched the old drone. It showed him views of Chiark while it gave him the latest news. Professor Boruelal still in retreat; Hafflis pregnant. Olz Hap away on a cruise with her first love, but coming back within the year to continue at the university. Chamlis still working on its history book.

Gurgeh sat, watching and listening. Contact had censored the communication, blanking out bits which, Gurgeh assumed, showed that the landscape of Chiark was Orbital, not planetary. It annoyed him less than he'd have expected.

He didn't enjoy the letter much. It all seemed so far away, so irrelevant. The ancient drone sounded hackneyed rather than wise or even friendly, and the people on the screen looked soft and stupid. Amalk-ney showed him Ikroh, and Gurgeh found himself angered at the fact that people came and stayed there every now and again. Who did they think they were?

Yay Meristinoux didn't appear in the letter; she'd finally grown fed up with Blask and the Preashipleyl machine and left to pursue her landscaping career in [deleted]. She sent her love. When she left she'd started the viral change to become a man.

There was one odd section, right at the end of the communication, apparently added after the main signal had been recorded. Chamlis was shown in the main lounge at Ikroh.

"Gurgeh," it said, "this arrived today; general delivery, unspecified sender, care of Special Circumstances." The view began to pan across to where, if no interfering interloper had changed the furniture around, there ought to have been a table. The screen blanked out. Chamlis said, "Our little friend. But quite lifeless. I've scanned it, and I had . . . [cut] send down its bugging team to take a look too. It's dead. Just a casing with no mind; like an intact human body with the brain neatly scooped out. There's a small cavity in the center, where its mind must have been."

The visuals returned; the view panned round to Chamlis again. "I can only assume the thing finally agreed to be restructured and they made it a new body. Odd they should send the old one here though. Let me know what you want done with it. Write soon. Hope this finds you well, and successful in whatever it is you're up to. Kindest re—"

Gurgeh switched the screen off. He got up quickly, went to the window and looked out at the courtyard beneath, frowning.

A smile spread slowly across his face. He laughed, silently, after a moment, then went over to the intercom and told his servant to bring some wine. He was just raising the glass to his lips when Flere-Imsaho floated in through the window, returning from another wildlife safari, its casing pale with dust. "You look pleased with yourself," it said. "What's the toast?"

Gurgeh gazed into the wine's amber depths and smiled. "Absent friends," he said, and drank.

The next match was a three game. Gurgeh was to face Yomonul Lu Rahsp, the star marshal imprisoned in the exoskeleton, and a youngish colonel, Lo Frag Traff. He knew that, going on form, they were both supposed to be inferior to Krowo, but the Intelligence chief had done so badly—he was unlikely to hold on to his post now—Gurgeh didn't think this was any indication he was going to have an easier game against his next two opponents than he'd had against the last one. On the contrary; it would be only natural for the two military men to gang up on him.

Nicosar was to play the old star marshal, Vechesteder, and the defense minister, Jhilno.

Gurgeh passed the days studying. Flere-Imsaho continued to explore. It told Gurgeh it had watched a whole region of the advancing fire-front being extinguished by a torrential rainstorm; it had revisited the area a couple of days later to find tinderplants re-igniting the dried vegetation. As an example of how integral the fire and the rest of the planet's ecology had become, the drone said, it was an impressive display.

The court amused itself with hunts in the forest during the daylight hours and live or holo shows at night.

Gurgeh found the entertainments predictable and tedious. The only faintly interesting ones were duels, usually males fighting each other, held in pits surrounded by banked circles of shouting, betting imperial officials and players. The duels were only occasionally to the death. Gurgeh suspected that things went on in the castle at night—entertainments of a different sort—which were inevitably fatal for at least one of the participants, and which he would not be welcome to attend or expected to hear about.

However, the thought no longer worried him.

Lo Frag Traff was a young apex with a very obvious scar running from one brow down his cheek, almost to his mouth. He played quick, fierce games, and his career in the Imperial Star Army bore the same hallmarks. His most famous exploit had been the sacking of the Urutypaig Library. Traff had been in command of a small ground force in a war against a humanoid species; the war in space had been fought to a temporary stalemate, but through a combination of great military talent and a little luck Traff found himself in a position to threaten the species' capital city from the ground. The enemy had sued for peace, making it a condition of the treaty that their great library, famous throughout the civilized species of the Lesser Cloud, be left untouched. Traff knew that if he refused this condition the fight would go on, so he gave his word that not a letter, not a pixel, on the ancient microfiles would be destroyed, and they would be left *in situ.*

Traff had orders from his star marshal that the library had to be destroyed. Nicosar himself had commanded this as one of his first edicts after coming to power; subject races had to understand that once they displeased the Emperor, nothing could prevent their punishment.

While nobody in the Empire cared in the least about one of

its loyal soldiers breaking an agreement with some bunch of aliens, Traff knew that giving your word was a sacred thing; nobody would ever trust him again if he went back on it.

Traff already knew what he was going to do. He solved the problem by shuffling the library, sorting every word in it into alphabetical order and every pixel of every illustration into order of color, shade and intensity. The original microfiles were wiped and re-recorded with volumes upon volumes of "the"s, "it"s, and "and"s; the illustrations were fields of pure color.

There were riots, of course, but Traff was in control by then, and as he explained to the incensed and—as it turned out, literally—suicidal guardians of the library, and to the Empire's Supreme Court, he had kept his word about not actually destroying or taking as booty a single word, image or file.

Halfway through the game on the Board of Origin, Gurgeh realized something remarkable; Yomonul and Traff were playing each other, not him. They played as if they expected him to win anyway, and were battling for second place. Gurgeh had known there was little love lost between the two; Yomonul represented the old guard of the military and Traff the new wave of brash young adventurers. Yomonul was an exponent of negotiation and minimum-force, Traff of the moves that smite. Yomonul had a liberal view of other species; Traff was a xenophobe. The two came from traditionally opposed colleges, and all their differences were displayed quite overtly in their game-styles; Yomonul's was studied, careful and detached; Traff's was aggressive to the point of recklessness.

Their attitude to the Emperor was different, too. Yomonul took a cool, practical view of the throne, while Traff was utterly loyal to Nicosar himself rather than the position he held. Each detested the beliefs of the other.

Nevertheless, Gurgeh hadn't expected them to more or

less disregard him and go straight for each other's throats. Once again, he felt slightly cheated that he wasn't getting a proper game. The only compensation was that the amount of venom in the play of the two warring military men was something to behold, undeniably impressive if distressingly self-defeating and wasteful. Gurgeh cruised through the game, quietly picking up points while the two soldiers fought. He was winning, but he couldn't help feeling the other two were getting much more out of the game than he was. He'd have expected they would use the physical option, but Nicosar himself had ordered that there be no betting during the match; he knew the two players were pathologically opposed, and didn't want to risk losing the military services of either.

Gurgeh sat watching a table-screen during lunch on his third day on the Board of Origin. There were still a few minutes before play resumed and Gurgeh sat alone, watching the news-reports showing how well Lo Tenyos Krowo was doing in his game against Yomonul and Traff. Whoever had faked the apex's play—not Krowo himself, who'd refused to have anything to do with the subterfuge—was making a good job of impersonating the Intelligence chief's style. Gurgeh smiled a little.

"Contemplating your coming victory, Jernau Gurgeh?" Hamin said, easing himself into the seat across the table.

Gurgeh turned the screen round. "It's a little early for that, don't you think?"

The old, bald apex peered at the screen, smiling thinly. "Hmm. You think so?" He reached out, turned the screen off.

"Things change, Hamin."

"Indeed they do, Gurgeh. But I think the course of this game will not. Yomonul and Traff will continue to ignore you and attack each other. You will win."

"Well then," Gurgeh said, looking at the dead screen. "Krowo will get to play Nicosar."

"Krowo may; we can devise a match to cover that. You must not."

"*Must* not?" Gurgeh said. "I thought I'd done all you wanted. What else can I do?"

"Refuse to play the Emperor."

Gurgeh looked into the old apex's pale gray eyes, each set in a web of fine lines. They gazed just as calmly back. "What's the problem, Hamin? I'm not a threat anymore."

Hamin smoothed the fine material at the cuff of his robe. "You know, Jernau Gurgeh, I do hate obsessions. They're so . . . blinding, yes?" He smiled. "I am becoming worried for my Emperor, Gurgeh. I know how much he wants to prove he is rightfully on the throne, that he is worthy of the post he's held the last two years. I believe he will do just that, but I know that what he really wants—what he always did want—is to play Molsce and win. That, of course, isn't possible anymore. The Emperor is dead, long live the Emperor; he rises from the flames . . . but I think he sees old Molsce in you, Jernau Gurgeh, and it is you he feels he must play, you he must beat; the alien, the man from the Culture, the *morat,* player-of-games. I am not sure that would be a good idea. It is not necessary. You will lose anyway, I feel certain, but . . . as I say; obsessions disturb me. It would be best for all concerned if you let it be known as soon as possible you will retire after this game."

"And deprive Nicosar of the chance to beat me?" Gurgeh looked surprised and amused.

"Yes. Better he still feels there's something still to prove. It will do him no harm."

"I'll think about it," Gurgeh said.

Hamin studied him for a moment. "I hope you understand how frank I've been with you, Jernau Gurgeh. It would be unfortunate if such honesty went unacknowledged, and unrewarded."

Gurgeh nodded. "Yes, I don't doubt it would."

A male servant at the door announced the game was about to recommence. "Excuse me, rector," Gurgeh said, rising. The old apex's gaze followed him. "Duty calls."

"Obey," Hamin said.

Gurgeh stopped, looking down at the wizened old creature on the far side of the table. Then he turned and left.

Hamin gazed at the blank table-screen in front of him, as if absorbed in some fascinating, invisible game that only he could see.

Gurgeh won on the Board of Origin and the Board of Form. The ferocious struggle between Traff and Yomonul continued; first one edged ahead, then the other. Traff went into the Board of Becoming with a very slight lead over the older apex. Gurgeh was so far ahead he was almost invulnerable, able to relax in his strongholds and spectate upon the total war around him before heading out to mop up whatever was left of the exhausted victor's forces. It seemed the only fair—not to mention expedient—thing to do; let the lads have their fun, then impose order later and tidy the toys back in the box.

Still no substitute for a real game, though.

"Are you pleased or displeased, Mr. Gurgeh?" Star Marshal Yomonul came up to Gurgeh and asked him the question during a pause in the game while Traff consulted with the Adjudicator on a point of order. Gurgeh had been standing thinking, staring at the board, and hadn't noticed the imprisoned apex approach. He looked up in surprise to see the star marshal in front of him, his lined face looking out, faintly amused, from its titanium and carbon cage. Neither soldier had paid him any attention until now.

"At being left out?" Gurgeh said.

The apex moved one rod-braced arm to indicate the board. "Yes; to be winning so easily. Do you seek the victory or the challenge?" The apex's skeletal mask moved with each action of the jaw.

"I'd prefer both," Gurgeh admitted. "I have thought of joining in; as a third force, or on one side or the other . . . but this looks too much like a personal war."

The elderly apex grinned; the head-cage nodded easily. "It is," he said. "You're doing very well as you are. I wouldn't change now, if I were you."

"What about you?" Gurgeh asked. "You seem to be getting the worst of it at the moment."

Yomonul smiled; the face mask flexed even for that small gesture. "I'm having the time of my life. And I still have a few surprises lined up for the youngster, and a few tricks. But I feel a little guilty at letting you through so easily. You'll embarrass us all if you play Nicosar and win."

Gurgeh expressed surprise. "You think I could?"

"No." The apex's gesture was the more emphatic for being contained and amplified in its dark cage. "Nicosar plays at his best when he has to, and at his best he will beat you. So long as he isn't too ambitious. No; he'll beat you, because you'll threaten him, and he will respect that. But—ah . . ." The star marshal turned as Traff strode across the board, moved a couple of pieces, and then bowed with exaggerated courtesy to Yomonul. The star marshal looked back at Gurgeh. "I see it is my turn. Excuse me." He returned to the fray.

Perhaps one of the tricks Yomonul had mentioned was making Traff think his conversation with Gurgeh had been to enlist the Culture man's aid; for some time afterward the younger soldier acted as though he was expecting to have to fight on two fronts.

It gave Yomonul an edge. He scraped in ahead of Traff. Gurgeh won the match and the chance to play Nicosar. Hamin tried to talk to him in the corridor outside the game-hall, immediately after his victory, but Gurgeh just smiled and walked past.

Cinderbuds swayed all around them; the light wind made shushing noises in the golden canopy. The court, the game-players and their retinues sat on a high, steeply raked wooden structure itself almost the size of a small castle. Before the stand, in a large clearing in the cinderbud forest, was a long, narrow run; a double fence of stout timbers five meters or more high. This formed the central section of a sort of open corral, shaped like an hourglass and open to the forest at both ends. Nicosar and the higher-placed players sat at the front of the high wooden platform with a good view of the wooden funnel.

At the back of the stand there were awninged areas where food was being prepared. Smells of roasting meat drifted over the stand and out into the forest.

"That'll have them frothing at the mouth," Star Marshal Yomonul said, leaning over to Gurgeh with a whirring of servoes. They were sitting side by side, on the front rank of the platform, a little along from the Emperor. Both held a large projectile rifle, fastened to a supporting tripod in front of them.

"What will?" Gurgeh asked.

"The smell." Yomonul grinned, gesturing behind them to the fires and grills. "Roasted meat. Wind's carrying it their way. It'll drive them crazy."

"Oh, great," muttered Flere-Imsaho from near Gurgeh's feet. It had already tried to persuade Gurgeh not to take part in the hunt.

Gurgeh ignored the machine and nodded. "Of course," he said. He hefted the rifle stock. The ancient weapon was single shot; a sliding bolt had to be operated to reload it. Each gun had slightly different rifling patterns, so that when the bullets were removed from the bodies of the animals, the marks on them would allow a score to be kept and heads and pelts to be allocated.

"You sure you've used one of these before?" Yomonul asked, grinning at him. The apex was in a good mood. In a few tens of days he would be released from the exoskeleton. Meanwhile, the Emperor had allowed the prison regimen to be relaxed; Yomonul could socialize, drink, and eat whatever he liked.

Gurgeh nodded. "I've shot guns," he said. He'd never used a projectile gun, but there had been that day, years ago now, with Yay, in the desert.

"Bet you've never shot anything *live* before," the drone said.

Yomonul tapped the machine's casing with one carbon-shod foot.

"Quiet, thing," he said.

Flere-Imsaho tipped slowly up so that its beveled brown front pointed up at Gurgeh. "'*Thing*'?" it said indignantly, in a sort of whispered screech.

Gurgeh winked and put his finger to his lips. He and Yomonul grinned at each other.

The hunt, as it was called, started with a blare of trumpets and the distant howling of the troshae. A line of males appeared from the forest and ran alongside the wooden funnel, beating the timbers with rods. The first troshae appeared, shadows striping along its flanks as it entered the clearing and ran into the wooden funnel. The people around Gurgeh murmured in anticipation.

"A big one," Yomonul said appreciatively as the golden-black striped beast loped six-legged down the run. Clicks all around the platform announced people preparing to fire. Gurgeh lifted the stock of the rifle. Fastened to its tripod, the rifle was easier to handle in the harsh gravity than it would have been otherwise, as well as being limited in its field of fire; something the Emperor's ever watchful guards no doubt found reassuring.

The troshae sprinted down the run, paws blurring on the dusty ground; people fired at it, filling the air with muffled cracking noises and puffs of gray smoke. White wood splinters spun off the run's timbers; puffs of dust burst from the ground. Yomonul sighted and fired; a chorus of shots burst out around Gurgeh. The guns were silenced, but all the same Gurgeh felt his ears close up a little, deadening the racket. He fired. The recoil took him by surprise; his bullet must have gone way over the animal's head.

He looked down into the run. The animal was screaming. It tried to leap up the fence on the far side of the run, but was brought down in a hail of fire. It limped on a little further, dragging three legs and leaving a trail of blood behind it. Gurgeh heard another muffled report by his side, and the carnivore's head jerked suddenly to one side; it collapsed. A great cheer went up. A gate in the run was opened and some males scurried in to drag the body away. Yomonul was on his feet beside Gurgeh, acknowledging the cheers. He sat down again quickly, exoskeleton motors whirring, as the next animal appeared out of the forest and raced between the wooden walls.

After the fourth troshae, several came at once, and in the confusion one scrambled up the timbers of the run and over the top; it started to chase some of the males waiting outside the run. A guard, on the ground at the foot of the stand, brought the animal down with a single laser-shot.

In the midmorning, when a great pile of the striped bodies had accumulated in the middle of the run and there was a danger some animals would climb out over the bodies of their predecessors, the hunt was stopped while males used hooks and hawsers and a couple of small tractors to clear the warm, blood-spattered debris. Somebody on the far side of the Emperor shot one of the males while they were working. There were some tuts, and a few drunken cheers. The Emperor fined the offender and told them if they did it again they'd find themselves running with the troshae. Everybody laughed.

"You're not firing, Gurgeh," Yomonul said. He reckoned he'd killed another three animals by then. Gurgeh had begun to find the hunt a little pointless, and almost stopped firing. He kept missing, anyway.

"I'm not very good at this," he said.

"Practice!" Yomonul laughed, slapping him on the back. The servo-amplified blow from the elated Star Marshal almost knocked the wind out of Gurgeh.

Yomonul claimed another kill. He gave an excited shout and kicked Flere-Imsaho. "Fetch!" he laughed.

The drone rose slowly and with dignity from the floor. "Jernau Gurgeh," it said. "I'm not putting up with any more of this. I'm going back to the castle. Do you mind?"

"Not at all."

"Thank you. Enjoy your marksmanship." It floated down and to the side, disappearing round the edge of the stand. Yomonul had it in his sights most of the way.

"You just let it go?" he asked Gurgeh, laughing.

"Glad to be rid of it," Gurgeh told him.

They broke for lunch. Nicosar congratulated Yomonul, saying how well he'd shot. Gurgeh sat with Yomonul at lunch, too, and went down on one knee as Nicosar's palanquin was brought up to their part of the table. Yomonul told the Emperor the exoskeleton helped steady his aim. Nicosar said it was the Emperor's pleasure that the device be removed soon, after the formal end of the games. Nicosar glanced at Gurgeh, but said nothing else; the AG palanquin lifted itself; the imperial guards nudged it further down the line of waiting people.

After lunch, people returned to their seats and the hunt went on. There were other animals to hunt, and the first part of the short afternoon was spent shooting them, but the troshae came back later on. So far, only seven of the two hundred or so troshae released from the forest pens into the run had made it all the way through the wooden funnel and out the far end to escape into the forest. Even they were wounded, and would anyway be caught by the Incandescence.

The earth in the wooden funnel in front of the shooting platform was dark with auburn blood. Gurgeh shot as the animals pounded down the sodden run, but aimed to just miss them, watching for the spatter of muddy ground in front of their noses as they tore, wounded and howling and panting, in front of him. He found the whole hunt somewhat distasteful, but could not deny that the infectious excitement of the Azadians had some effect on him. Yomonul was obviously enjoying himself. The apex leaned over as a large female troshae came running out of the forest with two small cubs.

"You need more practice, Gurgey," he said. "Don't you do any hunting at home?" The female and her cubs ran toward the wooden funnel.

"Not much," Gurgeh admitted.

Yomonul grunted, aimed at long range and fired. One of the cubs dropped. The female skidded, stopped, went back to it. The other cub ran on hesitantly. It mewled as bullets hit it.

Yomonul reloaded. "I was surprised to see you here at all," he said. The female, stung by a bullet in a rear leg, swung growling away from the dead cub and charged forward again, roaring at the tottering, wounded cub.

"I wanted to show I wasn't squeamish," Gurgeh said, watching the second cub's head jerk up and the beast fall at the feet of its mother. "And I have hunted—"

He was going to use the word "Azad," which meant machine and animal; any organism or system, and he turned to Yomonul with a small smile to say this, but when he looked at the apex he could see there was something wrong.

Yomonul was shaking. He sat clutching his gun, turned half toward Gurgeh, face quivering in its dark cage, skin white and covered in sweat, eyes bulging.

Gurgeh went to put his hand on the strut of the Star Marshal's forearm, instinctively offering support.

It was as though something broke inside the apex. Yomonul's gun swung right round, snapping the supporting tripod; the bulky silencer pointed straight at Gurgeh's forehead. Gurgeh had a fleeting, vivid impression of Yomonul's face; jaw clamped shut, blood trickling over his chin, eyes staring, a tic working furiously on the side of his face. Gurgeh ducked; the gun fired somewhere over his head and he heard a scream as he fell out of his seat, rolling past his own gun's tripod.

Before he could get up, Gurgeh was kicked in the back. He turned over to see Yomonul above him, swaying crazily against the background of shocked, pale faces behind him. He was struggling with the rifle bolt, reloading. One foot lashed out again, thudding into Gurgeh's ribs; he jerked back, trying to absorb the blow, and fell over the front of the platform.

He saw wooden slats whirling, cinderbuds revolving, then he struck, crashing into a male animal handler standing just before the run. They each thudded to the ground, winded. Gurgeh looked up and saw Yomonul on the platform, exoskeleton glinting dully in the sunlight, raising the rifle and sighting on him. Two apices came up behind Yomonul, arms out to grasp him. Without even glancing back, Yomonul swung his arms flashing round behind him; a hand smashed into the chest of one apex; the rifle slammed into the face of the other. Both collapsed; the carbon-ribbed arms darted back and Yomonul steadied the gun again, aiming at Gurgeh.

Gurgeh was on his feet, diving away. The shot hit the still winded male lying behind him. Gurgeh stumbled for the wooden doors leading under the high platform; shouts came from the platform as Yomonul jumped down, landing between Gurgeh and the doors; the Star Marshal reloaded the gun as he hit the ground on his feet, the exoskeleton easily absorbing the shock of landing. Gurgeh almost fell as he turned, feet skidding on the blood-spattered earth.

He pushed himself off the ground, to run between the edge of the wooden fence and the platform edge. A uniformed guard with a CREW rifle stood in his way, looking uncertainly up at the platform. Gurgeh went to run past him, ducking as he did so. Still a few meters in front of Gurgeh, the guard started to put one hand out and unhitch the laser from his shoulder. A look of almost comic surprise appeared on his flat face, an instant before one side of his chest burst open and he spun round into Gurgeh's path, knocking him over.

Gurgeh rolled again, clattering over the dead guard. He sat up. Yomonul was ten meters away, running awkwardly toward him, reloading. The guard's rifle was at Gurgeh's feet. He reached out, grabbed it, aimed at Yomonul and fired.

The Star Marshal ducked, but Gurgeh was still allowing for recoil after a morning shooting the projectile rifle. The laser-shot slammed into Yomonul's face; the apex's head blew apart.

Yomonul didn't stop. He didn't even slow down; the running figure, head-cage almost empty, trailing strips of flesh and splintered bone behind it like pennants, neck spouting blood, speeded up; it ran faster toward him, and less awkwardly.

It aimed the rifle straight at Gurgeh's head.

Gurgeh froze, stunned. Too late, he started to sight the CREW gun again, and began struggling to get up. The headless exoskeleton was three meters away; he stared into the silencer's black mouth and he knew he was dead. But the bizarre figure hesitated, empty head-shell jerking upward, and the gun wavered.

Something crashed into Gurgeh—from the back, he realized, surprised, as everything went dark; from the *back,* not from the front—and then came nothing.

His back hurt. He opened his eyes. A bulky brown drone hummed between him and a white ceiling.

"Gurgeh?" the machine said.

He swallowed, licked his lips. "What?" he said. He didn't know where he was, or who the drone was. He had only a very vague idea who he was.

"Gurgeh. It's me; Flere-Imsaho. How do you feel?"

Flear Imsah-ho. The name meant something. "Back hurts a bit," he said, hoping not to be found out. Gurgi? Gurgey? Must be his name.

"I'm not surprised. A very large troshae hit you in the back."

"A what?"

"Never mind. Go back to sleep."

". . . Sleep."

His eyelids felt very heavy and the drone looked blurred.

His back hurt. He opened his eyes and saw a white ceiling. He looked around for Flere-Imsaho. Dark wooden walls. Window. Flere-Imsaho; there it was. It floated over to him.

"Hello, Gurgeh."

"Hello."

"Do you remember who I am?"

"Still asking stupid questions, Flere-Imsaho. Am I going to be all right?"

"You're bruised, you've got a cracked rib and you're mildly concussed. You ought to be able to get up in a day or two."

"Do I remember you saying a . . . troshae hit me? Did I dream that?"

"You didn't dream it. I did tell you. That's what happened. How much do you remember?"

"Falling off the stand . . . platform," he said slowly, trying to think. He was in bed and his back was sore. It was his own room in the castle and the lights were on so it was probably night. His eyes widened. "Yomonul *kicked* me off!" he said suddenly. "*Why*?"

"It doesn't matter now. Go back to sleep."

Gurgeh started to say something else, but he felt tired again as the drone buzzed closer, and he closed his eyes for a second just to rest them.

Gurgeh stood by the window, looking down into the courtyard. The male servant took the tray out, glasses clinking.

"Go on," he said to the drone.

"The troshae climbed the fence while everybody was watching you and Yomonul. It came up behind you and sprang. It hit you and then bowled over the exoskeleton before it had time to do much about it. Guards shot the troshae as it tried to gore Yomonul, and by the time they dragged it off the exoskeleton it had deactivated."

Gurgeh shook his head slowly. "All I remember is being kicked off the stand." He sat down in a chair by the window. The far edge of the courtyard was golden in the hazy light of late afternoon. "And where were you while this was happening?"

"Back here, watching the hunt on an imperial broadcast. I'm sorry I left, Jernau Gurgeh, but that appalling apex was kicking me, and the whole obscene spectacle was just too gory and disgusting for words."

Gurgeh waved one hand. "It doesn't matter. I'm alive." He put his face in his hands. "You're sure it was I who shot Yomonul?"

"Oh yes! It's all recorded. Do you want to wa—"

"No." Gurgeh held up one hand to the drone, eyes still closed. "No; I don't want to watch."

"I didn't see that bit live," Flere-Imsaho said. "I was on my way back to the hunt as soon as Yomonul fired his first shot and killed the person on the other side of you. But I've watched the recording; yes, you killed him, with the guard's CREW. But of course that just meant whoever had taken control of the exoskeleton didn't have to fight against Yomonul inside it. As soon as Yomonul was dead the thing moved a lot faster and less erratically. He must have been using all his strength to try and stop it."

Gurgeh stared at the floor. "You're certain about all this?"

"Absolutely." The drone drifted over to the wall-screen. "Look, why not watch it on your—"

"No!" Gurgeh shouted, standing, and then swaying.

He sat down again. "No," he said, quieter.

"By the time I got there, whoever was jamming the exoskeleton controls had gone; I got a brief reading on my microwave sensors while I was between here and the hunt, but it switched off before I could get an accurate fix. Some kind of phased-pulse maser. The imperial guards picked up something too; they'd started a search in the forest by the time we took you away. I persuaded them I knew what I was doing and had you brought here. They sent a doctor in to look at you a couple of times, but that's all. Lucky I got there when I did or they might have taken you to the infirmary and started doing all sorts of nasty tests on you . . ." The drone sounded perplexed. "That's why I have a feeling this wasn't a straight security-service job. They'd have tried other, less public ways to kill you, and they'd have been all set up to get you into the hospital if it hadn't quite worked . . . all too disorganized. There's something funny going on, I'm sure."

Gurgeh put his hands to his back, carefully tracing the extent of the bruising again. "I wish I could remember everything. I wish I could remember whether I meant to kill Yomonul," he said. His chest ached. He felt sick.

"As you did, and you're such a bad shot, I'd assume the answer is no."

Gurgeh looked at the machine. "Don't you have something else you could be doing, drone?"

"Not really. Oh, by the way; the Emperor wants to see you, when you're feeling well."

"I'll go now," Gurgeh said, standing slowly.

"Are you sure? I don't think you should. You don't look well; I'd lie down if I were you. Please sit down. You're not ready. What if he's angry because you killed Yomonul? Oh, I suppose I'd better come with you . . ."

* * *

Nicosar sat in a small throne in front of a great bank of slanting, multicolored windows. The imperial apartments were submerged in the deep, polychromatic light; huge wall tapestries sewn with precious metal threads glittered like treasures in an underwater cave. Guards stood impassively around the walls and behind the throne; courtiers and officials shuffled to and fro with papers and flat-screens. An officer of the Imperial Household brought Gurgeh to the throne, leaving Flere-Imsaho at the other end of the room under the watchful eyes of two guards.

"Please sit." Nicosar motioned Gurgeh to a small stool on the dais in front of him. Gurgeh sat down gratefully. "Jernau Gurgeh," the Emperor said, his voice quiet and controlled, almost flat. "We offer you our sincere apologies for what happened yesterday. We are glad to see you have made such a rapid recovery, though we understand you are still in pain. Is there anything you wish?"

"Thank you, Your Highness, no."

"We are glad." Nicosar nodded slowly. He was still dressed in unrelieved black. His sober dress, small frame and plain face contrasted with the fabulous splashes of color from the raked windows overhead and the sumptuous clothing of the courtiers. The Emperor put small, ringed hands on the arms of the throne. "We are, of course, deeply sorry to lose the regard and the services of our Star Marshal, Yomonul Lu Rahsp, especially in such tragic circumstances, but we understand that you had no choice but to defend yourself. It is our will that no action be taken against you."

"Thank you, Your Highness."

Nicosar waved one hand. "In the matter of who plotted against you, the person who took control of our star marshal's imprisoning device was discovered and put to the question. We were deeply hurt to discover that the leading conspirator was our life-long mentor and guide, the rector of Candsev College."

"Ham—" Gurgeh began, but stopped. Nicosar's face was a study in displeasure. The old apex's name died in Gurgeh's throat. "I—" Gurgeh started again.

Nicosar held up one hand.

"We wish to tell you that the rector of Candsev College, Hamin Li Srilist, has been sentenced to death for his part in the conspiracy against you. We understand that this may not have been the only attempt on your life. If this is so, then all relevant circumstances will be investigated and the wrong-doers brought to justice.

"Certain persons in the court," Nicosar said, looking at the rings on his hands, "have desired to protect their Emperor through . . . misguided actions. The Emperor needs no such protection from a game-opponent, even if that opponent uses aids we deny ourselves. It has been necessary to deceive our subjects in the matter of your progress in these final games, but this is for their good, not ours. We have no need to be protected from unpleasant truths. The Emperor knows no fear, only discretion. We shall be happy to postpone the game between the Emperor-Regent and the man Jernau Morat Gurgeh until he feels fit to play."

Gurgeh found himself waiting for more of the quiet, slow, half-sung words, but Nicosar sat, impassively silent.

"I thank Your Highness," Gurgeh said, "but I would prefer there be no postponement. I feel almost well enough to play now, and there are still three days before the match is due to start. I'm sure there is no need to delay further."

Nicosar nodded slowly. "We are pleased. We hope, though, that if Jernau Gurgeh desires to change his mind on this matter before the match is due to start, he will not hesitate to inform the Imperial Office, which will gladly put back the starting date of the final match until Jernau Gurgeh feels fit to play the game of Azad to the very best of his ability."

"I thank Your Highness again."

"We are pleased that Jernau Gurgeh was not badly injured and has been able to attend this audience," Nicosar said. He nodded briefly to Gurgeh and then looked to a courtier, waiting impatiently to one side.

Gurgeh stood, bowed, and backed away.

"You only have to take *four* backward steps before you turn your back on him," Flere-Imsaho told him. "Otherwise; very good."

They were back in Gurgeh's room. "I'll try and remember next time," he said.

"Anyway, sounds like you're in the clear. I did a bit of overhearing while you had your tête-à-tête; courtiers usually know what's going on. Seems they found an apex trying to escape through the forest from the maser and the exo-controls; he'd dropped the gun they gave him to defend himself with, which was just as well because it was a bomb, not a gun, so they got him alive. He broke under torture and implicated one of Hamin's cronies who tried to bargain with a confession. So they started on Hamin."

"You mean they tortured him?"

"Only a little. He's old and they had to keep him alive for whatever punishment the Emperor decided on. The apex exo-controller and some other henchman have been impaled, the plea-bargaining crony's getting caged in the forest to await the Incandescence, and Hamin's being deprived of AGe drugs; he'll be dead in forty or fifty days."

Gurgeh shook his head. "Hamin . . . I didn't think he was that frightened of me."

"Well, he's old. They have funny ideas sometimes."

"Do you think I'm safe now?"

"Yes. The Emperor wants you alive so he can destroy you on the Azad boards. Nobody else would dare harm you. You can concentrate on the game. Anyway, I'll look after you."

Gurgeh looked, disbelievingly, at the buzzing drone.

He could detect no trace of irony in its voice.

Gurgeh and Nicosar started the first of the lesser games three days later. There was a curious atmosphere about the final match; a sense of anti-climax pervaded Castle Klaff. Normally this last contest was the culmination of six years' work and preparation in the Empire; the very apotheosis of all that Azad was and stood for. This time, the imperial continuance was already settled. Nicosar had ensured his next Great Year of rule when he'd beaten Vechesteder and Jhilno, though, as far as the rest of the Empire knew, the Emperor still had to play Krowo to decide who wore the imperial crown. Even if Gurgeh did win the game, it would make no difference, save for some wounded imperial pride. The court and the Bureau would put it down to experience, and make sure they didn't invite anymore decadent but sneaky aliens to take part in the holy game.

Gurgeh suspected that many of the people still in the fortress would as soon have left Echronedal to head back to Eä, but the coronation ceremony and the religious confirmation still had to be witnessed, and nobody would be allowed to leave Echronedal until the fire had passed and the Emperor had risen from its embers.

Probably only Gurgeh and Nicosar were really looking forward to the match; even the observing game-players and analysts were disheartened at the prospect of witnessing a game they were already barred from discussing, even among themselves. All Gurgeh's games past the point he had supposedly been knocked out were taboo subjects. They did not exist. The Imperial Games Bureau was already hard at work concocting an official final match between Nicosar and Krowo. Judging by their previous efforts, Gurgeh expected it to be entirely convincing. It might lack the ultimate spark of genius, but it would pass.

So everything was already settled. The Empire had new star marshals (though a little shuffling would be required to replace Yomonul), new generals and admirals, archbishops, ministers and judges. The course of the Empire was set, and with very little change from the previous bearing. Nicosar would continue with his present policies; the premises of the various winners indicated little discontent or new thinking. The courtiers and officials could therefore breathe easily again, knowing nothing would alter too much, and their positions were as secure as they'd ever be. So, instead of the usual tension surrounding the final game, there was an atmosphere more like that of an exhibition match. Only the two contestants were treating it as a real contest.

Gurgeh was immediately impressed by Nicosar's play. The Emperor didn't stop rising in Gurgeh's estimation; the more he studied the apex's play the more he realized just how powerful and complete an opponent he was facing. He would need to be more than lucky to beat Nicosar; he would need to be somebody else. From the beginning he tried to concentrate on not being trounced rather than actually defeating the Emperor.

Nicosar played cautiously most of the time; then, suddenly, he'd strike out with some brilliant flowing series of moves that looked at first as though they'd been made by some gifted madman, before revealing themselves as the masterstrokes they were; perfect answers to the impossible questions they themselves posed.

Gurgeh did his best to anticipate these devastating fusions of guile and power, and to find replies to them once they'd begun, but by the time the minor games were over, thirty days or so before the fire was due, Nicosar had a considerable advantage in pieces and cards to carry over to the first of the three great boards. Gurgeh suspected his only chance was to hold out as best he could on the first two boards and hope that he might pull something back on the final one.

The cinderbuds towered around the castle, rising like a slow tide of gold about the walls. Gurgeh sat in the same small garden he'd visited before. Then he'd been able to look out over the cinderbuds to the distant horizon; now the view ended twenty meters away at the first of the great yellow leaf-heads. Late sunlight spread the castle's shadow across the canopy. Behind Gurgeh, the fortress lights were coming on.

Gurgeh looked out to the tan trunks of the great trees, and shook his head. He'd lost the game on the Board of Origin and now he was losing on the Board of Form.

He was missing something; some facet of the way Nicosar was playing was escaping him. He knew it, he was certain, but he couldn't work out what that facet was. He had a nagging suspicion it was something very simple, however complex its articulation on the boards might be. He ought to have spotted it, analyzed and evaluated it long ago and turned it to his advantage, but for some reason—some reason intrinsic to his very understanding of the game, he felt sure—he could not. An aspect of his play seemed to have disappeared, and he was starting to think the knock to the head he'd taken during the hunt had affected him more than he'd first assumed.

But then, the ship didn't seem to have any better idea what he was doing wrong, either. Its advice always seemed to make sense at the time, but when Gurgeh got to the board he found he could never apply the ship's ideas. If he went against his instincts and forced himself to do as the *Limiting Factor* had suggested, he ended up in even more trouble; nothing was more guaranteed to cause you problems on an Azad board than trying to play in a way you didn't really believe in.

He rose slowly, straightening his back, which was hardly sore now, and returned to his room. Flere-Imsaho was in front of the screen, watching a holo-display of an odd diagram.

"What are you doing?" Gurgeh said, lowering himself into a soft chair. The drone turned, addressing him in Marain.

"I worked out a way to disable the bugs; we can talk in Marain now. Isn't that good?"

"I suppose so," Gurgeh said, still in Eächic. He picked up a small flat-screen to see what was happening in the Empire.

"Well, you might at least use the language after I went to the trouble of jamming their bugs. It wasn't easy you know; I'm not designed for that sort of thing. I had to learn a lot of stuff from some of my own files about electronics and optics and listening fields and all that sort of technical stuff. I thought you'd be pleased."

"Utterly and profoundly ecstatic," Gurgeh said carefully, in Marain. He looked at the small screen. It told him of the new appointments, the crushing of an insurrection in a distant system, the progress of the game between Nicosar and Krowo—Krowo wasn't as far behind as Gurgeh was—the victory won by imperial troops against a race of monsters, and higher rates of pay for males who volunteered to join the Army. "What *is* that you're looking at?" he said, looking briefly at the wall-screen, where Flere-Imsaho's strange torus turned slowly.

"Don't you recognize it?" the drone said, voice pitched to express surprise. "I thought you would; it's a model of the Reality."

"The—oh, yes." Gurgeh nodded and went back to the small screen, where a group of asteroids was being bombarded by imperial battleships, to quell the insurrection. "Four dimensions and all that." He flicked through the sub-channels to the game programs. A few of the second-series matches were still being played on Eä.

"Well, seven relevant dimensions actually, in the case of the Reality itself; one of those lines . . . are you listening?"

"Hmm? Oh yes." The games on Eä were all in their last stages. The secondary games from Echronedal were still being analyzed.

". . . one of those lines on the Reality represents our entire universe . . . surely you were taught all this?"

"Mm," Gurgeh nodded. He had never been especially interested in spatial theory or hyperspace or hyperspheres or the like; none of it seemed to make any difference to how he lived, so what did it matter? There were some games that were best understood in four dimensions, but Gurgeh only cared about their own particular rules, and the general theories only meant anything to him as they applied specifically to those games. He pressed for another page on the small screen . . . to be confronted with a picture of himself, once more expressing his sadness at being knocked out of the games, wishing the people and Empire of Azad well and thanking everybody for having him. An announcer talked over his faded voice to say that Gurgeh had pulled out of the second-series games on Echronedal. Gurgeh smiled thinly, watching the official reality he'd agreed to be part of as it gradually built up and became accepted fact.

He looked up briefly at the torus on the screen, and remembered something he'd puzzled over, years ago now. "What's the difference between hyperspace and ultraspace?" he asked the drone. "The ship mentioned ultraspace once and I never could work out what the hell it was talking about."

The drone tried to explain, using the holo-model of the Reality to illustrate. As ever, it over-explained, but Gurgeh got the idea, for what it was worth.

Flere-Imsaho annoyed him that evening, chattering away in Marain all the time about anything and everything. After initially finding it rather needlessly complex, Gurgeh enjoyed hearing the language again, and discovered some pleasure in speaking it, but the drone's high, squeaky voice became tiring after a while. It only shut up while he had his customary rather negative and depressing game-analysis with the ship that evening, still in Marain.

He had his best night's sleep since the day of the hunt, and woke feeling, for no good reason he could think of, that there might yet be a chance of turning the game around.

It took Gurgeh most of the morning's play to gradually work out what Nicosar was up to. When, eventually, he did, it took his breath away.

The Emperor had set out to beat not just Gurgeh, but the whole Culture. There was no other way to describe his use of pieces, territory and cards; he had set up his whole side of the match as an Empire, the very image of Azad.

Another revelation struck Gurgeh with a force almost as great; one reading—perhaps the best—of the way he'd always played was that he played as the Culture. He'd habitually set up something like the society itself when he constructed his positions and deployed his pieces; a net, a grid of forces and relationships, without any obvious hierarchy or entrenched leadership, and initially quite profoundly peaceful.

In all the games he'd played, the fight had always come to Gurgeh, initially. He'd thought of the period before as *preparing* for battle, but now he saw that if he'd been alone on the board he'd have done roughly the same, spreading slowly across the territories, consolidating gradually, calmly, economically . . . of course it had never happened; he always was attacked, and once the battle was joined he developed that conflict as assiduously and totally as before he'd tried to develop the patterns and potential of unthreatened pieces and undisputed territory.

Every other player he'd competed against had unwittingly tried to adjust to this novel style in its own terms, and comprehensively failed. Nicosar was trying no such thing. He'd gone the other way, and made the board his Empire, complete and exact in every structural detail to the limits of definition the game's scale imposed.

It stunned Gurgeh. The realization burst on him like some slow sunrise turning nova, like a trickle of understanding becoming stream, river, tide; tsunami. His next few moves were automatic; reaction-moves, not properly thought-out parts of his strategy, limited and inadequate though it had been shown to be. His mouth had gone dry, his hands shook.

Of course; this was what he'd been missing, this was the hidden facet, so open and blatant, and there for all to see, it was effectively invisible, too obvious for words or understanding. It was so simple, so elegant, so staggeringly ambitious but so fundamentally *practical,* and so much what Nicosar obviously thought the whole game to be about.

No wonder he'd been so desperate to play this man from the Culture, if this was what he'd planned all along.

Even the details Nicosar and only a handful of others in the Empire knew about the Culture and its true size and scope were there, included and displayed on the board, but probably utterly indecipherable to those who did not already know; the style of Nicosar's board-Empire was of a complete thing fully shown, the assumptions about his opponent's forces were couched in terms of fractions of something greater.

There was, too, a ruthlessness about the way the Emperor treated his own and his opponent's pieces which Gurgeh thought was almost a taunt; a tactic designed to disturb him. The Emperor sent pieces to their destruction with a sort of joyous callousness where Gurgeh would have hung back, attempting to prepare and build up. Where Gurgeh would have accepted surrender and conversion, Nicosar laid waste.

The difference was slight in some ways—no good player simply squandered pieces or massacred purely for the sake of it—but the implication of applied brutality was there, like a flavor, like a stench, like a silent mist hanging over the board.

He saw then that he'd been fighting back much as Nicosar might have expected him to, trying to save pieces, to make reasonable, considered, conservative moves and, in a sense, to ignore the way Nicosar was kicking and slinging his pieces into battle and tearing strips of territory from his opponent like ribbons of tattered flesh. In a way, Gurgeh had been trying desperately *not* to play Nicosar; the Emperor was playing a rough, harsh, dictatorial and frequently inelegant game and had rightly assumed something in the Culture man would simply not want to be a part of it.

Gurgeh started to take stock, sizing up the possibilities while he played a few more inconsequential blocking moves to give himself time to think. The point of the game was to win; he'd been forgetting that. Nothing else mattered; nothing else hung on the outcome of the game either. The game was irrelevant, therefore it could be allowed to mean everything, and the only barrier he had to negotiate was that put up by his own feelings.

He had to reply, but how? Become the Culture? Another Empire?

He was already playing the part of the Culture, and it wasn't working—and how do you match an Emperor as an imperialist?

He stood there on the board, wearing his faintly ridiculous, gathered-up clothes, and was only distantly aware of everything else around him. He tried to tear his thoughts away from the game for a moment, looking round the great ribbed prow-hall of the castle, at the tall, open windows and the yellow cinderbud canopy outside; at the half-full banks of seats, at the imperial guards and the adjudicating officials, at the great black horn-shapes of the electronic screening equipment directly overhead, at the many people in their various clothes and guises. All translated into game-thought; all viewed as though through some powerful drug which distorted everything he saw into twisted analogs of its latching hold on his brain.

He thought of mirrors, and of reverser fields, which gave the more technically artificial but perceivably more real impression; mirror-writing was what it said; reversed writing was ordinary writing. He saw the closed torus of Flere-Imsaho's unreal Reality, remembered Chamlis Amalk-ney and its warning about deviousness; things which meant nothing and something; harmonics of his thought.

Click. Switch off/switch on. As though he was a machine. Fall off the edge of the catastrophe curve, and never mind. He forgot everything and made the first move he saw.

He looked at the move he'd made. Nothing like what Nicosar would have done.

An archetypally Culture move. He felt his heart sink. He'd been hoping for something different, something better.

He looked again. Well, it was a Culture move, but at least it was an *attacking* Culture move; followed through, it would wreck his whole cautious strategy so far, but it was all he could do if he was to have even the glimmer of a chance of resisting Nicosar. Pretend there really was a lot at stake, pretend he was fighting for the whole Culture; set out to win, regardless, no matter . . .

At least he'd found a way to play, finally.

He knew he was going to lose, but it would not be a rout.

He gradually remodeled his whole game-plan to reflect the ethos of the Culture militant, trashing and abandoning whole areas of the board where the switch would not work, pulling back and regrouping and restructuring where it would; sacrificing where necessary, razing and scorching the ground where he had to. He didn't try to mimic Nicosar's crude but devastating attack-escape, return-invade strategy, but made his positions and his pieces in the image of a power that could eventually cope with such bludgeoning, if not now, then later, when it was ready.

He began to win a few points at last. The game was still lost, but there was still the Board of Becoming, where at last he might give Nicosar a fight.

Once or twice he caught a certain look on Nicosar's face, when he was close enough to read the apex's expression, that convinced him he'd done the right thing, even if it was something the Emperor had somehow expected. There was a recognition there now, in the apex's expression and on the board, and even a kind of respect in those moves; an acknowledgment that they were fighting on even terms.

Gurgeh was overcome by the sensation that he was like a wire with some terrible energy streaming through him; he was a great cloud poised to strike lightning over the board, a colossal wave tearing across the ocean toward the sleeping shore, a great pulse of molten energy from a planetary heart; a god with the power to destroy and create at will.

He had lost control of his own drug-glands; the mix of chemicals in his bloodstream had taken over, and his brain felt saturated with the one encompassing idea, like a fever; win, dominate, control; a set of angles defining one desire, the single absolute determination.

The breaks and the times when he slept were irrelevant; just the intervals between the real life of the board and the game. He functioned, talking to the drone or the ship or other people, eating and sleeping and walking around . . . but it was all nothing; irrelevant. Everything outside was just a setting and a background for the game.

He watched the rival forces surge and tide across the great board, and they spoke a strange language, sang a strange song that was at once a perfect set of harmonies and a battle to control the writing of the themes. What he saw in front of him was like a single huge organism; the pieces seemed to move as though with a will that was neither his nor the Emperor's, but something dictated finally by the game itself, an ultimate expression of its essence.

He saw it; he knew Nicosar saw it; but he doubted anybody else could. They were like a pair of secret lovers, secure and safe in their huge nest of a room, locked together before hundreds of people who looked on and who saw but who could not read and who would never guess what it was they were witnessing.

The game on the Board of Form came to an end. Gurgeh lost, but he had pulled back from the brink, and the advantage Nicosar would take to the Board of Becoming was far from decisive.

The two opponents separated, that act over, the final one yet to commence. Gurgeh left the prow-hall, exhausted and drained and gloriously happy, and slept for two days. The drone woke him.

"Gurgeh? Are you awake? Have you stopped being vague?"

"What are you talking about?"

"You; the game. What's going on? Even the ship couldn't work out what was happening on that board." The drone floated above him, brown and gray, humming quietly. Gurgeh rubbed his eyes, blinked. It was morning; there were about ten days to go before the fire was due. Gurgeh felt as though he was waking from a dream more vivid and real than reality.

He yawned, sitting up. "Have I been vague?"

"Does pain hurt? Is a supernova bright?"

Gurgeh stretched, smirking. "Nicosar's taking it impersonally," he said, getting up and padding to the window. He stepped out onto the balcony. Flere-Imsaho tutted and threw a robe around him.

"If you're going to start talking in riddles again . . ."

"What riddles?" Gurgeh drank in the mild air. He flexed his arms and shoulders again. "Isn't this a fine old castle, drone?" he said, leaning on the stone rail and taking another deep breath. "They know how to build castles, don't they?"

"I suppose they do, but Klaff wasn't built by the Empire. They took it off another humanoid species who used to hold a ceremony similar to the one the Empire holds to crown the Emperor. But don't change the subject. I asked you a question. What is that style? You've been very vague and strange the past few days; I could see you were concentrating so I didn't press the point, but I and the ship would like to be told."

"Nicosar's taken on the part of the Empire; hence his style. I've had no choice but to become the Culture, hence mine. It's that simple."

"It doesn't look it."

"Tough. Think of it as a sort of mutual rape."

"I think you should straighten out, Jernau Gurgeh."

"I'm—" Gurgeh started to say, then stopped to check. He frowned in exasperation. "I'm perfectly straight, you idiot! Now why don't you do something useful and order me some breakfast?"

"Yes, master," Flere-Imsaho said sullenly, and dipped back inside the room. Gurgeh looked up into the empty board of blue sky, his mind already racing with plans for the game on the Board of Becoming.

Flere-Imsaho watched the man grow even more intense and absorbed in the days between the second and final games. He hardly seemed to hear anything that was said to him; he had to be reminded to eat and sleep. The drone wouldn't have believed it, but twice it saw the man sitting with an expression of pain on his face, staring at nothing. Doing a remote ultrasound scan, the drone had discovered the man's bladder was full to bursting; he had to be told when to pee! He spent all day, every day, gazing intently at nothing, or feverishly studying replays of old games. And though he might have been briefly undrugged after his long sleep, immediately thereafter he started glanding again, and didn't stop. The drone used its Effector to monitor the man's brainwaves and found that even when he appeared to sleep, it wasn't really sleep; controlled lucid dreaming was what it seemed to be. His drug-glands were obviously working furiously all the time, and for the first time there were more tell-tale signs of intense drug-use on Gurgeh's body than there were on his opponent's.

How could he play in such a state? Had it been up to Flere-Imsaho, it would have stopped the man playing there and then. But it had its orders. It had a part to play, and it had played it, and all it could do now was wait and see what happened.

More people attended the start of the game on the Board of Becoming than had attended the previous two; the other game-players were still trying to work out what was going on in this strange, complicated, unfathomable game, and wanted to see what would happen on this final board, where the Emperor started with a considerable advantage, but on which the alien was known to be especially good.

Gurgeh dived back into the game, an amphibian into welcoming water. For a few moves he just gloried in the feeling of returning home to his element and the sheer joy of the contest, taking delight in a flexing of his strengths and powers, the readying tension of the pieces and places; then he curved out from that playing to the serious business of the building and the hunting, the making and linking and the destroying and cutting; the searching and destroying.

The board became both Culture and Empire again. The setting was made by them both; a glorious, beautiful, deadly killing field, unsurpassably fine and sweet and predatory and carved from Nicosar's beliefs and his together. Image of their minds; a hologram of pure coherence, burning like a standing wave of fire across the board, a perfect map of the landscapes of thought and faith within their heads.

He began the slow move that was defeat and victory together before he even knew it himself. Nothing so subtle, so complex, so beautiful had ever been seen on an Azad board. He believed that; he knew that. He would make it the truth.

The game went on.

Breaks, days, evenings, conversations, meals; they came and went in another dimension; a monochrome thing, a flat, grainy image. *He* was somewhere else entirely. Another dimension, another image. His skull was a blister with a board inside it, his outside self just another piece to be shuffled here and there.

He didn't talk to Nicosar, but they conversed, they carried out the most exquisitely textured exchange of mood and feeling through those pieces which they moved and were moved by; a song, a dance, a perfect poem. People filled the game-room every day now, engrossed in the fabulously perplexing work taking shape before them; trying to read that poem, see deeper into this moving picture, listen to this symphony, touch this living sculpture, and so understand it.

*It goes on until it ends,* Gurgeh thought to himself one day, and at the same time as the banality of the thought struck him, he saw that it was over. The climax had been reached. It was done, destroyed, could be no more. It was not finished, but it was over. A terrible sadness swamped him, took hold of him like a piece and made him sway and nearly fall, so that he had to walk to his stoolseat and pull himself onto it like an old man.

"Oh . . ." he heard himself say.

He looked at Nicosar, but the Emperor hadn't seen it yet. He was looking at element-cards, trying to work out a way to alter the terrain ahead of his next advance.

Gurgeh couldn't believe it. The game was over; couldn't *anybody* see that? He looked despairingly around the faces of the officials, the spectators, the observers and Adjudicators. What was wrong with them all? He looked back at the board, hoping desperately that he might have missed something, made some mistake that meant there was still something Nicosar could do, that the perfect dance might last a little longer. He could see nothing; it was done. He looked at the time shown on the point-board. It was nearly time to break for the day. It was a dark evening outside. He tried to remember what day it was. The fire was due very soon, wasn't it? Perhaps tonight, or tomorrow. Perhaps it had already been? No; even he would have noticed. The great high windows of the prow-hall were still unshuttered, looking out into the darkness where the huge cinderbuds waited, heavy with fruit.

Over over over. His — their — beautiful game over; dead. What had he done? He put his clenched hands over his mouth. *Nicosar, you fool!* The Emperor had fallen for it, taken the bait, entered the run and followed it to be torn apart near the high stand, storms of splinters before the fire.

Empires had fallen to barbarians before, and no doubt would again. Gurgeh knew all this from his childhood. Culture children were taught such things. The barbarians invade, and are taken over. Not always; some empires dissolve and cease, but many absorb; many take the barbarians in and end up conquering them. They make them live like the people they set out to take over. The architecture of the system channels them, beguiles them, seduces and transforms them, demanding from them what they could not before have given but slowly grow to offer. The empire survives, the barbarians survive, but the empire is no more and the barbarians are nowhere to be found.

The Culture had become the Empire, the Empire the barbarians. Nicosar looked triumphant, pieces everywhere, adapting and taking and changing and moving in for the kill. But it would be their own death-change; they could not survive as they were; wasn't that obvious? They would become Gurgeh's, or neutrals, their rebirth his to deliver. Over.

A prickling sensation began behind his nose and he sat back, overcome by the sadness of the game's ending, and waiting for tears.

None came. A suitable reprimand from his body, for using the elements so well, and water so much. He would drown Nicosar's attacks; the Emperor played with fire, and would be extinguished. No tears for him.

Something left Gurgeh, just ebbed away, burned out, relaxing its grip on him. The room was cool, filled with a spirit fragrance, and the rustling sound of the cinderbud canopy outside, beyond the tall, wide windows. People talked quietly in the galleries.

He looked around, and saw Hamin sitting in the college seats. The old apex looked shrunken and doll-like; a tiny withered husk of what he'd been, face lined and body misshapen. Gurgeh stared at him. Was this one of their ghosts? Had he been there all the time? Was he still alive? The unbearably old apex seemed to be staring fixedly at the center of the board, and for one absurd instant Gurgeh thought the old creature was already dead and they'd brought his desiccated body into the prow-hall as some sort of trophy, a final ignominy.

Then the horn sounded for the end of the evening's play, and two imperial guards came and wheeled the dying apex away. The shrunken, grizzled head looked briefly in his direction.

Gurgeh felt as though he'd been somewhere far away, on a great journey he'd just returned from. He looked at Nicosar, consulting with a couple of his advisors as the Adjudicators noted the closing positions and the people in the galleries stood up and started chattering. Did he imagine that Nicosar looked concerned, even worried? Perhaps so. He felt suddenly very sorry for the Emperor, for all of them; for everybody.

He sighed, and it was like the last breath of some great storm that had passed through him. He stretched his arms and legs, stood again. He looked at the board. Yes; over. He'd done it. There was much left to do, a lot still to happen, but Nicosar would lose. He could choose how he lost; fall forward and be absorbed, fall back and be taken over, go berserk and raze everything . . . but his board-Empire was finished.

He met the Emperor's gaze for a moment. He could see from the expression there that Nicosar hadn't fully realized yet, but he knew the apex was reading him in return and could probably see the change in the man, sense the sense of victory . . . Gurgeh lowered his gaze from that hard sight, and turned away and walked out of the hall.

There was no acclaim, there were no congratulations. Nobody else could see. Flere-Imsaho was its usual concerned, annoying self, but it too hadn't spotted anything, and still inquired how he thought the game was going. He lied. The *Limiting Factor* thought things were building up to a head. He didn't bother to tell it. He'd expected more of the ship, though.

He ate alone, mind blank. He spent the evening swimming in a pool deep inside the castle, carved out of the rock spur the fortress had been built upon. He was alone; everybody else had gone to the castle towers and the higher battlements, or had taken to aircars, watching the distant glow in the sky to the west, where the Incandescence had begun.

Gurgeh swam until he felt tired, then dried, dressed in trous, shirt and a light jacket, and went for a walk round the castle's curtain wall.

The night was dark under a covering of cloud; the great cinderbuds, higher than the outer walls, closed off the distant light of the approaching Incandescence. Imperial guards were out, ensuring that nobody started the fire early; Gurgeh had to prove to them he wasn't carrying anything which could produce a spark or flame before they would let him out of the castle, where shutters were being readied and the walkways were damp from tests of the sprinkler systems.

The cinderbuds creaked and rustled in the windless gloom, exposing new, tinder-dry surfaces to the rich air, bark-layers unpeeling from the great bulbs of flammable liquid that hung beneath their topmost branches. The night air was saturated by the heady stench of their sap.

A hushed feeling lay over the ancient fortress; a religious mood of awed anticipation which even Gurgeh would experience as a tangible change in the place. The swooshings of returning aircars, coming in over a damped-down swathe of forest to the castle, reminded Gurgeh that everybody was supposed to be in the castle by midnight, and he went back slowly, drinking in the atmosphere of still expectation like something precious that could not last for long, or perhaps ever be again.

Still, he wasn't tired; the pleasant fatigue from his swim had become just a sort of background tingle in his body, and so when he climbed the stairs to the level of his room, he didn't stop, but kept going up, even as the horn sounded to announce midnight.

Gurgeh came out at last onto a high battlement beneath a stubby tower. The circular walkway was damp and dark. He looked to the west, where a dim, fuzzy red glow lit up the edge of the sky. The Incandescence was still far away, below the horizon, its glare reflecting off the overcast like some livid artificial sunset. Despite that light, Gurgeh was conscious of the depth and stillness of the night as it settled round the castle, quieting it. He found a door in the tower and climbed to its machicolated summit. He leaned on the stonework and looked out into the north, where the low hills lay. He listened to the dripping of a leaking sprinkler somewhere beneath him, and the barely audible rustlings of the cinderbuds as they prepared for their own destruction. The hills were quite invisible; he gave up trying to make them out and turned again to that barely curved band of dark red in the west.

A horn sounded somewhere in the castle, then another and another. There were other noises too; distant shouting and running footsteps, as though the castle was waking up again. He wondered what was going on. He pulled the thin jacket closed, suddenly feeling the coolness of the night, as a light easterly breeze started up.

The sadness he'd felt during the day had not fully left him; rather it had sunk in, become something less obvious but more integral. How beautiful that game had been; how much he had enjoyed it, exulted in it . . . but only by trying to bring about its cessation, only by ensuring that that joy would be short-lived. He wondered if Nicosar had realized yet; he must have had a suspicion, at least. He sat down on a small stone bench.

Gurgeh realized suddenly that he would miss Nicosar. He

felt closer to the Emperor, in some ways, than he had ever felt to anybody; that game had been a deep intimacy, a sharing of experience and sensation Gurgeh doubted any other relationship could match.

He sighed, eventually, got up from the bench and went to the parapet again, looking down to the paved walk at the foot of the tower. There were two imperial guards standing there, dimly visible by the light spilling from the tower's open door. Their pale faces were tipped up, looking at him. He wasn't sure whether to wave or not. One of them lifted his arm; a bright light shone up at Gurgeh, who shielded his eyes. A third, smaller, darker figure Gurgeh hadn't noticed before moved toward the tower and entered it through the lit doorway. The torch beam switched off. The two guards took up positions on either side of the tower door.

Steps sounded within the tower. Gurgeh sat on the stone bench again and waited.

"Morat Gurgeh, good evening." It was Nicosar; the dark, slightly stooped figure of the Emperor of Azad climbed up out of the tower.

"Your Highness—"

"Sit down, Gurgeh," the quiet voice said. Nicosar joined Gurgeh on the bench, his face like an indistinct white moon in front of him, lit only by the faint glow from the tower's stairwell. Gurgeh wondered if Nicosar could see him at all. The moon-face turned away from him, looking toward the horizon-wide smudge of carmine. "There has been an attempt on my life, Gurgeh," the Emperor said quietly.

"An . . ." Gurgeh began, appalled. "Are you all right, Your Highness?"

The moon-face swung back. "I am unharmed." The apex held up one hand. "Please; no 'Your Highness' now. We're alone; there is no breach of protocol. I wanted to explain to you personally why the castle is under martial law. The Imperial Guard have taken over all commands. I do not anticipate another attack, but one must take care."

"But who would do this? Who would attack you?"

Nicosar looked to the north and the unseen hills. "We believe the culprits may have tried to escape along the viaduct to the reservoir lakes, so I've sent some guards there too." He turned slowly back to the man, and his voice was soft. "That's an interesting situation you've got me in, Morat Gurgeh."

"I . . ." Gurgeh sighed, looked at his feet. ". . . yes." He glanced at the circle of white face in front of him. "I'm sorry; I mean that it's . . . almost over." He heard his voice drop, and could not bear to look at Nicosar.

"Well," the Emperor said quietly, "we shall see. I may have a surprise for you in the morning."

Gurgeh was startled. The hazily pale face in front of him was too vague for the expression to be read, but could Nicosar be serious? Surely the apex could see his position was hopeless; had he seen something Gurgeh hadn't? At once he started to worry. Had he been too certain? Nobody else had noticed anything, not even the ship; what if he was wrong? He wanted to see the board again, but even the imperfectly detailed image of it he still carried in his mind was accurate enough to show how their respective fortunes stood; Nicosar's defeat was implicit, but certain. He was sure there was no way out for the Emperor; the game *must* be over.

"Tell me something, Gurgeh," Nicosar said evenly. The white circle faced him again. "How long were you really learning the game for?"

"We told you the truth; two years. Intensively, but—"

"Don't lie to me, Gurgeh. There's no point anymore."

"Nicosar; I wouldn't lie to you."

The moon-face shook slowly. "Whatever you want." The Emperor was silent for a few moments. "You must be very proud of your Culture."

He pronounced the last word with a distaste Gurgeh might have found comical if it hadn't been so obviously sincere.

"Pride?" he said. "I don't know. I didn't make it; I just happened to be born into it, I—"

"Don't be simple, Gurgeh. I mean the pride of being part of something. The pride of representing your people. Are you going to tell me you don't feel that?"

"I . . . some, perhaps yes . . . but I'm not here as a champion, Nicosar. I'm not representing anything except myself. I'm here to play the game, that's all."

"That's all," Nicosar repeated quietly. "Well, I suppose we must say that you've played it well." Gurgeh wished he could see the apex's face. Had his voice quivered? Was that a tremor in his voice?

"Thank you. But half the credit for this game is yours . . . more than half, because you set—"

"I don't want your *praise!*" Nicosar lashed out with one hand, striking Gurgeh across the mouth. The heavy rings raked the man's cheek and lips.

Gurgeh rocked back, stunned, dizzy with shock. Nicosar jumped up and went to the parapet, hands like claws on the dark stone. Gurgeh touched his blooded face. His hand was trembling.

"You disgust me, Morat Gurgeh," Nicosar said to the red glow in the west. "Your blind, insipid morality can't even account for your own success here, and you treat this battle-game like some filthy dance. It is there to be fought and struggled against, and you've attempted to seduce it. You've perverted it; replaced our holy witnessing with your own foul pornography . . . you've soiled it . . . *male.*"

Gurgeh dabbed at the blood on his lips. He felt dizzy, head swimming. "That . . . that may be how you see it, Nicosar." He swallowed some of the thick, salty blood. "I don't think you're being entirely fair to—"

"*Fair?*" the Emperor shouted, coming to stand over Gurgeh, blocking the view of the distant fire. "Why does anything have to be *fair?* Is life fair?" He reached down and took Gurgeh by the hair, shaking his head. "Is it? Is it?"

Gurgeh let the apex shake him. The Emperor let go of his hair after a moment, holding his hand as though he'd touched something dirty. Gurgeh cleared his throat. "No, life is not fair. Not intrinsically."

The apex turned away in exasperation, clutching again at the curled stone top of the battlements. "It's something we can try to make it, though," Gurgeh continued. "A goal we can aim for. You can choose to do so, or not. We have. I'm sorry you find us so repulsive for that."

"'Repulsive' is barely adequate for what I feel for your precious Culture, Gurgeh. I'm not sure I possess the words to explain to you what I feel for your . . . Culture. You know no glory, no pride, no worship. You have power; I've seen that; I know what you can do . . . but you're still impotent. You always will be. The meek, the pathetic, the frightened and cowed . . . they can only last so long, no matter how terrible and awesome the machines they crawl around within. In the end you will fall; all your glittering machinery won't save you. The strong survive. That's what life teaches us, Gurgeh, that's what the game shows us. Struggle to prevail; fight to prove worth. These are no hollow phrases; they are truth!"

Gurgeh watched the pale hands grasping the dark stone.

What could he say to this apex? Were they to argue metaphysics, here, now, with the imperfect tool of language, when they'd spent the last ten days devising the most perfect image of their competing philosophies they were capable of expressing, probably in any form?

What, anyway, was he to say? That intelligence could surpass and excel the blind force of evolution, with its emphasis on mutation, struggle and death? That conscious cooperation was more efficient than feral competition? That Azad could be so much more than a mere battle, if it was used to articulate, to communicate, to define . . . ? He'd done all that, said all that, and said it better than he ever could now.

"You have not won, Gurgeh," Nicosar said quietly, voice harsh, almost croaking. "Your kind will never win." He turned back, looking down at him. "You poor, pathetic male. You play, but you don't understand any of this, do you?"

Gurgeh heard what sounded like genuine pity in the apex's voice. "I think you've already decided that I don't," he told Nicosar.

The Emperor laughed, turning back to the distant reflection of the continent-wide fire still below the horizon. The sound died in a sort of cough. He waved one hand at Gurgeh. "Your sort never will understand. You'll only be used." He shook his head in the darkness. "Go back to your room, *morat.* I'll see you in the morning." The moon-face stared toward the horizon and the ruddy glare rubbed on the undersurface of the clouds. "The fire should be here by then."

Gurgeh waited a moment. It was as though he'd already gone; he felt dismissed, forgotten. Even Nicosar's last words had sounded as if they weren't really meant for Gurgeh at all.

The man rose quietly and went back down through the dimly lit tower. The two guards stood impassively outside the door at the tower's foot. Gurgeh looked up to the top of the tower, and saw Nicosar there on the battlements, flat pale face looking out toward the approaching fire, white hands clutching at cold stone. The man watched for a few seconds, then turned and left, going down through the corridors and halls where the imperial guards prowled, sending everybody to their rooms and locking the doors, watching all the stairs and elevators, and turning on all the lights so that the silent castle burned in the night, like some great stone ship on a darkly golden sea.

Flere-Imsaho was flicking through the broadcast channels when Gurgeh got back to his room. It asked him what all the fuss was about in the castle. He told it.

"Can't be that bad," the drone said, with a wobble-shrug. It looked back at the screen. "They aren't playing martial music. No outgoing communications possible though. What happened to your mouth?"

"I fell."

"Mm-hmm."

"Can we contact the ship?"

"Of course."

"Tell it to power up. We might need it."

"My, you're getting cautious. All right."

He went to bed, but lay awake, listening to the swelling roar of the wind.

At the top of the high tower, the apex watched the horizon for several hours, seemingly locked into the stone like a pale statue, or a small tree born of an errant seed. The wind from the east freshened, tugging at the stationary figure's dark clothes and howling round the dark-bright castle, tearing through the canopy of swaying cinderbuds with a noise like the sea.

The dawn came up. It lit the clouds first, then touched the edge of clear horizon in the east with gold. At the same time, in the black fastness of the west where the edge of the land glowed red, a sudden glint of bright, burning orange-yellow appeared, to waver and hesitate and disappear, then return, and brighten, and spread.

The figure on the tower drew back from that widening breach in the red-black sky, and—glancing briefly behind him, at the dawn—swayed uncertainly for a moment, as though caught between the rival currents of light flowing from each bright horizon.

Two guards came to the room. They unlocked the door and told Gurgeh he and the machine were required in the prow-hall. Gurgeh was dressed in his Azad robes. The guards told him it was the Emperor's pleasure that they abandon the statutory robes for this morning's play. Gurgeh looked at Flere-Imsaho, and went to change. He put on a fresh shirt, and the trous and light jacket he'd worn the previous night.

"So, I'm getting a chance to spectate at last; what a treat," Flere-Imsaho said as they headed for the game-hall. Gurgeh said nothing. Guards were escorting groups of people from various parts of the castle. Outside, beyond already shuttered doors and windows, the wind howled.

Gurgeh hadn't felt like breakfast. The ship had been in contact that morning, to congratulate him. It had finally seen. In fact, it thought there was a way out for Nicosar, but only to a draw. And no human brain could handle the play required. It had resumed its high-speed holding pattern, ready to come in the moment it sensed anything wrong. It watched through Flere-Imsaho's eyes.

When they got to the castle's prow-hall and the Board of Becoming, Nicosar was already there. The apex wore the uniform of the commander-in-chief of the Imperial Guard, a severe, subtly menacing set of clothes complete with ceremonial sword. Gurgeh felt quite dowdy in his old jacket. The prow-hall was almost full. People, escorted by the ubiquitous guards, were still filing into the tiered seats. Nicosar ignored Gurgeh; the apex was talking to an officer of the Guard.

"Hamin!" Gurgeh said, going over to where the old apex sat, in the front row of seats, his tiny, twisted body crumpled and hopeless between two burly guards. His face was shriveled and yellow. One of the guards put out his hand to stop Gurgeh coming any closer. He stood in front of the bench, squatting to look into the old rector's wrinkled face. "Hamin; can you hear me?" He thought, again, absurdly, that the apex was dead, then the small eyes flickered, and one opened, yellow-red and sticky with crystalline secretions. The shrunken-looking head moved a little. "Gurgeh . . ."

The eye closed, the head nodded. Gurgeh felt a hand on his sleeve, and he was led to his seat at the edge of the board.

The prow-hall's balcony windows were closed, the panes rattling in their metal frames, but the fire shutters had not been lowered. Outside, beneath a leaden sky, the tall cinderbuds shook in the gale, and the noise of the wind formed a bass background to the subdued conversations of the shuffling people still finding their places in the great hall.

"Shouldn't they have put the shutters down?" Gurgeh asked the drone. He sat in the stoolseat. Flere-Imsaho floated, buzzing and crackling, behind him. The Adjudicator and his helpers were checking the positions of the pieces.

"Yes," Flere-Imsaho said. "The fire's less than two hours away. They can drop the shutters in the last few minutes if they have to, but they don't usually wait that long. I'd watch it, Gurgeh. Legally, the Emperor isn't allowed to call on the physical option at this stage, but there's something funny going on. I can sense it."

Gurgeh wanted to say something cutting about the drone's senses, but his stomach was churning, and he felt something was wrong, too. He looked over at the bench where Hamin sat. The withered apex hadn't moved. His eyes were still closed.

"Something else," Flere-Imsaho said.

"What?"

"There's some sort of extra gear up there, on the ceiling."

Gurgeh glanced up without making it too obvious. The jumble of ECM and screening equipment looked much as it always had, but then he'd never inspected it very closely. "What sort of gear?" he asked.

"Gear that is worryingly opaque to my senses, which it shouldn't be. And that Guards colonel's wired with an optic-remote mike."

"The officer talking to Nicosar?"

"Yes. Isn't that against the rules?"

"Supposed to be."

"Want to raise it with the Adjudicator?"

The Adjudicator was standing at the edge of the board, between two burly guards. He looked frightened and grim. When his gaze fell on Gurgeh, it seemed to go straight through him. "I have a feeling," Gurgeh whispered, "it wouldn't do any good."

"Me too. Want me to get the ship to come in?"

"Can it get here before the fire?"

"Just."

Gurgeh didn't have to think too long. "Do it," he said.

"Signal sent. You remember the drill with the implant?"

"Vividly."

"Great," Flere-Imsaho said sourly. "A high-speed displace from a hostile environment with some gray-area effector gear around. Just what I need."

The hall was full, the doors were closed. The Adjudicator glanced resentfully over at the Guards colonel standing near Nicosar. The officer gave the briefest of nods. The Adjudicator announced the recommencement of the game.

Nicosar made a couple of inconsequential moves. Gurgeh couldn't see what the Emperor was aiming at. He must be trying to do something, but what? It didn't appear to have anything to do with winning the game. He tried to catch Nicosar's eye, but the apex refused to look at him. Gurgeh rubbed his cut lip and cheek. *I'm invisible,* he thought.

The cinderbuds swayed and shook in the storm outside; their leaves had spread to their maximum extent, and—whipped by the gale—they looked indistinct and merged, like one huge dull yellow organism quivering and poised beyond the castle walls. Gurgeh could sense people in the hall moving restlessly, muttering to each other, glancing at the still unshuttered windows. The guards stayed at the hall's exits, guns ready.

Nicosar made certain moves, placing element-cards in particular positions. Gurgeh still couldn't see what the point of all this was. The noise of the storm beyond the shaking windows was enough to all but drown the voices of the people in the hall. The smell of the cinderbuds' volatile saps and juices pervaded the air, and some dry shreds of their leaves had found their way in to the hall somehow, to soar and float and curl on currents of air inside the great hall.

High in the stone-dark sky beyond the windows, a burning orange glow lit up the clouds. Gurgeh began to sweat; he walked over the board, made some replying moves, attempting to draw Nicosar out. He heard somebody in the observers' gallery crying out, and then being quieted. The guards stood silently, watchfully, at the doors and around the board. The Guards colonel Nicosar had been talking to earlier stood near the Emperor. As he went back to his stoolseat, Gurgeh thought he saw tears on the officer's cheeks.

Nicosar had been sitting. Now he stood, and, taking four element-cards, strode to the center of the patterned terrain.

Gurgeh wanted to shout out or leap up; something; anything. But he felt rooted, transfixed. The guards in the room had tensed, the Emperor's hands were visibly shaking. The storm outside whipped the cinderbuds like something conscious and spiteful; a spear of orange leapt ponderously above the tops of the plants, writhed briefly against the wall of darkness behind it, then sank slowly out of sight.

"Oh dear holy shit," Flere-Imsaho whispered. "That's only five minutes away."

"What?" Gurgeh glanced at the machine.

"Five minutes," the drone said, with a realistic gulp. "It ought to be nearly an hour off. It can't have got here this quick. They've started a new fire-front."

Gurgeh closed his eyes. He felt the tiny lump under his paper-dry tongue. "The ship?" he said, opening his eyes again.

The drone was silent for seconds. ". . . No chance," it said, voice flat, resigned.

Nicosar stooped. He placed a fire-card on a water-symbol already on the board, in a fold in the high terrain. The Guards colonel turned his head fractionally to one side, mouth moving, as though blowing some speck of dust off his uniform's high collar.

Nicosar stood up, looking around, appeared to listen for something, but heard only the howling noise of the storm.

"I just registered an infrasound pulse," Flere-Imsaho said. "That was an explosion, a klick to north. The viaduct."

Gurgeh watched helplessly as Nicosar walked slowly to another position on the board and placed one card on another; fire on air. The Colonel talked into the mike near his shoulder again. The castle shook; a series of concussions shuddered through the hall.

The pieces on the board juddered; people stood up, started shouting. The glass panes cracked in their frames, crashing to the flagstones, letting the shrieking voice of the burning gale into the hall in a hail of fluttering leaves. A line of flames burst out over the tops of the trees, filling the base of the boiling black horizon with fire.

The next fire-card was placed; on earth. The castle seemed to shift under Gurgeh. The wind tore in through windows, rolling lighter pieces across the board like some absurd and unstoppable invasion; it whipped at the robes of the Adjudicator and his officials. People were piling out of the galleries, falling over each other to get to the exits, where the guards had drawn their guns.

The sky was full of fire.

Nicosar looked at Gurgeh as he placed the final fire-card, on the ghost-element, Life.

"This is looking worse and worse all—*grrreeeeee!*" Flere-Imsaho said, voice breaking, screeching. Gurgeh whirled round to see the bulky machine trembling in midair, surrounded by a bright aura of green fire.

The guards started shooting. The doors from the hall were thrown open and the people piled through, but in the hall the guards were suddenly all over the board itself, firing up into the galleries and benches, blasting laser-fire among the escaping crowds, felling the screaming, struggling apices, females and males in a storm of flickering light and shattering detonations.

"*Grrraaaaak!*" Flere-Imsaho screamed. Its casing glowed dull red and started to smoke. Gurgeh watched, transfixed. Nicosar stood near the center of the boards, surrounded by his guards, smiling at Gurgeh.

The fire raged above the cinderbuds. The hall emptied as a last few wounded people staggered through the doors. Flere-Imsaho hung in the air; it glowed orange, yellow, white; it started to rise, dripping blobs of molten material onto the board as it went, enveloped suddenly in flames and smoke. Suddenly, it accelerated across the hall as if pulled by some huge, invisible hand. It slammed into a far wall and exploded in a blinding flash and a blast that almost blew Gurgeh off his stoolseat.

The guards around the Emperor left the board and climbed over the benches and galleries, killing the wounded. They ignored Gurgeh. The sound of firing echoed through the doors leading to the rest of the castle, where the dead lay in their bright clothes like some obscene carpet.

Nicosar strolled slowly over to Gurgeh, stopping to tap a few Azad pieces out of his way with his boots as he advanced; he stamped on a little guttering pool of fire left from the molten debris Flere-Imsaho had trailed behind it. He drew his sword, almost casually.

Gurgeh clutched the arms of the seat. The inferno shrieked in the skies outside. Leaves swirled through the hall like dry, endless rain. Nicosar stopped in front of Gurgeh. The Emperor was smiling. He shouted above the gale. "Surprised?"

Gurgeh could hardly speak. "What have you done? Why?" he croaked.

Nicosar shrugged. "Made the game real, Gurgeh." He looked round the hall, surveying the carnage. They were alone now; the guards were spreading through the rest of the castle, killing.

The fallen were everywhere, scattered over the floor and the galleries, draped over benches, crumpled in corners, spread like Xs on the flagstones, their robes spotted with the dark burn-holes of laserburns. Smoke rose from the splintered woodwork and smoldering clothes; a sweet-sick smell of burned flesh filled the hall.

Nicosar weighed the heavy, double-edged sword in his gloved hand, smiling sadly at it. Gurgeh felt his bowels ache and his hands shake. There was a strange metallic taste in his mouth, and at first he thought it was the implant, rejecting, surfacing, for some reason reappearing, but then he knew that it wasn't, and realized, for the first time in his life, that fear really did have a taste.

Nicosar gave an inaudible sigh, drew himself up in front of Gurgeh, so that he seemed to fill the view in front of the man, and brought the sword slowly toward Gurgeh.

*Drone!* he thought. But it was just a sooty scar on the far wall.

*Ship!* But the implant under his tongue lay silent, and the *Limiting Factor* was still light-years away.

The tip of the sword was a few centimeters from Gurgeh's belly; it started to rise, passing slowly over Gurgeh's chest toward his neck. Nicosar opened his mouth as though he was about to say something, but then he shook his head, as though in exasperation, and lunged forward.

Gurgeh kicked out, slamming both feet into the Emperor's belly. Nicosar doubled up; Gurgeh was thrown backward off the seat. The sword hissed over his head.

Gurgeh kept on rolling as the stoolseat crashed to the ground; he jumped to his feet. Nicosar was half doubled-up, but still clutched the sword. He staggered toward the man, hacking the sword about him as though at invisible enemies between them. Gurgeh ran; to the side at first, then across the board, heading for the hall doors. Behind him, outside the windows, the fire above the thrashing cinderbuds obliterated the black clouds of smoke; the heat was something physical, a pressure on the skin and eyes. One of Gurgeh's feet came down on a game-piece, rolled across the board by the gale; he slipped and fell.

Nicosar stumbled after him.

The screening equipment whined, then hummed; smoke gouted from it. Blue lightning played furiously around the hanging machinery.

Nicosar didn't notice; he plunged forward at Gurgeh, who pushed himself away; the sword crashed into the board, centimeters from the man's head. Gurgeh picked himself up and leapt over a raised section of board. Nicosar came tearing and trampling after him.

The screening gear exploded. It crashed from the ceiling to the board in a shower of sparks and smashed into the center of the multicolored terrain a few meters in front of Gurgeh, who was forced to stop and turn. He faced Nicosar.

Something white blurred through the air.

Nicosar raised the sword over his head.

The blade snapped, clipped off by a flickering yellow-green field. Nicosar felt the weight of the sword change, and looked up in disbelief. The blade dangled uselessly in midair, suspended from the little white disk that was Flere-Imsaho.

"Ha ha ha," it boomed above the noise of the screaming wind.

Nicosar threw the sword-handle at Gurgeh; a green-yellow field caught it, propelled it back at Nicosar; the Emperor ducked. He staggered across the board in a storm of smoke and swirling leaves. The cinderbuds thrashed; flashes of white and yellow burst from between their trunks as the wall of flames above them beat toward the castle.

"Gurgeh!" Flere-Imsaho said, suddenly in front of his face. "Crouch down and curl up. *Now!*"

Gurgeh did as he was told, getting down on his haunches, arms wrapped around his shins. The drone floated above him, and Gurgeh saw the haze of a field all around him.

The wall of cinderbuds was breaking, the streaks and bursts of flame clawing through from behind them, shaking them, tearing them. The heat seemed to shrivel his face on the bones of his skull.

A figure appeared against the flames. It was Nicosar, holding one of the big laser-pistols the guards had been armed with. He stood just within and to the side of the windows, holding the gun in both hands and sighting carefully at Gurgeh. Gurgeh looked at the black muzzle of the gun, into the thumb-wide barrel, then his gaze moved up to Nicosar's face as the apex pulled the trigger.

Then he was looking at himself.

He stared into his own distorted face just long enough to see that Jernau Morat Gurgeh, at the very instant that might have been his death, looked only rather surprised and not a little stupid . . . then the mirror-field disappeared and he was looking at Nicosar again.

The apex stood in exactly the same place, swaying slightly now. There was something wrong though. Something had changed. It was very obvious but Gurgeh couldn't see what it was.

The Emperor went back on his heels, eyes staring blankly up at the smoke-stained ceiling where the screening gear had fallen from. Then the furnace gust from the windows caught him and he tipped slowly forward again, tipping toward the board, the weight of the hand-cannon in his gloved hands unbalancing him.

Gurgeh saw it then; the neat, slightly smoking black hole about wide enough to fit a thumb into, in the center of the apex's forehead.

Nicosar's body hit the board with a crash, scattering pieces.

The fire broke through.

The cinderbud dam gave way before the flames and was replaced by a vast wave of blinding light and a blast of heat like a hammer blow. Then the field around Gurgeh went dark, and the room and all the fire went dim, and far away at the back of his head there was a strange buzzing noise, and he felt drained, and empty, and exhausted.

After that everything went away from him, and there was only darkness.

Gurgeh opened his eyes.

He was lying on a balcony, under a jutting overhang of stone. The area around him had been swept clear, but everywhere else there was a centimeter-thick covering of dark gray ash. It was dull. The stones beneath him were warm; the air was cool and smoky.

He felt all right. No drowsiness, no sore head.

He sat up; something fell from his chest and rolled across the swept stones, falling into the gray dust. He picked it up; it was the Orbital bracelet; bright and undamaged and still keeping its own microscopic day-night cycle. He put it into his jacket pocket. He checked his hair, his eyebrows, his jacket; nothing singed at all.

The sky was dark gray; black at the horizon. Away to one side there was a small, vaguely purple disk in the sky, which he realized was the sun. He stood up.

The gray ash was being covered up with inky soot, falling from the dark overcast like negative snow. He walked across the heat-warped, flaking flagstones toward the edge of the balcony. The parapet had fallen away here; he kept back from the very edge.

The landscape had changed. Instead of the golden yellow wall of cinderbuds crowding the view beyond the curtain wall, there was just earth; black and brown and baked-looking, covered in great cracks and fissures the thin gray ash and the soot-rain had not yet filled. The barren waste stretched to the distant horizon. Faint wisps of smoke still climbed from fissures in the ground, climbing like the ghosts of trees, until the wind took them. The curtain wall was blackened and scorched, and breached in places.

The castle itself looked battered as though after a long siege. Towers had collapsed, and many of the apartments, office buildings and extra halls had fallen in on themselves, their flame-scarred windows showing only emptiness behind. Columns of smoke rose lazily like sinuous flagpoles to the summit of the crumbling fortress, where the wind caught them and made them pennants.

Gurgeh walked round the balcony, through the soft black snow of soot, to the prow-hall windows. His feet made no noise. The specks of soot made him sneeze, and his eyes itched. He entered the hall.

The stones still held their dry heat; it was like walking into a vast, dark oven. Inside the great game-room, among the dim shambles of twisted girders and fallen stonework, the board lay, warped and buckled and torn, its rainbow of colors reduced to grays and blacks, its carefully balanced topography of high ground and low made a nonsense of by the random heavings and saggings induced by the fire.

Buckled, annealed girders and holes in the floor and walls

marked where the observation galleries had been. The screening gear which had fallen from the ceiling of the hall lay half-melted and congealed in the center of the Azad board, like some blistered travesty of a mountain.

He turned to look at the window, where Nicosar had stood, and walked over the creaking surface of the ruined board. He crouched down, grunting as his knees sent stabs of pain through him. He put his hand out to where an eddy in the firestorm had collected a little conical pile of dust in the angle of an internal buttress; right at the edge of the game-board, near where a fused, L-shaped lump of blackened metal might have been the remains of a gun.

The gray-white ash was soft and warm, and mixed in with it he found a small, C-shaped piece of metal. The half-melted ring still contained the setting for a jewel, like a tiny rough crater on its rim, but the stone was gone. He looked at the ring for a while, blowing the ash off it and turning it over and over in his hands. After a while he put the ring back into the pile of dust. He hesitated, then he took the Orbital bracelet out of his jacket pocket and added it to the shallow gray cone, pulled the two poison-warning rings off his fingers, and put them there too. He scooped a handful of the warm ash into one palm, gazing at it thoughtfully.

"Jernau Gurgeh, good morning."

He turned and rose, quickly stuffing his hand into his jacket pocket as though ashamed of something. The little white body of Flere-Imsaho floated in through the window, very tiny and clean and exact in that shattered, melted place. A tiny gray thing, the size of a baby's finger, floated up to the drone from the ground near Gurgeh's feet. A hatch opened in Flere-Imsaho's immaculate body; the micromissile entered the drone. A section of the machine's body revolved, then was still.

"Hello," Gurgeh said, walking over to it. He looked round the ruined hall, then back at the drone. "I hope you're going to tell me what happened."

"Sit down, Gurgeh. I'll tell you."

He sat on a block of stone fallen from above the windows. He looked dubiously upward at where it must have fallen from. "Don't worry," Flere-Imsaho said. "You're safe. I've checked the roof."

Gurgeh rested his hands on his knees. "So?" he said.

"First things first," Flere-Imsaho said. "Allow me to introduce myself properly; my name is Sprant Flere-Imsaho Wu-Handrahen Xato Trabiti, and I am not a library drone."

Gurgeh nodded. He recognized some of the nomenclature Chiark Hub had been so impressed with, long ago. He didn't say anything.

"If I had been a library drone, you'd be dead. Even if you'd escaped Nicosar, you'd have been incinerated a few minutes later."

"I appreciate that," Gurgeh said. "Thank you." His voice sounded flat, wrung out, and not especially grateful. "I thought they'd got you; killed you."

"Damn nearly did," the drone said. "That firework display was for real. Nicosar must have got his hands on some equiv-tech effector gear; which means—or meant—the Empire has had some sort of contact with another advanced civilization. I've scanned what's left of the equipment; could be Homomda stuff. Anyway, the ship'll load it for further analysis."

"Where is the ship? I thought we'd be on it, not still down here."

"It came barreling through half an hour after the fire hit. Could have snapped us both off, but I reckoned we were safer staying where we were; I had no trouble insulating you from the fire, and keeping you under with my effector was easy enough too. The ship popped us a couple of spare drones and kept on going, braking and turning. It's on its way back now; should be overhead in five minutes. We can go safely back up in the module. Like I said; displacement can be risky."

Gurgeh gave a sort of half-laugh through his nose. He looked around the dim hall again. "I'm still waiting," he told the machine.

"The imperial guards went crazy, on Nicosar's orders. They blew up the aqueduct, cisterns and shelters, and killed everybody they could find. They tried to take over the *Invincible* from the Navy, too. In the resulting on-board firefight, the ship crashed; came down somewhere in the northern ocean. Biggish splash; tsunami's swept away rather a lot of mature cinderbuds, but I dare say the fire'll cope. There was no attempt to kill Nicosar the other night; that was just a ruse to get the whole castle and the game under the control of guards who'd do anything the Emperor told them."

"Why, though?" Gurgeh said tiredly, kicking at a blister of board metal. "*Why* did Nicosar order them to do all that?"

"He told them it was the only way to defeat the Culture and save him. They didn't know he was doomed too; they thought he had some way of saving himself. Maybe they'd have done it regardless, even knowing that. They were very highly trained. Anyway; they obeyed their orders." The machine made a chuckling noise. "Most of them, anyway. A few left the shelter they were supposed to blow up intact, and got some people into it with them. So you're not unique; there are some other survivors. Mostly servants; Nicosar made sure all the important people were in here. The ship's drones are with the survivors. We're keeping them locked up until you're safely away. They'll have enough rations to last until they're rescued."

"Go on."

"You sure you can handle all this stuff right now?"

"Just tell me *why,*" Gurgeh said, sighing.

"You've been used, Jernau Gurgeh," the drone said matter-of-factly. "The truth is, you *were* playing for the Culture, and Nicosar *was* playing for the Empire. I personally told the Emperor the night before the start of the last match that you really were our champion; if you won, we were coming in; we'd smash the Empire and impose our own order. If he won, we'd keep out for as long as he was Emperor and for the next ten Great Years anyway.

"That's why Nicosar did all he did. He wasn't just a sore loser; he'd lost his Empire. He had nothing else to live for, so why not go in a blaze of glory?"

"Was all that true?" Gurgeh asked. "Would we really have taken over?"

"Gurgeh," Flere-Imsaho said, "I have no idea. Not in my brief; no need to know. It doesn't matter; he *believed* it was true."

"Slightly unfair pressure," Gurgeh said, smiling without any humor at the machine. "Telling somebody they're playing for such high stakes, just the night before the game."

"Gamespersonship."

"So why didn't he tell me what we were playing for?"

"Guess."

"The bet would have been off and we came in all guns blazing anyway."

"Correct!"

Gurgeh shook his head, brushed a little soot off one jacket sleeve, smudging it. "You really thought I'd win?" he asked the drone. "Against Nicosar? You thought that, even before I got here?"

"Before you left Chiark, Gurgeh. As soon as you showed any interest in leaving. SC's been looking for somebody like you for quite a while. The Empire's been ripe to fall for decades; it needed a big push, but it could always go. Coming in 'all guns blazing' as you put it is almost never the right approach; Azad—the game itself—had to be discredited. It was what had held the Empire together all these years—the linchpin; but that made it the most vulnerable point, too." The drone made a show of looking around, at the mangled debris of the hall. "Everything worked out a little more dramatically than we'd expected, I must admit, but it looks like all the analyses of your abilities and Nicosar's weaknesses were just about right. My respect for those great Minds which use the likes of you and me like game-pieces increases all the time. Those are *very* smart machines."

"They knew I'd win?" Gurgeh asked disconsolately, chin in hand.

"You can't *know* something like that, Gurgeh. But they must have thought you stood a good chance. I had some of it explained to me in my briefing . . . they thought you were just about the best game-player in the Culture, and if you got interested and involved then there wasn't much any Azad player could do to stop you, no matter how long they'd spent playing the game. You've spent all your life learning games; there can't be a rule, move, concept or idea in Azad you haven't encountered ten times before in other games; it just brought them all together. These guys never stood a chance. All you needed was somebody to keep an eye on you and give you the occasional nudge in the right direction at the appropriate times." The drone dipped briefly; a little bow. "Yours truly!"

"All my life," Gurgeh said quietly, looking past the drone to the dull, dead landscape outside the tall windows. "Sixty years . . . and how long has the Culture known about the Empire?"

"About—ah! You're thinking we shaped you somehow. Not so. If we did that sort of thing we wouldn't need outsider 'mercenaries' like Shohobohaum Za to do the *really* dirty work."

"Za?" Gurgeh said.

"Not his real name; not Culture-born at all. Yes, he's what you'd call a 'mercenary.' Just as well, too, or the secret police would have shot you outside that tent. Remember timid little me nipping out of the way? I'd just shot one of your assailants with my CREW; on high X-ray so it wouldn't register on the cameras. Za broke the neck of another one; he'd heard there might be some trouble. He'll probably be leading a guerrilla army on Eä in a couple of days from now, I imagine."

The drone gave a little wobble in the air. "Let's see . . . what else can I tell you? Oh yes; the *Limiting Factor* isn't as innocent as it looks, either. While we were on the *Little Rascal* we did take out the old effectors, but only so we could put in new ones. Just two, in two of the three nose blisters. We put the empty one on clear and holos of empty blisters in the other two."

"But I was *in* all three!" Gurgeh protested.

"No, you were in the same one three times. The ship just rotated the corridors housing, fiddled with the AG and had a couple of drones change things round a bit while you were going from one to the other, or rather down one corridor, up another and back to the same blister. All for nothing, mind you, but if we *had* needed some heavy weaponry it would have been there. It's forward planning that makes one feel safe, don't you think?"

"Oh, yes," Gurgeh said, sighing. He got to his feet and went back out onto the balcony, where the black soot-snow fell steadily and quietly.

"Talking about the *Limiting Factor,*" Flere-Imsaho said cheerily, "the old reprobate is overhead now. Module's on its way. We'll have you aboard in a minute or two; you can have a nice wash and change out of those dirty clothes. Are you ready to leave?"

Gurgeh looked down at his feet, scuffed some of the soot and ash across the flagstones. "What is there to pack?"

"Not a lot, indeed. I was too busy keeping you from baking to go in search of your belongings. Anyway, the only thing you seem to be fond of is that tatty old jacket. Did you get that bracelet thing? I left it on your chest when I went exploring."

"Yes, thanks," Gurgeh said, gazing out at the flat black desolation stretching to the dark horizon. He looked up; the module burst through the deep brown overcast, trailing strands of vapor. "Thanks," Gurgeh said again, as the module swooped, dropping almost to ground level then racing across the scorched desert toward the castle, drawing a plume of ash and soot off the ground in its wake as it slowed and started to turn and the noise of its supersonic plummet cracked round the forlorn fortress like too-late thunder. "Thanks for everything."

The craft swung its rear toward the castle, floating up until it was level with the edge of the balcony parapet. Its rear door opened, made a flat ramp. The man walked across the balcony, stepped up onto the parapet, and into the cool interior of the machine.

The drone followed and the door closed.

The module blasted suddenly away, sucking a great swirling fountain of ash and soot after it as it climbed, flashing through the dark clouds above the castle like some solid lightning bolt, while its thunder broke across the plain and the castle and the low hills behind.

Ash settled again; the soot continued its soft and gentle fall.

The module returned a few minutes later, to pick up the ship's drones and the remains of the alien effector equipment, then left the castle for the last time, and rose again to its waiting ship.

A little while later, the small band of dazed survivors—released by the two ship's drones, and mostly servants, soldiers, concubines and clerks—stumbled into the daytime night and the soot-like snow, to take stock of their temporary exile in the once great fortress, and claim their vanished land.

# 4

## *The Passed Pawn*

Lazy-matching, dull-siding, the ship went slowly through one end of a tensor field three million kilometers long, over a wall of monocrystal, then started to float down through the gradually thickening atmosphere of the Plate. From five hundred kilometers up, the two slabs of land and sea, the one beyond them of raw rock under deep cloud, and the one beyond that of still forming land, showed clear in the night air.

Beyond its crystal wall, the farthest Plate was very new; dark and void to normal sight, the ship could see on it the illuminating radars of the landscaping machines as they moved their cargoes of rock in from space. Even as the vessel watched, a huge asteroid was detonated in the darkness, producing a slow fountain of red-glowing molten rock which fell slowly to the new surface, or was caught and held, molded in the vacuum before it was allowed to settle.

The Plate beside it was dark too, and near the bottom of its squared-off funnel a blanket of clouds covered it completely as its rawness was weathered.

The other two Plates were much older, and twinkled with lights. Chiark was at aphelion; Gevant and Osmolon were white on black; islands of snow on dark seas. The old warship slowly submerged itself in the atmosphere, floating down the blade-flat slope of the Plate wall to where the real air began, then set out over the ocean for the land.

A seaship, a liner on that ocean and bright with lights, blasted its horns and set off fireworks as the *Limiting Factor* went over, a kilometer up. The ship saluted too, using its effectors to produce artificial auroras; roaring, shifting folds of light in the clear, still air above it. Then the two ships sailed on into the night.

It had been an uneventful journey back. The man Gurgeh had wanted to be stored at once, saying he didn't want to be awake during the journey back; he wanted sleep, rest, a period of oblivion. The ship had insisted he think it over first, even though it had the equipment ready. After ten days it had relented and the man, who'd become increasingly morose during that time, went thankfully into a dreamless, low-metabolism sleep.

He hadn't played a single game of any description during those ten days, hardly said a word, couldn't even bother to get dressed, and spent most of his time just sitting staring at walls. The drone had agreed that putting him to sleep for the journey was probably the kindest thing they could do.

They'd crossed the Lesser Cloud and met with the Range class GSV *So Much for Subtlety,* which was heading back for the main galaxy. The inward journey had taken longer than the outward, but there'd been no hurry. The ship had left the

GSV near the higher reaches of a galactic limb and cut down and across, past stars, dustfields and nebulae, where the hydrogen migrated and the suns formed and in the ship's domain of unreal space the Holes were pillars of energy, from fabric to Grid.

It had woken the man up slowly, two days out from his home.

He still sat and stared at the walls; he didn't play any games, catch up on any news, or even deal with his mail. At his request, it hadn't signaled ahead to any of his friends, just sent one permission-to-approach burst to Chiark Hub.

It dropped a few hundred meters and followed the line of the fjord, slipping silently between the snow-covered mountains, its sleek hull reflecting a little blue-gray light as it floated over the dark, still water. A few people on yachts or in nearby houses saw the big craft as it cruised quietly by, and watched it maneuver its bulk delicately between bank and bank, water and patchy cloud.

Ikroh was dark and unlit, caught in the star-shadow of the three-hundred-and-fifty-meter length of silent craft above it.

Gurgeh took a last look round the cabin he'd been sleeping in—fitfully—for the last couple of ship nights, then walked slowly down the corridor to the module blister. Flere-Imsaho followed him with one small bag, wishing the man would change out of that horrible jacket.

It saw him into the module and came down with him. The lawn in front of the dark house was pure white and untouched. The module lowered to within a centimeter of it, then opened its rear door.

Gurgeh stepped out and down. The air was fragrant and sharp; a tangible clarity. His feet made cramping, creaking noises in the snow. He turned back to the lit interior of the module. Flere-Imsaho gave him his bag. He looked at the small machine.

"Goodbye," he said.

"Goodbye, Jernau Gurgeh. I don't expect we shall ever meet again."

"I suppose not."

He stepped back as the door started to swing closed and the craft began to rise very slowly, then he took a couple of quick steps backward until he could just see the drone over the rising lip of the door, and shouted, "One thing; when Nicosar fired that gun, and the ray came off the mirror-field and hit him; was that coincidence, or did you aim it?"

He thought it wasn't going to answer him, but just before the door closed and the wedge of light thrown over it disappeared with the rising craft, he heard the drone say:

"I am not going to tell you."

He stood and watched the module float back to the waiting ship. It was taken inside, the blister closed, and the *Limiting Factor* went black, its hull a perfect shadow, darker than the night. A pattern of lights came on along its length, spelling "Farewell" in Marain. Then it started to move, rising noiselessly upward.

Gurgeh watched it until the still-shown lights were just a set of moving stars, and fast receding in a sky of ghostly clouds, then he looked down at the faintly blue-gray snow. When he looked up again, the ship had gone.

He stood for a while, as though waiting. After a time he turned and tramped across the white lawn to the house.

He went in through the windows. The house was warm, and he shivered suddenly in his cool clothes for a second, then suddenly the lights went on.

"Boo!" Yay Meristinoux leapt out from behind a couch by the fire.

Chamlis Amalk-ney appeared from the kitchen with a tray. "Hello, Jernau. I hope you don't mind . . ."

Gurgeh's pale, pinched face broke into a smile. He put his bag down and looked at them both: Yay, fresh-faced and grinning, leaping over the couch; and Chamlis, fields orange-red, setting the tray down on the table before the banked fire. Yay thudded into him, arms round him, hugging him, laughing. She drew back.

"Gurgeh!"

"Yay, hello," he said, dropping his bag and hugging her.

"How *are* you?" she asked, squeezing him. "Are you all right? We annoyed Hub until it told us you were definitely coming, but you've been asleep all this time, haven't you? You didn't even read my letters."

Gurgeh looked away. "No. I've got them, but I haven't . . ." he shook his head, looked down. "I'm sorry."

"Never mind." Yay patted his shoulder. She kept one arm round him and took him to the couch. He sat, looking at them both. Chamlis broke up the damp sawdust banking on the fire, releasing the flames beneath. Yay spread her arms, showing off short skirt and waistcoat.

"Changed, haven't I?"

Gurgeh nodded. Yay looked as well and handsome as ever, and androgynous.

"Just changing back," she said. "Another few months and I'll be back where I started. Ah, Gurgeh, you should have seen me as a man; I was dashing!"

"He was unbearable," Chamlis said, pouring some mulled wine from a pot-bellied jug. Yay threw herself onto the couch beside Gurgeh, hugging him again and making a growling noise in her throat. Chamlis handed them gently steaming goblets of wine.

Gurgeh drank gratefully. "I didn't expect to see you," he told Yay. "I thought you'd gone away."

"I went away." Yay nodded, gulping her wine. "I came back. Last summer. Chiark's getting another Plate-pair; I put in some plans . . . and now I'm team coordinator for farside."

"Congratulations. Floating islands?"

Yay looked blank for a second, then laughed into her goblet. "No floating islands, Gurgeh."

"Plenty of volcanoes, though," Chamlis said sniffily, sucking a thread of wine from a thimble-sized container.

"Perhaps one little one," Yay nodded. Her hair was longer than he remembered; blue-black. Still as curly. She punched him gently on the shoulder. "It's good to see you again, Gurgeh."

He squeezed her hand, looked at Chamlis. "Good to be back," he said, then fell silent, staring at the burning logs in the fireplace.

"We're all glad you're back, Gurgeh," Chamlis said after a while. "But if you don't mind my saying so, you don't look too good. We heard you were in storage for the last couple of years, but there's something else. . . . What happened out there? We've heard all sorts of reports. Do you want to talk about it?"

Gurgeh hesitated, gazing at the leaping flames consuming the jumbled logs in the fire.

He put his glass down and started to explain.

He told them all that happened, from the first few days aboard the *Limiting Factor* to the last few days, again on the ship, as it powered out of the disintegrating Empire of Azad.

Chamlis was quiet, and its fields changed slowly through many colors. Yay grew slowly more concerned-looking; she shook her head frequently, gasped several times, and looked ill twice. In between, she kept the fire stocked with logs.

Gurgeh sipped his lukewarm wine. "So . . . I slept, all the way back, until two days out. And now it all seems . . . I don't know; deep-frozen. Not fresh, but . . . not decayed yet. Not gone." He swilled the wine around in his goblet. His shoulders shook with a half-hearted laugh. "Oh well." He drained his glass.

Chamlis lifted the jug from the ashes at the front of the fire and refilled Gurgeh's goblet with the hot wine. "Jernau, I can't tell you how sorry I am; this was all my fault. If I hadn't—"

"No," Gurgeh said. "Not your fault. I got myself into it. You did warn me. Don't ever say that; don't ever think it was anybody's responsibility but mine." He got up suddenly and walked to the fjord-side windows, looking down the slope of snow-covered lawn to the trees and the black water, and over it to the mountains and the scattered lights of the houses on the far shore.

"You know," he said, as though talking to his own reflection in the glass, "I asked the ship yesterday exactly what they did do about the Empire in the end; how they went in to sort it out. It said they didn't even bother. Fell apart all on its own."

He thought of Hamin and Monenine and Inclate and At-sen and Bermoiya and Za and Olos and Krowo and the girl whose name he'd forgotten . . .

He shook his head at his image in the glass. "Anyway; it's over." He turned back to Yay and Chamlis and the warm room. "What's the gossip here?"

So they told him about Hafflis's twins, both talking now, and Boruelal leaving to go GSV-ing for a few years, and Olz

Hap—breaker of not a few young hearts—being more or less acclaimed/embarrassed/forced into Boruelal's old post, and Yay fathering a child a year back—he'd get to meet mother and child next year probably, when they came for an extended visit—and one of Shuro's pals being killed in a combat game two years back, and Ren Myglan becoming a man, and Chamlis still hard at work on the reference text for its pet planet, and Tronze Festival the year before last ending in disaster and chaos after some fireworks blew up in the lake and swamped half the cliffside terraces; two people dead, brains splattered over lumps of stonework; hundreds injured. Last year's hadn't been half so exciting.

Gurgeh was listening to all this as he wandered round the room, reacquainting himself with it. Nothing much seemed to have changed.

"What a lot I've miss—" he began, then noticed the little wooden plaque on the wall, and the object mounted on it. He reached out, touched it, took it down from the wall.

"Ah," Chamlis said, making what was almost a coughing noise. "I hope you don't mind. . . . I mean I hope you don't think that's too . . . irreverent, or tasteless. I just thought . . ."

Gurgeh smiled sadly, touching the lifeless surfaces of the body that had once been Mawhrin-Skel. He turned back to Yay and Chamlis, walking over to the old drone. "Not at all, but I don't want it. Do you?"

"Yes, please."

Gurgeh presented the heavy little trophy to Chamlis, who went red with pleasure. "You vindictive old horror," Yay snorted.

"This means a great deal to me," Chamlis said primly, holding the plaque close to its casing. Gurgeh put his glass back on the tray.

A log collapsed in the fire, showering sparks up. Gurgeh crouched and poked at the remaining logs. He yawned.

Yay and the drone exchanged looks, then Yay reached out and tapped Gurgeh with one foot. "Come on, Jernau; you're tired; Chamlis has to head back home and make sure its new fishes haven't eaten each other. Is it all right if I stay here?"

Gurgeh looked, surprised, at her smiling face, and nodded.

When Chamlis left, Yay put her head on Gurgeh's shoulder and said she'd missed him a lot, and five years was a long time, and he looked a lot more cuddleable than when he'd gone away, and . . . if he wanted . . . if he wasn't too tired . . .

She used her mouth, and on her forming body Gurgeh traced slow movements, rediscovering sensations he'd almost forgotten; stroking her gold-dark skin, caressing the odd, almost comic unbuddings of her now concaving genitals, making her laugh, laughing with her, and—in the long moment of climax—with her then too, still one, their every tactile cell surging to a single pulse, as though alight.

Still he didn't sleep, and in the night got up out of the tousled bed. He went to the windows and opened them. The cold night air spilled in. He shivered, pulled on the trous, jacket and shoes.

Yay moved and made a small noise. He closed the windows and went back to the bed, crouching down in the darkness beside her. He pulled the covers over her exposed back and shoulder, and moved his hand very gently through her curls. She snored once and stirred, then breathed quietly on.

He crossed to the windows and went quickly outside, closing them silently behind him.

He stood on the snow-covered balcony, gazing at the dark trees descending in uneven rows to the glittering black fjord. The mountains on the far side shone faintly, and above them in the crisp night dim areas of light moved on the darkness, occluding star-fields and the farside Plates. The clouds drifted slowly, and down at Ikroh there was no wind.

Gurgeh looked up and saw, among the clouds, the Clouds, their ancient light hardly wavering in the cold, calm air. He watched his breath go out before him, like a damp smoke between him and those distant stars, and shoved his chilled hands into the jacket pockets for warmth. One touched something softer than the snow, and he brought it out; a little dust.

He looked up from it at the stars again, and the view was warped and distorted by something in his eyes, which at first he thought was rain.

. . . No, not quite the end.

There's still me. I know I've been naughty, not revealing my identity, but then, maybe you've guessed; and who am I to deprive you of the satisfaction of working it out for yourself? Who am I, indeed?

Yes, I was there, all the time. Well, more or less all the time. I watched, I listened, I thought and sensed and waited, and did as I was told (or asked, to maintain the proprieties). I was there all right, in person or in the shape of one of my representatives, my little spies.

To be honest, I don't know whether I'd have liked old Gurgeh to have found out the truth or not; still undecided on that one, I must confess. I—we—left it to chance, in the end.

For example; just supposing Chiark Hub had told our hero the exact shape of the cavity in the husk that had been Mawhrin-Skel, or Gurgeh had somehow opened that lifeless casing and seen for himself . . . would he have thought that little, disk-shaped hole a mere coincidence?

Or would he have started to suspect?

We'll never know; if you're reading this he's long dead; had his appointment with the displacement drone and been zapped to the very livid heart of the system, corpse blasted to plasma in the vast erupting core of Chiark's sun, his sundered atoms rising and falling in the raging fluid thermals of the mighty star, each pulverized particle migrating over the millennia to that planet-swallowing surface of blinding, storm-swept fire, to boil off there, and so add their own little parcels of meaningless illumination to the encompassing night . . .

Ah well, getting a bit flowery there.

Still; an old drone should be allowed such indulgences, now and again, don't you think?

Let me recapitulate.

This is a true story. I was there. When I wasn't, and when I didn't know exactly what was going on—inside Gurgeh's mind, for example—I admit that I have not hesitated to make it up.

But it's still a true story.

Would I lie to you?

As ever,

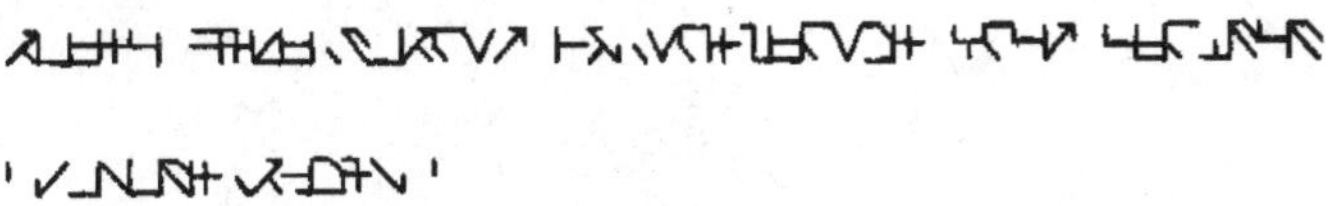

Sprant Flere-Imsaho Wu-Handrahen Xato Trabiti
("Mawhrin-Skel")

# extras

# meet the author

*John Foley*

Iain Banks came to controversial public notice with the publication of his first novel, *The Wasp Factory,* in 1984. *Consider Phlebas,* his first science fiction novel, was published under the name Iain M. Banks in 1987. He is now widely acclaimed as one of the most powerful, innovative and exciting writers of his generation. Iain Banks lives in Edinburgh, Scotland. Find out more about Iain M. Banks at www.iainbanks.net.

# introducing

**If you enjoyed**
**THE PLAYER OF GAMES,**
**look out for**

## MATTER

*by Iain M. Banks*

A light breeze produced a dry rattling sound from some nearby bushes. It lifted delicate little veils of dust from a few sandy patches nearby and shifted a lock of dark hair across the forehead of the woman sitting on the wood and canvas camp chair which was perched, not quite level, on a patch of bare rock near the edge of a low ridge looking out over the scrub and sand of the desert. In the distance, trembling through the heat haze, was the straight line of the road. Some scrawny trees, few taller than one man standing on another's shoulders, marked the course of the dusty highway. Further away, tens of kilometers beyond the road, a line of dark, jagged mountains shimmered in the baking air.

By most human standards the woman was tall, slim and well muscled. Her hair was short and straight and dark and her skin was the color of pale agate. There was nobody of her specific kind within several thousand light-years of where she sat, though if there had been they might have said that she was somewhere between being a young woman and one at the very start of middle age. They would, however, have thought she looked somewhat short and bulky. She was dressed in a pair of wide, loose-fitting pants and a thin, cool-looking jacket, both the same shade as the sand. She wore a wide black hat to shade her from the late morning sun, which showed as a harsh white point high in the cloudless, pale green sky. She raised a pair of very old and worn-looking binoculars to her night-dark eyes and looked out toward the point where the desert road met the horizon to the west. There was a folding table to her right holding a glass and a bottle of chilled water. A small backpack lay underneath. She reached out with her other hand and lifted the glass from the table, sipping at the water while still looking through the ancient field glasses.

"They're about an hour away," said the machine floating to her left. The machine looked like a scruffy metal suitcase. It moved a little in the air, rotating and tipping as though looking up at the seated woman. "And anyway," it continued, "you won't see much at all with those museum pieces."

She put the glass down on the table again and lowered the binoculars. "They were my father's," she told the machine.

"Really," the drone said, with what might have been a sigh.

A screen flicked into existence a couple of meters in front of the woman, filling half her field of view. It showed, from a point a hundred meters above and in front of its leading edge, an army of men—some mounted, most on foot—marching along another section of the desert highway, all raising dust which piled into the air and drifted slowly away to the southeast. Sunlight glittered off the edges of raised spears and pikes. Banners, flags and pennants swayed above the heads of the mass of moving men. The army filled the road for a couple of kilometers behind the mounted men at its head. Bringing up the rear were baggage carts, covered and open wagons, wheeled catapults and trebuchets and a variety of lumbering wooden siege engines, all pulled by dark, powerful-looking animals whose sweating shoulders towered over the men walking at their sides.

The woman tutted. "Put that away," she said.

"Yes, ma'am," the machine said. The screen vanished.

The woman looked through the binoculars again, using both hands this time. "I can see their dust," she announced. "And another couple of scouts, I think."

"Astounding," the drone said.

If the woman heard the sarcasm in the machine's voice, she chose to ignore it. She drained the water glass, placed the field glasses on the table, pulled the brim of her hat down over her eyes and settled back in the camp seat, crossing her arms and stretching her booted feet out, crossed at the ankle. "Having a snooze," she told the drone from beneath the hat. "Wake me when it's time."

"Just you make yourself comfortable there," the drone told her.

"Mm-hmm."

Turminder Xuss (drone, offensive) watched the woman Djan Seriy Anaplian for a few minutes, monitoring her slowing breathing and her gradually relaxing muscle-state until it knew she was genuinely asleep.

"Sweet dreams, princess," it said quietly. Reviewing its words immediately, the drone was completely unable to determine whether a disinterested observer would have detected any trace of sarcasm or not.

It checked round its half-dozen previously deployed scout

and secondary knife missiles, using their sensors to watch the still distant approaching army draw slowly closer and monitoring the various small patrols and individual scouts the army had sent out ahead of it.

For a while, it watched the army move. From a certain perspective it looked like a single great organism inching darkly across the tawny sweep of desert; something segmented, hesitant—bits of it would come to a stop for no obvious reason for long moments, before starting off again, so that it seemed to shuffle rather than flow en masse—but determined, unarguably fixed in its onward purpose. And all on their way to war, the drone thought sourly, to take and burn and loot and rape and raze. What sullen application these humans devoted to destruction.

About half an hour later, when the front of the army was hazily visible on the desert highway a couple of kilometers to the west, a single mounted scout came riding along the top of the ridge, straight toward where the drone kept vigil and the woman slept. The man showed no sign of having seen through the camouflage field surrounding their little encampment, but unless he changed course he was going to ride right into them.

The drone made a tutting noise very similar to the one the woman had made earlier and told its nearest knife missile to spook the mount. The pencil-thin shape came darting in, effectively invisible, and jabbed the beast in one flank so that it screamed and jerked, nearly unseating its rider as it veered away down the shallow slope of ridge toward the road.

The scout shouted and swore at his animal, reining it in and turning its broad snout back toward the ridge, some distance beyond the woman and the drone. They galloped away, leaving a thin trail of dust hanging in the near-still air.

Djan Seriy Anaplian stirred, sat up a little and looked out from under her hat. "What was all that?" she asked sleepily.

"Nothing. Go back to sleep."

"Hmm." She relaxed again and a minute later was quietly snoring.

The drone woke her when the head of the army was almost level with them. It bobbed its front at the body of men and animals a kilometer distant while Anaplian was still yawning and stretching. "The boys are all here," it told her.

"Indeed they are," the woman said. She lifted the binoculars and focused on the very front of the army, where a group of men rode mounted on especially tall, colorfully caparisoned animals. These men wore high, plumed helmets and their highly polished armor glittered brightly in the glare. "They're all very parade ground," Anaplian said. "It's like they're expecting to bump into somebody out here they need to impress."

"God?" the drone suggested.

The woman was silent for a moment. "Hmm," she said eventually. She put the field glasses down and looked at the drone. "Shall we?"

"Merely say the word."

Anaplian looked back at the army, took a deep breath and said, "Very well. Let us do this."

The drone made a little dipping motion like a nod. A small hatch opened in its side. A cylinder perhaps four centimeters wide and twenty-five long, shaped like a sort of conical knife, rolled lazily into the air then darted away, keeping close to the ground and accelerating quickly toward the rear of the column of men, animals and machines. It left a trail of dust for a moment before it adjusted its altitude. Anaplian lost sight of its camouflaged shape almost immediately.

The drone's aura field, invisible until now, glowed rosily for a moment or two. "This," it said, "should be fun."

The woman looked at it dubiously. "There aren't going to be any mistakes this time, are there?"

"Certainly not," the machine said crisply. "Want to watch?" it asked her. "I mean properly, not through those antique opera glasses."

Anaplian looked at the machine through narrowed eyes for a little, then said, slowly, "All right."

The screen blinked into existence just to one side of them this time, so that Anaplian could still see the army in the distance with the naked eye. The screen view was from some distance behind the great column now, and much lower than before. Dust drifted across the view. "That's from the trailing scout missile," Turminder Xuss said. Another screen flickered next to the first. "This is from the knife missile itself." The camera in the knife missile registered the tiny machine scudding past the army in a blur of men, uniforms and weapons, then showed the tall shapes of the wagons, war machines and siege engines before banking sharply after the tail end of the army was passed. The rushing missile stooped, taking up a position a kilometer behind the rear of the army and a meter or so above the road surface. Its speed had dropped from near-supersonic to something close to that of a swiftly flying bird. It was closing rapidly with the rear of the column.

"I'll sync the scout to the knife, follow it in behind," the drone said. In moments, the flat circular base of the knife missile appeared as a dot in the center of the scout missile's view, then expanded until it looked like the smaller machine was only a meter behind the larger one. "There go the warps!" Xuss said, sounding excited. "See?"

Two arrowhead shapes, one on either side, detached from

the knife missile's body, swung out and disappeared. The monofilament wires which still attached each of the little warps to the knife missile were invisible. The view changed as the scout missile pulled back and up, showing almost the whole of the army ahead.

"I'll get the knife to buzz the wires," the drone said.

"What does that mean?"

"Vibrates them, so that whatever the monofils go through, it'll be like getting sliced by an implausibly sharp battle axe rather than the world's keenest razor," the drone said helpfully.

The screen displaying what the scout missile could see showed a tree a hundred meters behind the last, trundling wagon. The tree jerked and the top three-quarters slid at a steep angle down the sloped stump that was the bottom quarter before toppling to the dust. "That took a flick," the drone said, glowing briefly rosy again and sounding amused. The wagons and siege engines filled the view coming from the knife missile. "The first bit's actually the trickiest . . ."

The fabric roofs of the covered wagons rose into the air like released birds; tensed hoops of wood—cut—sprang apart. The giant, solid wheels of the catapults, trebuchets and siege engines shed their top sections on the next revolution and the great wooden structures thudded to a halt, the top halves of some of them, also cut through, jumping forward with the shock. Arm-thick lengths of rope, wound rock-tight a moment earlier, burst like released springs, then flopped like string. The scout missile swung between the felled and wrecked machines as the men in and around the wagons and siege engines started to react. The knife missile powered onward, toward the foot soldiers immediately ahead. It plunged into the mass of spears, pikes, pennant poles, banners and flags, scything through them in a welter of sliced wood, falling blades and flapping fabric.

Anaplian caught glimpses of a couple of men slashed or skewered by falling pike heads.

"Bound to be a few casualties," the drone muttered.

"Bound to be," the woman said.

The knife missile was catching glimpses of confused faces as men heard the shouts of those behind them and turned to look. The missile was a half-second away from the rear of the mass of mounted men and roughly level with their necks when the drone sent,

—Are you sure we can't—?

—Positive, Anaplian replied, inserting a sigh into what was an entirely nonverbal exchange. —Just stick to the plan.

The tiny machine nudged up a half meter or so and tore above the mounted men, catching their plumed helmets and chopping the gaudy decorations off like a harvest of motley stalks. It leapt over the head of the column, leaving consternation and fluttering plumage in its wake. Then it zoomed, heading skyward. The following scout missile registered the monofil warps clicking back into place in the knife missile's body before it swiveled, rose and slowed, to look back at the whole army again.

It was, Anaplian thought, a scene of entirely satisfactory chaos, outrage and confusion. She smiled. This was an event of such rarity that Turminder Xuss recorded the moment.

The screens hanging in the air disappeared. The knife missile reappeared and swung into the offered hatchway in the side of the drone.

Anaplian looked out over the plain to the road and the halted army. "Many casualties?" she asked, smile disappearing.

"Sixteen or so," the drone told her. "About half will likely prove fatal, in time."

She nodded, still watching the distant column of men and machines. "Oh well."

"Indeed," Turminder Xuss agreed. The scout missile floated up to the drone and also entered via a side panel. "Still," the drone said, sounding weary, "we should have done more."

"Should we."

"Yes. You ought to have let me do a proper decapitation."

"No," Anaplian said.

"Just the nobles," the drone said. "The guys right at the front. The ones who came up with their spiffing war plans in the first place."

"No," the woman said again, rising from her seat and, turning, folding it. She held it in one hand. With the other she lifted the old pair of binoculars from the table. "Module coming?"

"Overhead," the drone told her. It moved round her and picked up the camp table, placing the glass and water bottle inside the backpack beneath. "Just the two nasty Dukes? And the King?"

Anaplian held on to her hat as she looked straight up, squinting briefly in the sunlight until her eyes adjusted. "No."

"This is not, I trust, some kind of transferred familial sentimentality," the drone said with half-pretended distaste.

"No," the woman said, watching the shape of the module ripple in the air a few meters away.

Turminder Xuss moved toward the module as its rear door hinged open. "And are you going to stop saying no to me all the time?"

Anaplian looked at it, expressionless.

"Never mind," the drone said, sighing. It bob-nodded toward the open module door. "After you."